R. M. Kozan

Breakaway: 1977

Fresh Blue Ink
Ottawa

Fresh Blue Ink
is an imprint of
Fresh Blue Inc.
33 Jackson Court, Kanata, Ontario, Canada K2K-1B6

FreshBlueInk.ca

ISBN-13: 978-0-9920119-0-1

Cover illustrations copyright © Fresh Blue Inc.

Opening quotation credits:
Sylvia Anderson (My Fab Years, 2007, p.100).
Barry Morse (1979 interview by R.M. Kozan)

First Canadian printing: September 2013
First USA printing: September 2013

Acknowledgements and Thanks

For their gracious feedback on the early drafts of this novel: Patricia Balcom, Lois Crowe, Nancy Curran, Lucie Kearns, James Kozan, Karl Meinert, and Nicholas Rudd.

For their enthusiasm in creating the cover illustrations, the good people at telefar.com: Anne Bella, Abhilash Vijayan, and Shifin Salim.

For answering my CKOS-related questions at an ungodly pre-dawn hour: Linus Westburg.

For providing the first official review of this work, plus additional feedback, the author of <u>Destination: Moonbase Alpha</u>, Robert E. Wood.

Finally, for their years of exciting TV science fiction entertainment, I am grateful for the creators of *Space: 1999*, Gerry and Sylvia Anderson.

Breakaway: 1977

"It is not that we originate mental problems, but [the power of film and television] can certainly incite and inspire them by over-stimulating an already confused imagination."
- Sylvia Anderson
Co-creator, *Space: 1999*

"Oh there'll be other series. I shall show up as somebody's scientific uncle again before long."
- Barry Morse
Professor Victor Bergman, *Space: 1999*

Lionel's Introduction (Lionel O'Neill, 1988)

In my youth I was kidnapped by a spaceship from the future.
Well, not literally. Back in 1975, when I was fourteen years
old, my life was a mess. But then I encountered something that
filled me with wonder and a whiff of hope: the television series
Space: 1999. Here I found a fantastic future in which anything
was possible and people worked together in a spirit of
cooperation and tolerance so unlike my experiences to that
point in this world.

Sadly, *Space: 1999* survived only two years: the first year
or 'season' ran in 1975 as I endured Grade 8; the second ran the
following year. The fiery, yet sensitive personality of
Commander John Koenig of Moonbase Alpha became my role
model. Here was a dark-haired man whose face demanded no
terror nor betrayed any fear. His loyalty-inspiring integrity
required few words. He was a man innately good. More often
than not, he persevered against great odds to save his loyal
crew of Moonbase Alphans.

That first year, or Year One as we fans dub it, my parents
began the terminal process of divorce that would unravel our
lives and accelerate the disintegration of my threadbare sanity.
Part of my problem was that I had matured physically and
intellectually much faster than the other kids. By the time I hit
fourteen, although only recently surpassing five feet in height, I
had long, dark, wiry hair, Jon Entwistle sideburns, and sported
a more thorough mustache than any other boy in my grade.

My advanced physical maturation could have paid off in
rock god status among my peers had it not been for my
shortness, plus a shyness with both girls and boys prompted by
my moderate, but always inconvenient, stutter. I was both book
and math smart, but I had few social skills and therefore few
friends.

I lived in Yorkton, a small city of 15,000 in southeastern
Saskatchewan. The leading industry there was Morris Rod
Weeder, a manufacturer of farm equipment. Most of the local
economy was geared towards supplying and servicing the

surrounding farms. Saskatchewan of course is big on wheat. See the crest of Saskatchewan: three golden wheat sheaves. Pretty exciting stuff it was not.

I had read virtually every interesting book in the Yorkton Public Library, scouring both the adult and child sections. I preferred to look outward, toward the mysteries and secrets of the wider world because my family had its own secrets. I had secrets. By the time I met Roger Kay and Samantha Renfield, I was accelerating toward complete isolation from everyone who had ever bothered or needed me before.

Sam, Roger, and I had our fascination with *Space: 1999* in common and when we became aware of a local fan organization called the Association Of Alphans, my friends encouraged me to divert all my creative frustration and energy into that channel. For this period in my life, I am grateful. For an all too brief oasis of time, our triangle of friendship held firm and we gazed optimistically into a future we thought would be wonderful and somehow seemed certain to be entirely within our grasp. For me, this was not to be.

Roger's Introduction (Roger Kay, 1994)

When I was younger, I spent a lot of time writing instead of doing, probably because I was very uncertain about myself and feared others would detect this inadequacy and think worse of me for it. So I kept my counsel to myself, thinking better to be thought a fool than to open my mouth and confirm it. Instead, I wrote.

I wrote in my diary. I wrote space stories, asteroid station tales. I created my own alternate universe. I wrote episode summaries and fan fiction for the television show *Space: 1999*.

Way back then I shared these tales with my two closest, or really *only* friends and it provided a prism or perhaps shadow puppet play stage where we could engage our minds and feelings in a detached and safe search for the truth of life and identity. The early stories we experienced, and often ourselves created, were critical ingredients that immediately and unconsciously shaped us. They were the pivot points of our maturation. We eagerly analyzed our own responses to these stories. In them we strove to see our own reflections. They could hardly be considered distractions or time-wasters!

I wish I could look back upon everything positively at this later stage in life, now more than fifteen years on, but the truth does not discount my friend Neil *[Editor's note: 'Neil' refers to Lionel O'Neill]* and his destiny. His is a wake-up call. There are lambs slaughtered in these woods. I cannot believe anything has changed, despite any of my other statements to the contrary.

This collection of documents charts a personal tragedy that extends to more than one person. Although my diaries make up the bulk of the text, the story is really Neil's.

I must admit I am amazed at the longevity of my old Sony and BASF cassettes. My archive of sometime surreptitious audio taping from the 1970s consists of literally hundreds of 30, 60, and 90 minute cassette tapes capturing both the living and the dead, but even the living have changed so completely that the old voices now all whisper like shy ghosts.

The Freedom of Information Act here in Canada has been invaluable in providing police records and documents critical to completing this story. Without their release acting as levee breakers, I might never have obtained the flood of other statements that added so much to this story.

I would like to thank the Association of Alphans for their sharing of archival materials, including the exclusive Barry Morse interview. Also, extraordinary efforts were made by Nancy O'Neill to obtain the more recent material for this book. As well as being the instigator of this project, she also excelled in her wearying role as editor. Finally, I must thank Neil and Sam for their honesty and openness. Despite their obvious shortcomings, this time they did the right thing.

Entries from Roger Kay's 1975 Diary

[Editor's note: During the creation of this book, these diary entries were subjected to spell check. If this diminishes the authentic feel of the original diaries, I regret it.]

Tuesday, September 2, 1975

School started today. After a terrible, lonely summer I've decided to keep a diary of my activities. Perhaps this will help me understand why I have such a hard time finding and keeping friends.

It was a very dull summer. I planned to hang out with Arvid and Ken but Arvid seemed more interested in playing softball than hanging out and Ken was continually away in Regina.

I hate stupid sports because you have to be good at them or you get in trouble. Every time I try to play a game it winds up that the opposing team cheers me and my own team hates me. Not a recipe for fun. I don't understand why they call them 'games' if everyone takes them so seriously. And who comes up with this stuff anyway? Chasing a ball and running over the same piece of ground again and again, how is that fun? I'm much happier with a book or a good space movie.

I rode my bike around all summer and didn't see another soul except the little kids playing ball at Victoria School. It was like *On The Beach*, except the adults survived.

Anyway, I'm back at school now. My homeroom teacher is Mr. Windleigh. He seems pretty nice but talks very slow. He rolls his head around and stares at the ceiling to appear thoughtful.

We have a six day schedule instead of a five day schedule so it'll be hard to track what we're supposed to be doing each day. Way to go school administrators! This semester I have: Math, Music, Art, Science, Social Studies, English, Guidance, Study Period and Phys-ed. Plus French and Economics. I took French instead of Ukrainian, because I'll need the French credits to get into university obviously. Also, I chose Economics instead of Christian Ethics. St. Joe's is a combined school, with both public school and Catholic system kids. The Catholic kids take Christian Ethics and us public school heathens take Economics.

Wednesday, September 3, 1975

Today I learned not to cross Mr. Windleigh. I drew a cartoon of him and labeled it 'Mr. Windy'. I drew him staring up at the ceiling and words spilling down into a big pile on the floor while the people in the desks beside him had word balloons with 'zzzz' above them. I thought it was pretty funny but when I passed it to Arvid, Mr. Windleigh intercepted it. He said it was a waste of talent and if I don't spend my time and energy trying to learn then I would surely end up becoming a failure in life. And did I want to be a failure in life? I didn't really make the connection of life failure with my humorous drawing but once he quits looking at the ceiling and stabs you with those intense eyes, you don't want to disagree with him. I must learn to think about consequences before I do things.

Friday, September 5, 1975

In Science today we found out that we will definitely have to learn the Metric System. Eventually we will no longer use the foot and pounds Imperial system. I worked it out that instead of being 5'1" and 87 pounds I will be 155 centimeters tall and weigh 40 kilograms! Sounds like it doesn't mean anything.

Arvid was being a jerk today. I wore my new platform shoes to school and was enjoying the perspective from two inches of extra height when he started bugging me about my pants being floods. Well yeah, I'll have to get the hems let down I guess to make up for my new shoes, but a real friend shouldn't need to make a big deal out of it. He kept making a 'flood siren' noise every time I turned to him. I just hope Mom can fix all my good bell bottoms.

Sunday, September 7, 1975

Ken and I were throwing oranges into a tree, or trying to. One hit me in the head. Mom was mad when she found the oranges missing.

Monday, September 8, 1975

Today was not a good day. I've been spending lunch hour with Ken every day so far this year. We go hang out under the gymnasium stage to eat. In the visitor entrance area, at the front of the school, which is the main entry when they are using the gymnasium as a theater, there are these low doors into the storage area under the stage. They keep hundreds of chairs stacked and lying sideways on these long wooden wheeled things and then push them into the storage area. This leaves a little space on the side of each wheeled thing where you can sneak in. I bring my little pocket flashlight with me and we are able to see fine. I told Ken it is not hard to see in there; it is elegantly dim like a fancy restaurant and we dine in complete privacy and peace.

This worked great all last week. We were being really careful not to leave any garbage in there so the teachers wouldn't find out, but today Lucky discovered us. I think we were talking and he heard us because he pulled open the door and said "Hey it's the mole people!". Then he took his juice drink and poured it on the floor so that we'd have to crawl through the puddle to get out.

I got real messy and sticky and by the time I was out, Principal Whyte was standing there, hands on his hips, scolding us. So now it looks like we'll never get to eat lunch in there again. Also Lucky now knows that we live in fear so things are likely to get worse.

Tuesday, September 9, 1975

Ken and I found a new place to have lunch: the chapel! It is a nice dark quiet room where Lucky is not likely to show up. You just have to be a little bit careful because the entrance is by all the offices. But today we got inside and there was no one there.

To make sure we are not spotted by anyone else coming in, we sit in the confession booths. You can talk to each other if you are side by side and I don't think they can hear you in the chapel. I must 'confess' lunch is now much more peaceful! Ha ha!

Wednesday, September 10, 1975

School was a drag again. Sometimes I'd like to murder that Lucky Tuttosi. He was bugging me after I got out of Phys-ed and he followed me all the way home, calling me names without stop. At the end of second period Science I had been explaining to Ken and Arvid about the Apollo-Soyuz docking that had occurred in July. Finally an American and a Soviet spacecraft had docked in Earth orbit! I admit I am enthusiastic about international cooperation in outer space but I'm not a commie. Lucky thinks any kind of enthusiasm or knowledge is nerdy.

Cher has her own TV show since she left Sonny, and I've seen it a couple of times, but tonight she was a guest on the Carol Burnett show. She still looks amazing.

Petersen's Book of Man In Space:
A Description in 400 Words
(Roger Kay, 1975)

Petersen's Book of Man In Space is a five volume set that describes all the accomplishments of the space age. So far!

Volume 1 covers the fathers of modern rocket science, Goddard and Tsiolkovsky, the first use of rockets such as the V-2 by the Germans during WWII, the first successful true satellite: the Russian Sputnik in 1957, plus the many disastrous early American efforts finally resulting in the successful Explorer 1 satellite in early 1958.

After that, animals were sent into Earth orbit: two dogs courtesy of the Russians, and a monkey on behalf of the Americans.

Finally, in 1961, as promised, man in space! First up was the Russian Yuri Gagarin aboard the Vostok. Then came U.S. Project Mercury: a series of launches carrying a single astronaut aboard a Mercury capsule atop a Redstone rocket. Mercury yields the first American in space: Alan Shepard. Both firsts occur in 1961.

Volume 2 moves on to Project Gemini, a series of orbital two-man flights that occurred in 1965 and 1966. While the Russians chalk up first woman in space and first spacewalk, the American's Gemini program attains the first docking of two spacecraft. Also, new information and pictures of the Moon are obtained by the Ranger, Surveyor and Lunar Orbiter programs.

Volume 3 focuses on the early Apollo program including details of the previous Saturn 1 booster and then the famous Saturn 5: the massive launch vehicle used in the Apollo program. Disaster soon follows for both the U.S. and the Russians: a fire on the launch pad kills the three American astronauts aboard Apollo 1, and the solitary cosmonaut does not survive a flawed re-entry aboard the Russian Soyuz 1.

Volume 4 takes us from Apollo 7 through Apollo 11. The first orbit of another celestial body by a manned spacecraft is accomplished with Apollo 8: it orbits the Moon during

Christmas 1968. Apollo 11 achieves the historic first manned Moon landing on July 20, 1969!

Volume 5 covers Apollo 12 through 17 which are subsequent manned Moon landings including the first "moon car": the Lunar Roving Vehicle, a glorified golf cart for the cosmos.

Beyond Apollo 17 there is mention of a space shuttle for development by 1979, a year still almost half a decade into the future. No drawings of the promised craft are included in the final volume, but anyway they are not required as my imagination enjoys the thrill of speculation: what will come next?

On Arvid and Ken (Roger Kay, 1994)

I wasn't friends with either Arvid or Ken until I entered Grade 7. They came from a different elementary school, I forget which. I think we gravitated to each other that first year of junior high because we were all low in the pecking order.

I remember the first Grade 7 science lab period we had, back in September 1974. We were new to St. Joe's and a bit overwhelmed by the huge building complex with its many mysterious areas. We descended into the basement of the old building, a faded and worn subterranean realm imbued to my youthful eyes with storied antiquity. The science lab had perhaps six tables, each seating four or more students, and high enough that we had to perch upon bar stools. At the center of each table were several chrome spigots which provided the natural gas to feed the Bunsen burners which the higher grades used in their chemistry experiments. I had never been in a lab like that before, and the scientific ambiance thrilled me.

That first day the teacher came in and said "the first thing we want to do is to make sure these natural gas valves are always closed". The gas supply was off but he wanted to be sure that when a later class came in, and the main supply valve was opened, there would be no open student valves. So we all made a show of opening and then making sure the valves were fully closed.

The teacher went on to the next topic but Ken was still fiddling with the valve in front of me. In retaliation, I opened the valve in front of him. We each closed our own valves. The teacher went out of the room to get something and while Arvid was distracted, looking at something across the room, Ken opened the valve in front of him. In a few seconds Arvid saw the sabotage, but instead of retaliating he began a speech about the importance of friendship. How the friends you make in school can last a whole lifetime, how you need people to depend on, and that a true friend would not do this type of thing. I was very impressed with his maturity and marked him as a friend on that day. Ken later apologized to both Arvid and I, and we three were best friends for the rest of the year.

Looking back on it, and realizing that Arvid probably didn't know who had opened his valve, his engaging speech now seems a very astute Machiavellian move if not to gain friends then at least to confuse his enemies.

Later that school year, in the spring, the movie *Legend Of Boggy Creek* came to town and Arvid, Ken and I went together to see it. The movie is about Sasquatch, or Bigfoot if you prefer, and although now it seems a bit silly, at the time it petrified me. I was not prone to believing in ghosts or monsters. I thought all supernatural phenomena were bullshit but this was a documentary; the monster was scientist-validated. So, maybe it really could exist!

As we walked back from the Tower Theatre, I shivered with fright. The night was dark and quiet. We seemed very alone and vulnerable, even though we were walking down a city street. Then something spooked me. In the grip of irrational fear, I grabbed Arvid's arm. He pushed me away immediately and said 'you fag'. Ken teased me, saying I was Sasquatch's girlfriend and Arvid found this hilarious. The teasing seemed to last for weeks and I don't think my trust in our friendship ever recovered after that. I was a flag of convenience.

That summer Arvid spent his time playing baseball with some much younger kids from his church. He was a star.

Ken spent most of the summer in Regina. I was told he was visiting relatives, but I think he had a lot of health problems and had gone there for some special medical care. Ken wouldn't talk about his health problems but it was clear he had some. He was thin, sickly, and missed a lot of school.

The next year, as Grade 8 started, they were still the best friends I had, but I didn't trust them much.

Entries from Roger Kay's 1975 Diary

Thursday, September 11, 1975
Met a new friend today. His name is Lionel but I just call him Neil cause it sounds more like a first name, although it is actually his last name (well, O'Neill). He is a fan of space too and digs Neil Armstrong. I invited him over to see my Apollo rocket. He knows his Service Module from his Lunar Landing Module, I'll give him that!

I lent him my cassettes of the new *Six Million Dollar Man* and *Bionic Woman* episodes. It is pretty cool this season because instead of the usual cops and robbers they are dealing with a sasquatch who is actually an alien robot. Neil isn't a big fan, but after he hears these episodes he might get more interested.

Saturday, September 13, 1975
Neil lives by the corner of Darlington and 5th Avenue North, just a block from my house, so I went over there this afternoon. I knocked on the back door for a while but no one answered. I went around the front and heard a TV, so I knocked there too. His Mom finally came to the door but said Neil wasn't in the house and she didn't know where he was.

Dad was stippling my ceiling today so I have to sleep in the basement. Stayed up real late watching a movie: *The Invisible Woman*. Pretty cool.

Monday, September 14, 1975
Today Arvid was bugging me about hanging out with Neil. He said that Neil's father is a bad man but wouldn't explain what he meant by that no matter how I pressed him. The only thing he'd say is that he knows something because of his connection with the Jewish temple. Apparently Neil's family are some type of lapsed Jews. I said I didn't care if he was a lapsed Satanist, he is a good guy and my friend. If Arvid tries to make me choose between them, he'll find out he's hanging by a very thin thread.

Tuesday, September 15, 1975

Today I ate lunch with Neil. Sometimes he stutters, but if you wait him out, you'll hear something worthwhile. Ken and Arvid found us near the end of lunch but when they sat down, Neil got quiet. When Neil did try to say something, his words were sticking. Ken rolled his eyes and Arvid kept trying to put words in his mouth. Before they interrupted us, Neil had been telling me all about some books he was reading in his fast whisper, but after they sat down, he pretty much just let them talk. They sound like kindergartners next to him.

Wednesday, September 16, 1975

If I ever doubted I live in the most boring place in the world, I was wrong. Saskatchewan is one square place (okay rectangular). In Social Studies we looked at the different areas, uplands, lowlands, parkland, and we spent a long time looking at pictures of the Great Sand Hills. Mounds of sand which slowly change over time.

Gripping? I was gripping my desk trying not to fall onto the floor in a dead sleep. How can you get excited about so much of nothing? Sometimes I think we are just the pause between interesting provinces.

I note that the most boring states in the US are also the most geometric. Maybe that lack of imagination in drawing the boundary carries over into everything local. I wonder what I would be like if I had been born in a big city, Vancouver or Toronto, or even Los Angeles or New York? I don't think I'd be spending my time reading about sand hills, great or not.

Thursday, September 17, 1975

Today we started a new thing in English called ORA, or Optimum Reading Achievement. It is the latest technology for measuring and improving reading skills. Next to 8-23 is the special classroom used for ORA. Instead of open individual desks, there are rows of closed-type desks each equipped with an ORA machine. You put your reading material on the bottom of the machine, set the reading speed, then the teacher turns out the lights and you read the words on the page as they are lit by a moving bar of light from the ORA machine. You are supposed to read no faster or slower than the light travels. We started at a very slow speed today and it was quite painful. I bet I am much faster than most.

Neil brought back my tapes today. I'm very impressed he didn't just keep them. I remember I lent my tape of *Jack: A Flash Fantasy* to Arvid and he put me off for months before finally returning it, and then without the case! Finally, an intelligent and reliable person I can be friends with. Now I have his phone number too!

Friday, September 18, 1975

I got 8/10 on my economics quiz. Not bad at all! School was pretty quiet. I think the Grade Nines were away somewhere.

Didn't see Neil today. When I phoned his place, his mom didn't know where he was. Called Arvid and we rode down to Bowes Creek and threw stones in.

Saturday, September 19, 1975

Called Neil's today but again his mom said he wasn't around. Where does he go?

I was bored so I walked downtown. There is an art gallery in a tiny old house just around the corner of 4th on Smith. I went in and they had lots of pictures made with wheat and straw and bits of things. Cool. The woman in charge was eyeing me nervously and didn't sit down again until I was heading out the door.

Thursday, September 30, 1975

Today in music we are studying *Tommy* by The Who. Far out, man! There is a movie about it too, but we are listening to the double album from 1969. Some pretty cool music. I can relate to the kid Tommy. Perhaps it would be easier to be deaf, dumb and blind. Or if I could just not feel the blows of my tormentors. Called Neil later but he still wasn't there.

Friday, October 3, 1975

I think Neil doesn't like Arvid or Ken much. If I'm hanging out with them, he stays away. I'm not surprised because they talk about a lot of stuff that he is plain not interested in.

Today Neil and I took off at lunch and walked past Sacred Heart. It wasn't that cold out. We talked about space and the future. We are definitely going to get off this planet sometime.

I asked him where he goes all the time, and he told me that usually he's in one of two places: the shed in his backyard (his folks won't call him to the phone if he's out there) or the public library. He has an older brother who listens to music all the time in the shed but when his brother's friends show up, Neil gets kicked out. I said I'd go to the library with him sometime.

On The Public Library as Sanctuary
(Lionel O'Neill, 1988)

While my parents were mostly able to ignore my shed-dwelling music-loving brother Jerry's activities, except perhaps at meal time when we were all thrown together by common need, I was able to escape most conflicts by keeping my own nose stuck in a book, or better yet, a entire library.

I spent a lot of time inside the Yorkton Public Library. Back then it was located at the corner of 4th Avenue North and Broadway Avenue. The main building was an old, wood and brick two storey. The collections were housed on the main floor. Probably they had storage in the basement. I think upstairs were some unrelated offices.

You had to step down and over an uneven floor join to enter the adult section, which was actually located in a smaller, single storey building directly adjacent. This is where I discovered the fiction of Arthur C. Clarke, Ben Bova, Philip K. Dick, Harry Harrison, Pierre Boule, Frederik Pohl, and many other SF greats.

The music section was at the front of the library, near the entrance, and that is often as far as Jerry would need to go when he occasionally accompanied me. Directly behind the records and tapes were the newspapers and magazines. At least one librarian was invariably present and observant behind the long counter facing all this. The children's book collection occupied the rear section of the building.

I preferred the adult section, well out of view of the librarians behind their check-out counter. Here I remember was where I came to sit on the floor and read novel after novel for those months in 1975 and 1976 when my parents' battle was reaching a climax. The staff were kind, first telling me that I could sit on a chair instead of the floor. I just thought that they wouldn't want my snow-wet clothes on the few chairs that they had, chairs for their important, adult clients.

So I would read another and another book there, maybe checking it out, but usually not. I did not often take books home. I was also very conscious that they might get soiled, so hardcovers or very new books I would just leave at the library. This had its own risks. One time a fine hardcover copy of <u>Planet of the Apes</u> escaped before I could read its last fifty pages. It finally did reappear on the shelf, but I spent a two week interlude mentally kicking myself for letting it go.

Later that year Roger began to meet me at the library on those days when my mental state allowed company. He encouraged me to take my loans home, and generally convinced me I was a valid customer, and not a real or potential annoyance and inconvenience to the staff.

On St. Joseph's Layout and Architecture
(Roger Kay, 1994)

St. Joseph's Junior High School was a sprawling polygon of edifice compared to Victoria School, the little brick box where I spent grades one through six. One of only two junior highs in the city, it accommodated about 600 kids and was located directly across the street from both high schools that Yorkton offered: the public Yorkton Regional High School to the west, and the private (Roman Catholic) Sacred Heart High School to the north. This concentration of secondary schools meant the area was swarming with adolescents. Saint Joe's, as we called it, started out as a Catholic men's college but by 1973 it was a junior high school, housing grades seven through nine.

The complex had been built in two phases. The old building, the east-facing first phase, was square, four storey (including basement), and built long before I was born. The basement level housed the science labs plus some very decrepit and oddly shaped rooms used as far as I could tell only for Economics and Christian Ethics classes.

The three levels above this were notably refurbished in comparison.

The main or ground level held the Industrial Arts and Home Economics labs. The 'Home Ec' lab was a large open space with multiple kitchen areas. The Industrial Arts area included a large, open workshop space plus a photography dark room with a very nifty purpose-built convoluted entry hall that obviated the need for any door yet kept the inner room in perpetual blackness.

There was also an Art room, which was a large, well-windowed area behind the original entrance to the old building. That doorway was never used but the grand steps leading to it were a favorite hangout for the older kids at lunchtime.

On the second level was the library, sometimes referred to as the Resource Center, plus a modern media room labeled with splashy '70s graphics as the ETV (educational television) room. The ETV room was used both for TV production by senior Industrial Arts students and by all grades for the viewing of videotapes or TV programs.

The top level of the old building held the Grade 9 classrooms and lockers. Unlike the other classroom areas, the relative value and maturity of its denizens was emphasized by the fact that it was freshly painted in vibrant and boldly modern (for that time) colors and fully carpeted.

Beyond the old building was the newer, larger remainder of the complex which was probably built in the sixties. A classroom wing faced north but sprawled west behind the old building. It had two stories: Grade 7 classrooms on the main floor, Grade 8 on the second. Lockers adjacent to classes.

Beyond that, there was an administration wing that faced west onto Gladstone Avenue, with a view of the Regional High School across the street. This would be considered the back by students, but the front by adults. It contained only disciplinary destinations: the offices of the Principal and Vice Principal.

Past the admin wing, on the southwest corner of the complex, an atrium provided a grand entrance to the gymnasium to the south, and served multiple purposes for internal events as well as a greeting and coatcheck area for adult guests during external events. The gymnasium also contained a stage for theater and assemblies.

Adjacent to the gymnasium but further east were the change rooms, and Physical Education (Phys-ed we call it) offices. Connecting this area back to the old building and the classroom wing was a long mezzanine, half full of rows of lockers which completed the hollow square that was the newer portion of St. Joe's.

In the center of the hollow square was a smaller, round building which contained a chapel on the second storey, accessible only from the admin wing, and a music room on the main floor, accessible only from the mezzanine.

The student entrance was on the east side, facing the mostly empty remainder of the school's full city block which contained the bike stands, some marginally grassy areas, and a baseball diamond at the far east end.

I remember my friend Neil describing the ancient historical basis for the architectural concept of St. Joe's. Neil was knowledgeable about most anything you could read in a book and was probably the only Grade 8 kid I had ever met, myself included, who had heard of Frank Lloyd Wright.

He said St. Joe's was based on the feudal idea of the citadel. In the middle ages a community of peasants would be housed in a compact town surrounded by a protective wall. A small, fortified enclave, the citadel, was located at the heart of the town and this is where the feudal lord, the ruler of his society, and his knights would live.

In Neil's analogy, the feudal city was the hollow square delineated by the old building, the classroom wing, the admin wing, the gymnasium, and the mezzanine locker area. The citadel was represented by the round building inside the hollow square, which in this case contained only a chapel and below that, the music room. The feudal lord and his knights, represented by our principal and the teachers, did occasionally gather in the chapel to validate their divine authority and to plan the work of the peasants, meaning us, the students.

Neil certainly believed in the impact of rock music on the development of political identity and philosophy for the modern teenager. The music room was situated directly below the chapel, and its doorway faced the opposite direction. Its music spilled out onto the mezzanine level to rattle the lockers, while the silence of the empty and serene upper room, the chapel, did not disturb the powers of status quo in the administration wing.

There was music, secret and subterranean, alien to the church and yet inside the perimeter of the citadel. This juxtaposition of architectural spaces, the chapel versus the recital room, was more than a coincidence to Neil. It was predictive: music would supplant religion in the hearts and minds of the new generation.

Entries from Roger Kay's 1975 Diary

Monday, October 6, 1976

In ORA today I managed to hit 550 words per minute and still passed the comprehension test. I think I am the fastest reader in the class! Ken and Arvid both barely passed at the 400 level and Brian was at 300 and failing. I'm starting to like this class.

Friday, October 10, 1975

After school I finally got to go inside Neil's house. It is not as nice as ours and quite a bit smaller. His mom seems very unhappy and tired in person. When I bring a friend over, I have to beg my Mom to leave us alone, else she will be pestering us with cookies and questions. Neil's mom hardly noticed we were there. She just laid on the couch, listening to CJGX.

We came in through the back porch, which was filled with empty beer cartons, into their little kitchen, and what a mess that was! There were containers and all sorts of things, a lot of it not food-related, lying on all the surfaces. Dirty dishes in the sink. Maybe they had a big party the night before. When Neil introduced me to his mom, she just looked at me with dead eyes and said, okay, don't make a mess honey. Everything was already a mess so I'm not sure what she was talking about.

Later Neil got us a snack, some stale animal crackers he was hiding in his room, and some Kool-Aid he made himself, right next to the sink, as I watched. I never make Kool-Aid myself (Mom always keeps a jug ready in the fridge) but I'm pretty sure you need to use a whole packet of powder for each jug. Today Neil used half a packet and when I pointed out that he should use the whole packet, he just stopped moving for a second and then said no, I have to leave half for me and my brother's supper. I dropped the subject.

Neil has a lot of interesting drawings in his room, not really drawings like art, but more technical stuff. He has a chart of how tall King Kong is versus other more familiar objects, including a six foot man, a giraffe, the Yorkton post office building, and finally the water tower (slightly taller).

Also a very strange blueprint for the interior of the saucer from *The Day The Earth Stood Still*, showing a rest/stow area for the robotic guardian Gort, also one for the humanoid Klaatu, as well as a cockpit with a glass floor, all of which never actually appeared in the movie.

Friday, October 17, 1975

Tonight at 10 there is a show called *Space 1999*. I hope by space they mean outer space!! I'm going to have a bath and then tape it on my ever trusty Lloyd's tape recorder. How's that for optimistic?

Saturday, October 18, 1975

Neil saw *Space 1999* last night too. We hung out in Shaw Park, despite the cold wind, and talked about it all afternoon. We both feel like something really big is happening and for once we are there to see it. I had a notebook and we were both trying to sketch that Eagle spacecraft used by the Moonbase Alpha astronauts but we couldn't really agree what it looks like beyond the nosecone.

I taped the show on cassette, of course, but that doesn't help our drawing efforts. I invited Neil to come in and listen to it but he was on his way downtown to meet his brother.

On Breakaway (Roger Kay, 1994)

I remember the night of Friday, October 17, 1975 very vividly.
The Yorkton Enterprise newspaper made your hands filthy.
The ink was cheap and smeared at first touch. If you read that
pure black ink and then touched a wall, you could leave a hand
print and cause yourself some trouble. My parents were quite
earnest in their advocacy of clean walls.

Despite these dangers, I was always eager to check the TV
listings on the lookout for possible SF or horror movies. We
had one channel, CKOS Television, channel 3, so it didn't take
long to scan the listings. The results were usually
disappointing.

Another frustration was that most of the good (i.e. SF or
horror) movies that played were very old and run only late at
night. On weekends my parents were accommodating and let
me stay up late to watch movies, as long as I used our old black
and white TV in the basement and made very little noise. If the
movie timeslot interfered with a school night, I was out of luck.

At that time, *Star Trek* was unknown to me. It had been
cancelled in the late sixties and had never played on CKOS. It
was later that year before I managed to finally see part of a few
Star Trek episodes while on painful shopping trips with my
parents to Regina, the capital city of Saskatchewan. By then it
was too late - I was inoculated with 1999 and immune to the
full force of Trek's charms.

On this particular day however, I spotted something in the
TV listings with the enticing name "Space: 1999". There was
no synopsis or other details given but the combination of the
futuristic date, plus the word 'space' intrigued me. Was it
something to do with the space program, or could it be a new
science fiction show?

The premiere episode played fairly late that evening, 10 pm
for some reason, but I was wide awake and eager to see what
this strange program might be. The first episode is of course
"Breakaway" and deals with Commander John Koenig's arrival
as the newly appointed commander of Moonbase Alpha.

Koenig's job is to deal with a mysterious sickness affecting the local moon base astronauts, as well as the crew chosen for an interplanetary mission to the newly discovered planet Meta, a planet from which a mysterious mathematical signal emanates.

The first few scenes are reminiscent of *2001: A Space Odyssey* (which I had not seen at the time) in that the new Commander transits from Earth orbit aboard a stewardess-bearing shuttle in order to arrive at a moon base to deal with a top-secret problem. In the case of 1999, the problem was not the discovery of an alien monolith under the lunar surface, but a strange disease possibly connected with subsurface nuclear waste storage facilities.

By the time the first episode is over, the Meta spacecraft crew are dead, both of the two lunar nuclear waste areas have exploded, and the Moon has hurtled free of Earthly orbit. Commander Koenig has made a tough command decision: retreat to Earth is impossible; Moonbase Alpha will be the Alphans' home as they travel the cosmos.

It appears the Alphans are headed towards Meta. Fade out on the mysterious sinusoidal wave signal.

On Breakaway (Lionel O'Neill, 1988)

The night of Friday, October 17, 1975 was a watershed for me. Two extraordinary events happened that day, both with effects that colored everything that came after.

The first event was the departure of my father, Earl, in a police car. He wasn't driving. The second was my exposure to the very first episode of the series *Space: 1999*, titled "Breakaway".

When I got home from school that afternoon there was already a fight percolating. I think it had been payday. Earl was sitting in the living room with a bottle. Mom was in the kitchen cleaning. They were bellowing at each other, flinging dismissive comments back and forth though they were in different rooms and not actually facing each other. Earl shouted that the house was always a mess and that Mom could not cook, was worthless, a hypochondriac, and many other things I've tried to forget since.

Mom seemed to be standing her ground for once. She screeched back with similar ardor. He was a drunkard who didn't bring home enough money to raise all the children he had created. The implication that *he* had created all the children, not her, and was somehow more responsible for our pathetic lives, was a new twist to me. I had become accustomed to hearing Earl complain about how hard he worked and how ungrateful and lazy we all were, how he had put the roof over our heads but none of us raised a finger to help out. I didn't think this fair of course because we all helped Mom around the house and we all lived in fear of his temper. Earl complained we were lazy but after his day of work he would just plop down into a chair, open a bottle, and watch TV. I was the one who did the bulk of the chores, and a lot of the shopping too. I tried to stay out of their way, and that meant being out of the house a majority of the time.

This particular day however I stuck around, hiding in the bedroom I shared with my dear brother Jerry. I couldn't help but overhear their verbal sparring and it escalated as the dark came on, around 7 pm that evening. Mom had prepared something she called Sportman's Steak for supper which on a normal night would have evoked only the usual complaint from Earl that one would indeed need to be a sport to call this meat a steak. Tonight however they were taking things to a new limit. When we assembled in the kitchen to get our portion of Mom's cooking, Earl asked Mom, very unfairly and unkindly, where she had wasted the rest of his money. She said something like, this is all we can afford on your peon wages. This set him off. He backhanded her and she fell against the counter. I was shocked, being accustomed only to verbal explosions. Jerry took me firmly by hand and pulled me outside, directing me to go into his shed. But as Jerry went back into the house I hid near the back door to watch.

Jerry walked right past Earl and opened the front door. Maybe he intended to invite or push Earl out that door. He turned to confront Earl. Jerry raised his hand and shook his index finger in Earl's face and firmly instructed him never to hit Mom again. This enraged Earl and he re-directed his abuse toward Jerry, but this was ineffective: Jerry stood his ground between them. Earl then pushed Jerry backwards through the rear porch door and started throwing things around in the kitchen. Mom was a lump on the floor, crying. Jerry told me to go across the alley to a neighbour's and call the police, which I did.

The neighbours were elderly and not inclined to accompany me. I returned alone only a couple of minutes later, to find everyone still in the living room. Mom was on the couch, nursing her bruised face in shaky hands. Earl and Jerry were standing deadlocked, face to face. Each had grabbed the other's arms. Earl warned Jerry that he had to listen to him or get the hell out of his house. Jerry swore and threatened Earl, saying he would pay for hurting Mom. Soon they were struggling to break free of each other. Jerry managed to get an arm loose and connected a punch to Earl's face, which forced him back a couple of steps. Fists rained for a minute but Jerry, with the advantage of being sober and focused, slowly got the better of Earl. Earl fell back on the couch at one point right on top of Mom, but Jerry pulled him off and swung him around. This caused a lot of damage throughout the living room.

Around this time the RCMP showed up. One officer smelled Earl's boozy breath and hauled him out to the police car. Another two threw Jerry on the carpet and handcuffed him. After they talked to Mom and heard her injuries were solely the work of Earl, they let Jerry up, took off the cuffs, and asked if he was okay. When Jerry said he was, they ordered him to take me out of the house so they could talk to Mom alone.

Jerry and I sat in the shed with the door open so we could see into the house through the back door. At one point I remember I peeked around the side of the house and saw Earl sitting in the back of the police car. He looked out of it, almost asleep, head bowed and eyes closed.

Jerry was scraped and shaken. I moistened a cloth using the outside faucet and used that to wipe his face a bit.

We came back into the house only after the police took Earl away. Mom was crying and she hugged Jerry and me, but very soon, much too soon for me, she was wailing in fear about what we were going to do without Earl. The police had not been clear on when Earl would return. By then it was well past eight o'clock. By nine, she had gone to bed and Jerry had gone out. And not just to the shed.

I tidied up the kitchen, putting broken dishes in the garbage and wiping up food from the floor and walls. In the living room I straightened the furniture and our meager possessions. I didn't throw anything out, even if it was broken.

When ten o'clock came, I turned on the television and had the most wonderful surprise. A new science fiction show, with beautiful spaceships, a spacious and stylistically minimalist moon base housing a complement of astronauts who live in a future where talented, caring humans struggle with complicated, exciting and important issues like nuclear waste storage and interplanetary missions. I was transfixed, lost in this new, better world. At the end of that first episode, when the

Moon breaks free from Earth orbit, and the Alphans leave our solar system, I went with them most willingly.

Earl did return after a couple of days. He threatened Mom with divorce. That didn't happen right away for a variety of reasons, but a series of escalating separations did result. Meanwhile the drinking and fighting continued. After that, other than to eat or sleep, Jerry rarely came in from the shed, his 'clubhouse'.

Entries from Roger Kay's 1975 Diary

Monday, October 20, 1975
Mom got a phone call before breakfast. Aunt Doris died in her sleep. Today Neil was very distant. He seemed sleepy in class and in recess he just sat down beside a tree and wouldn't talk. I really hope he isn't mad at me.

Tuesday, October 21, 1975
Everything is better today. Neil is his old self and we spent study period designing interstellar spaceships.

Wednesday, October 22, 1975
In Science class we had to dissect a worm. We were split into groups of four and I was with Ken, Sandra Sprong and Gloria Zaharia. Nobody wanted to cut the worm open but eventually Ken did, all the while making worm terror noises: "Help me! Ahhh!"

When I did the report cover I drew a worm bent upright, with hands in a prayer-like pose, saying, "Please, no, don't..."

Thursday, October 23, 1975
Today on the way home William, who is in Grade 9 and a lot bigger than me, caught up to my bicycle and forced me to stop. He had two friends with him but quickly assured me he wasn't planning to beat me.

He showed me a piece of lettuce and said I had to tell them what it tasted like before they'd let me go. I didn't want to, but he kept threatening me and said if I just tasted it once I could go. Lettuce doesn't have much taste so I did put it in my mouth and chewed it a little. Only then did he tell me that they had been dissecting a frog in Science and that the piece of lettuce was actually frog skin. I started to retch and they pedaled away, laughing. How can I be so stupid?

Friday, October 24, 1975
Neil saved my butt in Phys-ed class this morning. We had a combined Phys-ed class with 8-23 and we were supposed to run all the way around JayCee beach. Of course everyone who knows anything takes the shortcut through the bike trails. I did too, and after I rounded the last treacherous bit, where the path

becomes quite narrow and very angled as it passes up the edge of a little hill and makes a sharp turn, wham I'm facing Lucky and a couple of his goons who hassle me for clinging onto the branches as I maneuver around the sharp, steep curve.

Hey why don't you just fly over that part, they say. Don't you have your license yet? I take the bait and ask: what license? Your fairy license.

I was feeling cocky for some reason, maybe a little light headed from the unusual exertion, so I tell them: I'm into science fiction, not fantasy, and didn't trolls like them belong below the trail, not on it? They were moving in for the kill, grabbing me, when Neil comes around curve. He walks right up to Lucky, without a word, reaches up and clamps his neck in one hand.

"You mess with my friend again and you'll be eating broken teeth" he says, waving his fist in Lucky's face. Lucky's friends instantly vanish and he quickly backs down saying: sorry, sorry.

Nobody ever stuck up for me like that. It was great! Neil might be short but he is very strong, and his facial hair makes him look menacing too.

On the Importance of Family (Lionel O'Neill, 1988)

Most days, after my father came home after work, he would drop himself in front of the television and commence ingesting beer. This would continue all night with only a short intermission called while my mother served supper. It is clear to me now that my mother suffered from depression; she was endlessly enervated and listless, doing the minimum required to get through each day and avoid Earl's wrath. Our evening meal was consistently dismal, some warmed over leftovers or something she had frozen long ago and now emerged from the freezer like an alien autopsy ready for dissection and classification.

Supper was a time for battle between my parents and my older brother, Jeremiah, or Jerry as I called him. In 1975 I was fourteen, and Jerry was nineteen. He had finished high school two years prior but was perpetually under or unemployed. Jerry spent much of his considerable free time behind our house, in our shed, his clubhouse, listening to rock music, reading an eclectic array of books, and generally avoiding the next dirty, low-paying job.

Jerry was like a god to me. He did not sit down for the abuse my parents paid him, hence the battlefield of suppertime. I learned more about rock groups of the seventies from his defense of his latest LP purchase than from my peer group. While Jerry wore his hair long, much to our parents dismay, mine was still relatively short, only onto the shoulders and not over them and down the back like Jerry. I tried to stay clear of these rock battles. Jerry was focused on the sixties and seventies; I was focused on the future.

I remember telling Jerry this early on, but he insisted that rock and roll was the future and that when the current older generation was out of the way, things would change rapidly. No more discrimination against longhairs, their music, and or their 'sacrament' (one of the code words he used to reference marijuana). At first I found this hard to reconcile.

Jerry first encouraged me to experiment with drugs around this time. His clubhouse was crammed full of his stuff, books, records, drawings, a half-disassembled motorcycle that never ran, and just enough space for Jerry and a couple of his friends to sit on stolen lawn chairs and hang out.

Stu 'College' and Steve Bishop were Jerry's best friends. Stu had a beautiful new black and yellow Monza Spyder. If his friends were around, Jerry might quickly dismiss me. If they were absent, it was a different story. He would encourage me to hang out and listen to music with him. Around the time I entered Grade 8, he offered me my first toke.

I remember it felt really good, much better than cigarettes, like all my troubles added up to nothing in the face of this new experience. Just the fact that Jerry would share this secret activity with me made me love him and it all the more.

At first I could not reconcile the drug taking with my love of knowledge and science fiction but Jerry made efforts to convince me our interests were not so far apart. I remember Jerry playing different albums and showing me that each had a science fiction angle: the Rolling Stones' "20,000 Light Years From Home", Black Sabbath's "Iron Man", also their "Into The Void", Jimi Hendrix's "EXP" and "Third Stone From The Sun". He made me see how rock and roll and SF were related, or at least not necessarily diametric opposites nor mutually exclusive.

Entries from Roger Kay's 1975 Diary

Saturday, October 25, 1975

Saw my second episode of *Space 1999* today! Taped it. It is called "War Games"! Moonbase Alpha is under attack by aliens who are using 'Mark 9 Hawks', ships similar but a little pointier around the nosecone than the Eagles. The moonbase is destroyed in a giant battle with mysterious, smooth-headed aliens who sit around in glass boxes, but at the end of the episode, time rewinds and they get a second chance because when they, this time, choose not to destroy the Hawks, the aliens also do not attack but instead send a message saying, "You may have saved yourself, but because of your warlike ways, you can never come to our planet." So much for settling on planet Meta.

Sunday, October 26, 1975

Had to get up early today, put on my suit, and go to church. We go to the United Church on Smith Street and the pastor is Reverend Jones. He is an old guy with only a little remaining white hair, but tall and sort of powerful-looking, with a booming voice. Sunday School for my age is held in a smaller hall on the main floor of the annex building. We have to sit around and listen to Bible readings and have silly discussions about Jesus' supposed love for Man. Not very convincing considering the world we live in.

Monday, October 27, 1975

Discussed "War Games" with Neil today. He showed me his sketches of the Hawk spacecraft, and also some new Eagle sketches. They are very good! I can never make things look three dimensional like that. We're still not sure if the planet Meta was where those aliens came from.

Wednesday, October 29, 1975

Today after school Neil and I went to the Co-op. I was looking for a costume. They have a lot of stuff this year, a real big Halloween area in the basement. It's cool going in there because they have one of the few elevators in Yorkton that John Q. Public can ride. Funny that it only goes between the main floor and basement. At St. Joes there are old parts which are four stories high but still no elevator.

Anyhow, I only had a buck to spend but I knew what I wanted. I picked up a bald wig for 75 cents. Neil bought some face paint crayons for 50 cents. I asked him what he was going to go as, but he just said: I'll think of something.

Thursday, October 30, 1975

I spent most of the evening working on my Halloween costume. I wanted to be one of those mysterious and powerful aliens from "War Games" so I needed a bald head, some little blobs to replace my eyebrows and a long flowing robe. Mom found an old silk bathrobe of hers that was worn out and she converted it into an alien toga for me. Also I made new eyebrows out of painted, unpopped popcorn kernels mounted on a backing of cardboard. The final touch is the bald wig I found at the Co-op yesterday. The only problem is that I have very thick hair and even though it is not really that long, it makes my bald wig look a little lumpy.

Friday, October 31, 1975

Halloween! Right after supper I put on my costume, tried to smooth out my head lumps (not very successfully), then grabbed a pillowcase and headed out. I did my own block plus the next down 5th, then did a short block down Darlington other side before crossing back to Neil's house. He was just finishing with his face paints (I didn't recognize what he was trying to do, but I didn't ask) and we soon left to do 6th, which we covered entirely from Smith to Henderson St.. Then we did 4th all the way from Smith St. to York Road. We slipped over to 3rd Avenue then and began to work our way back but by the time we got to the Kinsmen park, we were out of time. No way I'm missing an episode of 1999! And I already had a heavy pillowcase of candy.

Some kid in a pirate costume kept yelling at me "Hey brain tumor alien!" Not sure who that was.

Space 1999 was called "Collision Course" and I taped it. This time a giant planet is right in the path of the Moon and Moonbase Alpha and when Commander Koenig takes an Eagle to go check it out, he is intercepted by this huge alien ship. Onboard he meets a very old female alien (Arra) who assures him that his, and the Alphans', destiny is not to be crushed by the planet and therefore he must do nothing to interfere with her plans. Back on Alpha they are busily planning to explode some nukes between the Moon and the planet to create a shockwave to change the Moon's path. When Koenig tries to stop them, they think he is nuts and confine him to quarters.

As the critical moment approaches Koenig (and fearless Eagle pilot Alan Carter) escape from detention and hold Main Mission hostage, preventing the Alphans from carrying out their shockwave plan. At the last moment, just as Koenig thinks Arra has abandoned him, he cries out to her in despair. Then the planet winks out of existence and all is well. Next time the Alphans will know better than to question Koenig!

It was a very exciting episode but I feel a little sick now because I was scarfing candy the whole time I watched it.

Monday, November 3, 1975

I think I know why Neil is so short. He smokes! His brother gives him the occasional cigarette and you can also buy them in singles from the corner store. I never heard of that before.

The last class before lunch was Health class and it was about puberty and sex. On the way home for lunch I saw Neil at the corner store and he was smoking. I asked him if he had had the same class and he said yeah, but sex is for animals and that he didn't need to hear about grownup bullshit. I asked if he wanted kids when he grew up and he said: no way!

Thursday, November 6, 1975

It rained this morning. The temperature was definitely way above freezing. Then the sun came out in the afternoon and it was really quite nice!

Neil told me he was going to build an Eagle out of clay and he knew where to get the clay and today was the perfect day to get some. So after school we headed down Gladstone to York Road. We walked to Leon's Manufacturing and then snuck beside it, along the railway tracks, until we were behind it. There is a valley behind there which I've never seen before, with fairly gentle sloping sides, and only a tiny bit of water at the very bottom. We went a ways down the side and we were leaving big foot prints, sinking into the squishy slope. Neil had a bag with him and scooped up some of the ground. He says he only has to dry it out then he can use it for clay. He said he and his brother used to get clay from there long ago. We walked back to his place and he laid the clay out beside his shed, squishing it flat so the Sun could dry it quickly tomorrow.

Later at supper I told my folks about Neil's resourcefulness and they were aghast. They said our valley is actually a drainage ditch for the water treatment plant, and the water at the bottom was actually sewage. Yuck! They made me promise not to go back there again.

Friday, November 7, 1975

Today I told Neil what I learned about the drainage ditch. He said yeah it was possible but didn't think it was a big deal. There was nothing there, he shrugged, and you don't go all the way down the side anyway. He says it is too cold for his clay to dry properly so I guess I won't be seeing a clay Eagle anytime soon.

Space 1999 was called "Force of Life". I taped it. A mysterious ball of blue light descends from space and enters one of their nuclear technicians, Anton Zoref, and he winds up becoming a life-sucking zombie, who leaves a trail of frozen corpses but remains undetected because he reverts back to normal after each attack. Finally he absorbs all the energy in one of Alpha's nuclear reactors and then leaves as a slightly larger (and I assume happier) ball of blue light.

Going to Junior High, I know something about life-sucking zombies, so this episode hits home!

Monday, November 10, 1975

Accidentally brought my Science textbook to Math class, so I have homework. Oops. Talked to Neil about Anton Zoref during lunch. He pointed out that it doesn't make sense that the blue ball would leave the Moon after absorbing all the energy from the single nuclear reactor it caused to explode. Why wouldn't it stick around and finish off the other reactors as well? I suggested it might already be full and was heading home to feed its young. Damn, I'm smart.

Friday, November 14, 1975

Neil promised to give me a copy of his best Eagle sketch so I needed an extra dime today. We photocopied it during recess and I paid the office people.

I taped 1999. It was called "Death's Other Dominion". The Moon encounters a frozen planet, Ultima Thule, where the remnants of a human colony from a crashed spaceship live underground in caves. Somehow they exist on a different timeline- the colony is over two hundred years old and the inhabitants are immortal! When the Alphans are invited to join the Thulians, they consider it and attempt to bring the leader back to Alpha for discussion. That's when they find out Thulians turn into a steaming pile of decomposing muck when they attempt to leave the special environment of their chilly planet. Scratch that planet off the potential homes list! Some great acting in this episode. The snowy blowy planet surface makes me think of our winter. You might as well be on a hostile planet when you're stumbling around in the whiteout conditions of a Saskatchewan flurry.

Already it is getting very cold some mornings. I've had to bring out my mitts and scarf which just brings me more razzing at school. I can't help it though as I am very sensitive to cold. Probably because I'm skinny. No fat or muscle to cushion and protect me from chilly weather, or the blows of the stupid.

Sunday, November 16, 1975

Today I had to get dressed up and go to church. I hate it there because everyone is so fake and smiley. The teachers all talk about love and God's plan for us then when they turn around it is all-out war. I got an elastic band in the face today. I should have brought some thumb tacks with me.

On Religion (Lionel O'Neill, 1988)

Religion was complicated but distant for me. My father is Catholic, but my mother was Jewish and they never reconciled this difference. I don't think I ever stepped into the Jewish Temple. A circumcision did occur at some point, although thankfully I do not recall it. Likewise, I never did attend church as a Catholic. The closest to church attendance I had was taking the Christian Ethics class instead of Economics at St. Joe's.

I personally do not believe in any gods, God, or G-d. The world is too messed up for anyone to be looking after it. The only explanation is that random chance has left us here to fend for ourselves. My brother Jerry certainly believed this too.

I believe in love, but I do not believe in selfless or supernatural love.

In later life I thought perhaps I had become an entheogenist, contacting core reality through altered states. Certainly I've seen Hell, but I've yet to see Heaven. Regardless of my views, the universe must have pleasure in being alive, otherwise it would not exist.

On the Utility of Violence (Lionel O'Neill, 1988)

When I was very young I did not question my parents, or any authority figures. My brother Jerry introduced me to the idea of resistance and self-respect but it came a bit too late. It was only when I saw him stand up to our father that I came to understand that violence could sometimes be necessary and a good thing. Without the ability to fight to defend oneself, you wound up a victim and injustice persisted unchecked.

By the time I was in Grade 8, I had thoroughly absorbed this lesson. I fought to protect myself and my friends. I recall coming across Roger Kay being pummeled against his locker. I liked Roger. He was one of the few people who didn't ostracize me for having a stutter plus we shared an affection for science fiction. I didn't hesitate to punch his attacker right in back of the head. He collapsed on the ground and I just kept moving. Both Roger and I escaped any blame for my victim's injury. The bullies' Law of Silence works both ways.

Entries from Roger Kay's 1975 Diary

Monday, November 17, 1975

Ken and I went downtown after school to look for a birthday present for Mom. He suggested the book <u>The Eagle Has Landed</u>, but I noticed it was not about Apollo 11, instead it was about some Germans in WWII. Who cares about that? He also suggested <u>Jaws</u> or <u>The Moneychangers</u> but I wasn't too sure. I think he was just messing around. I found an interesting book on the Bermuda Triangle, but eventually bought a Sydney Omarr Scorpio horoscope book instead. She can read it everyday and think of me!

Tuesday, November 18, 1975

Today is Mom's 42nd birthday so we went to the Broadway Café for Chinese food. Sweet and sour spareribs! Yum! When we came home Mom opened her presents. Dad got her something called a microwave oven. It sits on the countertop and cooks with microwave energy instead of heat, so the oven itself does not get hot. It is an Amana Radar Range and is very impressive looking with lots of chrome and smooth 'touch-pad' button where you enter the cooking time. Even Moonbase Alpha doesn't have that futuristic type of button!

Wednesday, November 19, 1975

I told Ken and Arvid about our new oven today. What a mistake that was. They said it was a waste of money and that it would fry my brain. No way Dad would buy something unsafe I said and the argument started. They invoked such experts as Brian Woloschuk who emphasized the faulty design of the microwave by punching me in the stomach and stealing my pencil. Had to do my multiple choice Economics test in pen so I didn't do as well as I should have. Now Brian is calling me 'Richie Rich'. What a bunch of jerks. I wish Neil was in my homeroom cause he'd straighten them out (I'm in 8-21 but he's in 8-23).

Had Chinese leftovers for supper, warmed up with the Amana. Tastes great and I'm not growing a second head or anything.

Thursday, November 20, 1975

Today in Math, Brian kept poking me in the back when we were supposed to be doing our questions. I said "What?" but he just looked surprised and said "What?" Then he was firing spitballs at me. I didn't notice at first but then I felt all these little blobs in my hair. I was freaking a bit as I pulled them out, trying to figure out what they were. How juvenile. Halfway through the period I had gotten nothing done. When I told him to lay off, he said "What are you going to do, microwave me?" As a result, I still have most of my math questions to do.

We had double Phys-ed at the end of the day. At first I was glad because Mr. Dutchak said we were not going outside, and it is pretty cold out, but then we wound up running laps from 2:25 until 3:35. My legs were sore after that and I had a hard time walking home. When I grow up, no doubt I'll have a job that requires running for hours at a time. Yeah, right. If I do, please just shoot me.

Friday, November 21, 1975

What a terrible week at school. When the other kids bugged me about wearing warm clothing I said you'd have to be stupid to just suffer from the cold. They took that to mean that I thought I was much smarter than they, so they started calling me Professor. Lucky kept coming up to me and saying, which hand am I going to hit you with Professor? There's no good answer to that.

Today's episode of *Space 1999* was called "Voyager's Return" and I taped it. The story is that an automated Earth space probe threatens Alpha with the deadly exhaust of its advanced propulsion system. Luckily the scientist who created the drive is on Alpha and is able to remotely deactivate it before it totally blasts Alpha. Unluckily, some aliens show up and their home worlds have already been destroyed by the drive and now they want to hold the whole of Moonbase Alpha responsible. Eventually the old scientist who had created the drive sacrifices himself by destroying the aliens and himself with his 'Keller Drive'. Goodnight!

Saturday, November 22, 1975

This afternoon I walked down to Accent on Books in the Broadway Park Plaza with Neil. I had a dollar to spend on a new paperback and I found a *Space: 1999* book called <u>Breakaway</u>. It has a picture of an Eagle hovering over Moonbase Alpha on the cover and contains the stories for several episodes. Neil lent me thirty two cents because the book is actually $1.25 plus of course 5% provincial sales tax.

On the way back from the mall, Neil came in to have a look at the Amana. He joked that hopefully aliens won't show up at my house and claim the Amana heat rays are causing destruction on other planets. That kind of joke I can take.

We practiced some Eagle drawings, using the cover of my new book as a reference, then he left just before supper.

Spent the evening reading <u>Breakaway</u>. It has a different order than the TV episodes. Instead of the "War Games" planet, the first thing they encounter after "Breakaway" is a planet they name Terra Nova.... Not Meta?!

Ran out of time and have to sleep now.

Sunday, November 23, 1975

We had to go to church today because I was being confirmed. What a joke. I only did it for my parents' sake. I don't really believe in God. Being confirmed means I no longer have to go to Sunday school and instead can sit in the upstairs sanctuary and listen to the real sermon. But if I have my choice I'll never go. Truth is, we only go sometimes. Since Aunt Doris died however it seems like we are going every week. What a drag.

Tuesday, November 25, 1975

In English today we had to write a paragraph describing a character and then read it to the class. I am still mad at Brian so I wrote a parody of him called 'Crian Wussachuk' that says in part, "Crian had a sloping forehead indicative of monkey-level brain activity, and he continually smelled of unwashed underwear. When he wasn't complaining about the work that he hadn't yet done, he liked to pester his betters".

Brian didn't like that at all but he couldn't do anything because I changed the name. Mr. Mitchell thought it was quite funny and gave me a B+.

Friday, November 28, 1975

1999 was called "Alpha Child". A child (the first born on Alpha) starts to grow at an amazing rate and very quickly is fully adult. It seems normal in other ways, but does not speak. Soon it becomes clear that the child is possessed by an alien. Then the mother also gets possessed and the rest of Alpha is in a fight not to get taken over by these aliens who turn out to be renegades on the run from a genetically controlled society.

In the end their aliens pursuers arrive, destroy the renegades, and return the Alphan child and mother to normal, which is good because Alpha needs some new population! In every episode at least one Alphan dies. I did tape it of course.

Saturday, November 29, 1975

Neil came over to the house this afternoon. I showed him my tape collection. I have quite a few movies as well as a lot of *Six Million Dollar Man* episodes. Now I also have seven *Space: 1999* episodes! I have to quit taping Six Mill Man otherwise I will not have enough cassettes. Already I am taping over some old cassettes but I don't want to tape over all of them since they are nicely labeled.

Supper was Kentucky Fried Chicken. Yum! I went with Dad to pick it up.

Tonight on TV I saw *The Omega Man* with Charlton Heston. Taped over two old Six Million $ Man episodes to get it.

Sunday, November 30, 1975

On the news they said that the Canada Post strike should now be over. It has gone on for more than a month! Why do they always go on strike before Christmas? Makes negotiations more fun no doubt. I just hope things get back to normal quickly so no presents are delayed. I get a lot of good stuff from my Aunts and Uncles through the mail.

Friday, December 5, 1975

Tonight's 1999 episode was amazing! "Dragon's Domain" follows this Alphan, Tony Cellini, who has nightmares about a space probe mission a few years previous which he barely survived. He returned alone from that mission in a survival capsule claiming the rest of the crew had been killed by a monster that lives in a spaceship graveyard.

Tony Cellini is having nightmares about that monster just as Alpha encounters the same graveyard of spaceships. You'd think they would believe him but they don't really and he has to take the battle to the monster by stealing an Eagle and confronting it himself. Only when the team of Alphans chasing Tony's stolen Eagle docks with the same graveyard ship do they meet the monster and kill it, but of course it is too late for Tony. Pretty dark stuff. The monster was very chilling with a giant green glowing eye, waving tentacles, and all the sound and fury of your worst nightmare. It sucks you into its under area then spits out a steaming skeleton!

Time for some nightmares of my own. Good night!

On My First Dance (Roger Kay, 1994)

I remember back when I was in Grade 7, one study period
Gloria Zaharia told me that Cindy Burke liked me and pushed
me to ask her to the sock hop of the following week.

I was quite excited about this, but wary because Cindy was
a very nice looking girl and I couldn't figure out what was
behind her liking me. I'm a decent looking guy, I suppose, but
it seemed to me that girls usually went for taller, more athletic
guys. So I was a little doubtful.

When I did manage to screw up the courage to talk to her,
she impressed me as nice but I also noted she didn't share many
of my interests. She was mostly interested in dancing. Maybe
she had the idea that I knew how to dance. Possibly one of my
'friends' mischievously planted that idea with her.

Friday, December 13, 1974 was the big day. The school
had canceled the final two periods so that everyone, from us
little Grade 7s to the big post-pubescent Grade 9s, could attend.

The gymnasium was dark and so full and you couldn't find
anyone easily. Eventually I bumped into Arvid and we hung
near the front, close to the stage. Then I spotted Cindy. I spent
a couple of songs fighting with myself before finally, during a
waltz, I summoned the nerve to ask her to dance. I calculated a
waltz would be much easier to execute than any of the modern
forms of dance which require a level of spontaneity quite
impossible to me under the pressure of a crowded sock hop.
Cindy seemed a little reluctant to agree at first, which seemed
strange considering her earlier avowed desire to dance with me,
but finally, after some prodding, she said okay.

At that time I was oblivious to the fact that most kids in my
grade didn't dance during these waltzes. I had waltzed a bit at
family weddings so I actually could foxtrot. What I didn't
understand was that in the context of a junior high sockhop the
songs I considered 'waltzes' were in fact 'slow dances',
something very different.

Slow dancing involves pressing your body tightly against
your partner and hardly moving. Only a few couples were

dancing, and they were all Grade 9s, no doubt already dating. I made a fool of myself by taking Cindy onto that dance floor and then foxtrotting her energetically around the gym at arm's length.

I guess everyone in my class saw and laughed their asses off at me for dancing this old-fashioned dance. Cindy was embarrassed too, I now realize, because directly after that, when I still didn't realize what a fool I had made of myself, I asked her for a modern dance, and she declined. I was forever marked as a nerd in the eyes of her and her friends.

Entries from Roger Kay's 1975 Diary

Friday, December 12, 1975

Today there was a big sock hop at school for all the grades. Our double English period was cancelled and instead my whole homeroom was marched down to the gymnasium and told to have a good time, although they did discourage us from close, slow dancing and said they would be on the watch-out for people making out, smoking, or trying to leave early.

I spent the hour and a half in a comfortable shadow in the far corner of the gym, away from the entrance and away from the stage. After last year's fiasco, I have no illusions about any of the girls in my grade. I just hung back, listened to the music, and tried to blend with the scenery. It worked. I escaped mentally or physically unharmed.

1999 was "Mission Of The Darians". I taped it. What happens is that Alpha encounters a huge spaceship or space city that is sending out a distress call. When they board the giant ship they discover the call is on automatic and that the disaster happened long ago. Now the ship is occupied by two classes of these aliens, or Darians: the primitive lower class are descendants of those who were exposed to the radiation and now no longer understand they are on a spaceship; and the upper crust of pure, unmutated Darians who know the score.

The Alphans upset the balance when they reveal to the lower class that the upper class are not Gods but just Darians, the same as them. The Alphans convince them that they all need to cooperate to save what remains of the Darian race. An amazing space city and some very beautiful and scantily clad elite Darians. Wow!

Friday, December 19, 1975

Last day of school before Xmas break. Got a 75% on my French assignment. Yes! And handed in my music report on ELO. Neil walked home with me after school and I gave him his present. He didn't have anything for me yet, but maybe soon.

I taped 1999 and it was "The Black Sun". The Moon is headed for a black hole, an area of space where there is incredible gravity and nothing can escape. The Alphans build a force field to cover the Moonbase but they don't have much hope it will work. When they finally do cross into the black hole there is some kind of intelligence inside and it saves them, letting them pass into a new area of space filled with lots of planets.

Saturday, December 20, 1975

Slept in cause I stayed up late last night and watched *Escape From the Planet of the Apes*. It was great! It is about two talking apes, Cornelius and Zira, who come from the so-called planet of the apes and land on this Earth. They are treated well at first, like celebrities, but then the humans eventually decide they must be killed to safeguard the Earth. In the end, the two intelligent apes die but their baby lives on, concealed in a zoo among normal apes. Sometimes I feel like it is me who has landed on the wrong Earth, and who the humans are out to get.

In the afternoon Neil and I hung out downtown. He was looking for a present for his cool brother Jerry for Xmas so we wandered around the Met, then Woolworths, then walked as far as MacLeods before he declared "Jerry needs music". So we turned back to The Stereo Hut on Betts Avenue and looked at their LPs. They were playing the new Queen LP, *A Night At The Opera* and we considered that carefully. They also had a new *Greatest Hits* by Nazareth but I thought the song "Love Hurts" was just too sappy for a real rock band. Finally Neil decided on this new group Rainbow, which was started by Deep Purple's guitarist. It is a little cheaper than the Queen album and Jerry is a big Deep Purple fan.

On the way home, Neil complained about all the fighting between his parents. Apparently Jerry just stays out in the shed and Neil stays far away from the house whenever he can. Neil spends a lot of time at the public library. Ever since his mom said she wanted a divorce, things have gotten a lot worse. This explains why a lot of the time when I go looking for him, Neil is not there and I can't find him. I feel bad for him. Why don't the parents of all the stupid bullies in the world get divorced instead? Why should it be Neil?

Thursday, December 25, 1975

Xmas!! I've got a lot of thank you letters to write to my Aunts and Uncles. Grandma sent me some Thank You Notes (she's no fool) plus 5 dollars. Mom and Dad did well by me. They got me: an Eagle model, two book sets, one by Isaac Asimov and one by Andre Norton, 18 blank cassettes (the 120 minute kind!), a couple of nifty cassette cases, a game called Radar Search, a photo album, two 24 exposure films for my 110 Haminex camera (plus some batteries for the integrated electronic flash), brown earmuffs, a shirt, a sweater, blue corduroy pants, some hangers, winter boots and socks.

My aunts and uncles got me: a game called Boggle and another one called Password, some shaving lotion (as if I need it), a deck of cards, a 1957 Chevy model, a keychain, some pens, and another 5 dollars.

We had to go to church in the morning but when we came back it was Christmas cookies and treats, and present opening time. I played with my new stuff until about 7 when we had a very late but excellent turkey dinner. Grandma stayed all day and so did Uncle Tim and Auntie Rose. They don't have any kids so I guess they like to come over to watch me open presents. I'm very good at it. Ha ha!

Friday, December 26, 1975

Today is Boxing Day so everything is closed. Hung around the house and played with my new stuff most of the day. Called Neil in the afternoon and told him about all my presents. Sounds like he didn't get much. I think his mom is Jewish, but I've seen a cross in his house too. His brother got him a paperback copy of One Flew Over The Cuckoo's Nest and we are planning to go see that movie this weekend.

Space: 1999 tonight was called "Guardian Of Piri". The Moon encounters a strange planet with a female alien called the Guardian played by the very sexy Catherine Schell, who was the Phantom's wife in *The Return of the Pink Panther*.

The Alphans cannot detect any life on Piri but the Guardian stops the moon in its tracks and somehow drugs the Alphans so that they only want to come to the planet and lounge around, sighing deeply. For some reason Commander Koenig does not fall under the influence of the Guardian and winds up alone, wandering an abandoned Alpha. Eventually he discovers that the antidote to the general sleepiness of life on Piri is strong emotion. He heads back to Piri and starts a fight with Morrow, Carter, and everyone. Once the violence beings, the others snap out of their stupor and realize they cannot stay on the planet. Koenig destroys the Guardian, and the scattered broken pieces prove she was a robot.

Saturday, December 27, 1975

Spent all morning working on my Eagle model. My head was getting a little dizzy from the Varsol at the end but now I'm almost done. Everything is painted, decals applied, and the main pieces are done and ready for a final gluing.

In the afternoon Neil and I walked down to Bowes River. To get there you head East down Darlington for several blocks until you get to Dracup Avenue, the edge of town. Then you cross Highway 9 and there is a gravel road which curves into a wooded area and dips just a bit, and when you get to the end, there is a pile of rocks. Just past the rocks, you have Bowes River. There is an old car, from the 1940s, that is partially covered by the water. Now that the river (it is more of a pond) is frozen, we can finally get to the car and crawl up on the hood, which is a great place to contemplate the universe.

We discussed yesterday's 1999 episode about the planet Piri. I thought it was quite evil for the Guardian to drug the Alphans and enslave them with a false sense of bliss, but Neil took the opposite idea: the Guardian was just trying to help the Alphans but did not understand their actual needs as human beings. I countered that by asking what happened to the original aliens who lived on Piri, did they die by accident or was there something about the Guardian's help that killed them? Neil admitted that perhaps there was something about the Guardian's bliss that was harmful to more than just humans.

Still, if the Guardian really wanted to harm the Alphans, it would not have given them bliss, but hostility and violence instead. Neil told me that there is a drug which causes violence and destruction and it is not some illegal drug. It is alcohol. He swore me to secrecy, then told me his father has a drinking problem and this has caused violence in the past. I feel bad for him. He left around 9.

I did the final gluing of components just before bed. I have an Eagle! Mere words cannot describe its beauty.

Sunday, December 28, 1975

Still eating Xmas leftovers today. Turkey and cranberry jelly sandwiches, yum!

Neil and I went down to the Tower Theater at 7 to see *One Flew Over The Cuckoo's Nest* but it was Restricted so we couldn't get in. We were M-A-D. It wasn't horribly cold so we went to Shaw Park and hung out on a bench and he told me the story anyway. I can see why he relates to the book, the mental ward in the hospital is similar to our own jail, St. Joe's, and some of the teachers are quite as evil as Nurse Ratched. Plus there is a character Billy Bibbit who stutters like Neil, only worse.

Came home around 9 and watched some TV.

Wednesday, December 31, 1975

Tonight Mom and Dad are going to a party at the house of Dad's boss. My Aunt Karen will be babysitting me and a couple of my friends. I've invited Neil and Arvid over and told them to bring a couple of records each. Probably Karen will watch TV upstairs and talk on the phone all night with her boyfriend, so we'll be able to play records in the basement all night.

Well what a disaster that was. It is like Neil and Arvid are not the same age at all. Neil brought over Black Sabbath *Sabotage* and something called Blue Oyster Cult. They are his brother's LPs. Black Sabbath look like real hippies and the music is real crazy, dark and furious sounding. During one part the singer screams "Suck me!". I was worried Karen might come down and bug us but she stayed upstairs the whole time.

Arvid didn't like it at all. Neil was explaining all the space-related songs that Black Sabbath has. Despite the name that sounds like a horror flick, they also dig outer space. This album didn't really show that.

Then there was the Blue Oyster Cult LP. One song, "The Last Days Of May" talks about these drug smugglers. It is pretty interesting stuff and no doubt what a lot of the older kids listen to.

On the other hand... this is what Arvid brought and it was all 45s, no LPs: "Thank God I'm A Country Boy" by John Denver, "Rhinestone Cowboy" by Glen Campbell, and "Philadelphia Freedom" by Elton John. I kidded him and asked if these were his grandmother's 45s and he didn't like that at all.

We listened to them all once to keep him happy, but it was clear we didn't like his choices. The B-side of the Elton John 45 had a Beatles song with John Lennon on it. I asked Arvid why he didn't bring some real Beatles LPs but he didn't have any because his parents thought they were hippies on drugs. Beatles might be old but it is still rock. I don't think you can classify this other stuff as rock and roll.

We listened to Neil's LPs all the way through, twice. We replayed "The Last Days of May" a few times, trying to hear all the lyrics and figure out how the story went. Arvid didn't seem happy during this. In fact he started to sulk as soon as we had finished with his records and moved on to Neil's. He couldn't say anything nice about Neil's music. Neil was trying to explain about the other work by these artists but Arvid kept interrupting and asking stupid questions. Soon Neil started stuttering and then could hardly speak so we just sat there and listened.

Arvid left about 10 but Neil stayed until just after midnight. My folks got home around 1 in the morning. They seemed in a good mood but Dad drove Karen home right away and I had to go to bed before he got back.

Entries from Roger Kay's 1976 Diary

Thursday, January 1, 1976
So begins 1976. I hope it is better than 1975, which although it was the United Nations' Year of the Woman, didn't seem to help me in meeting one.

Looking at last year's diary, I see I did quite well for a lot of the time, especially after August, but there are also some huge holes. This year I will strive to write every single day.

Part of my problem is that last year I was using a regular diary, which only allows one page per day. Some days I struggled to fill the page, and some days I ran over into the next day (or two!) because of too much going on in a single day. This caused me to skip some days because there was just no room to write. Therefore I have started this diary in an ordinary notebook. This will allow me to write as much or as little as needed each day. But I will write everyday, I pledge to you.

Friday, January 2, 1976
No 1999 today!? Damn! After school Neil and I went to the pool hall on Betts Ave. I know I'm not supposed to. Some guys were smoking out front. Neil asked one for a smoke and he said sure. We walked in, Neil bought a pop, and then we hung out in the back alley.

Neil told me how his dad was so upset with his sister when she got pregnant that he smashed things and yelled in her face that he wished she had been a homo, a lesbian, instead of what she was now, a slut. So there can be something worse than being a fag it seems. At least for women.

Solomon (guy from pool hall) says that at least with women they "can go into movie business". He thought that was real funny and I eventually got it later.

Saturday, January 3, 1976
This morning I told Mom and Dad that I am looking for a job. They already give me an allowance (a dollar a week) and a little bit more when I shovel snow or cut the grass, but with

some extra money I could buy lots of books, a few records, and see more movies too.

Well I went out for a while with Neil this afternoon and when I got back Mom told me that she had talked to her friend Betty Cuthbert, whose husband brings in the Leader Post from Regina everyday. She said they have some openings for paperboys so I called her husband, Fred, back right away and he offered me the route for downtown and 6th Avenue. It is perfect for me, a small route, 19 papers, which is nice cause I can't carry too much weight, but still it means an extra twelve dollars every two weeks! I just have to show up at the Mediterranean Restaurant on Monday after 4 and there will be a stack of Leader Posts for me and a list of addresses to deliver them to.

Watched a bunch of mindless TV with the folks. No science fiction.

Sunday, January 4, 1976

Thank God no church today. I had to work on my book report anyway. I wrote about Pierre Boule's <u>Planet Of The Apes</u>. I discussed the differences between the book and the very excellent movie.

I'm very excited about starting my paper route tomorrow!

Monday, January 5, 1976

So today was the second day of school in 1976. I'm still getting used to it. I'm still writing 1975 on everything. 1976 just seems so strange.

Today I started my paper route! It is very cool. I get to deliver to these places: Mediterranean Restaurant (three papers!), the bowling alley, the library, a Leader Post reporter's office, another office called P.C.C., the Balmoral Hotel (Room 11), Castle Feed & Seed, 60 Turbo, and about nine houses on 6th, just a block from my own house. The bag was quite heavy when I first filled it so I struggled a bit downtown, but by the time I start down 6th it was okay. Today it was very cold and my nose kept running, but I managed to get the whole route done in less than an hour. It should go even faster next time now that I know where everything is. In the summer, on my bike, I could probably do the whole thing in 30 minutes. My first job!! I'm in the money!! (almost)

Mr. Cuthbert stopped by after supper and gave me the collection book. There is a sheet for each customer and when they pay, I rip out the square token for the period and give it to them as proof they paid. No problem!

Friday, January 9, 1976

After school I did my first collection. Because I started in the middle of the two week period, I won't get to keep most of this money but at least I got to meet my customers for the first time. Collecting from the businesses was easy, but with the houses it was about half and half. Half paid and half didn't answer their door. The exception was 159 6th Avenue North., the Youngs, who didn't pay although they did answer their door. She is a little old lady and said they would have the money for me on Monday. I hope this doesn't turn out to be a valuable life lesson or anything.

Also I found out that the Morris house (37 6th Ave. North) is indeed George Morris's house, the owner of Morris Rod Weeder. You'd think he'd be really rich, but his house is only a dated 1.5 storey. Nice, but not really fancy.

Space: 1999 was called "End Of Eternity". Alpha encounters an asteroid on a collision course with the Moon. They set some explosive charges to re-direct the asteroid but after an initial explosion, when the Alphan astronauts again crawl about on the rocky surface, they discover a habitable chamber inside the asteroid containing an unconscious alien and a bunch of paintings. The alien is badly injured so they take him back to Alpha to treat him. Big mistake. Turns out Balor is an immortal who believes the meaning of life is pain, but mostly other people's pain! So he starts causing mayhem and it takes some doing before Koenig can lure him into an airlock and push the eject button. So long very menacing character!

Saturday, January 10, 1976

After my route I met up with Neil at the public library. I found out he's not always completely honest. While he was checking a book out, the librarian asked him if Jeremiah was his brother. Yes, he admitted. Well he has some records overdue for a long time, and we can't get a hold of him. She then directly asked Neil, does Jeremiah live with you? No, says Neil, he doesn't stay at our house, he moved to Saskatoon. That ended their conversation.

I didn't say anything until we were outside and Neil danced around the lies. Jerry doesn't stay in the house much, and he did live in Saskatoon with his grandparents last summer (as did Neil). Neil says he doesn't believe in stealing, and has never stolen anything from the library, he says. He wouldn't admit that Jerry had stolen anything and just said, he has good reasons for everything he's done. I didn't press him on it.

I took out Black Sabbath's *We Sold Our Soul For Rock and Roll*. I'm amazed they have such cool rock at the library. When you open the double album, inside is a photo of a woman in a coffin. Yikes! I like the song "Iron Man".

Also got the book <u>1984</u> by George Orwell. Neil says it is a 'dystopia' (spelled correctly) which is the opposite of a utopia.

Sunday, January 11, 1976

Minus 31 with wind chill today. Did my route but practically froze my nose off. I wore my earmuffs. I don't care what anyone says.

That Black Sabbath double record I got from the library yesterday is pretty wild. It starts out with a graveyard human sacrifice scene in the song "Black Sabbath". "Children of the Grave" ends with a lot of spooky ghost sounds. I like the heavier rock too, and this stuff is heavier than anything I've heard. It has faeries, wizards and the Devil.

Neil told me the songs "Sweet Leaf" and "Snowblind" are about drugs. "Sweet Leaf" is about grass, which the hippies smoke, and "Snowblind" is about cocaine, which is a powder you put up your nose, or at least rock stars do!

Friday, January 16, 1976

Need to do another book report for English and I think I will use Orwell's <u>1984</u>. It is not quite what I expected but interesting. The author has invented a whole new set of words for his future dystopia. The book is "doubleplusgood". There are no spaceships or futuristic technology, except the television which watches you back as you watch it! But the government it portrays is quite scary. They make you do exercises in front of the TV each morning, and don't like people who think for themselves.

1999 was called "A Matter of Life and Death". Alpha arrives at a new planet, Terra Nova, which appears to be an excellent potential home for them. However when the reconnaissance Eagle returns to Alpha, the pilots are dead and they discover onboard only a stowaway, the unconscious body of Dr. Helena Russell's husband, Lee. The problem is that Lee Russell disappeared on a space voyage five years before and was presumed dead.

When Lee eventually awakes he is not welcoming to the Alphans. Instead he warns them to stay away from the planet. They don't believe who he is, or what he is saying but it turns out he and the entire planet are made of anti-matter so when the Alphans ignore him and head to the planet as a group, things start exploding. Paul is killed, Sandra is blinded, and even the Moon explodes! Then a huge wind storm and an avalanche kills Koenig. Only a dirty, disheveled and crying Helena is left, but Lee reappears and reverses all the destruction. Revived, Koenig realizes they cannot stay and cancels Operation Exodus. The Alphans must continue their mission aboard the moonbase!

This is the story that follows "Breakaway" in my E.C.Tubb novel. Seems like CKOS is getting the episodes in the wrong order.

Saturday, January 17, 1976

Slept in until 11. I phoned Neil and he came over and we went downtown. First to the Broadway Café. He wanted lunch but I didn't have any money to spend so I just had a water. He ordered a steak and the waitress looked at us, unsure, and asked to see his money. I guess they don't know him there like they do at the Yorkton Hotel. Plus the steak was like three dollars! He was really hungry.

We hung out there a while and discussed yesterday's episode. The fact that Helena was previously married was a surprise to us, but I guess we should have expected it. I said the good thing is that now the husband is out of the way and Koenig can move in if he wants! I was suggesting that, by then in the future, Free Love would have become the norm so husband and wife would not mean so much. Neil disagreed saying that these professional people on the moonbase would not want to be distracted by all that and likely there was not much sex on the moonbase. With such a small population I argued they would have to avoid the competition and jealousies that conventional morality would bring.

Neil is super cool, even when he disagrees with you, he'll frame it in a way that you end up agreeing with him. So yeah while the Earth might have fully absorbed the Free Love lessons of the sixties, on the Moon they are still all virgins! Ha ha!

After that we crossed the street to OK Economy because he had to buy some stuff for his mom.

I stayed up late to watch *Robinson Crusoe On Mars*. It was pretty cool. 1:20 a.m.! Good night.

Friday, January 23, 1976

Did my collections today. My first full paper period! Only a couple of houses didn't answer the door. The Youngs paid in full. Mrs. Morris asked me to put her paper in the slot on their inner door, inside their front porch. I said no problem and she gave me a fifty cent tip!

Space: 1999 was "Earthbound". Alpha encounters a spaceship that is heading to Earth and contains several aliens in suspended animation. The Alphans accidentally kill one alien when they try to open its suspension chamber. The rest of the aliens then wake up but they are not too angry and the head alien (Peter Cushing!) even offers them the now empty chamber so that one Alphan can travel back to Earth with the aliens. But who will it be?

Koenig decides to ask computer to choose, but bitter old Commissioner Simmonds takes matters into his own hands and takes hostages until Koenig agrees to give him the spot on the alien ship. The aliens and Alphans, especially Dr. Russell, worked together trying to make the suspension technology work for an Alphan but it turns out the work is incomplete when Simmonds forces the matter. So he winds up stuck in the alien suspension box, wide awake after only a few minutes asleep. He realizes he is doomed to starve or suffocate, locked inside that glass box.

The Alphans can hear him over the commlock system saying, "Help me, Koenig, help me!" But there is nothing Alpha can do. That's a nasty way to die, but he is to blame for his own doom.

Saturday, January 24, 1976

Today I called Neil and he came over and we went downtown to the Med *[Editor's note: the Mediterranean Restaurant]* for a coffee. I don't really drink coffee - it's just an expression! I had a Coke (50 cents).

We talked about "Earthbound". Not sure what rock Commissioner Simmonds crawled out from under. He was not in any episode except the first, "Breakaway". So maybe this is actually the second episode? This plus the planet Meta question really make us wonder if the episodes are being shown in the wrong order. Maybe in a few months there will be an episode with the Moon finally catching up to Meta?

I have decided that I will spend more time writing episodes summaries. Perhaps if I have a good summary for every episode, I can create a book out of it. I have always wanted to be a writer.

I am also working on a short story about *Space: 1999*. In it, the Alphans receive a message from Earth. There is new technology available, and they can all be transported back to Earth quite soon. All they have to do is fill out some paperwork.

But when the paperwork arrives, it is ridiculously lengthy and involved. By the time they complete it, they are told that there is new, additional paperwork on the way. The new paperwork keeps arriving faster than they can complete it!

Therefore, Earth is, once again, out of reach and the Alphans must continue their quest through deep space.

Episode Summary: "The Full Circle" (200 words)

[Editor's note: this summary is omitted. Roger's complete, original summaries for only four of the forty eight episodes are included because his progressively lengthy and detailed synopses could fill another entire book. The word count information provided for each omitted episode summary demonstrates Roger's increasing dedication to his writing effort. As an alternative to this lengthy content, Roger has provided much more recent and compact commentary regarding each episode in order to establish a context for their discussion in this book.]

Comments on "The Full Circle" (Roger Kay, 1994)

Alpha loses contact with the landing party sent to an Earth-like planet. When the Eagle is returned via remote control, it contains only a dead caveman.

The next expedition, led by Commander Koenig and Dr. Russell, completely disappears. Eagle pilot Alan Carter and Main Mission operative Sandra Benes are then dispatched to the planet, but Carter gets stuck in a pit trap and Sandra is kidnapped by cave people.

Favorite scene: While trying to escape, Sandra bashes the head caveman, who looks suspiciously like a dirty and hirsute Koenig, on the head with a hefty rock. She escapes but later is re-captured and a cavewoman (who looks a lot like Dr. Russell) takes revenge by trussing Sandra up and dangling her over an open fire in preparation of sacrificing her. Way to wear a fur, Sahn!

Entries from Roger Kay's 1976 Diary

Friday, January 30, 1976

Space: 1999's episode tonight was called "The Full Circle". I wrote two drafts of my summary.

I wonder if there could be a mist which would do the opposite: instead of sending you back in time to be a caveman, would push people into the future? They come out of the mist with all their prejudice and small-mindedness gone. They care more for intellect than strength. They value character more than looks. I'd like to send our whole school through a mist like that. Would we come out looking like those aliens you always see with UFOs?

Saturday, January 31, 1976

There is a new record store in town! It is called Sam The Record Man and is in a new modern gray stone multi-store building on the corner of Broadway and 6th, basically around the corner from CKOS TV. It is on the 6th Avenue side. Neil says his brother Jerry told him about it and we checked it out today.

They have all sorts of stuff but not the *Space: 1999* soundtrack. The owner is Rudy and he is very friendly. He says he can special order the soundtrack for $11.99. Plus 5% tax of course. I said I'd get back to him. I'm doing okay with my paper route, but not that okay.

On the corner there is a little coffee shop called the Summit Café. I bought Neil a pop there and we talked about yesterday's episode of 1999. He says that the mist implies evolution is true, so Catholics won't like the episode. I don't really see a conflict. Who says God could not have devised evolution? But anyway I don't think I believe in God. The world is too messed up for anyone to be watching over it, unless maybe God is a bully and that is how he gets his jollies.

Tonight I am starting to write a novel about a space base that was built on an asteroid. The adventure begins when another asteroid collides with it and knocks it out of the solar system. Kind of similar to *Space: 1999* I guess, but I have all different characters.

Thursday, February 5, 1976

Neil wasn't in school today. Yesterday he told me he had to go to Saskatoon with his mom, on the bus, to see a divorce lawyer. He thinks his mom's family is paying for the lawyer, because her family lives near Saskatoon. Otherwise, why would they have to go so far? I hope it is not too hard on him.

We had double Phys-ed but there was a problem with a burst pipe near the gym so they canceled it. It was too cold to exercise outside so we had a double study period instead and I finished all my homework. Thank you merciful universe!

Friday, February 6, 1976

Started collecting again today. Still need to go back to the Young's, and the Dietz house.

1999 was called "Another Time, Another Place". I wrote a good summary of it. I like these time travel paradox ideas. Actually right now I have The Man Who Folded Himself by David Gerrold out from the library and I'm halfway through. The Alphans didn't have THAT much time travel trouble!

Episode Summary: "Another Time, Another Place"
(364 words)
[Omitted.]

Comments on "Another Time, Another Place"
(Roger Kay, 1994)

The Moon encounters a strange space phenomenon in which everything seems to split into two and they are hurled a great distance through space toward a new solar system, but it turns out to be THE Solar System and the Moon comes to rest in orbit around the Earth! At first the Alphans are overjoyed to be home, but with no radio signals and few life signs from Earth they soon discover that the planet is in much worse shape than when they left it.

Despite this, they are enthusiastic about launching Operation Exodus, but then a second Moon emerges from behind the Earth. There is a second Moonbase Alpha!

Favorite scene: Koenig and Carter take an Eagle to reconnoiter the second Moon. There they find Alpha evacuated, deserted, plus two dead bodies in a crashed Eagle: it is them.

Entries from Roger Kay's 1976 Diary

Saturday, February 7, 1976

It was very cold so Neil just came over and we hung out in the basement. We played records so our conversation could not be overheard.

He told me about seeing the lawyer in Saskatoon, yes his mom's folks are paying. His parents are no longer living together, but his dad is sometimes in the house on weekends. Neil wishes his dad would just stay away. He brings money into the house, but he also causes a lot of destruction. Things are so bad that whenever his brother Jerry and his dad are in the house at the same time an argument starts and his mom ends up crying. I don't know how he stands it. I guess if I had to choose between parents who are too strict and parents who fight all the time, I'd take the strict ones. And that's what I've got so I'm not complaining!

We talked about the alternate Alpha in "Another Time, Another Place" and time paradoxes. For example, you cannot go back in time and kill your own grandfather, although if your father was already born, you could perhaps get away with it. He suggested I read <u>Up The Line</u> by Robert Silverberg. He says they have it at the YPL *[Editor's note: Yorkton Public Library]*.

Friday, February 13, 1976

1999 was "The Infernal Machine". I taped it and wrote a summary.

One strange thing about this episode is that Paul is missing from Main Mission and a fellow named Winters is in his chair. Koenig does mention that Paul has a broken rib and some fractures at the start of the episode but we never find out how or why.

A very excellent episode. I like the line "Alone, we cease to have personalities" although I'm not sure it is true.

Episode Summary: "The Infernal Machine"
(318 words)
[Omitted.]

Comments on "The Infernal Machine"
(Roger Kay, 1994)

A strange, awkwardly shaped spacecraft shows up at Alpha and a voice asks for help and permission to land. Koenig reluctantly agrees but then the voice demands that Koenig, Helena and Bergman all go over to the craft.

When they board, it soon becomes apparent that the voice is actually the spacecraft itself which is an advanced computer that has its own personality. There is only one very old man on board, Companion, and he calls this machine "Gwent".

Gwent makes demands for supplies but when Koenig asks for assurance that they will be released once the supplies are handed over, things turn nasty. Soon it becomes clear that Companion is dying and the Alphan visitors will become his replacements.

Favorite scene: When the supplies finally arrive, Gwent demands one long black rod be immediately inserted in a specific round receptacle. Koenig recognizes the importance of this fuel rod and, instead of obeying Gwent's orders, he defiantly hurls it to the floor, smashing it into hundreds of pieces. Koenig is not one to capitulate.

Entries from Roger Kay's 1976 Diary

Saturday, February 14, 1976

When I got up, there was a bag on the kitchen table with a chocolate heart in it. Thanks Mom! I ate it before starting my route. Afterwards I met Neil at the YPL and we walked to the Yorkton Hotel. Neil had some fries and gravy and I ordered a Coke.

We talked about "The Infernal Machine" and agreed it was a shame Gwent destroyed himself at the end. Once Gwent set Koenig and the others free, he (it?) could have extended the hand of friendship. Gwent's technology would have helped the Alphans and in return they could have provided him the companionship he craved.

It was strange that such an advanced being/computer would be blind. If the Alphans had helped create artificial eyesight for him it might have gone a long way towards curing his paranoia. It is the weaknesses in people that can lead to fear and hatred, which then lead to paranoia and aggression. Bullies are aggressive because they are stupid; they sense the weakness of their own minds and have to overcompensate by using their strong bodies to terrorize others.

Gwent, blind and isolated, became his own worst enemy- literally as his weary companion was the living version of his computer self! If Gwent had reached out to the Alphans, he might have made a great addition to the show: humans and an alien computer intelligence working together. Perhaps he could even have returned them to Earth! But in the end, no good came of it. Alpha was damaged and Gwent was destroyed. The part of me that has no sympathy for bullies was glad to see him destroyed, but the part of me that sees the possibility in what Gwent might have become, senses the appalling waste of his/its death.

Nothing good on TV. Did some writing and zzzzz.

On Speech Therapy (Lionel O'Neill, 1988)

I've stuttered ever since I was nine years old, that would be 1970, the year my oldest sister Nancy left home. Mom told me that was when she first noticed anything unusual. There was a big fight between Earl and Nancy one night when she was in Grade 12. It was near the end of May, so she was very close to graduating. The guy she was seeing had been arrested, I don't know for what, and Earl was livid. Jerry later explained that there were other things Nancy was doing, or had done, which Earl couldn't stomach and this was why he made her leave. Jerry wouldn't be more specific than that.

In hindsight, I suspect the issue was she was using birth control. There might have been a question of drug use as well. Regardless, Earl did not want her in the house anymore and so off she went, just shy of her Grade 12 graduation. I know she moved to Regina after that and eventually did graduate with a degree in Social Work from the University of Regina. Where Nancy got the money to do this, I don't know, but she did seem to be able to pull herself out of the slump the rest of the family was in.

I can recall Nancy saying goodbye to me, but nothing else from that day. On that cruel, sunny day in 1970 there was a lot said in our living room, and Jerry claims I was present the whole time. He says Earl ranted and raged, declaring that his life was a waste, we had all destroyed his dreams, and the future was utterly worthless. Earl wasn't talking to me specifically, but Jerry said I was there, heard, and cried the whole day. Not bawling, just standing around with tears in my eyes and a quivering chin.

A few years later, when I was in Grade 6, we moved from our comfortable, contemporary, four bedroom bungalow duplex in the crescents of south Yorkton to the much smaller, much older house on Darlington Avenue, amid the rectangular grid of the established north end. This was almost exactly one year after Earl lost his good job and began to perfect his drinking.

It wasn't long after that, probably June, that Marilyn, my other sister, revealed she was pregnant. The news was hushed up and she was hastily sent to live with my Mom's sister in Canora. Marilyn successfully gave birth, but no one celebrated. My little nephew Joey lives there still, in the same house. I remember Marilyn as gentle and very kind back then but she was also always out, hanging around with boys, just not sticking around home much.

That first supper after Marilyn had gone, it was just the four of us at the table, very quiet and tense. I remember Earl stopped eating at one point, put down his fork and knife, looked at Jerry and I, and said "So, two down and two to go. How are you boys going to disappoint me?" I don't think I ever called him Dad again after that.

Then there were long stretches where both Mom and Earl were gone and Jerry looked after me. He made sure I got up and went to school, assembled my sandwich for lunch, and boiled us Kraft Dinner for supper. Jerry cut up sausages and put it in with the bright yellow noodles. I still like that food.

I remember being about five years old and playing marbles (always funsies, never keepsies) behind Victoria School with Jerry. I think he often let me win, but at the time I thought if I can beat my older, wiser brother, I must be pretty good. I remember feeling good about myself and the future when Marilyn was looking after me. We played 20 Questions and Hangman and she was always encouraging me, even when I didn't come close to winning.

After Nancy and Marilyn were gone, I don't recall feeling like that again. I was always tense and became more introverted. Jerry was also affected. He steered clear of our parents as much as he could. I think they liked it that way. After raising my sisters, they were apparently drained of energy and empathy. Certainly there was none left for me.

Jerry had spent his childhood watching these dramas play out: first the feminist Nancy is ejected from the house, and then the 'corrupted' Marilyn. So my folks were pretty pissed off with popular culture and modern ideas. Then when Jerry crested adolescence, he listened to hippy music but was generally careful to stay out of the way. And me: my eye was always on the sky, something far away. Perhaps the farther the better.

Jerry kept a lot of the books that Nancy had left behind, saving them to read himself and eventually share with me. I remember one time Earl spotted Jerry reading Nancy's copy of Everything You Always Wanted To Know About Sex (But Were Afraid To Ask). He ripped it up right there and then.

Because the house on Darlington only had two bedrooms, once Marilyn was gone Jerry and I moved from our nightly camp in the living room into her bedroom. He and I did not celebrate escaping the couch and floor respectively however. A bullet does not celebrate having increased privacy and escape from the elements when it moves from the ammunition belt to the rifle chamber. I felt like we were about to be fired.

I told all this to my speech therapist at the Psychiatric Centre of the Yorkton Union Hospital. In February 1976 I began my speech therapy with Elizabeth Snow. The first session was on a Saturday afternoon, but I convinced her to move the next appointment to earlier in the morning because it was less conspicuous. I did not want anyone to know I was going to the Psychiatric Centre. I was so worried someone would find out about the therapy that I would walk all the way west down Darlington and then to the far opposite side of town, by going south down Gladstone. This long and indirect path completely avoided downtown and I was therefore, I hoped, unobserved in my travels. But it was a long walk and my legs were always rubber by the time I passed the spider-shaped wings of the brand new seniors complex which was the penultimate building along my route to the Yorkton Union Hospital.

Every trip there I made, I was careful to enter the hospital through the original, dated main entrance and then make my way down the seeming miles of white and gray, pipe-infested and disused subterranean corridors connecting the old yellow brick edifice with the new construction of the very modern psychiatric wing. I would never directly present myself at the actual entrance of the psychiatric wing for fear of someone seeing me and making an assumption about why I was there. Mental illness, even in the variety of a harmless verbal disfluency, was a shameful and taboo topic.

My speech therapy continued for about a year. Ms. Snow gave me a lot of homework. I had to phone businesses and ask them simple questions: how much to dry-clean a shirt? Are you open late on Thursday night? Most of these tasks I did without too much effort. Usually I did okay one on one so these exercises didn't seem very appropriate or useful. When I had to deal with more than one person, or I was being directly challenged, then my fluency quickly ended. This meant that if someone was teasing or bullying me I would rarely reply verbally. By the time I entered junior high, my attitude towards the world had changed. My default response to ill treatment was a punch to the head of the oppressor. So I did not endure much teasing.

However, I was still stuck with the problem of public speaking being nearly impossible. Also it was very frustrating to me that some people did not understand speech impediments, and assumed I was intellectually impaired, to me an odious aspersion.

Entries from Roger Kay's 1976 Diary

Monday, February 16, 1976

Today was a day that went from interesting and new to stupid and old real quick. Mr. Mitchell was sick so we had a substitute teacher for English, Ms. Koch. She is in her 20s and good looking. All the boys were saying sexy stuff about her in the hallway. I think she is nicer than Mr. Mitchell who can be short-tempered.

We had double Phys-ed for the whole first half of the afternoon. We did a bunch of exercises and then, already exhausted, started a relay game. I didn't get a turn before the bell rang but I was on the losing team so we had to run the relay all over again. By this time it was late and the girls who had Phys-ed next were already in the gym and stood around watching us. Very embarrassing. When it was finally over we headed to the change room. As I was entering, Donald Gorchynski, who was already changed and leaving, shoved me against the door frame on his way past. I fell down and I heard him say 'loser'. I have a big bruise on my back from the door frame.

No homework today. Ms. Koch asked us to read some stuff but I didn't bother.

My paper route was uneventful. Pretty cold today so I moved as fast as possible, not easy in the deep snow. Some people don't shovel their walks! Still I was home by 4:36. Supper was hot dogs. Did some writing.

Tuesday, February 17, 1976

Mr. Mitchell was back today. School was very boring. I aced the ORA test, got the highest score in my class: 770 words per minute! Very windy today and my lips were chapped after I did my route. Mom gave me some Lipsol.

Worked on my Asteroid Beta novel. Introduced a character called Donald Gorski, a nasty fellow who only got to where he was because he was related to the first Moonbase Alpha commander (yes my story shares the same universe as Space 1999, although in my universe it is Asteroid Beta and not the

---

Moon that leaves orbit). In this chapter some aliens lay eggs in his ears and take over his mind. He becomes increasingly deranged as the eggs mature and at the end of the chapter, as Commander Hargreaves is getting ready to finish him off, Donald is lying on the ground wounded, the eggs hatch and alien worm creatures crawl out of his ears and he dies an excruciating death before Hargreaves can even shoot him. Then the Commander orders the area cleared and opens the airlocks to kill the worm creatures.

Friday, February 20, 1976

Did my collections today after school. Have to go back to the Balmoral because Curtis Loew wasn't around. Maybe he finally found a job.

In the evening Mom and Dad were watching Profile, which is the horrible local talent program that CKOS puts on. Linus Westberg is the host and he always says something nice no matter how bad the talent sounds (I use the word 'talent' loosely). Tonight was a husband and wife who wore cowboy clothes and sang some awful country and western songs. I don't normally listen to Profile but Dad was trimming my hair so I had to sit in the kitchen while Mom was watching TV in the living room. There was no escape.

I got in a fight with Dad over my hair length. I want to grow it longer but he wants to cut it all off! It is not just hippies who have long hair, I told him. Lots of people do, like everyone at school. There is also this guy on *Space: 1999* who I see in Main Mission sometimes. I don't know his name but he has long, dark hair. If Dad cuts mine too short, I'm sure I'll have even more problems at school.

Space 1999 was "Ring Around The Moon".

Episode Summary: "Ring Around The Moon"
(538 words)
[Omitted.]

Comments on "Ring Around The Moon"
(Roger Kay, 1994)

A strange orange sphere appears over the Moon and causes technician Ted Clifford to become a super-strength zombie who operates the main computer keypad with amazing speed, transmitting data to points unknown. Then he collapses. A beam of orange light emerges from the alien sphere and encircles the Moon. A voice issues a warning: "Do not resist. You are the captives of the planet Triton."

An Eagle is sent to investigate the orange sphere, but it fails and crashes during its return to the Moon. As the medical team approaches the wreck, walking along the lunar surface, a ball of orange light descends and kidnaps Dr. Helena Russell.

Favorite scene: Koenig and Carter fly toward the orange sphere aboard an Eagle specially equipped with an anti-gravity generator that they hope can negate the Tritonian force field. The plan works at first, but when the alien forcefield is suddenly reversed, the occupants of the Eagle lose consciousness due to the high velocity.

Entries from Roger Kay's 1976 Diary

Saturday, February 21, 1976

Very cold outside today and this makes my route less fun. I like the money and the responsibility but I can't handle too much cold. I don't wear earmuffs to school but on my route I sometimes wear them. And of course halfway through my route, just as I was heading down the hill on 6th, Brian W and his dad drive by. I don't know if he noticed my earmuffs but he gave me the finger anyway.

When I got to the YPL I couldn't find Neil. I picked up a couple of new comics at Logan's Drugs.

I'm working on another chapter in my book <u>Asteroid Beta</u>. Commander John Hargreaves and two other Betans (the asteroid and its base are officially called Asteroid Beta) have been thrown back in time five years and are on the Earth trying to stop the disaster which originally caused their asteroid to be knocked out of its solar orbit. The idea is quite promising and I wrote a bunch of pages.

Monday, February 23, 1976

Handed in my social studies paper on a prominent political figure. I did Martin Luther King. We had to do a thirty second oral presentation just saying who we had picked and why. I said I chose MLK because he believed in the equality of all people and this was an important political idea that still needed some attention today. Plus his assassination makes for a good story. I don't think Mr. Windleigh liked that I chose an American. Everybody else was choosing Tommy Douglas, Allan Blakeney, or Pierre Trudeau. Ken chose Robert Stanfield and that got a laugh from the class.

I finally caught up with Neil after school. He said he had to go with his mom on an appointment this Saturday but wouldn't give me any details. More divorce stuff maybe? He came over and we played Radar Search for about an hour.

Tuesday, February 24, 1976

I wasn't prepared for the French quiz today. I got six out of ten. Oops.

After lunch this Glen guy from 8-23 comes up to me and asks if I'm friends with 'Lionel'. I said yeah and he said do you know your friend is a retard? I said no, that's not right, he is probably the smartest guy in the whole school. Glen started to laugh and then did an imitation of a retard stuttering. I started to walk away and he called me a fag. I just kept going. That guy doesn't have a clue what he is talking about.

I walked home with Neil and told him about it. He turned red and said: I know Glen. I don't think I'd like to be Glen tomorrow.

Neil told me how he hates speeches and today when he gave his overview of a political figure (he picked Leonid Brezhnev of the USSR by the way) he was stuttering and couldn't finish. I felt for him. I doubt most Grade 8s even know who Brezhnev is. Neil is a newspaper junkie, and very often when I catch up to him at the YPL on Saturdays, he has his nose buried in The Regina Leader Post or The Winnipeg Free Press or some other paper. So just who exactly, in truth, is retarded and who is advanced around here?

Friday, February 27, 1976

1999 was "Missing Link" and I taped it. Peter Cushing played Raan, the head alien. I remember him as Dr. Frankenstein and just in a whole lot of horror movies.

I worked hard on a summary for this episode. I think Helena is in love with Koenig. She was crying before she turned his life support off.

Episode Summary: "Missing Link" (627 words)
[Omitted.]

Comments on "Missing Link" (Roger Kay, 1994)

Unable to land due to unknown, destabilizing forces, an Eagle exploration crew is returning after attempting to survey a very blue planet. Approaching the Moon, the Eagle loses control and crashes 100 miles from Alpha. Of the Eagle crew, the worst injured is Commander Koenig, who remains in a coma.

From Koenig's perspective, he is the least injured survivor. He walks all the way back to Alpha, but finds it deserted. Soon he meets Raan of the planet Zenno who admits everything he sees is actually on Zenno and made from light. The Zennons are very advanced and can transmute matter into any form they wish simply by using the power of their minds. Koenig desires a return to Alpha but Raan wants him to stay on Zenno as his study subject. Humans are the missing link for Zennons, Raan claims. When Koenig meets Raan's daughter Vana and they fall in love, things become decidedly more complicated for Raan.

Meanwhile back on Alpha, Alan Carter cannot accept Koenig's terminal prognosis. As the doctors consider pulling the plug, Carter turns to violence to safeguard his Commander.

Favorite scene: Koenig wakes up in Medical Centre with Bergman at his side. At first Koenig is relieved to be back, but that soon turns to worry as Professor Bergman acts strangely, saying that they are all doomed to never get off this rock, the Moon, and that Alpha will be their tomb. Bergman offers Koenig a chance to escape Alpha with a few others because one of the planets in the area can sustain life, but only for a few people. Of course this is unacceptable to Koenig and he succinctly tells Bergman to check himself out an airlock if he doesn't like it. The room dissolves into a Zenno-like orange mist and Koenig realizes he has been played for a fool. This was not the real Alpha.

Entries from Roger Kay's 1976 Diary

Saturday, February 28, 1976

Met up with Neil at the YPL after I finished my route. We went next door to the bowling alley and watched for a while. Too cold to hang outside.

We wondered when Koenig and Helena will get together. Every episode it seems that they are being drawn together. There are only three hundred people on Alpha so their options are very limited. It makes sense for them to be together because he is the Commander and she is the head of Medical. They wind up going on the same missions all the time anyway! The fact that Koenig falls in love with Vana this time around might slow this process down. If Helena finds out about that, it might derail it altogether.

Neil says that Koenig and Helena are husband and wife in real life (Martin Landau and Barbara Bain) so this makes it even more likely something will develop. Neil says before this they both starred on a spy show called *Mission Impossible*, which I've never seen. I guess I should just be very glad CKOS is even showing *Space: 1999*.

Friday, March 5, 1976

Did my collection today. Almost 18 dollars! Of course I'll only get to keep about one third of that. It was rainy and I was filthy with ink and my carrier bag soaked by the time I got home.

I taped 1999. It was called "The Last Sunset".

Episode Summary: "The Last Sunset" (1098 words)
[Omitted.]

Comments on "The Last Sunset" (Roger Kay, 1994)

Alan Carter is piloting an Eagle to have the first look at the planet Ariel, a small blue planet with an attractive atmosphere, when a small alien object is detected approaching him. Carter tries to outmaneuver the small object, but no luck. It strikes the Eagle, but instead of exploding, it has gently attached itself to the Eagle nosecone. Koenig orders the Eagle back to Alpha and as they examine the alien artifact it begins to spew gas. Soon hundreds more of the alien devices land on the Moon and they all emit the same gas, a mix of breathable gases. Soon the outside pressure rises and the Moon has a life-supporting atmosphere! Rain clouds form and the first ever lunar rainstorm begins.

Because of this, the Alphans forget the planet Ariel and focus on their own celestial body. As Alpha is located at the bottom of a crater and therefore vulnerable to flooding, they need to relocate to higher ground. A survey Eagle is dispatched but caught in a sudden thunderstorm, suffers lightning strikes, and plummets. Helena, Paul, Alan, and Sandra survive the crash, but their communication gear and supplies do not. As they suffer through choking dust storms and extreme thirst, Paul finds a mysterious food growing on the surface. Is it manna from the good people on planet Ariel or a door to madness?

Favorite scene: It is a sunny day on the Moon. Koenig walks over to one of the windows in Main Mission and opens it. Fresh air comes in.

Entries from Roger Kay's 1976 Diary

Saturday, March 6, 1976

It wasn't that cold today. Did my route and as usual saved my last paper for the YPL. I finish downtown and all of 6th before returning to Broadway for that last paper. Met Neil at the YPL. We stopped in at the House of Hobbies on Betts and checked out the spacecraft models. Nothing new. Then we went across the street to the pool hall. Neil got a smoke from that Solomon guy. Then we just hung around St. Gerard's parking lot and talked about "The Last Sunset".

The aliens on the planet Ariel wanted to keep the Alphans away at all costs because of human primitiveness. This makes a lot of sense to me. The Alphans are heroic, but humans in general are a much less positive force. The aliens on the "War Games" planet said the same thing: humans are too impulsive and destructive to ever co-exist with us. Of course a lot of these aliens are not so great themselves!

Neil told me about how Mexican Indians use hallucinogenic mushrooms during religious rituals so the 'manna from the gods' that Paul found is based on reality. Also, some hippies use a similar mushroom for their own purposes. I said you'd have to have some kind of hallucination to believe in religion and Neil agreed. The mushrooms used by young people, called shrooms, are not just used for fun, but are for transcendental experience, which means something that takes you out of the ordinary and lets you see reality from a higher perspective. How can you see or understand something when you are deep inside it? The drug gives you the outside-of-it perspective.

There is another drug called LSD, or acid, which does the same thing but is much stronger. Acid was legal in the sixties but not anymore. This guy called Timothy Leary was a psychology scientist and did a lot of LSD tests on people. He led the psychedelic (means 'mind expanding') movement with the slogan "Turn on, tune in, drop out" which a lot of the hippies followed. I found out that Black Sabbath is considered acid rock. When they sing "smoking and tripping is all that you do", the smoking refers to grass and the tripping to acid. I asked Neil if he had ever smoked grass or done acid and he said no, but maybe his brother has.

We had Shake 'n Bake chicken for supper. Yum!

This evening I re-arranged the furniture in my room. I moved the bed closer to the window so I can look out into the back yard without getting out of bed. I like to read in bed.

Friday, March 12, 1976

Space: 1999 was called "Space Brain".

*[No comments provided because Roger's complete, original
summary is included below.]*

Episode Summary: "Space Brain"
(Roger Kay, 1976, 942 words)

This episode opens with Koenig finishing a jigsaw puzzle in
his office. He puts the last piece in place then gets up and tells
Paul and Sandra, the only ones in a dark Main Mission, he's
turning in for the night. As he walks to his living quarters, he
tries to use a communications post to talk to Paul, but it just
displays a torrent of alien hieroglyphics. Koenig heads back to
Main Mission and dispatches Eagle 1 to investigate.

Waylon and Cousteau are the standby team and fly into the
source of the alien transmissions. As they get close, they report
strange colored lights and shapes forming. Soon their Eagle
appears to be coated in some white sticky substance. Next,
contact is lost.

Koenig sends Carter to pilot a rescue Eagle. As the rescue
Eagle heads to the area a meteorite whizzes by, barely missing
them, and slams into the Moon right next to Moonbase Alpha.

When they analyze the meteorite composition, they realize
it is Eagle 1, crew included. Koenig immediately orders the
rescue Eagle to return, but Kelly, Carter's co-pilot, is already
on a spacewalk, trying to get a visual confirmation of any
remainder of the first Eagle. Koenig orders the rescue Eagle
back immediately, but Carter cannot abandon Kelly and
performs a spacewalk himself to grab the now inert Kelly.

Back on Alpha, Kelly is examined in the Medical Centre.
His body is fine, but his brainwaves are going crazy. A monitor
which should show his condition, starts to spew alien
hieroglyphics and strange graphics. Kano, the computer expert,
calls from Main Mission to say he has determined that the main
computer is sending data to Kelly, and Kelly is sending it to
orbital reference 397, where the first Eagle was crushed. When
Kano tries to cut the flow of info from main computer, Kelly

regains consciousness and fights his way out of Medical Centre.

Kelly heads to the computer section where he starts tapping away at the computer keypads with inhuman speed. Koenig tries to question him, but Kelly just shoves Koenig away. When Koenig shuts down the computer power, Kelly displays anguish and retreats to his living quarters, where his wife tries to comfort him as he whimpers "I have to do it, make them understand..."

A command conference is called. All the section heads gather at the round table in Koenig's office. They agree they cannot change the Moon's course and instead come up with the idea of delivering some nuclear charges into the heart of the space anomaly, hoping the explosion would weaken it enough to let them pass through unharmed. The Moon will reach the area where the first Eagle was crushed in less than two days so they immediately dispatch a nuke-laden Eagle.

Professor Bergman finds that the bits of the space anomaly that were mixed up in the meteorite (Eagle 1) have reverted to their normal form, resembling soap foam, and claims that 'in sufficient quantity' this stuff could crush anything.

Helena muses that Kelly's condition has only gone from bad to worse since they cut off his link to main computer. Meanwhile, Koenig is having second thoughts about the space anomaly. When Bergman tells him that the info obtained by the anomaly mostly concerns the path of the Moon and its gravitational variables, Koenig considers that maybe the anomaly is trying to help them avoid crashing into it. The only way to know for sure is to establish contact so Koenig suggests Helena put Kelly and he into a symbiotic state so that he can know what Kelly is thinking. Helena protests, but Koenig overrides her concern and the symbiosis goes ahead.

Koenig emerges unscathed and understanding the space anomaly is actually a living brain involved with a whole galaxy (or many galaxies) of alien civilizations. Kelly regains consciousness at that time too, and states that the brain is trying to help them and that is why it is talking with main computer.

They all go to Main Mission and the main computer spits out more hieroglyphics. These Kelly can interpret as precise data on where to lay nuclear charges along the Moon's equator to increase its spin and avoid passing through the center of the space brain.

Koenig orders the nukes back, but there is a problem with the Eagle onboard system and although the Eagle does reverse course, they have lost control over it. Koenig pilots another Eagle in a race to get to the nuke-heavy Eagle before it can return and obliterate them. He manages to defuse the nuclear charges, but cannot seem to nudge the Eagle out of its path, so he struggles with it until they are both nearly upon Alpha. He ditches the failing Eagle and it crashes near a launch pad. The nukes are lost.

Bergman has an idea that they can increase the air pressure in Alpha to counteract the crushing forces of the space brain. A long shot, but all they have.

As the Moon approaches the space brain, the space foam starts rolling in. Pretty soon most of the surface installations are evacuated and only Main Mission is left. Helena is forced to abandon Medical Centre after the windows burst and the foam starts pouring in. They hold out in Main Mission and, after some tense moments, the Moon has passed through the anomaly and the foam begins to recede.

Helena voices regret about Kelly, but Koenig tells her that she is no more responsible for his death than they are for the death of the space brain. And what of all the civilizations that depended on the brain, what have they lost?

Entries from Roger Kay's 1976 Diary

Saturday, March 13, 1976

Had a lazy morning watching cartoons. Did my route right after lunch and caught up with Neil at the YPL. It was pretty nice out, above zero. We walked to Shaw Park and hung out on a bench.

Our usual discussion of the previous night's episode went ahead. I should tape these sessions to use as discussion points in my planned episode guide book. Neil always raises fascinating points and has huge knowledge of areas I know little about. For example, today we talked about "Space Brain". Was the fact that it was killed a good or bad thing?

The episode made it seem sort of sad, but Neil told me about a philosopher named Neechie *[Editor's note: Friedrich Nietzsche]* who believes that God is dead and that this is a great thing because it gives humans the freedom to decide things for themselves without fear of being second guessed by an all-powerful being. So the death of the Space Brain actually frees those aliens who previously thought they needed it.

Neil said God is like a drug. It starts out with a hope for transcendental experience and greater understanding and then leaves you dependant and dull when, finally, the drug is all you can see. People who believe in God are like this: they see God everywhere but don't seem to see the real world or real people anywhere.

Picked up a Lighthouse record from the YPL: "Ain't nothing better in the world you know than lying in the sun with your radio!" They must have some good radio stations where that song was written. Maybe it should be lying in the sun with your record player, or your cassette recorder! Still, I can't wait for summer to get here.

Wednesday, March 17, 1976

Today after lunch our double Phys-ed class was canceled so we could go to Sacred Heart and see their play *Fiddler on the Roof*. They did a good job, although I'm not into musicals. But I approve whenever Art replaces Sport. We were supposed to return to St. Joe's for a study period at 2:30, but I misheard (sure I did) and just left. Got my route done early.

Friday, March 19, 1976

Did my collection after school. Everyone paid. The planets must be aligned!

Tonight I watched and taped "The Troubled Spirit". One thing I liked especially was the use of exotic guitar music throughout the episode giving a special and chilling quality to the eerie scenes.

Episode Summary: "The Troubled Spirit" (1254 words)
[Omitted.]

Comments on "The Troubled Spirit" (Roger Kay, 1994)

A séance-like experimental session hosted by scientist Dan Mateo as an attempt to communicate with plants goes horribly wrong. He is injured and a mysterious temperature drop is recorded in the Hydroponics Lab.

Mateo rapidly recovers and is released from Medical Centre but soon his girlfriend and then his unsympathetic boss die suspicious deaths. A mysterious and powerful but disfigured apparition now stalks the Alphans.

Favorite scene: In the opening sequence a group of Alphans is attending a music recital. A bearded longhair is playing a black guitar, starting with some strange, psychedelic noises, and then picking up tempo to a gallop as it becomes more Eastern-sounding.

As the opening scenes play out, as the four Alphans in Hydroponics hold hands around a table in their pseudo-séance, as Mateo's boss comes in and tries to break the circle, as he succeeds and Mateo falls to the floor unconscious and then, as a cold wind rushes through all the corridors of Alpha, disturbing Paul and the others in Main Mission, the tempo of the music continues to increase. Finally the frigid gust reaches the recital room causing the performance to end abruptly just at the climax of the music: the guitar player seems to have lost electrical power and the audience jumps to its feet, not to applaud, but in confusion.

Entries from Roger Kay's 1976 Diary

Saturday, March 20, 1976

Snowing again today. When will it end? I have to trudge through piles of snow and new piles of muck and snow. The salt they use on the roads gets everywhere and makes your clothes stiff and stained. I did my route and then Neil and I went to the Med for coffee.

We discussed Mateo's experiments with plant communication. What a crazy idea. What would a plant have to say other than: don't eat me? Maybe, don't step on me! No wonder they tapped such an angry vein with their séance. Neil suggested I write a short story about the final thoughts of a sentient radish as it waits in a buffet and its friends are eaten one by one. We both agreed it was great to see the Alphans relaxing at a recital and get a glimpse of what the sound of rock could be like in the year 1999.

Came home, changed clothes, watched TV. Tried to write some but feeling lazy today.

Comments on "Testament Of Arkadia"
[No comments provided because Roger's complete, original summary is included below.]

Episode Summary: "Testament of Arkadia"
(Roger Kay, 1976, 992 words)

The episode opens with Koenig sitting in his office writing a log or memoir longhand. He writes that events on the planet Arkadia have caused the Alphans to reconsider their purpose on their odd journey. We continue in flashback mode: Koenig is practicing some kind of martial arts with Luke when Paul alerts him to an emergency.

In Main Mission, Koenig discovers they are approaching a new planet, but suddenly the course of the Moon changes to take them much closer to the planet than they had calculated. Bergman says gravitation and magnetism cannot explain it. Kano notes that there is a small power loss from their generators. Then the Moon unexpectedly accelerates towards the planet, and abruptly stops dead!

The power loss slowly but steadily increases and the Alphans can find no cause for it. They have only 48 hours until all their power is gone so they must look to the planet for a safe refuge. A well-equipped Eagle is dispatched to the planet with Koenig, Helena, Bergman, Alan as pilot of course, a couple of security guards, and two other individuals to be picked by main computer on the basis of general experience and skills. A round trip is thirty hours so they have scant time to either choose the planet or find the answer to their power loss dilemma.

Once they land, the Alphan team discover the planet is not really dead, but in stasis, waiting for the return of bacteria so that the soil can begin to support life again. Luke, Koenig's martial arts partner from the start of the episode, is on the Eagle team, as is Anna, a language expert.

Meanwhile, the power loss on Alpha is up to 30% and the power cuts are making life chilly in Main Mission. The staff don heavier clothing.

On the planet, Bergman and Helena stumble upon a cave with a table of humanoid skeletons and an inscription carved into the rock wall. Bergman tentatively identifies the writing as Sanskrit, an early Earth language, and soon Anna translates it. This 'Testament of Arkadia' explains that the planet was destroyed but that some of the people left with seeds to start again elsewhere in the cosmos, and those who are now guided to Arkadia must make it fertile and live again. Luke and Anna then make a startling announcement: the trees they had earlier examined were oak, pine, etc, Earth trees! They must therefore conclude that the Arkadians traveled to Earth in the past and are the true ancestors of humanity.

Koenig considers the possibility of evacuating to the planet, but it will take two years for the soil to become fertile, and all the rations they have could only last six months. And Alpha has less than 24 hours before completely losing power.

While Koenig narrates the flashback, we see Luke and Anna, while working in the cave, have a mystical experience: the skeletons at the table momentarily come back to life. Koenig says that something happened in the cave that profoundly altered their personalities. Luke and Anna are elated when Koenig beeps their commlocks and tells them the plan is to evacuate Alpha. They are eager to live on the new planet.

In the Eagle on the way back to Alpha, Koenig is preparing to order Operation Exodus but the power loss suddenly stabilizes at 50%. He cancels the evacuation plan for the time being. When he lands back at Alpha, Helena confirms that the Alphans could scrape by with 50% power so he completely cancels Operation Exodus.

Luke and Anna go to Koenig's office to plead with him to let them live on the planet surface. Koenig says it is completely out of the question and that the only way the two of them could survive on the planet would be to take half of Alpha's supplies, which would likely doom Alpha. He orders them out of his office.

Luke threatens Kano with a stun gun and demands the access code for the protein storage. When he has it, he commlocks the code to Anna who stuns two guards and successfully unlocks the protein storage room. Before Luke can leave Main Mission, Kana manages to hit the Red Alert button. Luke seizes the bystanding Helena as a hostage, then demands an Eagle, a moonbuggy and three years of supplies. Koenig appears to give in. When Luke and Anna board the getaway Eagle, Koenig pleads again for Helena to be released, but Luke is wily. He wants an unarmed Eagle to escort them out of range before he will hand over Helena. Koenig has no choice.

Traveling toward the planet, Luke and Anna apologize to Helena but she argues with them, saying their actions are condemning all of Alpha to death. Helena also argues that Luke and Anna will be the only two living creatures on the planet and so they are going to a living hell. They counter, no, we're going home.

Now close to the planet, Carter's unarmed Eagle docks with the kidnappers' ship and Helena is given back. As soon as he is in range, Carter alerts Alpha that Helena is safe. Koenig then commands two pursuit Eagles to prepare for launch. The plan is to retrieve the stolen supplies which also contain one item not requested: a tracing beacon.

But just as the pursuit Eagles are ready to lift off, the Moon lurches. It is moving again! The power loss has also begun to reverse itself. Realizing that the supplies will not be critical if their power returns, Koenig cancels the pursuit Eagles and advises Carter to go full throttle to catch up with the now rapidly departing Moon.

On the planet surface, Anna and Luke are unpacking supplies when they are startled to see the Moon restart its journey.

Back on Alpha, Carter and Helena have returned safely. Helena laments that Luke and Anna will be all alone. Koenig counters that it was their decision. Helena questions him: was it really?

Entries from Roger Kay's 1976 Diary

Friday, March 26, 1976

Today our whole class had to stay late. Mr. Windleigh says
that every period he counts how many minutes we waste
talking and then when the total reaches thirty, he will keep us
for an extra half hour. So today we stayed until 4:10. Way to
punish us for your being unable to control us. I feel this is very
unfair. The kids who talk should be punished, not the whole
class. Had to rush through my paper route.

Tonight's 1999 episode was "Testament of Arkadia".
Shades of predestination! Did Luke and Anna really have a
choice? Did Mateo from last week? Maybe we are predestined
never to find out! Ha ha!

Saturday, March 27, 1976

It rained all day. This helps get rid of the snow, but is pretty
dreary for delivering newspapers. Found Neil at the YPL. Not
wanting to get soaked even worse, we didn't go far, just around
the corner to the Med.

Yesterday's 1999 episode was awesome. Because it is told
in flashbacks, and seems to explain the reason why the Moon
originally left orbit we are worried that this might be the last
episode of the season. Please, no!

The predestination theme is strong in this one. We've seen
similar episodes before (like "Collision Course", or "Black
Sun") where the fate of the Alphans is part of a great cosmic
plan. Cases where they clearly should be destroyed by
circumstance but emerge unharmed. I guess their space brain
isn't dead!

Thursday, April 1, 1976

A deeply stupid day. I woke with Mom coming into my
room at 7:45 saying: Hurry up, we need to get packed, Canada
has joined the U.S. and we're moving to Alaska today! I was
confused and worried for a moment until she said: April Fools!

In homeroom Mr. Windleigh said that we were taking a trip
to the Mud Pie factory in Melville today but that the bus had
broken down so we would have to walk there. Melville is about

thirty miles away. There is no Mud Pie factory. There were varying degrees of disbelief and excitement about this, depending on the IQ, but I knew it was bull.

In Science class Mr. Mulligan told us that he was going to show us how to turn lead into gold. We thought it was a joke at first but he said he could do it. When I objected that this was totally impossible he said, well it is not alchemy, it is more economics. Then he talked the whole period about the stock market, the price of gold and lead, and how if one could see that the price of one was going up, and the other going down, you could make 'gold' (money) by selling gold on the market and buying lead. He said something about 'futures' and 'hedge funds'. It seemed a very elaborate and roundabout way to avoid admitting he was full of it. I understood his very thin and rather silly argument but most of the class just sat there waiting for his fever to pass. I like Mr. Mulligan. He is enthusiastic but sometimes goes a bit too far into things that are beyond most of the class.

Ken passed me a note in the afternoon saying that Neil had been killed on the soccer field. More bullshit. I said that if you pull a prank after noon on April Fool's, then you are the fool. He said no I'm not kidding, he's really dead. Bullshit.

Walked home with Neil after school and told him about it. He just laughed. He told his brother Jerry this morning that Robert Plant was leaving Led Zeppelin and the new vocalist was going to be Burton Cummings, and if this wasn't enough, their next hit would be a heavier version of "Stand Tall". Jerry didn't believe him but thought it was funny.

At supper, I told Mom and Dad all about the stupid happenings today. I asked Mom if she really thought that Canada was going to join the U.S. someday and she said she didn't know but that if we keep on electing the NDP it might have to happen when the province goes bankrupt. My folks are pro-business Progressive Conservatives.

Still struggling with the second draft of my Asteroid Beta story about time travel. I'm calling it "I'd Like To Change The World" as an ironic nod to the song of the same name.

Friday, April 2, 1976

I actually forgot to do my collection today! How bizarre is that? It is not as if I don't need the money!!

I taped 1999 and hooray it was another new episode: "The Last Enemy".

Episode Summary: "The Last Enemy" (1101 words)
[Omitted.]

Comments on "The Last Enemy" (Roger Kay, 1994)

The Moon approaches a new star system and this time they find two planets, each on the opposite side of their star, situated so they cannot see each other directly. Soon a large military craft arrives from the left hand planet, Betha, and opens fire. Its missiles are destined for the right hand planet, Delta.

Retaliation follows. Missiles arrive from Delta and destroy the nearby Bethan gunship. A small escape craft emerges from the wreckage and Dionne, the leader and only survivor of the Bethan gunship pleads with the Alphans for asylum.

Now the Alphans understand the Moon has become a strategic military high ground. How can they placate Dionne without getting further involved in the destruction and mayhem of this war of the worlds?

Favorite scene: Koenig can lie convincingly when required. Near the end of the episode, when things look bad for Alpha, Koenig pleads for Dionne to allow him to come to her ship, alone and unarmed, in a moon buggy. This surprises Dionne and she asks him if he is willing to abandon his people. Koenig shouts I didn't say that, but then grabs Carter's stun gun and threatens the other Alphans. Bergman cuts off the transmission and Koenig admits to his crew he is playing a game. He orders Bergman to re-open the communication link, and then he advances the subterfuge that will save Alpha.

Entries from Roger Kay's 1976 Diary

Saturday, April 3, 1976

A sunny Saturday finally! I went out early and got my route done by 11. Did my collection too, and got most of it except from Balmoral Curtis. Neil wasn't at the library so on the way home I wandered over to his house. The place was dark and there was a padlock on the shed.

Got bored and walked all the way down to Broadway Park Plaza and it was well worth it. Accent on Books had a package of Starship Enterprise blueprints for five dollars! I asked them if I could open the snap on the plastic pouch and unfold one of the pages to see what it was like and they reluctantly agreed. It was an amazingly detailed blueprint of every single room on the Enterprise. Now I've seen very little of *Star Trek*, but I have read some of the episodes in book format and it actually is good stuff. I just had to have these blueprints and so I handed over a large part of my collection money to get them. Spent the rest of the day in my room, poring over the incredible starship details. They need to put out blueprints for Moonbase Alpha! I'd pay even more for that.

Sunday, April 4, 1976

Neil called in the afternoon and we went to hang out in Shaw Park. He said he was missing yesterday because he had to go to the hospital with his mom. He didn't want to tell me more so I dropped it. I told him about my new *Star Trek* blueprints and he came back to the house to check them out.

Had a boring night watching TV with the folks. *Walt Disney*, *This Is The Law*, *W-5*, *Switch*. That's enough sucking at the glass teat for tonight. Ha ha!

Friday, April 9, 1976

Today 1999 was "War Games", a repeat. Another chance to see the gorgeous Mark IX Hawks in action but I guess this means we've seen all the episodes for this year.

I knew the end of the season would come, but still this is a very sad day.

Sorry for not writing much, dear diary, but I am spending more of my effort on my <u>Asteroid Beta</u> novel. I am learning to type now too. Dad gave me his old Smith Corona typewriter and now my desk looks like a real writer's desk. If I start to use it for my assignments, I think my teachers will be very impressed. I have a lot of handwritten material that needs typing. It is going to be a lot of work but it will be worth it to look professional. My marks will soar!

Saturday, April 10, 1976

It was cloudy and windy when I got up at 10. I rushed out to do my papers before it started to rain, but I was too late and got soaked anyway. Met Neil at the YPL and there was really nobody in there so we just sat by the magazines and quietly chatted.

I told him about my latest chapter on <u>Asteroid Beta</u>. I've also decided that Hawks should be used by my asteroid base. Being further out from Earth, the Hawks could be protection against the bandits that lurk in the Asteroid Belt. Now that the asteroid has broken free and is wandering the galaxy, the Hawks will be handy for dealing with hostile aliens. Neil says he would like to draw a blueprint of my asteroid base. He promised to come over and make notes based on what I've written so far.

Thursday, April 15, 1976

I was late for school today. The temperature is hovering around freezing and the rain from yesterday is now ice. I tried to hurry but wiped out in a puddle of slush in front of Dr. Brass Elementary. I swear some of the little kids there were laughing at me. I missed homeroom entirely and they were into English period when I finally got to my desk. Kind of creepy coming in and going to your locker when everyone else is in class.

In the afternoon it had warmed up and for Phys-ed we had to go out running in the muck of course. My legs were caked with grit and soaked with dirty water by the time I got back.

While I was doing my papers, William (not sure of his last name, but he's in Grade 9 and much bigger than me) got in my way on 6th and wouldn't let me pass. He kept saying that I was a fag and I should admit it but I wouldn't. Eventually he hit me and I fell down, crying, I admit. Mr. Jacobson, one of my customers, came out on his front step and yelled at William who fled. It was very embarrassing. If I were a grownup I could have shot him in self-defense or at least called the cops. But I'm just a worthless little kid and no one gives a crap. Earth sucks.

Friday, April 16, 1976

Neil came over after supper with a new record for me to tape. It is called *2112* and the group is Rush. I'd never heard of them but he says they are a heavy Canadian band that already has several records.

The entire first side of the record is the story of *2112*: it is a future where music is unknown and the government controls what everyone thinks. The hero, or narrator, finds an old guitar. He is amazed with the beauty and freedom of making your own music and tries to convince his powerful high priests that this guitar, and music, are something wonderful. Of course they disagree. He despairs and lies bleeding, dying of suicide, but too quickly has he despaired because at that moment spaceships arrive and overthrow the old order.

The second side has some cool songs too, like "Something for Nothing". Neil had to leave early to get the record back before his brother notices it missing. I also told Neil about my problem with William from Grade 9. He says not to worry, he'll fix him.

I listened to my new *2112* tape twice before going to bed.

Saturday, April 17, 1976

Did my route and met Neil at the YPL. He insisted I take out this book called <u>Anthem</u> by someone named Ayn Rand. It is about a future society where individualism is wiped out and even the word 'I' has been lost.

We went to Sam The Record Man's to look at the previous Rush albums. None of them are space related.

We hung out in the Summit Café and Neil told me that the *2112* concept is based on the ideas of this Ayn Rand, a woman who is actually a philosopher not just a writer. He has read some of her books, stuff way longer than <u>Anthem</u>, plus some philosophical essays.

Rand is an American who believes that the individual is more important than the group and in something called 'the virtue of selfishness'. The idea is that you should not live your life for someone else; it should never be a 'hand-me-down' life. Only you can determine what is the meaning and value of your own life. You should not just blindly follow your family, church, government, culture, whoever. Makes sense to me. I mean I'm loyal to my family, but everyone else can just go to Hell.

Sunday, April 25, 1976

Nice day. Helped Dad paint the back fence in the afternoon.

Went over to Neil's in the evening and hung out. He showed me his brother's new Led Zeppelin album *Presence* and we listened to the whole thing. He says this is real hippy music and that his brother and his friends smoke grass sometimes and listen to it. In the future all music will be rock, Neil claims, and scientists and astronauts would listen to these groups too.

I didn't see any science fiction connection but he pointed out that the mysterious, featureless, black object in all the photos on the album was similar to the obelisk in *2001: A Space Odyssey*. I still have not seen the movie (please CKOS! Put it on soon!) but I have read Arthur C. Clarke's book and I know that the obelisk is a doorway to another galaxy or perhaps universe.

Neil says this object on the album is the same thing: it is a silhouette of a bong, a water-filled pipe used to smoke grass, which is also a doorway to another universe, but this one hidden deep inside your mind.

Neil's brother showed up around 9 with a friend. He gave Neil some cigarettes for 'guarding his clubhouse' and Neil walked me home. I was getting ready for a bath when Mom smelled my clothes and came storming into my bedroom. Why did my clothes smell like cigarette smoke? Had I been smoking? I tried to tell her that I hadn't, but she was mad and not listening. Neil's house smells like smoke, the shed smells like smoke, shit, Neil smells like smoke sometimes! She tried to tell me I couldn't be friends with Neil any more, but I defended him standingly. I think I finally convinced her that I don't smoked myself, but it was a big fight.

Monday, April 26, 1976

At breakfast Mom was asking why I don't invite Ken or Arvid over anymore. I tried to tell her that we are no longer interested in the same things. I hope she gets over this soon. I know when I go inside Neil's shed again, she'll smell me and I'll be in trouble. Neil may smoke, but he is an A student and spends most of his time reading. How is that for a model citizen? Plus if I didn't have him for a friend I'd be dead by now. How many times I've wished he was in my homeroom. Mom says I need to make new friends but I will not descend to the level of the bulk of my ill-learned contemporaries. I'd rather be dead than like them. If I have to spend the whole summer alone, that's what I'll do if that shows her.

Spent all day at school worrying about this. I was walking down to 8-24, preoccupied, when Lucky snuck up behind me and pushed the books out from under my arm. My binder hit the floor and exploded. I scooped everything up but many pages had come free of the rings and were out of order. What a pain.

In English I got back an A+ for my writing assignment: a summary of "The Testament of Arkadia".

Paper route went smoothly.

I spent the evening working on Asteroid Beta Chapter 2. Finally my time traveling asteroid-dwellers make it back from Earth unharmed, but they did not avert the disaster which originally threw Asteroid Beta out of the solar system. I'm ready for Chapter 3!

Wednesday, May 5, 1976

That William from Grade 9 was bugging me again. Neil and I were in the Resource Center near the end of lunch period, looking at magazines. William came by and swept all our stuff off onto the floor. Neil got up to confront him but William just stared him down and said: you wanna settle this outside? I've never seen Neil back down, but William is large and crazy, a bad combination. Neil just sat down and said: let it go. Ken saw the whole thing and he was snickering afterwards. What a jerk. You don't laugh at the people who have the same problems as you do. Not very mature. I fear this could be the end.

Thursday, May 6, 1976

Today at lunch for some reason Neil insisted we eat outside, on the steps of the old building. This did not seem wise to me as some large and nasty people tend to congregate there. William was there, and some other very evil-looking people from Grade 9.

Neil was acting strangely, bragging about how his brother is working at the new McDonald's which just opened on East Broadway. He claimed that his brother could get him free food there anytime he wanted. McDonald's is the type of modern restaurant they have in big cities, so we were all impressed with this. Neil seemed to brag the whole time we ate our lunch. I had some cookies in my lunch and William demanded that I give them to him. Neil didn't stop him from taking my cookies and even seemed to be paying him some kind of respect that he doesn't deserve in the least.

After school I walked with Neil and asked him what was going on. He said: just trust me and go along with whatever I do. Fine. It may cost me some cookies to find out what he has planned. Then this evening I got a rare call from Neil. He wanted to make sure that I'd be in school tomorrow and I'd be eating my lunch on the old building steps again. He said he'd be late but I absolutely had to be there. This may cost me my neck, but I have to trust Neil. What would have happened if Alan Carter had not believed Koenig in "Collision Course"? I am up to the test.

Friday, May 7, 1976

Today at noon, despite my fears, I grabbed my lunch and headed to the old building front steps. Before I could even sit down, William demanded my cookies. I handed them over meekly. He said okay, sit over there, pointing at the lowest step.

In a few minutes, I saw a cool black sports car pull up on Catherine Street. (I later found out it is Neil's brother's friend's car.) Neil climbed out of the back seat and walked over. He was carrying a McDonald's bag and a giant McDonald's milkshake. He just sat next to me without looking at anybody else and said in a very soft voice: only eat the fries. Then he unpacked the bag, carefully laying out his spread on the concrete ledge siding the stairs: a Big Mac hamburger, a large, red cardboard sleeve of french fries, a gigantic chocolate milkshake, some packages of ketchup and salt, and a pile of napkins. In a much louder voice he said: geez I gotta take a leak. He grabbed the hamburger but left everything else behind.

As soon as he was out of sight, William came right down and demanded some fries. I tried to give him just a few but soon he took the whole package and started passing them around to his friends. Then he grabbed the milkshake and took off with a couple of his cronies.

When Neil finally came back I said I was sorry but there was no way I could stop William from stealing his stuff. Neil just said never mind, come on, and we walked into the playground center, where he added: don't tell anyone that I brought McDonald's today. If anyone asks, just deny deny deny. Sure. But I don't understand why the victim should be the one to cover up the crime. Perhaps he poisoned the milkshake? I'd lie to the police for Neil, you can count on that.

Monday, May 10, 1976

Today at lunch all hell broke loose. We did not go anywhere near the old building front steps, but William came and found us as we sat on the concrete ledge behind the old building. He was totally angry, shouting: you sick fuck! He grabbed Neil and they rolled on the ground until some teachers came and separated them. The teachers asked who started the fight and we all could honestly say it was William. Later that day we heard that William was expelled. On the way home from school Neil told me that he had put a piece of dog shit in the milkshake because he was sure William would steal it. I don't think I ever laughed so hard.

Tuesday, May 11, 1976

Neil has a black eye and some scuff marks on his face! I think he got in a fight last night, but he said it was nothing. For lunch today, he insisted we go sit on the old building front steps. The Grade 9s there got up and left when we arrived. Then there were a few other kids who came to sit on the steps, but no bullies. I can't believe I've gone from hiding under the gym stage to eat my lunch at the start of the year, to now sitting at the top of this prized landing. Neil is a god.

Wednesday, May 12, 1976

I need a short story by the end of the month for English, so I am going to use my first chapter of <u>Asteroid Beta</u>. I want it to look professional so I need to type it up. This may take a long time. Have to start now. See you later, diary.

Sunday, May 16, 1976

I've spent the last few nights working feverishly to get Chapter 1 typed up, so this morning Dad comes into my bedroom and says you need some fresh air, you're going to help me with the garden. So I spent all day turning over soil in the back yard, and pulling weeds in the planters. It was a hot day and by supper I was a wreck, burned from the sun, sweaty, sore, tired. Next time I need some fresh air I'll open a window.

Friday, June 4, 1976

Got my Asteroid Beta story back from Mr. Mitchell. He gave me an A+ and asked if I had other chapters. I said I do have a Chapter 2, but it is not quite typed up yet. He was very encouraging. To be honest, since I've been putting all that work into typing Chapter 2, I've not even thought about how Chapter 3 will go.

Friday, June 11, 1976

Sorry for ignoring you so much lately, my dear diary. What have I been doing you ask? Just the usual, delivering my newspapers, school work, taping good TV shows and movies, hanging out at the library, getting beat up, typing. Why do people want to hurt others? I know that their remarks have no basis in reality; they choose their insults for effectiveness, not accuracy. I'm looking forward to summer vacation. My marks are really good so far this year but M and D are still pushing me to see how well I can do.

Again, sorry for not writing lately. I will do better!

Sunday, June 20, 1976

Neil came over this afternoon for a while. We were drawing pictures of possible spaceships for my Asteroid Beta base. Then he dropped a bomb. He is going to be staying on Earl's parents farm and help them out this summer. It is lots of work and not much fun but he doesn't have a way out of it. His brother Jerry is going too, but Jerry will actually be paid a few bucks, unlike Neil. His grandparents are pretty poor, or pretty stingy, or maybe both. Sounds like another crappy summer on my own coming up, but I resolve this year to get something done, like finishing my Asteroid Beta book.

Monday, June 21, 1976

Had my English final exam this morning from 10 until 11:30. It wasn't too bad. I like final exam week because I get to sleep in. In the afternoon we had the Economics final. It was a little tougher but mostly multiple guess and I think I did okay.

Did my route and when I got home Mom was saying, what do you want to do this summer? I said I didn't know, maybe look for a job. Well how about a full time job for your Uncle Tim at Pic-A-Pop? I was floored. He is offering a dollar fifty an hour! He wants me as soon as possible so I have to quit my paper route right away. I phoned Fred Cuthbert right then and he said he'd try to arrange for someone to take over my route starting next week. $1.50 an hour works out to $60.00 a week! If I do that all summer I'll have tons of money. I am really happy!

[Editor's note: Roger apparently abandoned his diary for July and most of August.]

Saturday, August 21, 1976

This afternoon I went downtown to Logan's Drugs looking for #44 of *Kamandi, The Last Boy On Earth*. I met a girl there named Samantha. She was holding a magazine with a cover that showed Kirk, Spock (the main characters from *Star Trek*) and the U.S.S. Enterprise in the foreground, and a spectacular black hole behind them. It wasn't *Official UFO* or any of that Myron Fass crap I could tell because the inside page was also glossy. I asked her if it was a *Star Trek* magazine and then nervously admitted that I hadn't really seen much of *Star Trek*, but I was a big *Space: 1999* fan. She said so was she and we talked a while! She will be in Grade 9 at St. Joes just like me this fall. I said can I call you 'Sam' and she said sure and she hoped I'd be in her homeroom class! I almost forgot to buy a copy of the magazine. It is called *Starlog* and this is the very first issue. Finally a decent SF magazine!

Starlog #1 has oodles on *Star Trek*, including an episode guide, but it also has news on *Space: 1999*. There is a second season in the works and Catherine Schell (from "Guardian of Piri") will be playing a resident alien (yeah, like Spock) who can physically transform herself into other life forms. That should add a twist! Also there will be more humor, plus Koenig and Helena will finally get together romantically. Sounds like lots of good changes coming.

I am hoping and dreaming that Sam will be in my homeroom class. She seems like one of those great dreams you have where everyone likes you and you end up kissed by the pretty girl.

In the evening Neil called and we went to the Yorkton Hotel. He was broke so I bought him a drink. He told me about his summer. It was a lot of mindless manual labour and he was glad to be back in Yorkton. I told him all about *Starlog* and he wanted to come over and see it but it was getting late.

I just realized I didn't tell him about Samantha. I'm not sure why.

On Moving to Yorkton (Samantha Renfield, 1994)

I was born and lived in Regina until I was thirteen years old
when my father got a job as a copy editor with CJGX radio in
Yorkton. He also wrote commercials and helped the
announcers with their material. Understandably I wasn't too
thrilled to move as it meant starting again in a new, strange and
smaller, city with no friends.

My history with science fiction to that point: my older
brother James had turned me on to Star Trek and we watched
all the re-runs with messianic fervor. I especially liked Spock.
He valued logic above all else, and kept a tight rein on his
emotions. Probably logic could not explain his deep bond with
Kirk and McCoy but he only admitted that bond under extreme
circumstances, and therefore was able to retract any emotional
statements as soon as the situation stabilized. Spock could
reason it was time for an emotional outburst, I think Dr.
McCoy once noted. That degree of personal control was
attractive to me.

I loved to read and my interest in science fiction was not
exclusive to *Star Trek*. When I first encountered *Space: 1999* I
was struck by the quality of the special effects, and the very
mysterious nature of the fictional cosmos that confronted the
Moonbase Alphans each week. Certainly it was a weaker
cousin of *Star Trek*, but family nonetheless.

When I moved to Yorkton in the summer of 1976 it was
unexpectedly a step up from my Regina circles. Although *Star
Trek* syndication did not play in Yorkton, it was here I finally
found other science fiction buffs to share my interests with, and
here also I experienced my first real brush with infatuation, in
the guise of Lionel O'Neill.

On Meeting Samantha Renfield (Roger Kay, 1994)

I met Samantha Renfield in front of the magazine rack inside Logan's Drugs. I was trolling for new science fiction magazines. My lucrative summer job with Pic-A-Pop financed my growing addiction to science fiction. I was working 40 hours a week for the first time that summer and Saturdays I inevitably ended up at Logan's to plan my next expenditure.

In late August 1976 I found her there, flipping through the newly arrived *Starlog* #1. I was so startled to find a girl at my destination, doing what I intended to do, that I overcame my shyness and asked her if she was a SF fan. I remember the elation of finding someone who liked outer space, and therefore indirectly, could be said to like *me*. And she was a girl! Not bad looking at all. She had long, straight, very dark red hair. Almost a wine color. Very pale skin, a shy smile and when she finally focused her gaze upon you it was like an alien mind probe; I had no defense and had to trust in the benevolence of the greater intelligence.

Later that year she blossomed. Sprouted amazing breasts. After that, I noticed how round her hips were or had become. She was no ectomorph, but no way was she fat either. I didn't understand why she wasn't higher in the social pecking order at school. She was not sporty, but she was very intelligent. Both of those probably worked against her. Perhaps it was the mouthful of silver braces. Hanging out with SF geeks like Neil and I certainly could not have helped.

Entries from Roger Kay's 1976 Diary

Thursday, August 26, 1976

Last day of work today. Uncle Tim and the rest of the staff got together at lunch and presented me with a snazzy Pic-A-Pop bottle opener. I really liked working there. Once school starts Uncle Tim says I can work part time, but we haven't figured out when. I'm not sure I want to work Saturdays. Now I suppose I can get another paper route, but it'll be hard to go back to so little money, and I can't get another real job because I'm not legally old enough to work. Right now I've got over two hundred and fifty dollars in the bank which sounds good but I do need to save up a lot more to buy a car for when I'm sixteen.

When I got home, Mom had a bunch of school supplies for me, including a calculator! It is smaller than the one Dad got for work a couple of years ago and much more advanced. Instead of hitting a special button to see what is behind the decimal point, it actually displays the decimal point right in the answer. Very cool. Each digit is created based on picking which of seven segments (light-emitting diodes, or 'LEDs') arranged in a figure eight to light. Very nifty!

Watched *New Avengers* and then had a bath. Starting to feel depressed because I can no longer ignore the fact that school starts tomorrow.

Friday, August 27, 1976

Well school started today. I am now in 9-31 up on the fourth floor of the old building, far away from the 7s and 8s in the class room wing. Paradoxically, the Grade 9 floor in the old building has been renovated so that it looks like the newest area of St. Joes. There is wall to wall carpeting in the classrooms and hallway, and the walls are a bold red. Very modern!

Neil is in 9-32 and so is Samantha Renfield. I wish I was too, but no luck. I also found out that Jocelyn Bjornson is not coming back to school - she got pregnant! She is my age. How crazy is that? I've never even kissed a girl.

My homeroom teacher is Mr. Peebles, but people call him Mr. Pebbles, or Mr. Pebblerock, like he was a Flintstone! Brian Woloschuk is in my class again. He has grown a lot over summer and is now very, very tall. Probably not good. But he does seem maybe a bit more mature. Or perhaps he is just holding back because his friends are not in this class. Ken and Arvid are both in my class, but they seem to want to keep to themselves. I think they are mad I made friends with Neil and that I didn't try to call them during the summer. This means I don't have any friends in my homeroom. Anyway, we again have the stupid six-day schedule, with: English, Social Studies, French, Economics, Music, Phys-ed, Algebra, Industrial Arts, Health, Science, Art, plus a double-period for study (Friday morning) and a homeroom period (last thing Monday).

I like my new locker. It is around the corner from 9-34, near the back stairs, the next to last locker on that side. Also, Neil's locker is almost right across from me. I calculate this greatly decreases the chance of my getting stuffed into my locker.

I didn't see Samantha today.

Monday, August 30, 1976

Second day of school. Finally caught up with Samantha. At lunchtime I approached her and said, hey you wanna sit with the science fiction fans, meaning Neil and me, and she said YES!

She is very interesting and well-read. Her brother James is very cool and even sneaks her into R movies sometimes. She told us about a movie called *The Man Who Fell To Earth* about an alien who comes from a dying, water-starved planet and tries to make a lot of money by introducing advanced alien technology on Earth. Eventually the government finds out, kidnaps him and messes him up, so his mission is a failure. Sam says there is an old novel that the movie is based on. She mentioned a critical scene where the alien goes into an elevator and even the gentle force of the elevator accelerating upward is more than his delicate alien skeleton can handle. Bones break and he is hurt pretty bad. Interesting that one could grow up very weak just by living on a relatively low gravity planet.

She is also a big fan of the guy who played the lead role in the movie, David Bowie. He has a record called *Ziggy Stardust and The Spiders From Mars.* That's not science fiction but he did an earlier song in the sixties called "Space Oddity". "Can you hear me Major Tom...?" I've heard that, and I like it.

Neil seemed to be having a little trouble speaking to her at first, but by the end of lunch when it was clear she didn't hold his stutter against him or think him an idiot, he was doing fine. This year is starting off much better than last year.

Tuesday, August 31, 1976

Sam ate lunch with us again today. Some people think we're strange because we are two guys and a girl.

Brian walked by and called me fag for eating lunch with a girl, but Neil followed him into the stairwell. Later he told me that he just asked Brian if it made sense to accuse someone of being a fag for hanging around a girl and Brian voluntarily agreed it might not, and retracted his accusation. I bet Neil left something out of the description of his persuasion technique.

At lunch we talked about starting a *Space: 1999* fan club and I said we should have a weekly meeting and record everything. Sam was intrigued when I told her about my Sony tape recorder and my tape collection.

After school I couldn't find Neil so I walked home alone. Practiced my typing, and then watched *M*A*S*H* and *King of Kensington.*

Friday, September 3, 1976

At lunch Sam told us how some of the girls in her class are bugging her about eating lunch with two guys, especially because those two guys are Neil and I. Apparently stupidity is not limited to males of the species as they were telling her to beware becoming pregnant and asking what it was like to kiss a loser. That hurts. It is one thing to have the guys insult you, another entirely for the girls to do it. For this reason I did not share that Marvin Miller had called her a slut in homeroom just before lunch. If he does it again I'll tell Neil, and he'll straighten him out.

Neil and I told Sam that we are planning to meet on Sunday in Shaw Park around 3 to discuss the new *Space: 1999* season. We invited her and she seemed interested but said her family is going to Regina this weekend so she can't make it.

Did more typing. I'm actually getting pretty good.

Saturday, September 4, 1976

Today the new (second) season of *Space: 1999* started! At 4 o'clock with great anticipation I set up my cassette recorder downstairs, then watched "The Metamorph" upstairs on the color TV. Wow! There are new uniforms, Main Mission is replaced with a new Command Centre, and Dr. Russell even has a new haircut. They also changed the opening credits and theme song. I wrote a good summary of the new episode.

Comments on "The Metamorph"
[No recent comments provided because Roger's complete,
original summary is included below.]

Episode Summary: "The Metamorph"
(Roger Kay, 1976, 1682 words)

Helena dictates into her log that it is now 342 days since
breakaway, and they have recently been catapulted six light
years by a space warp. No one was hurt, however one life
support system was damaged and a supply of the rare element
titanium will be required to repair it.

A survey Eagle sent to a nearby planet flies above the
rocky and volcanic landscape before confirming there is
titanium present. The Eagle starts to head back to Alpha, but a
ball of white light emerges from the planet, overtakes it, then
envelopes it. As pilot Bill Fraser cries for help, the ball of light
retreats to the planet and his wife collapses, sobbing on the
floor of Command Centre, a compact one storey rectangular
underground control room which replaces the sprawling old
Main Mission of last year.

Koenig questions a Command Center officer, no name
given, who claims that he has scanned the planet and found no
life. He further insists the planet is an environmental hell on
which no life could ever possibly exist. Proving the officer
mistaken, an alien appears on the big screen, and introduces
himself as Mentor.

Mentor claims the Eagle occupants are well, but the Eagle
itself has been destroyed. Millions of deaths occurred on
Mentor's planet when armed space vehicles previously visited,
he says, so now they take defensive action.

Koenig pleads that their intentions are non-hostile, and the
Alphans are only seeking mineral supplies. Mentor becomes
friendlier and suggests they should visit his planet. He requests
that Koenig send a technical officer to discuss their mineral
requirements, plus a medical officer as one of the Eagle

occupants was slightly injured. Koenig agrees, but on condition that they meet in space, not on the planet.

Overhearing their discussion is Mentor's beautiful and plungingly neck-lined daughter Maya, who knows the secrets of molecular transformation. She is in the physical form of a large lioness, but then transforms to her usual humanoid shape to talk with her father.

Maya says the Alphans are a much more attractive people than the others they've met. Mentor agrees that they appear to be a similar to Psychons, although not as advanced. He assures her the Alphans will soon be helping restore their beloved home planet Psychon.

The Alphans prepare an Eagle with extra booster units to allow them to get back in a hurry if things do not go well. Koenig and Carter are in the nosecone, while Helena, and a technical officer, the unnamed Alphan from Command Centre, are in the back compartment.

When the Eagle reaches the rendezvous point, Mentor sends a ship to meet them, but the scan of it from Alpha reveals that it is not carrying the two pilots, Fraser and Torrens. It is a trap!

The alien ship begins to emit strong magnetism and tries to draw the Eagle down to the planet. Only with the help of the extra boosters does the Eagle finally break free. They seem to be escaping but then the alien ship turns into a ball of light and Koenig's Eagle is captured, just like the first Eagle.

When the lightball sets them down on the planet, the Alphans see they have landed in a graveyard of spaceships. They cannot contact Alpha, but Mentor re-appears on their screens, asking for patience. Suddenly Fraser appears in the background and breaks in shouting: they're lying Commander, we're prisoners!

Mentor claims Fraser is feverish and requests that the Alphans remain in their ship for the time being. Soon the Alphans grow impatient and decide to ignore Mentor's request and head for a nearby cave entrance.

On Alpha, Sandra cannot get any reading from the planet surface. Something is interfering. Tony (Koenig's new second-in-command) expresses worry that Fraser's wife is going to crack up. Sandra reassures him that she, Fraser's unnamed wife, will be okay as long as she knows Fraser is okay. She asks Tony to cut the wife some slack because they have only been married for two months.

Meanwhile, inside the cave, Helena has found some chunks of rock she thinks are titanium. She asks the unknown Alphan for confirmation, calling him Lou. He confirms that they only need a couple more similarly chunks.

Further into the cave they see a diversity of humanoids working the rocks like primitive miners. They move clumsily, robotically, and appear to be brain damaged. Koenig spots the first Eagle's co-pilot, Torrens. He is climbing down a ladder and does not recognize them.

When Koenig tries to touch Torrens, a force field repels him. This is noticed by a sentry, who raises a transparent wand at the Alphans, but Koenig fires first and the sentry turns to rock. Lou muses this is another example of molecular transformation, like the alien ship and the balls of light.

Mentor appears and demands they drop their weapons but it is just an energy field around his image. Koenig asks Lou if they can get around the image and Lou suggests a laser might disrupt it.

Mentor warns that any force they use will be turned against them, but before Koenig can stop him, Lou fires the laser rifle at the image. The laser beam is reflected back at Lou, and he is vaporized.

Guess we didn't really need to know his last name!

The Alphans head back down the cave passage to try to escape, but a ball of light comes after them and they are gone, somehow captured.

Koenig wakes up in an orange cell with a large lioness watching him, licking its chops. The lioness transforms into Maya, and she apologizes on the off chance she startled him.

Koenig suggests this was indeed her purpose, and as he casually approaches her, a force field sizzles into life and violently throws him back.

Maya apologizes again, saying she should have warned him of it. She introduces herself and asks why he is so unfriendly.

Koenig lists reasons such as being lied to, being assaulted, his people being tortured and killed. Maya denies her father is capable of any of this. She deactivates the force field and invites Koenig to accompany her to see Mentor.

When they get to his lair, Mentor asks Maya to leave them alone. She chafes and stalls at this a bit because she wants to see him soothe Koenig's anger which she doesn't understand, but Mentor insists she leave.

Alone with Koenig, Mentor explains his master console of bubbling colored liquids in tall cylinders: it is Psyche, a biological machine that can perform molecular transformation on a grand scale. It will be used to restore his glorious planet, Psychon.

The only catch is that Psyche requires the minds of intelligent beings as a power source. Mentor insists their destinies are linked, but Koenig disagrees, horrified by his new understanding of what has happened to the cave workers, and Torrens.

Mentor demonstrates his powers by causing several explosions on the Moon.

Koenig admits that the Alphans cannot fight him, but instead of co-operation offers only frustration. Koenig dares Mentor to destroy them.

This presents Mentor with a catch-22 but he breaks the stalemate by showing Koenig that he has bolted Helena, Carter and Fraser into the brain-sucking apparatus, and they will be fodder for Psyche unless he agrees.

Koenig relents; he sends a message to Alpha: the planet has subterranean areas which are habitable and the Alphans should evacuate to it as soon as possible under Directive Four.

Helena, Carter, and Fraser are shocked at Koenig's bargain. One of the sentries has to stun Carter as he lunges at Koenig.

Meanwhile back on Alpha, the main computer will not tell Sandra what Directive Four is, but Tony knows very well. It means: ignore the rest of this message, just destroy the place of origin of this message. It is mandatory and cannot be countermanded. On Tony's command, an Eagle with explosives is launched towards Psychon.

When Mentor scans the Eagle and detects explosives but no life forms, he rages that Koenig has betrayed him. He appears to Koenig in his cell and berates him for being a liar.

Helena, Carter and Fraser realize that Koenig, instead of betraying them, has hatched a suicidal plan to destroy Psychon. Despite their still perilous position, they are relieved and congratulate Koenig.

Maya overhears that the approaching Eagle was sent to destroy Psychon and rushes to confront the captive Alphans. Koenig tries to tell her the truth but Maya cannot believe that Psyche is harmful or that her father is a murderer. Koenig pleads again and again for her to go and see what is in the caves until finally Maya transforms into a dove and flies into the full horror of the mining caverns.

As Mentor again threatens Koenig, showing him a view of Alpha with buildings exploding, Maya returns from the caves and overhears.

Koenig quickly convinces her to free them on the promise he will attempt only to stop, not harm, Mentor.

When Koenig gets to Mentor's lair, he starts to smash the bubbling liquid-filled tubes of Psyche. Mentor howls that his will unleash the full power of Psyche and destroy Psychon, pure madness! But Koenig does not relent and a cascade of explosions ensue.

Meanwhile, Helena and Fraser are trying to save what is left of Torrens, but when they enter the mining cave, explosions have already buried Torrens in rubble.

As the flames engulf him, Mentor cries out for Koenig to save Maya, to take her away.

Maya struggles with Koenig, transforming into, by turns, a falcon, a German Shepherd dog, a huge black ape.

Finally she realizes she must escape with the Alphans to the Eagle, which lifts off just in time as the entire planet explodes.

On their way back to Alpha, Fraser get a grateful hello and a kiss blown from his wife on Alpha.

Koenig and Helena comfort Maya. They thank her for saving their lives, but she thinks her life is over, saying on every planet but Psychon she'll be an alien. Koenig makes it clear that she is welcome by saying: we're all aliens until you get to know us.

Entries from Roger Kay's 1976 Diary

Sunday, September 5, 1976

Neil and I hung out in Shaw Park and discussed the new 1999 episode. The sky was grey. Neil was annoyed that Professor Bergman, Paul Morrow, plus a few others are missing from the new series. He did admit the planet Psychon looked amazingly real and Maya would be an interesting new character, but he also looked a bit perturbed.

I told Mom that I was out of Kleenex but she said she wouldn't be buying any for two weeks!

Monday, September 6, 1976

We are going to study black and white photography in Industrial Arts! They have 35mm cameras to lend us, and we just have to pay for film and photographic paper. Mr. Voerstadt wants two dollars for a roll of film before you get a camera. I paid him at the end of the class and he said come back after last period to pick up the camera. In Math we started doing decimals. This is where the calculator really makes things easier, saving on a lot of long division calculations.

At lunch, Sam joined us. I was worried she wouldn't. Last week she had lunch with Sandra Sprong and that group a couple times, but now she says she'd rather eat with us because we are much more interesting. This might be social suicide on her part, to hang out with a couple of misfits like us, but we are happy to have her.

I told her all about my <u>Asteroid Beta</u> novel and she says she wants to read it! No one other than Neil has read the whole thing yet and he read the longhand version. I am almost done typing up the second chapter, so I said she could read the first two chapters very soon.

In Phys-ed this afternoon. I managed 31 laps in 16 minutes, which I thought was pretty good, even if no one else did.

Picked up the 35mm camera after the final bell. Mr. Voerstadt showed me how to load the film, really he loaded it for me.

I did a series of photos of my Eagle model. It was tied on a string to my curtain rod. The birch tree in the backyard formed the backdrop. Tried a few shots after dark as well.

Friday, September 10, 1976

Took the camera back to school today and in Industrial Arts we learned how to use a machine to print contact strips of our negatives. The contact strip is a print that comes directly from your negative being pressed up against the photographic paper, so the print is the same size as the negative: very small! The idea is that contact strips give you a glimpse of your work without having to use much paper or chemicals. You then pick what you want to print full size.

Some kids who didn't pay had to all share one film and take like two pictures each. I'm eager to pay for another whole roll! I did learn one important thing from my first roll when I printed the contact strip. Night shots on windows do not look good: you can see reflections from lights inside my room. Some of the daytime shots worked very well though and Mr. Voerstadt even wanted a print for himself of my best shot: a noble Eagle in profile, lifting off in front of the birch tree.

I thought Grade 9 was going to be much more civilized than Grade 8 but stupidity again burst into my life today. Brian and Marvin were hanging around the outer room of the photo lab when I came out, quite late as I had bought another roll of film and struggled for some time to load it myself. When they saw me at first they were saying: hey you wanna earn some money? They wanted to give me 25 cents if they could take a picture of my bare butt. I said no way, thinking this would only get me into a much worse situation, so they started bugging me and it escalated until they held me with my head pushed out the window, threatening to make me fall. But I said: you better just push me then, and eventually they let me go. I almost forgot my camera on the way out. This is getting out of hand.

Saturday, September 11, 1976

Today at 4 *Space: 1999* was a new episode called "The Exiles".

Episode Summary: "The Exiles" (1493 words)
[Omitted.]

Comments on "The Exiles" (Roger Kay, 1994)

In Command Centre the calm is broken when fifty small red metal craft, space bees someone suggests, approach the Moon and go into orbit. Soon the Alphans have freed a young couple, the male Cantar, and the female Zova from the stasis of their space coffins. The aliens claim their craft are in family groups and that a small ruthless group has unfairly exiled them from their home Golos, 'the peace planet' (haven't we heard that before?).

Cantar pleads with Koenig to rescue and revive the remaining exiles but Koenig argues their life support systems are already strained. Cantar offers to use his advanced technology to greatly increase Alpha's life support capabilities. Koenig agrees but once Cantar starts working in the Life Support Unit, a painfully loud high frequency noise disables the Alphans but has no effect upon the exiles, who smile evilly.

Favorite scene: Maya is in Helena's living quarters and Koenig is due to arrive. Maya asks Helena if she is sure Koenig has a sense of humor. Encouraged by the answer, Maya transforms into a second Helena. Koenig comes in and is confronted with two Helenas. They each kiss him, then ask him to determine which is the real Helena. He says there was no difference whatsoever. When the real Helena reacts negatively to the remark, Koenig points out she has given away the game.

Entries from Roger Kay's 1976 Diary

Sunday, September 12, 1976

Met up with Neil and Sam in Shaw Park this afternoon. We talked about the new 1999 episode. Neil called Maya a 'fish out of water' and suggested we might see some interesting episodes about her adapting to Alphan society.

Already it appears Maya is headed for a love interest with the new security chief Tony Verdeschi. We're not sure where Tony came from. He seems to have replaced Paul Morrow (Koenig's right hand man!) in the storylines. Other Main Mission staff that are now officially missing include: Professor Victor Bergman, computer chief Kano, operator Tanya Alexander, and that guy with the long, dark hair.

It is also very clear that Maya is aware that Koenig and Helena are an item. The kiss test demonstrated this. Sam says this saves Koenig from the 'Captain Kirk Syndrome' where the leading man becomes involved with a new girl every week.

Did more typing tonight and just have three more pages to go before Chapter 2 is ready for Sam.

Monday, September 13, 1976

In Phys-ed we had a really difficult obstacle course. I did not do well. Some of the guys were having showers after Phys-ed but there's no way I'm taking off my clothes anywhere near that school.

Neil and I were at the House of Hobbies and I found a Moonbase Alpha model! I had to buy it right then, even though it was over eight dollars. I went to the Royal Bank, took out ten dollars, and ran right back to buy it. They only had one so I made them promise not to sell it until I got back. I was moving fast.

Neil is very interested in the shapes of the buildings because he wants to create a blueprint set for the whole of Alpha, a very ambitious idea. This evening he came over and made sketches of the different pieces. I need some gray paint for the lunar surface. The model is a lunar landscape and external view of Alpha, about one foot by eighteen inches, and then on the corner of that, is a larger scale version of just Main Mission and the Commander's office, maybe three by five inches. There are tiny Eagles to sit on the launch pads, and tiny Alphans to populate Main Mission. Cool!

I just noticed that "Breakaway" is exactly 23 years from today!

Friday, September 17, 1976

Today was pretty easy. Had a couple of quizzes, Math and French. Did all my homework in study period.

Neil and I walked down to Sam The Record Man after school and I found the *Space: 1999* soundtrack LP and it was only $7.99! I went to the Royal Bank to get some money, but it was already closed! Rushed home and begged Mom to lend me the money until Monday which, after some arguing about me 'wasting' my money, she finally lent me a ten. I left Neil looking at albums and he was amused I took so long to get back. The new album is the Year One music!

Neil came over this evening and we listened to my new purchase. I taped a cassette copy of it for him and he was very happy. Neil was impressed with my Alpha model especially all the careful painting. It took two full evenings but I did a lot of detail painting, even the different colored sleeves for the little Main Mission figures!

Stayed up late to watch the movie *Colossus 1980*. It is about an army super-computer that takes over the world. Very well done and chilling but I'm tired now, 1:20 a.m. Good night!

Saturday, September 18, 1976

Slept in until 10:30. When I got up Mom suggested I call Uncle Tim and see if I can work there part-time. She thinks I'm spending all my money just because I've bought a few things this week. But I've still got over two hundred dollars in the bank, a fortune!

I gave in however and called him. Now I'm planning on working there 7 to 9 on Monday, Wednesday and Thursday evenings. I'll still be making a buck and a half an hour so that works out to $9 a week, about 150% of what I made on the paper route. Cool!

Taped a new episode today: "Journey To Where". Wrote a great summary. Strange thing with this episode is where is Sandra Benes? Yasko seems to be taking her place?

Episode Summary: "Journey To Where" (1578 words)
[Omitted.]

Comments on "Journey To Where" (Roger Kay, 1994)

Alpha receives a transmission from Planet Earth! It is Dr. Logan from Texas City Space Station 1. The year is 2120 and neutrino transmission technology makes instant communication over great distances possible. There is an associated instant transport technology for people but the Alphans must build the transmitter based upon Dr. Logan's specifications, test the device, and transfer all the Alphans within 72 hours else a constellation will move between the Earth and Alpha making the transfer impossible for the foreseeable future. Despite the fact that everyone on Earth now lives in domes, and everywhere outside is uninhabitable, the Alphans still desire to return there.

The Alphans manage to build the machine, but earthquakes back on planet Earth throw the calculations off so Koenig, Helena, and Alan Carter wind up in Scotland in 1339. Worse still, Helena has caught viral pneumonia and the locals think she has the plague!

Favorite scene: Koenig, Helena and Alan are herded into a cave-like prison cell. Helena is now very sick, sweating, shaking and coughing. She says she has only six to eight hours to live without treatment and that the others will die too if they cannot escape the cell and get away from her. Koenig then kisses her on the mouth. He has no plans to live without her. Helena realizes the significance of the kiss and starts to cry.

Entries from Roger Kay's 1976 Diary

Sunday, September 19, 1976

As planned I met up with Neil and Sam at Shaw Park this afternoon. Sam was still dressed in her church clothes. She looks very different than in her usual jeans and t-shirt. Today she looked a lot older than us, or at least older than me. For some reason this made me a little shy. Also, I noticed Neil was stuttering more than usual.

We discussed the "Journey To Where". This episode really marks a watershed moment for the Alphans. Forever more after this they will never dream of returning to Earth. They now know that the Earth is in bad shape and not much more Earth-like than Alpha. They may still dream of finding a planet, but it won't be Earth. Neil mentioned that because they have accepted the 'who needs Nature' idea, maybe the Alphans would now be happy to just stay put on Alpha. Maybe they will give up entirely their quest for a planet. Later episodes will test this theory.

I raised the issue of Sandra, and Neil brought up the entire list of missing Alphans. Certainly there are some questions about the transition to Year Two. I also noted I was happy to hear about the abolishment of competitive sports in 2026. Too bad its fifty years too late for me. Neil suggested sports bring out the animal instincts in people and an advanced society would certainly want to rid itself of that type of poison. He even suggested that, in the far future, humans would evolve beyond the need for physical bodies completely. We would become entities of pure energy, like the people from planet Zenno, made of light.

I gave Sam the typewritten sheets for the first two chapters of Asteroid Beta and she seems eager to read it. I am nervous but excited. I don't have a lot of feedback on my writing yet.

Monday, September 20, 1976

This week we're finally back in the photo lab for Industrial Arts. Mr. Voerstadt showed us how to use chemicals to develop our film. First you have to put your film into a light tight container, then you add various chemicals, being very careful to time each operation. It is definitely more tricky than just throwing the film into the machine like we did before but you definitely feel more professional doing the tray method.

After school I walked home with Neil and Sam and told them about my job at Pic-A-Pop. They seemed impressed and Neil said he'd love a job like that. Problem is, as long as you're under sixteen the government says you can't have a real job. I'm just lucky that I have an uncle with a business who is willing to pay me 'under the table'.

Back at Pic-A-Pop after supper. I moved some stock to the front for them, and cleaned up in the back as well by stacking up some pallets of all one flavor. I love that they trust me to use the pallet mover and I am super careful to go very slow and not brake or start quickly. The fact that anything I break comes out of my pay is another motivation. The two hours went by quickly and Uncle Tim sent me home right at 9, locking the door behind me.

Listened to my 1999 soundtrack as I wrote this.

Thursday, September 23, 1976

At lunch Neil told me about this Grade 11, Ron, from the Regional who runs a *Space: 1999* non-profit organization. Walking home yesterday, Neil stopped at the Darlington Confectionary to buy some smokes. Ron was also in there, noticed all the Eagle doodles on Neil's duotang, and started talking about 1999 with him. He probably didn't realize that Neil was younger than him. Once you start to talk to Neil, however, you realize that he is more intelligent than even high school students. Well, unless he stutters. Ron's organization publishes something called *The Association of Alphans Newsletter*. He is looking for 1999-related fiction, drawings, and whatever he can get his hands on. The first issue is not yet out but he says that it will be by the end of the year. Neil is working on some technical drawings he hopes Ron will publish. He just lives a few doors down the back alley from Neil, on 4th, just a couple of houses past Victoria School.

Neil says I should polish up some fiction and he'll present it to this guy. I'd love to be published! This is an incredible opportunity. Neil also said the guy has info on something called the Moonbase Alpha Technical Notebook, which is published by *Starlog* and contains all sorts of information and drawings of the technology used in 1999. Neil wrote down the ordering details because he thought I'd want to buy one. Of course he would too, but I know he doesn't have the money.

Had to work tonight but I got my first pay since summer. At the end of the evening, Uncle Tim personally paid me my nine dollars for the week.

Friday, September 24, 1976

Neil is full of surprises. At lunch he told Sam and I about a film class at the Regional High School that he will be taking. It is the same as what they offer the high school kids, except it is for exceptional younger kids and happens in the evenings, Monday and Wednesday. He says his brother Jerry did the class and knows the teacher (Mr. Focault) very well. Neil is very excited and happy.

After school I scrambled down to the Post Office to get a money order so I could order the Moonbase Alpha Technical Notebook. I have the letter and envelope all ready, so I just had to put the M.O. in, buy a stamp, seal it, and off it went. Please hurry *Starlog*!

Worked a bit on chapter 3 of Asteroid Beta. In this one, the Betans discover a city of robots inside another passing asteroid. Unlike in most science fiction, these robots don't understand English and they cannot communicate with the crew of Beta. I've got the landing party in there, had them captured by the robots, but now I'm not sure how to progress.

Saturday, September 25, 1976

Rainy this morning so I worked on Beta. I've now written the Chapter 3 ending. The Betans rescue their crew by altering one of the robots to act by remote control. They mount a mini-camera in its skull so they can see where they are going, and then use it to walk into the robot city and wheel their people out concealed in a garbage container. The Reverse Trojan

Horse! This way they don't have to solve the communication problem and they don't have to fight the powerful robots. Because they don't understand the robots or what they want, their only solution is to get away from them.

Spent the evening working on the summary for today's 1999 episode "One Moment of Humanity".

Episode Summary: "One Moment Of Humanity"
(1138 words)
[Omitted.]

Comments on "One Moment Of Humanity"
(Roger Kay, 1994)

Zamara from the planet Vega appears in Command Centre and demonstrates she has the capability to leave Alpha powerless. She instantly transports Helena and Tony to her planet.

At first Vega seems hospitable. The people and surroundings are beautiful. Helena and Tony are offered food and served by robots. But they soon discover that the attractive Vegans are really robots, and the robots are the actual Vegans, living behind masks, fearful that if the robots ever learn violence by example they would slaughter all the Vegans. This is what the Vegan robots desire most, the knowledge of violence.

The Vegans try to provoke Tony and Helena verbally. When that fails, they agree to send them back to Alpha, but when they arrive Alpha is mysteriously empty. This is just an elaborate ruse to provoke a paranoia of each other. When this fails, Zamara returns to Alpha just long enough to peruse the moonbase library and determine that jealousy is an excellent accelerant for human violence. Now she will kidnap Koenig and Maya as well. She has two pairs for which jealousy might be combustible.

Favorite scene: When they first arrive on Vega, Helena and Tony are offered food. Robots place bowls in front of them. One robot whispers to Helena that she must not react as they expect, and that if they show aggression, they will be killed.

When they taste the food it is awful but Helena, mindful of the warning, insists it is 'interesting'. Zamara calls her a lying cow. When Tony tastes some food, he grimaces, and then catching a meaningful look from Helena, declares it delicious. Zamara's male companion, Zarl, calls him a spineless liar. Tony struggles not to react.

Entries from Roger Kay's 1976 Diary

Sunday, September 26, 1976

Today Sam came over to my house for the first time. It was so rainy I thought she might not show up, but at one o'clock I saw her standing out by the table where we had agreed to meet. Our living room window has a good view of Shaw Park so I just opened the front door and called her over. I was impressed she even showed up in this rain.

She brought back the first two chapters of <u>Asteroid Beta</u>, carrying them inside her raincoat, pressed close to her. She preserved them dry and warm. She says she liked my story but we didn't discuss it much. Our attention was focused on "One Moment of Humanity". Neil found a bunch of holes in it. He is right that the show is changing. I taped our discussion.

Supper was oven burgers. Kind of greasy.

Watched *Sonny & Cher*, *Switch*, *Marketplace* and *Ombudsman*. Waste of time.

Roger: Okay, today we'll be discussing "One Moment of Humanity", the fourth episode of the new *Space: 1999* year. Our experts this week are Samantha Renfield...

Sam: Um, hello.

Roger: And Lionel O'Neill....

Neil: Good day.

Roger: Let's start with you Neil. How would you rate this episode?

Neil: Well I'm sad to say this is one of the weakest episodes yet. I mean it's still visually stunning but ... some of the reactions ... not very realistic. For example, when Zarl is dancing with Helena, trying to make Koenig jealous, why would he get jealous? This is some alien android dancing with Helena, not Tony or Alan. Zarl's not the competition. Koenig doesn't have to worry about Helena falling for this robot, no matter how well it dances!

(general laughter in background)

Roger: *(singing)* I'm just a love machine, and I won't work for nobody but you...

(sound of Sam's laughter)

Neil: Right. Also the ending was kinda fake. Why did Zarl die? When he felt that moment of humanity, or love, for Helena, this is what killed him? If these androids can't handle strong emotions, well what about hate then? Wouldn't that also kill them? If any strong emotion kills them, then aren't they in fact harmless, and the whole plot just null and void? There's a bad contradiction here. The alien androids can turn off Alpha's life support but they can't hit you in the face? Why didn't they just turn off the heat in their own cities? That would have eliminated the Vegan people without any violence.

Roger: Yeah. The planet surface sure did look freezing.

Neil: Uh huh. Another great problem here is, after saving everyone on the planet from the evil androids, our Alphans just go on their merry way, without any reward. Don't you think they would have been offered a place on the alien planet? Koenig was ready to do Operation Exodus for Ultima Thule, so it's not they just don't like cold planets... and the alien instant transport technology would make Operation Exodus a snap!

Roger: Yeah that's strange. They missed a few opportunities. In "Journey To Where" they use a transporter from 22nd century Earth. After that, what happens to it? Couldn't they use it to transport to a third point, bypass whatever is in the way, and then jump over to Earth? Why's it gotta be a direct line, a single jump?

Neil: Good question.

Roger: They've already tested the equipment once. Why didn't Earth just send them all the technical details so they could build the entire device themselves? You know, rather than having Earth run the transfer, just radio all the technical discoveries that made it possible and let Alpha build its own device.

Sam: Wow yeah. If you're going down that road, howabout Maya? She is this super intelligent alien who knows all sorts of planets. There was a whole graveyard of ships on Psychon. Couldn't most of those go faster than light? So shouldn't Maya have some clue how to build one?

Roger: Maybe she's holding out on the Alphans.

Sam: She doesn't want Tony to find a nice Italian wife!

(general laughter)

Sam: Even in "The Exiles", once Cantar and Zova are defeated, why didn't the people on Golos offer the Alphans sanctuary?

Roger: They rely heavily on some fragile equipment... Maybe they just can't support any more people.

Sam: For Alpha, I could understand that. Limited resources. But Golos is a whole planet, with great technology, including a transporter. They could've shared the plans for their transporter at the very least!

Roger: Instead they got the commemorative spoon.

Sam: More like a fork in the back!

(general laughter)

Neil: Maybe all this just reinforces the idea that the Alphans are now much more comfortable aboard their moonbase and not so interested in finding a planet to live on. This changes the dynamic of the show, from one of a desperate search and struggle against time, to one of exploration and adventure. In other words, a second *Star Trek*. I fear we are dealing with the creeping Star Trekization of 1999.

Entries from Roger Kay's 1976 Diary

Tuesday, September 28, 1976

We did contour maps in Science today. Easy and boring. Had an ORA session in English: I am up to 1100 words per minute! The only other person in my class to come close was Sandra Sprong. She was bragging about breaking 1000. No one tried to trump that, so I think I do have high score, but I won't say anything or it will only cause trouble for me. At lunch I told Sam and Neil. They had ORA first period and both broke 1000. Neil got 1300 and Sam did 1150. Should I be glad I have smart friends or should I be trying harder? I have to take the first choice.

Neil had his first film class at the Regional last night and he was telling us all about the types of camera movements you can do. I remember zoom, tilt, pan, truck, dolly shot. He had a long list.

Industrial Arts this afternoon was our last photography class. Next time is going to be TV production when we will finally be let into the mysterious ETV room beside the Resource Centre.

In the evening Neil invited me over for the first time in a long time. We hung in their shed and listened to some of his brother's cool rock LPs. I like the Spirit song "Mr. Skin". That's the nickname for their bald drummer. We also listened to *Captain Beyond*, which has some really great hard rock guitar on it. Neil's brother Jerry showed up at about 9. He actually looks a lot like the guy on the cover of *Captain Beyond* with his super long hair, purple shirt, and jewelry. Even his face really. Jerry had two friends with him and promptly, but gently, kicked both Neil and me out.

We went for a walk and wound up sitting on this ledge; there is a large house (divided into apartments) on 3rd, one house in from Darlington with a large garage behind it which is on a bit of a hill, much higher than the back alley. A small ledge runs along one side of the garage where you can edge out onto. It is not that far to fall, maybe six feet. We crawled out onto it and just hung out.

Saturday, October 2, 1976

Slept in late this morning. In the afternoon Neil and I went downtown. We stopped at the pool hall and played a couple of games of pinball. Solomon was there and we all hung in the alley while he and Neil smoked cigarettes. Solomon, or "Solo Man" claims to be a great guitar player. He knows Neil's brother Jerry, that is how Neil knows him. We stopped at Sam The Record Man and Neil found a new double live album by Led Zeppelin, a group his brother likes. We didn't buy anything. Had to get home fast after that. Today's 1999 episode was "Brian the Brain". I taped it then worked on the summary all evening.

Episode Summary: "Brian The Brain" (1073 words)
[Omitted.]

Comments on "Brian The Brain" (Roger Kay, 1994)

The Alphans encounter the sole survivor of a 1997 interstellar mission that included three Superswifts and a mothership. All the crew have died on the poisonous Planet D. The one survivor is a surprisingly jocular square-bodied computer that calls itself Brian. They soon discover that Brian's levity is a mask for a psychopathic personality.

Favorite scene: Brian holds Koenig and Helena hostage on his ship as they approach Planet D. He asks them if they love each other and they deny it so he forces them to participate in a 'love test'. He seals them into separate airlocks and explains he will slowly release the air from each. If they desire, they can hit a black button to send their remaining air to the other airlock. The decompression begins and they start to gasp for air. As the situation becomes critical, they each reach for their black button simultaneously. Brian is delighted and lets them out of the airlocks saying, you do love each other!

Entries from Roger Kay's 1976 Diary

Sunday, October 3, 1976

Sam and Neil came over this afternoon. Neil showed us his 1999 spaceship guide project. For each spaceship he has created a drawing and defined its complement, maximum speed, propulsion system, armament, and planet of origin. He included everything from Year One. He says he'll present his work to the Association of Alphans (really his friend Ron) and maybe it'll get published. I just realized that, for some reason, the Eagle was not included...

We had a long discussion about "Brian the Brain". Neil was not that impressed with this episode, saying it was an inferior remake of "The Infernal Machine". He is also a little upset that the last three episodes have really shown Koenig and Helena in love. I think he preferred their stoic and independent Year One personalities. Sam takes the position that the new scripts are making the Alphans more human. Neil says they are only making them more ordinary and less heroic. Good thing we can agree to disagree.

Wednesday, October 6, 1976

Today in Industrial Arts we started the TV production segment. This will go on for five weeks as we learn about switching, camera operation, production and even performance. The ETV room has two TV cameras, a switching console with monitors, and a videotape machine to record and play back everything. Today was just a lecture and Mr. Voerstadt went over some of the same topics Neil was talking about. When you roll the camera on its tripod towards the subject, it is called 'trucking in' or 'dollying in'. You can also just zoom in, which can be smoother, although it looks slightly different. The switching console seems simple enough to operate. There are some connections to keep straight - microphones for each channel, camera input for each channel, output to the videotape recording machine. The cameras are only black and white and have to stay in the ETV room but we will each get a timeslot to go there and play with them, trying to produce something.

The first four sessions will be note taking and discussion, then we will have some hands-on examples, then finally we will get a chance to produce our own show in November. I need to write a TV script!

At Pic-A-Pop I went through hundreds of returned bottles. I had to clean some. Others were cracked and had to be discarded. We have to be more careful what we take back, Uncle Tim says. Came home, had a bath then just watched *Cimarron Strip*. I don't usually like cowboy shows, but this one is actually pretty good.

Friday, October 8, 1976

I discussed my TV production project with Neil and Sam at lunch. I will need some actors for it and I don't trust anyone in my class not to mess it up, so maybe they would be interested? A lot of the production slots are at lunch, during spares, or even after school, so they might be able to make it. As well, I offered my services as an actor to Neil for his project.

Sam doesn't have this project because she takes Home Economics, not Industrial Arts, not by choice of course. She says it is criminal that they don't offer these courses to girls. It is not entirely true: at the end of the year, we each switch for two weeks and the guys take Home Ec. while the girls take Industrial Arts. Still, they usually don't get a chance to do the photography or TV production projects.

I stuck my head into the ETV room after lunch, and some guys from 9-30 were in there. They quickly told me to get out, that I was ruining their shot. I didn't think I was. The cameras were pointing the other way, and I opened the door very quietly.

Afternoon was fairly painless. Had a quiz in Social Studies and then another one in Health.

After school Neil and I walked down to the brand new, all modern, indoor mall east of town: the Parkland Mall. It is way bigger than the Broadway Park Plaza, and the focus is on the inside; the smaller stores don't have entrances on the exterior. The grand opening was yesterday. It has a giant Kmart, which I suppose will compete with the Zeller's at the other end of town in the BPP, and a whole bunch of little stores, including clothing stores, a pet store, a hobby store, and some less interesting stuff.

I was mostly interested in the new hobby store, Yorkton Hobby Center, but it didn't have anything you couldn't get at the House of Hobbies on Betts downtown. This new mall has an enormous parking lot and really isn't designed to walk to.

Inside, along the superwide corridor, there are a few walk-up service food places and a bunch of tables and chairs stuck out in the middle, with a few potted trees trying to give it an outdoorsy, courtyard feel. I bought Neil a drink and we sat there watching the shoppers swarm. At one point I saw Lucky in the crowd. I know he saw me because our eyes met and he said something to his accomplice. I thought he would come confront me but then he probably saw Neil because he just faded back into the crowd.

Saturday, October 9, 1976

Rainy day. I stayed home and contemplated existence. 1999 at 4 was a new one called "New Adam, New Eve". I taped it and spent the evening crafting an excellent summary. Late movie was some gangster thing. Not worth my time.

Comments on "New Adam, New Eve"
[No comments provided because Roger's complete, original summary is included below.]

Episode Summary: "New Adam, New Eve"
(Roger Kay, 1976, 1618 words)

Helena dictates into her log: it is now 1095 days since breakaway. The Alphans are having problems with their sensors. Some type of magnetic turbulence is enveloping the Moon. A mysterious headache, like thunder, goes around Command Centre and Helena scans each person, concerned but not yet worried. The big screen shows some strange churning patterns, with a blue planet behind the turbulence appearing then disappearing in short flashes. The patterns are replaced with other strange shapes, like cells or amoeba. Then a figure appears with a long flowing cape and hair; he states that he is their creator.

This God asks Koenig if he doubts his credentials, and Koenig asserts he has not provided any. The God snaps his fingers and a sumptuous meal on silver plates and white linen appears. Koenig says it is too old-fashioned. With a snap the food disappears and a beautiful woman in a skimpy white outfit appears with a tray of drinks. This is a high protein ambrosia that could sustain you for a month, he claims. Koenig and Tony refuse a glass, and Carter is about to take one when Koenig says "Leave it".

The God introduces himself as Magus and notes that the Alphans are skeptical. This should not be a surprise to you, our creator, says Koenig. Magus agrees but says other species would fall on their knees or offer a sacrificial goat. Koenig smirks that they are a bit low on sacrificial goats. Magus says, well then, power is something you always did respect, and he promptly melts then explodes an Eagle on its launch pad.

Koenig gives in and says what do you want? Magus says he will give something to the Alphans that he has given to no other species: a second chance. Will we be returned to Earth, they ask? No, you will be given a new Earth. The blue planet then re-appears on their screens. Magus claims it is Earth-like and they should settle there. No, we must have a careful look first, argues Koenig. Fine, but the team to do it will be Koenig, Helena, Maya and Tony, stipulates Magus. Koenig counters that he should be making the decision on landing team, but eventually relents when Magus appears to compromise by agreeing they can take an Eagle as opposed to his transport method. However, when they are aboard the Eagle and it starts to lift off, Magus transports it instantly to the planet surface, where radio contact with Alpha is blocked.

Magus shows them around the planet, claiming there are wild boar, horses, pure water, good soil, in all a garden of Eden Mark Two. The Alphan team is impressed and Koenig indicates he wants to bring a task force down to examine the planet closer but Magus says there will be no one else. You four will start humanity anew. To make matters worse, Magus decrees that Maya will be pair-bonded with Koenig, and Helena with Tony. The offspring will be incredible, Magus promises. Hold on Santa Claus, says Tony. Helena objects too, saying it is bad psychology and possibly bad biology. No, Magus replies, he has worked everything out carefully and they must submit. He gives the Alphans one final rule, they must not leave the glade they are in; a ring of rocks clearly marks its limits. Magus then disappears, the sun sets, and the Moon rises. They try to return to the Eagle, but it has disappeared. Maya says it is molecular diffusion: the Eagle is still there, but disrupted and not visible.

When they return to their camp fire, they sample Magus' food. Tony reaches to touch Maya but they are both instantly and painfully stung. The same occurs when Koenig touches Helena. This is how Magus will enforce his chosen pair-bonds.

The food must be spiked because they start to see each other in soft lights and when Maya goes to help Koenig fetch some wood their hands touch and Koenig says "You can't fight city hall forever". Meanwhile Tony is kissing Helena.

These developments are interrupted when a fracas between two aliens is overheard. A giant ape like creature is beating up a humanoid that looks a bit like a humanoid-shaped brain, all ridges and bumps. The brain is getting the worst of it but Maya transforms into the Creature from the Black Lagoon and attacks, driving the aggressor away. Koenig prepares to follow the tracks of the victim, the brain creature, into a cave but Magus appears in the sky, angry at his rule being broken, and drives them back into the glade with lightning bolts from his eyes.

When the Alphans awake, the sun has risen and Magus is standing in front of them. Koenig asks him what he was trying to hide last night and Magus says he was just protecting them and that humans are known for two things: asking endless questions and hurting themselves.

Koenig states humans require free will.

Just a myth, Magus replies.

Koenig claims he has the right to leave the glade.

No, Magus says, but you have the right to try.

Koenig sprints to the edge of the glade, but as he reaches its limit, a forcefield blasts him back. (During the previous conversation Maya has stepped behind Magus and scanned him.) Before he leaves, Magus creates a silver tray with goblets for them, but Koenig knocks it over.

Once Magus is gone Maya reveals her scan results: Magus has a mechanical power source on him that enables his great powers. The fact that the Moon is much closer to the planet indicates that Magus is using some of his power to stop the planet from being pulled apart by the gravitational effects. Also, where are the rescue Eagles from Alpha? Magus must be using his powers to ensure they cannot approach the planet. All this takes energy and Magus' power, although great, is not infinite. They muse Magus' earlier verbal slip-up, that he could 'ill afford' the energy to create the forcefield around the glade. Koenig throws a stone over the forcefield and it falls to the ground outside the glade. Maya sees her opportunity, transforms into an owl and flies out of the glade.

Meanwhile on Alpha, Carter has a freshly modified Eagle, one with four extra booster rockets strapped on and pointed downward. As Carter attempts liftoff again, we see Magus on the planet concentrating, shaking and sweating. This continues for a minute, then Carter gives up. Magus looks relieved and raises his arms towards the sun. It is the source of his power.

Magus sees the owl and compels it to land on his arm. He mutters he thought owls were extinct on this planet, then lets it go. Maya reports back to Koenig and team that Magus may be super human but he is not supernatural because he did not realize Maya was the owl. Also, Maya has spotted an entrance to a cave inside the glade that may connect with the cave outside, but the opening has recently been covered with rocks. They use their lasers to clear the cave entrance and begin to explore.

Some giant reptiles block their way and the Alphans fry them with their hand weapons. One of the humanoid brain creatures drops down onto Koenig and starts to fight with him, albeit very weakly, saying "Shoot...". Koenig stops fighting and questions the creature who then admits he and his kind are part of an earlier experiment by Magus and they wish only to die, which is why they fight the ape creatures. The brain creature reveals that Magus is the last of the cosmic magicians and is seeking answers regarding the creation of life. That is why he brings creatures together to reproduce and then experiments with the results. Koenig lets the unfortunate alien go.

When the Alphans exit the cave, Magus is waiting and furious. He sends a bolt of energy at Tony who collapses on the ground. Helena lashes out at Magus calling him a liar and a fraud. Magus explains that he knows Earth well, and has been there many times, as Nostradamus and other historical figures. He pleads that they must work as a team to discover the secrets of creation together. When Koenig still refuses, Magus shows them an exterior view of Alpha and then causes several explosions. Koenig finally cries stop! He agrees to at least talk about Magus' terms and Magus is satisfied and says he will return in the morning.

While Magus is gone, the Alphans begin to unravel the mystery of his powers. They deduce that because he only appears in person during daylight, he must use light as his power source. Maya agrees that Magus might possess the advanced technology of a light decelerator, a crystal imbedded in his brain stem which would allow him to direct power with his thoughts. How to beat so powerful an entity? By doing the unexpected and being primitive, says Koenig. Next they build a pit trap and cover it with branches and leaves.

When Magus arrives the next morning he wants Koenig's answer, but Koenig lays out some demands. Unnerved by this impertinence, Magus strides towards Koenig and falls into the pit. The others quickly throw additional cover on the pit to block any light and as Magus screams that they must let him out or the planet will explode, the planet begins to do exactly that. The Eagle re-appears, sitting just where they left it. The Alphans run toward it, except Koenig who returns to the cave to offer the mutants an escape from the planet. The mutants refuse and Koenig makes it back to the Eagle just in time to avoid being caught in the complete planetary destruction.

Entries from Roger Kay's 1976 Diary

Sunday, October 10, 1976

Sam and Neil came over this afternoon. I told them for my ETV project I'm going to write a short story based on my Asteroid Beta universe and I hoped they would be my actors. They said yes! Now I just need to come up with something I can shoot quickly and entirely within the ETV room.

We discussed "New Adam, New Eve" and I taped our session.

I asked Mom if Sam and Neil could stay for supper (Thanksgiving turkey and all!) and she said sure. Sam couldn't stay because her family expected her, but Neil said he'd stay no problem. He ran home to tell his brother (not his mom?) and came right back. My Mom makes great stuffing and I had a load of it with my turkey, plus mashed potatoes with mushroom gravy. Both Neil and I had second helpings.

Dad started asking a lot of questions about Neil's parents, but he didn't get much out of him. Just that his dad is sometimes around, but mostly not, and his mom is not really well. He and his brother mostly run the household, buying the groceries, making meals, cleaning up. Dad wanted to know about their Thanksgiving, wouldn't they be having a special meal? Oh yes, Neil said, but it would be later that evening so he was glad to eat here too. Dad didn't say much after that. Mom started up with asking Neil what his brother did for a living. Not much was the answer. After supper Neil left pretty quick. His brother would need some help making their supper.

My folks were a little shocked at Neil's appetite, but at the same time I hope they feel more sympathetic towards him. I don't talk about his family problems so this is the first time they've got a glimpse of his home life. Neil also told them that he quit smoking cigarettes, which isn't exactly true.

10 October 1976
(audio tape from collection of Roger Kay)

Roger: Okay. Today we are discussing the *Space: 1999* episode "New Adam, New Eve". On our panel is the esteemed Lionel O'Neill, and the perspicacious Samantha Renfield.
Sam: Perspicacious, holy crap!
Neil: No fair. Her adjective has more syllables!
(general laughter)
Roger: So guys what is our rating for this episode? Out of ten. Sam?
Sam: I give it a seven. Anything with an alien and an alien planet I give more.
Neil: I think maybe six. For a cosmic magician, Magus wasn't too swift. Getting pushed into a hole, he didn't see that coming? You think he'd be listening in on their conversations, making sure their escape plans didn't get anywhere. I mean, he knew their names when he showed up at Alpha. He can read their computer or somehow he's been observing Alpha for some time. Why suddenly leave them all alone and unmonitored once they're on the planet surface? That's when the experiment *begins*, right? That's where he should be watching them very very closely. Doesn't make sense... And why appear in the flesh? It's just too dangerous. If he can project a hologram in the sky during the night, he should do the same thing during the day. Stay well away from the captives. A hologram is more impressive anyway.
Sam: It's a thing with villains. They have to make grave mistakes, because usually they start with big advantages over the heroes. The heroes have to be in a very dismal position to start with, otherwise it's not very exciting. You know, the heroes can come up with good ideas to overcome bad odds, but a lot of luck has to fall on their side, and a lot of that luck is really the villian's stupidity.
Neil: Oh yeah. That's not just 1999. That's any television show.
Sam: Exactly.

Roger: Harlan Ellison would have something to say about that, that quality is always a problem with TV. Okay. What about Maya's comment that the Psychons found their creator and that it was just a creature created by another power in another universe?

Neil: They just dropped that in there. It makes sense. I mean, what proof is there that God is *not* a solar-powered, psychopathic alien?

Sam: Maya asked if you discover the source of divine power, is it still divine? Like magic, divine power is indistinguishable from sufficiently advanced technology.

Roger: Asimov.

Neil: I like what you're saying about the hero starting out with a great disadvantage. I think they blow things out of proportion for dramatic effect. Like Magus shaking with concentration as Carter tries to lift off. I mean, it clearly takes lots of effort for Magus to hold that Eagle on the launch pad. But that's the same guy who's holding the Moon in place, and holding the entire planet together! As soon as he falls into that dark hole, he loses control, the Moon starts to move away, and the planet breaks up. But the force required to control the Moon and planet has to be much more than stopping a single Eagle. Was he really stretched that close to breaking point? If the planet was two percent bigger, would he not have been able to handle it? I'm just saying that they exaggerate some things in a not realistic way just to have an extra intense scene.

Sam: I'm sure that's true. It's TV. If you only have an hour to tell the story, you'll have to fudge some things and just smooth over a lot of reality complications.

Neil: One thing I did like about this episode though, is that Koenig, at least in the very beginning before he knew Magus was a big problem, did seriously consider the planet for Operation Exodus. I don't like the idea of Alphans happy to exist on Alpha, their biggest worry scheduling their time off together. The overriding concern should be getting off that rock and finding a planet. That's what gives the series its bite. They are living precariously. Their systems can fail anytime.

Sam: The odds of getting anywhere near a planet are so remote that anything they approach should be looked at very carefully.

Roger: Yeah they did consider the planet. Briefly. What else. Did you guys notice that this episode should actually come before "Brian the Brain", according to the number of days since breakaway in Helena's log?

Neil: Yup. We're getting episodes out of order this season too.

Roger: Thanks a lot CBC!

Sam: So Roger, you got your ETV story yet?

Roger: No. Not really. Trying to come up with different settings without leaving the ETV room. That'll be the trick. There's not much for props either. I mean I could just tape a discussion like this, like a talk show, but that'd be pretty boring, no offense. I'd rather have like a short story and then film it.

Neil: You mean tape it.

Roger: Yeah videotape it.

Sam: How about have a black backdrop and you say you're on the planet surface, but it's after dark. Or maybe you're inside a cave?

Roger: Yeah that's a good idea. I could have Asteroid Beta pass close to a planet, and they send down one person, or they send down a team, but one person reports back, at night, or from a cave, and the other actor is back in Beta's Mission Control monitoring the progress. I'm gonna give you script consultant credit!

Sam: Cool. (*sarcastically*) Now do you have any ideas for my Home Ec. cookie project?

Roger: Eagle-shaped cookies?

Neil: Or a cookie shaped like each section on Alpha? Then you put all the cookies together and they form a model of Alpha?

Sam: You guys are *so* much help. See what I'm missing? God damn sexual segregation.

(general laughter)

Sam: How long does your story have to be?

Roger: Ten to fifteen minutes.

Sam: I can't wait to see what you come up with!

Roger: Thanks! Do I have a volunteer for the planetary expedition?

Sam: I'll do it!

Neil: Hey...

Roger: Too late. You snooze! Sam's on the planet, and you're back in Mission Control.

Neil: When do you think you'll have a draft of the script?

Entries from Roger Kay's 1976 Diary

Monday, October 11, 1976
Spent most of the day trying to come up with an idea for my ETV project. Finally started to get something this afternoon. I roughed it out on scrap paper then typed up the first draft this evening. I was done by 9:15. Working title of my script: *Planet Zygov*.

Pic-A-Pop was closed today because of Thanksgiving. Nice to have the time off, but I like my money too you know!

Tuesday, October 12, 1976
Had a strange dream about *Planet Zygov*. I was the Commander and Neil and Sam were both on the planet. I tell them we cannot save them and they start kissing! In the dream, I'm upset but it is not clear why.

During Algebra we were doing questions and Brian kept shooting spit balls into my hair. When I just flicked them off and ignored him he tried a different tack, saying what do you think of Samantha's tits? I got angry and this excited him. I said she's more than just tits. He latched onto this and was singing "more than tits" like it was a car commercial jingle for the rest of the period.

Neil and Sam and I had lunch at our usual spot, just outside the music room, against the windows. We've been there for the last week. Some of the little Grade 7s walk by and look at us with wonder: a co-ed group. They don't even realize that we're the nerds, not the cool kids. Neil was telling us about some 1999 fanzines he saw over at his friend Ron's house. They have names like *Eagle 1*, *Comloc*, and *Photo Fiends*. I said we should invite him over to our 1999 discussion session on Sundays, but Neil said the guy is pretty age conscious and not willing to hang out with anyone younger. That's just prejudiced. He made the exception for Neil no doubt because he looks and sounds older. Neil is still working on some drawings for Ron's first *Association of Alphans Newsletter* but nothing definite yet.

School day died a slow death in a double Social Studies period. They say Canada is based on Peace, Order, and Good Government. That must be excluding junior high schools.

Wrote a second draft of *Planet Zygov*.

Wednesday, October 13, 1976

Today in ETV I asked Mr. Voerstadt if Neil and I could be partners for the TV production project even though we're in different classes. Everyone else is in groups of three or four in my class and I don't want to join any of those do-nothing groups. He said as long as we got the work done, he was okay. He also said Sam could play a role in our show, but she wouldn't get any credit.

At lunch I showed Sam and Neil my script for *Planet Zygov* and they thought it was "brilliant". Neil liked how all my scenes could be shot so simply. I wrote it like that because we can't do any editing. Well you can rewind the tape and record over stuff, but then how do you track how much time you are using and avoid taping over the next scene? The solution is to record the scenes in their correct order so we can have as many takes as required and then just move on to the next scene. There will be some small props needed and we discussed how to create a believable control console, a communicator, a small hand weapon. I need a picture of an asteroid next to a planet. For clothing, I suggest we just use jeans and a black t-shirt. If all the actors are wearing the same thing, it'll look like a uniform. If I don't become a writer, I want to get involved in TV or film production. Science fiction of course!

Friday, October 15, 1976

After school today I went over to Neil's and we hung out in the shed. They have an electric heater so it's fairly comfortable, although I still wear my coat. He played me some more of his brother's LPs. He has a lot! We discussed Zygov. He wants to switch roles, so he can be Victor, and I'll be the Commander. I think he just wants that role because it has fewer lines. The better role is the Commander, and I want him in that role, not just so that I can direct, but because he looks more like a

Commander than me. Who is gonna believe the pale, skinny kid with the soft voice is the Commander? He's got a deep voice, is muscular, and has facial hair. Also, as far as being shy about playing the lover of Helena (Sam will play Helena obviously), they are not even in the same room during the whole show: they talk over the radio! It is not like they have kissing or love scenes... I think I eventually convinced him, although he looks worried again.

I'm going to listen to side one of *2112* in bed now. Good night!

Saturday, October 16, 1976

Went to the library this morning and found Neil reading The Fountainhead by Ayn Rand. I don't know why but he usually doesn't take books home with him. He just goes in there and sits around reading. I scoured the LP section for new finds but same old. We went for coffee at the Summit Café.

Taped "The Mark of Archanon" at 4 and used the tape to write up my summary. Hey, maybe that Association of Alphans would be interested in my episode guide! Not that it is near completion yet.

Episode Summary: "The Mark Of Archanon"
(1607 words)
[Omitted.]

Comments on "The Mark Of Archanon"
(Roger Kay, 1994)

An alien chamber containing two frozen figures is found in a cavern on the Moon. It bears a symbol that Maya identifies as a pan-galactic warning but, too late, a mining explosion has already cracked open the chamber.

The Alphans manage to revive the ancient aliens but do not realize that the elder of the father-son pair has a disease that causes homicidal outbursts. The symbol on the forehead will glow whenever the disease is active; this is the Mark of Archanon.

Note that the episode ends with Koenig kissing Helena.

Favorite scene: Alan Carter's successful bonding with the alien son, Etrec. Carter has left Etrec alone in the Rec Area as the Alphans deal with his violent father, Pasc. When Carter later re-enters the Rec Area, he does not see that Etrec has wrapped his hands around the neck of one of the doves kept there, and his Mark of Archanon is glowing. Etrec lets the dove go, but keeps his back to Carter. As Carter explains a blood sample from Etrec would help the Alphans investigate and cure the dangerous Archanon virus, Etrec says that an Archanon cannot give blood. He picks up a small kitchen knife and prepares to strike Carter, but at the last moment, cannot, and cuts his own forehead instead, gouging the Mark.

There, he says, here is some Archanon blood for you.

Entries from Roger Kay's 1976 Diary

Sunday, October 17, 1976

Sam couldn't come over because she has relatives visiting. But Neil came over and we discussed "Mark of the Archanon". With just us two, I didn't bother to tape the discussion. We can have a three way with Sam when she's available.

For this episode, I think Neil liked most of it, but he was frustrated that the Archanons didn't really help the Alphans. They had a transmitter that has a range of "whatever is necessary" and spaceships that could get to Alpha on very short notice, but they don't offer the Alphans a ride back to Earth, or even share any technology. They think of themselves as Peace Bringers, but they are not very helpful in other respects. I was joking about the Mark and how maybe we should apply it to humans known to be violent. There are some people in my school who could benefit from being frozen until help arrives.

Neil is really into his film class. He says that it's opening his eyes to how shows are shot. We went over my *Planet Zygov* script again and he suggested I add a final scene, where Victor admits he is wrong. I like that idea.

Adventures of Asteroid Beta: Planet Zygov
Roger's ETV project script (Oct. 17, 1976)

Characters:
John Hargreaves: Commander of Asteroid Beta
Helena Proudfoot: Chief Medical Officer
Victor Bugliosi: Science Officer

Scene 1: Picture of asteroid and strange planet against black, starry sky.

VOICE OVER:

It is the year 2121. Far beyond the orbit of Mars, a scientific base with a crew of 600 is situated on the north side of the asteroid named Beta. It suffers near catastrophe as a mysterious rogue comet is hurled from the direction of the star Sol and strikes it.

Asteroid Beta is knocked out of the Solar System with a tremendous velocity, however the base, also named Beta, is not completely destroyed. There, some 500 scientists and engineers still struggle for survival and dream of finding a new planet as a home among the stars.

Scene 2: John is sitting at his command desk, dictating his log.

JOHN:

It is now 666 days since leaving Sol orbit. We have been approaching a double-star system for several weeks and are now close enough to see that there is an interesting planet in the temperate orbital zone. We must examine this planet and decide if it is a potential home for our people before we travel too far past it.

On a personal note, Helena Proudfoot and I have decided to get married. This will be the first wedding on Beta since this asteroid careened away from our solar system.

(Victor approaches John from stage left)
                    VICTOR:
Is this a good time?
                    JOHN:
Certainly. Just finishing up my log.
                    VICTOR:
Have you decided on the landing party yet?
                    JOHN:
(Nodding)
Helena will perform the analysis and Alan will fly the
Falcon.
                    VICTOR:
Helena? Are you sure? You don't want her to be late for the
wedding...
                    JOHN:
Victor, she's the best person for the job. If I start letting my
personal feelings into important command decisions, then we're
all going to be in a heap of trouble.
                    VICTOR:
Yes, I do agree. Very well. I will let them know.
                    JOHN:
Thanks Victor.

Scene 3: Helena is standing, holding a communicator, blue
sky behind her.
                    HELENA:
Falcon 1 to Beta, are you receiving me Beta?
                    JOHN'S VOICE:
Yes we copy. Go ahead Falcon 1.
                    HELENA:
John, the planet looks very good. There is water and
vegetation. We've seen no dangerous animals yet. I think we
could live here.
                    JOHN'S VOICE:
Excellent news! Continue to send your data and we will
process it for you on priority.

HELENA:

One thing, John. We are reading some large underground caverns, and some of the ground seems unstable. We have detected Falcon 1 settling several feet into the ground since landing. Also my bacterial scan is not yet complete.

JOHN'S VOICE:

Okay. Keep a close eye on things. Beta out.

Scene 4: John is at his desk, shuffling papers. After a few seconds, Victor approaches from stage left.

VICTOR:

John, have you heard from Helena?

JOHN:

She should be reporting in any-

HELENA'S VOICE:

Falcon 1 to Beta, Falcon 1 to Beta...

(John smiles at Victor)

JOHN:

Hello Falcon 1. We were just talking about you.

HELENA'S VOICE:

Something good I hope?

JOHN:

(Smiling)

What could we possibly-

HELENA'S VOICE:

(As if falling)

Aaaaaaah!

JOHN:

Falcon 1! Falcon 1! Helena! Respond! Falcon 1!

VICTOR:

(Glances at his handheld communicator)

John, sensors indicate that Falcon 1 is now *below* the surface of Planet Zygov.

(John looks at Victor with dread. Fade out.)

Scene 5: In the commander's office. John's desk is messy, covered with papers and coffee cups. He dictates his log.

JOHN:

It is now 667 days since leaving Sol orbit. The landing team has fallen into a crevice or a cave-in on planet Zygov and we are readying a rescue team to retrieve them.

VICTOR:

(Enters stage left)
John, some disturbing news.

JOHN:

(Clicks a knob to stop the log. Looks carefully at Victor and settles back into his chair before speaking.)
What is it, Victor?

VICTOR:

Ah, I've complete the analysis of Helena's bacterial scan data.
(Pause)
It is not good. There are some bugs down there that we cannot afford to be exposed to. We have to isolate ourselves from that planet.

JOHN:

What about the rescue mission?

VICTOR:

(Shaking his head)
No. We can't risk it. No one else can *go* to that planet, John.

JOHN:

But Helena … and Alan?

VICTOR:

And no one can come *from* the planet. You have to cancel the rescue mission.

JOHN:

But that is *Helena* down there.

VICTOR:

The choice is Helena, or the rest of us.

JOHN:

(Stares off into space and rubs his head for ten seconds)
You're sure about the bacteria scan?

VICTOR:

Absolutely. I'm sorry John. We must abort Falcon 2. We can't let them get anywhere near that planet!

JOHN:

I can't do that Victor. Helena means everything to me. I won't stop Falcon 2 from rescuing them.

VICTOR:

But the base John, we don't know what that bacteria will do. We can't take the chance!

JOHN:

But there is a chance Victor. Maybe we're wrong. Maybe we'll be okay. How can I throw Helena's life away based on a probability?

VICTOR:

You don't want us all to be *very probably* dead... We must contact Falcon 2 and stop them from entering Zygov's atmosphere!

(Victor starts to raise his communicator but John pulls a weapon from his desk and aims it at Victor)

JOHN:

Victor. Don't. I won't let you. I will shoot!

VICTOR:

John, I've known you since you were a little boy. You pulled me out of that swamp when we were ten. You've pulled us all out of all sorts of space swamps since we've left the solar system. I can't believe you would turn your back on all that, turn your back on the five hundred and twelve men and women aboard this base. That is just not the John Hargeaves I know. If you must shoot me, you must. But I must do what I must.

(Victor raises his communicator and very deliberately presses a button)

This is Victor Bugliosi. Falcon 2, do not approach planet Zygov, repeat do not approach planet Zygov. Return to base immediately.

JOHN:

(Lowers his weapon slowly, then drops it and collapses onto his desk, head in hands. Fade out.)

Scene 6: Helena is in darkness. Only her face is seen in the glow of her communicator.

HELENA:

John do you read me?

JOHN'S VOICE:

We're here Helena.

HELENA:

Alan's got two broken legs. I'll need some splints and a stretcher to move him.

JOHN'S VOICE:

Helena, we've got a problem ... the bacterial scan came back. It's bad. We can't let anyone else go down there, and we can't let you come back. We have to cancel the rescue mission.

HELENA:

No that can't be. You can't leave us here. Alan is in pain. I'm ... I'm....

JOHN'S VOICE:

I am so sorry Helena.

(A long silence follows)

HELENA:

John we can't die down here. That scan could be wrong.

JOHN'S VOICE:

I'm sorry. Victor says it's impossible to ignore this. We can't risk it!

HELENA:

Victor says? You can't?? You're the commander. You can make the decision. You can save us!

JOHN'S VOICE:

I'm sorry Helena. I've made my decision.

HELENA:

Your decision? You're sorry?? You can't leave us to die! You've got to do something! Bring us back and quarantine us, disinfect us!

JOHN'S VOICE:

You know that's impossible. I am so sorry, my love...

HELENA:

You can save us! I love you... what's wrong with you? Do something! Do something!!

(Sobbing)

Please...do something ...Hargreaves!!

(Fade out)

Scene 7: John is slumped at his command desk, doing nothing. Lights are low. Five seconds pass. Victor enters slowly from the left.

VICTOR:

John? John... I was ... wrong...

JOHN:

(Picks up the gun from his desk and looks at it, then at Victor, then back at the gun. Fade out.)

THE END

Entries from Roger Kay's 1976 Diary

Thursday, October 21, 1976

Sam is getting totally screwed by the school over our TV production. They want her to write a 500 word essay on her experience, what she learned by working with Neil and me. Then when the girls in her homeroom switch from Home Ec. to Industrial Arts for one day later this year, she will have to sit it out. The guys get two weeks of ETV production and the girls get zero. Totally sexist.

I think Voerstadt expects Sam will join us for the taping of Zygov, but not be involved in the pre or post production. He says he'll set up our production slots so that they match her study or free periods. No arrangement for her to miss any class periods of Home Ec. I plan on working on the pre and post production not just during class time so that Sam can join us and be a true member of the project.

Why is Voerstadt squeezing her out? Is he threatened by a girl with interest in TV production? If she doesn't write the paper, they say she'll get a failing grade for the project, no matter what grade Neil and I get! It makes no sense. We talked about this all lunch. It seems they are trying everything to discourage her from working with us. But we will work together. Us Alphans must stick together, no matter whom we are up against.

Episode Summary: "The Rules Of Luton" (1169 words)
[Omitted.]

Comments on "The Rules Of Luton" (Roger Kay, 1994)

Koenig and Maya are dropped off to check out a very promising planet. They survey the vegetation and declare it safe but when Koenig plucks some berries and Maya plucks a flower, a voice cries out "Murderers!"

Vegetation rules the planet of Luton and the Alphans have transgressed bigtime. For their crimes Koenig and Maya will be forced into guerilla combat with a squad of three other unlucky aliens. Maya may be Koenig's ace card, but he doesn't know that each of his opponents has been given a special power by the Judges of Luton.

Favorite scene: Koenig and Maya have a revelatory tete-a-tete during a quiet moment between battles.

Maya recounts the Psychon outmigration that occurred as the surface temperature of her now destroyed home planet rose year after year. Her brother was among the one thousand Psychons that escaped. By the end there was only Mentor left, and Maya too but only because she would not abandon him. Love also prevented Mentor from leaving; the tomb of Mentor's wife, Maya's mother, was on Psychon.

When Maya asks Koenig about his family, he does not admit to having any, other than a wife who died in the 1987 war to end all wars, the war in which prejudice was finally wiped out. When Maya asks what his wife was like, Koenig says she was like, well… Helena.

Entries from Roger Kay's 1976 Diary

Sunday, October 24, 1976

Neil came over around 1:30 and Sam arrived about 1:45.
Mom made some cookies yesterday and although I couldn't
have any last night, today she put them out. My guests were
impressed with the cookies.

We discussed "The Rules Of Luton". We seem to be falling
into a pattern. Sam and I defend the new episode, while Neil
savages it. He had problems with the talking plants in this one.
Maybe if they were just telepathic, that might be okay, he said,
but we clearly heard the shriek of all the plants when the first
flower was plucked, at the start of the episode. And then later,
the three trees who are the Judges of Luton communicate over
Koenig's commlock. These are some powerful trees. They can
also make the planet disappear from scanner sight. If they can
do all this, why didn't they send a message to the approaching
Eagle, "Hey you, don't land here cause you'll crush our
citizens!" No, they wait until it is too late, then extract a blood-
thirsty revenge on the landing party.

I suggested maybe they do have a telepathic ability, maybe
Koenig wasn't really seeing them on the commlock at all, he
just thought he did. Perhaps their ability is very limited by
distance, so they couldn't warn the Eagle or Moonbase Alpha
early on.

Sam suggested perhaps the plants assumed the Alphans
were strictly meat-eating and therefore no threat.

Neil then pointed out that if there is no animal life on the
planet, what maintains the atmosphere? Humans breath in
oxygen and exhale carbon dioxide. Plants do the opposite. If
either process is missing, eventually the atmosphere will
contain only the wrong gas. So if the animals had all died out,
soon the plants would all die too. Also there is a problem with
pollination. No bees means big problems for pollinating plants.
Neil is way smarter than the script writers. I suggested we
should write an episode and send it to Gerry Anderson. Maybe
they need some scripts for the third year…

I should have taped our lively discussion today but I need to go to Radio Shack to buy some more cassettes. They left a little after 4.

We had ham for supper. Yum! For desert, for some reason, the cookies were suddenly unavailable again.

Friday, October 29, 1976

Today my <u>Moonbase Alpha Technical Notebook</u> arrived! I couldn't believe it when I got home but there it was: a red three-ring binder with a golden emblem and lettering on it. It has sections on the history of each character, a full episode guide (Year One <u>and</u> Year Two!!), plus drawings of the uniforms, spacesuits, commlock, stun gun, floor plans for living quarters, Main Mission, Command Centre, Medical Centre. There are also fold out drawings for the entire moonbase, showing what each building is for, and how the travel tubes connect it all together. Plus there is also a timeline from 1981 to 1999 for the *Space: 1999* universe!

So much new information in it I need to absorb. There is a coupon you clip out in the back and send back in so they can notify you when additional pages come out. Because it comes in a binder, you can just add pages to it! The thing is just beautiful beyond words.

I called Neil after supper and he came over right away. We spent several hours poring over the MATN's wonders.

Saturday, Oct 30, 1976

Didn't sleep in much today. Got up around 9:30 and got ready to go downtown. Neil came over at 10 and we went to the YPL to photocopy some of my MATN. We had to get them to load the 11x17 paper so that we could xerox the fold out pages. After that we just came back here, hung out, and discussed the MATN. He stayed right until 5; we watched 1999 together while I taped it. I spent the evening working on my new episode summary.

Episode Summary: "All That Glisters" (1478 words)
[Omitted.]

Comments on "All That Glisters" (Roger Kay, 1994)

A specially-equipped laboratory Eagle is dispatched to survey a distant planet for milgonite, a rare mineral used in the Alphan life support systems.

Aboard are Koenig, Carter, Helena, Tony, Maya and an Texan-Irish geologist named Dave who is attracted to Maya and flirts with her, much to Tony's dismay. They discover a glowing rock formation that, despite some optimism, does not turn out to be milgonite. They slice free a piece of the rock for study, but soon find it is an alien life form with dangerous powers: Tony is struck down, and thereafter operates only in zombie-slave mode or lies comatose. Now that they have a sample of this dangerous rock aboard the Eagle, how will they ever get rid of it? And they only have three hours until Alpha is out of range.

Favorite scene: When the rock takes control of the Eagle computer, numerous star charts flash by. It is clearly looking for a new place to live. It has a deadline to leave this planet or it will die, muses Koenig. I know the feeling, says Alpha's best pilot, Alan Carter.

Entries from Roger Kay's 1976 Diary

Sunday, October 31, 1976

Sam and Neil came over this afternoon. Sam was very impressed with the MATN *[Editor's note: acronym for Moonbase Alpha Technical Notebook]*. I think it distracted her from our discussions of "All That Glisters". I tried to defend it as best I could but it really is a weaker episode. This time instead of plants attacking, it is rocks. So we spent more time discussing the MATN than yesterday's episode.

We discovered that the timeline in the MATN actually does explain what happened to Bergman, Morrow and Kano. In just one sentence each, it says Morrow and Kano died in an Eagle crash, and Bergman died from a faulty spacesuit. All this occurs between Year One and Year Two. Very sad to finally read this. They won't be coming back.

Also the MATN timeline confirms that the episodes were shown on CBC in the wrong order. Terra Nova is indeed the first planet that Alpha encounters, but it is still not clear if it is the same planet as Meta, so it's probably not. Which makes sense. What are the odds that the Moon would be knocked onto a path that would take it near Meta?

Today is Halloween but I just stayed home and handed out treats. We have little chocolate bars and little bags of licorice. I was giving out mostly licorice until Mom noticed and told me to be more fair. She says the younger kids come earlier, so I should give them the chocolate bars and then if we run out, the older kids who come later can have licorice. My plan was to hold out on the chocolate bars until as late as possible. This is apparently not acceptable. What a drag it is getting old.

I was moping a bit over this but after all the kids had been and gone, Mom pulled out another bag of chocolate bars and gave them to me! Then I felt kind of silly for being greedy.

Tuesday, November 2, 1976

Today after school I went to Logan's Drugs and found the second issue of *Starlog*! I was beginning to think they'd never put out another issue, that it was a one-issue wonder, like so many Myron Fass space rags. But there it was finally, and on the cover, I couldn't believe it, a beautiful painted artwork of Moonbase Alpha, with Koenig and Russell heads floating above it. There is a major section on 1999: an episode guide, and details about the changes we're now seeing in the Year Two episodes.

I knew Neil would kill to see this, so I called his house around 6. Amazingly, he did answer the phone and then came right over. We read my new, hot-off-the-presses *Starlog* #2.

The article writer seems a little ambivalent about 1999, saying that most of the first year episodes failed to make sense because they used a 'mysterious unknown force'. I don't agree with that. Their attitude seems to be that 1999 is the best new thing on TV, but still isn't very good. Neil and I think there might be a pro-Trek bias in *Starlog*. There is also an article saying that a *Star Trek* movie is in the planning stages. I don't think any television series has ever been made into a movie before, so it seems a bit unlikely.

Wednesday, November 3, 1976

I have a VHS videotape cassette sitting right now on my desk. It is much larger than an audio cassette, perhaps the size of a couple paperbacks, but it comes in a plastic case similar to tapes. Unlike an audio tape however you cannot turn the wheels to manually rewind. Only the video machine knows how to move the tape. The magnetic tape inside looks just like audio tape except it is like an inch wide, not 1/5 of an inch. My videotape contains the first three scenes from *Planet Zygov* and it was much harder to put it together than I thought it would be. I knew I had the ETV room for third period, and 9-32 has a study period then, so as Voerstadt promised Neil and Sam could come and help me.

When I got to the ETV room there were people loitering inside. After I taped our first graphic to the wall, I had to tell everyone to be quiet over and over as we shot the opening scene; I played my cassette with the ending theme for 1999 Year One's closing credits over a tight zoom in on our opening graphic. The setup shot. I cranked the volume and held the microphone right next to the tape player but still I had to repeat it a few times because people kept talking in the background. Finally I got them to stop yakking during the music but as soon as I turned the volume down to begin the voice-over, people would start up talking again! Neil and Sam were sitting quietly in the corner, poring over the script together, leaving me to deal with the technical details, and crowd control.

When I finally had the a good take of the first scene, we started the second, which is Neil at the command desk and me, as Victor, walking on. Neil was having a hell of a time with his lines. He kept stuttering and flubbing them. Not a very believable commander. The script was right there on his desk too.

We did a few takes and then I just said, everybody out. Anybody who stays, I'm taking names and we'll be using your slot if you stay and mess with ours! So when they eventually left, time was almost up and we had to rush to get a couple more takes of Scene 2, and then one take of Scene 3, which is mostly Sam.

Scene 3 went smoothly because we could hold the script up above the camera, and Sam could just read it. Neil has some lines too, but is off camera so he can just read those also. We're ready for Scene 4 but we only have one more period in the ETV room to record the rest of the seven scenes. I could write a book about how hard it is to direct.

Thursday, November 4, 1976

Still a little angry about yesterday's problems in the ETV room. I thought, if other people can hang out during my period, I should go there and check out the competition during their periods. So during study period (3:00 to 3:35) I went back to the ETV room. I pretended I was working on my script and stayed pretty quiet. There were two teams in there. One was Brian Woloschuk, Dwayne Dodson and Terry Sunquist, from 9-31. The other team was James Hopkins, Bob Lee, and Mike Webb, from 9-32.

Brian's team were just taking turns sitting at the table and reading from their script, which was a kind of travelogue for

Yorkton that I guessed Terry had written and was foisting on the other, lazier team members. It was just a list of dry, boring facts: Yorkton the parkland jewel, home of the Parkland Mall, Morris Rod Weeder, Leon's Manufacturing, blah blah. Brian just read his part quickly and left, but not before sneering at me and slapping the air in front of my face. What a jerk.

The second team did a fake interview, James interviewing Bob, something about hockey. Mike was operating both cameras at the same time. He would run from one camera to the other, zooming in and out, panning abruptly, and then run back to the switching board to change which camera was feeding the tape. I don't think that'll turn out too great. The interview sounded like they were just reading the script, which they were. They had scripts on the interview table and they weren't shy about pausing in mid-sentence to flip the page.

I stayed until the end, pretending I needed to look at the switching board again. Sure, that's what I was waiting around for. Eventually Mr. Voerstadt showed up to check the equipment. He asked me to help clean up the cables the other teams had left all over the place. I coiled them properly. As he locked up, he said that he had read all the scripts and that mine was the most creative! I left the school for once feeling happy. I had confirmation of my talent both from the mouth of an intelligent teacher and by my own direct observation and evaluation of the competition.

It was very busy at Pic-A-Pop. I swapped countless pallets from the back and created no broken glass to deal with!

Saturday, Nov 6, 1976

A rainy morning and a soggy cold afternoon. I dropped over to Neil's after lunch and we walked to Mark's Confectionary to pick up some smokes for his mom. After that we came back to my place. He stuck around for 1999 which was better than the last couple of times we both agreed. Supper was spaghetti and meatballs. Worked on my episode summary after that.

Episode Summary: "The Taybor" (1153 words)
[Omitted.]

Comments on "The Taybor" (Roger Kay, 1994)

Taybor of the spacecraft S.S.Emporium is an intergalactic trader who offers his services to Moonbase Alpha. He is also a rotund blowhard with a penchant for liquor. He entices the Alphans with a schematic of his jumpdrive which would allow them to propel the Moon where they wanted, perhaps back to Earth if they only knew where it was. In return, Taybor wants Maya, but he would be happy to settle for an Alpha-created cyborg resembling her. Or would he?

Favorite scene: Koenig, Helena, Tony and Maya hold a welcome supper for Taybor, who is jovial and full of stories. Taybor squeezes Maya's leg and says it is only a friendly gesture, so she partially transforms and her now grotesque, giant claws grab him under the table and squeezes. He gasps in pain and Maya says, *now* we're friends.

Entries from Roger Kay's 1976 Diary

Sunday, November 7, 1976

Sam and Neil both arrived just before 2. We all liked "The Taybor" more than the last two episodes. Neil claimed the fact that the Taybor was a drunk foreshadowed his evil intent. It seems to me the scene was included just for the laughs, but I didn't want to contradict him. Sam doesn't know about Neil's family's problems with alcohol so I just let it drop.

Neil wants Sam and I to help him with his film project at the Regional! He says it is almost finished, which surprised me since he hasn't talked about his project at all. Sure he talks about what he's learning in the class, but he never mentioned that he was working on a script! He's working with two high school guys, both from Sacred Heart. He says they are okay, but they are tall, from rich families, and a bit stuck up.

Their projects are not like our ETV projects. They work in groups of three. Each of them has their own film project, and they each have to help the others on their projects as well as lead their own project. They are using Super 8 sound cameras so they have an 8 millimeter wide film that can be edited like larger, professional film formats, not just record-over do-overs like with our videotapes in ETV.

Most of Neil's scenes have already been shot, but he says he needs a couple minor characters for the final scenes and wants Sam and me to play them. He needs to shoot it very soon so I said Tuesday or Friday nights are good for me. Sam didn't say much. She only seems to be available on Sunday afternoons. She left around 4.

Neil came back over after supper and we hacked a script out for his last two scenes. It will be very dramatic!

Monday, November 8, 1976

In third period, study period, I went to the Resource Center. 9-32 was in there for their English period, looking for magazine articles to summarize. Their class had paired off for this 'research'. Mrs. Wilson had stuck Sam with a female partner who needed some help. Nothing spells team like enforced servitude. Neil did not have a partner and had already written a summary of whatever was on page 1 of the Leader Post yesterday so we chatted and drew Eagles.

Neil was talking about Eagle propulsion systems, how the different rockets were used for different purposes (thrusters, maneuvering jets, landing rockets) when Mike Webb from Neil's class came over and asked how much room you'd need to land an Eagle without getting scorched. Neil went through a long calculation and thought process and finally said that you didn't need much room if there weren't any combustibles in the area. "Combustibles"? Who uses a word like that? For some reason I found it really funny. I don't think Mike expected a serious answer. He was just looking for weakness in Neil's intellectual armor but I don't think he found any.

Tuesday, November 9, 1976

Today at lunch Neil dropped another bomb on us. He is going to get to meet Barry Morse! Neil is amazing at holding secrets. He mentioned this as he casually unwrapped his sandwich. If it was me, I would have phoned him last night, or mentioned it in the hall between classes. Last night was Neil's final film class at the Regional but it turns out they are going to use volunteers from his class as projectionists for the Yorkton International Film Festival coming up next week. He's not making this up. He showed me a pamphlet that says the festival is running from next Monday through Saturday and Barry Morse is one of the judges. Professor Victor Bergman will be in Yorkton! Turns out Mr. Focault knows that Neil is a huge 1999 fan and he's gonna make sure that Neil gets to run the projector for at least some of the films Mr. Morse will see. The judges will have private screenings of the films, totally apart from the screenings for the general public. Sam and I were very impressed and a bit jealous. I suggested Neil ask Mr. Morse for an interview, which he can later sell to the Association of Alphans. This guarantees him a chance to talk meaningfully with Mr. Morse. I'm so brilliant!

After school Neil, Sam, and I went across the street to the Regional. They have a very nice theater with padded seats and we've seen a play or two in there but otherwise I've never been in that endlessly huge complex. We went in at the main entrance, near the theater, then walked into the center of it all where there is a square atrium with a glass building in the middle. You walk past the main offices then you are in a glass corridor, with one side looking out into the open air of the atrium, and on your other side, curving inward, the glass wall of the round library in the middle. We completed the curve around in the glass corridor and then entered the main library door.

The librarian seems to know Neil. She smiled and said hello. Neil introduced Sam and me to her (I forgot her name). The library is an open space donut, with the donut hole being a central enclosed room (the librarian's offices) that has a stairwell going up one side, where they are more rows of book shelves up on a loft atop the offices. On the other side is a stairwell going down to the basement where the film and TV area is. Down there is a large round room with doors going off into various production labs. A 3-camera TV production system is in one area, and some film viewing and editing machines are in another. We found Mr. Focault talking to some students, but in a minute he came over and welcomed us saying "Lionel's" was a very interesting project. Then Neil signed out a camera and took the bag of props he had already sorted.

The shooting location for our first scenes was just behind the school. Near the chain link fence that secures the automotive shops on the west edge of the building. There are a few vehicles there, some decrepit ones for student learning and some trucks for maintenance (like snow clearing). Mr. Focault had made sure we were permitted to shoot there this afternoon. The janitor came out to see if we were the right film crew (how many film crews are there lurking in this giant building?) and then said, come get me when you're done so I can lock up.

For this scene, Neil plays a security guard at a government motor pool, and I play his murderer. Our bag of props included a clipboard, a police-style hat, and a plastic cap gun. Neil explained the camera and handed it over to Sam so she could film our speaking scene. She shot a few segments of Neil opening and closing the metal gate and walking around looking thoughtful with a clipboard. Then it was time for the dialogue shots.

The murderer (me) asks Neil if he is Cain California. Yes I am, he says. I pull out the gun and shoot him. When the cap explodes Neil clutches his chest, hangs his head forward so the hat falls off, falls to his knees, painful expression, then falls forward. No blood but still I thought it was pretty convincing. Neil directed Sam to film his death a second time. With me firing the cap pistol off-screen, Neil slowly, painfully collapses onto the road again. Perfect. We call the janitor and he locks up the gate.

For the final scene we head back into the school, downstairs to Mr. Focault's kingdom again. He was still there, but no other students this time. We put a table and couple of chairs in a corner, and turn down the lights. Neil gave me a white striped convict-style shirt to put on. He gave Sam a plastic badge to pin to the front of her shirt. I, the murderer, am being questioned by her, the police. There are papers spread on the table. One of them, right in front of me, is the relevant script page. This makes it easier to remember the lines, plus Neil is now handling the camera and we are shooting in short segments, so we have time to review our lines between each shot.

Neil took some two-shots of Sam and I at the table, but most of the dialogue is done as one-shots, the talking head, then the reaction shot of the other actor. Not having to rewind and fuss over possibly overwriting good stuff makes extra takes much more fun. We'll fix it in editing, is now my favorite expression. For the very last scene I needed to be crying so we took some drinking fountain water in a cup and dribbled it onto my face.

When we finished the shoot, Neil said you guys can go. He had to stick around to unload the camera and get the film ready for processing. I wanted to snoop about the school a bit, but Sam was anxious to get home so we didn't. It was almost 6 and getting quite dark. I walked her to the corner of 2nd and Darlington, as far as she ever lets me go.

Nothing good on TV. Wrote this long entry. Had a bath. Good night!

Thursday, November 11, 1976

Did the final taping for *Planet Zygov* in third period. I almost forgot the videotape this morning. That would have been a complete disaster. But things went fairly smoothly. Most of the other teams are done their projects, so we finally had the ETV room to ourselves.

I very carefully cued up the videotape again, you have to make sure that you stop the tape just as the ball of static that occurs between shots starts to form. If you leave it a fraction of a second too late, then you have the first bit of the shot you want to record over still peeking through. If you come in too early, you destroy stuff you want to keep. It is a fine line but we've been letting the shots linger a bit at the end just for this reason.

Things went fairly smoothly. We had to do a couple of takes of Scene 6, which has lots of dialogue. We just finished the final scene, I'd performed a fade out and was letting the darkness run for a few seconds when the bell rang. Perfect!

After school, I handed the tape in to Mr. Voerstadt. It is out of my hands now, literally and figuratively. I leave my fate in the hands of the academy. Ha ha! Maybe I'll get a Golden Sheaf for it? (That's the award they give at the Yorkton International Film Festival.)

Work was pretty boring. It ain't Hollywood!

Friday, November 12, 1976

Today at lunch Sam gave me the sheets of foolscap on which she's written her 500 word essay for Mr. Voerstadt. She wants me to type it up for her. She plans to make photocopies and if the school gives her a hassle, she swears she'll go to the newspaper about this discrimination. I read her essay right then and was struck by her bravery. She's not "making nice". I'm worried how the school will respond. Neil read her essay right there too and he thought it was great. At first I thought he said 'typical' which confused me, but he really said 'epochal', which I looked up later.

Phys-ed was medicine ball games and I almost got my neck broke when Brian launched the ball right at my head when I wasn't looking. I was sore after that and the day dragged on. Did my math questions during math period so no homework as usual.

When I got home I took about an hour to carefully type up Sam's paper. She's a great writer, probably better than me, but she used the word 'husband' in a weird way that she insists is correct. I myself made only two small mistakes and managed a very professional-looking (I hope) job of whiting out the problems. Double spaced it comes to most of two pages. I hope she's doing the right thing.

What I Learned In ETV by Samantha Penfield (9-32)

I am being punished for my sex. Is there a female word for artist? We have heroes, and heroines, policemen and policewomen, artists and …? Maybe the fact that there is no word for something means that we do not want it to exist.

In my school I am not encouraged to be creative as a girl. Even though I do better in math than most boys, I am stuck in a ghetto of Home Economics, not real Economics. I am allowed Arts but banned from Industrial Arts. Is my only purpose and destination that of a future slave to some male who demands he husband all my resources?

Why are all the books we read written by men? Why is all the history we learn about the doings of men? Will this ever change if we continue to treat our females as second class citizens?

I predict that someday in the future women and men will together explore the planets and the stars. Together we will unlock the mysteries of the universe. But it will be hard for that day to come if the educational system segregates and stereotypes its female students, forcing upon them failure to reach their true potential.

The future of our planet depends upon people of intellect and good will working together. If that includes only males, then we are losing half of our potential! I don't know of any other case where people are satisfied with a system that operates at half of its capability. Certainly it is crazy to allow this for something as important as the quality of our next generation.

Is there something in capable and talented women that threatens men? I don't think there is any reason for this. It was a man, but a smart man, who said "There is nothing to fear but fear itself!" Let's not shoot our nose off to spite our face. Treat females equally!

Working with Roger and Lionel on a television production project was a very worthwhile experience for me. I helped with the technical production: operating a TV camera, checking sound levels, checking lighting and transitions in playback, setting up the cabling for a multi-camera system, performing camera switching during recording, cueing up videotape for re-shooting of scenes. Also I helped with the creative aspects of the production: designing the sets, creating graphics for special effects and credits. As well as learning about all these technical activities, I acted in a major speaking role.

I am fascinated by this new electronic media of videotape and glad to learn more of its possibilities and limitations. But more importantly, this experience has revealed to me that even now, directly after the UN's International Year of the Woman, and still in the middle of the UN's International Decade of Woman, we are still mired in primitive thinking from dark, olden days. What else can you call it when a female has to work twice as hard as a male and is rewarded with only a fraction of the credit she deserves? This has still not changed. This I cannot ever accept. I will fight the power. This I have learned.

Entries from Roger Kay's 1976 Diary

Saturday, Nov 13, 1976

No Neil at the library today. Not sure where he is. I was gonna walk down to Accent on Books, but it was too cold and wet. I stopped in at Sam The Record Man and found a new LP called *If I Were Brittania I'd Waive The Rules* by a group called Budgie. I never heard of this before and Rudy didn't have one open to play, but the cover was amazing: budgies in spacesuits, flying through the air, amid some sort of futuristic battle. I wonder if Jerry knows about this! It was $6.99 but I'm making good money and I had to have it. When I got it home, I wasn't disappointed. Budgie is some far out heavy rock.

1999 was "Seed Of Destruction" today, a really great episode where Koenig gets replaced by an evil twin and his crew mutinies. But hey, read my synopsis why don't you? I just spent all evening writing it! One thing I did notice is that Sandra is back in the Command Centre.

Episode Summary: "Seed Of Destruction"
(1372 words)
[Omitted.]

Comments on "Seed Of Destruction" (Roger Kay, 1994)

An Eagle with Koenig and Carter aboard lands to investigate a small jewel-like asteroid. Koenig enters a cavern with much crystal outcropping and many mirrored surfaces. He takes a sample of the crystalline rock but is suddenly frozen and trapped inside one of the reflective honeycombs. His mirror double emerges from another honeycomb and returns to the Eagle.

Back on Alpha, the mirror-Koenig is a harsh commander. He demands his crew build a energy transfer beam to send all of Alpha's power to the asteroid. He insists this is necessary for Alpha's survival, to break the asteroid's grip on them, but as he drains Alpha's power and systems begin to fail, doubts emerge among the Alphans and mutiny is brewing.

Favorite scene: When Helena confronts Koenig about his erratic behavior, she touches his hand and finds it inhumanly cold. At this point Helena understands this is not her Koenig but she must assiduously conceal this knowledge, as well as her fear of him.

Entries from Roger Kay's 1976 Diary

Sunday, November 14, 1976

Neil showed up around 1:30. I asked him where he got to yesterday, but he just said sorry, I couldn't make it, and asked me what I did. I showed him the Budgie album and started to play it. He liked it and thinks Jerry would be interested too. The day I can show the worldly Jerry new and worthwhile music will be something.

We both thought "Seed of Destruction" was one of the best episodes so far this season however I wanted to tape a session about other issues in 1999, and when Sam showed up closer to 2:00, I rolled the tape, and we did. This time Sam wound up on offense and Neil and I on defense, or at least it seemed that way!

I gave Sam the typewritten sheets for her ETV project essay. Neil and I are both amazed she is going to hand it in. It is a slap in the face to the system.

The folks were busy with some paperwork so I had free reign over the TV. Watched a movie *The Outer Space Connection* on CICC (channel 10). It claims the world will end on December 21, 2012. What, no Xmas? They make some interesting arguments, but I'm not convinced.

14 November 1976
(audio tape from collection of Roger Kay)

Roger: We're rolling. And we're discussing issues in *Space: 1999*, Year One or Year Two. I have with me Samatha Renfield, our expert on *Star Trek*, extra-terrestrial psychology and issues of women in space. Also we have, uh, Lionel O'Neill, our space tech expert. Let's begin with Year One. Sam, what particular issues do you see with 1999 Year One versus *Star Trek*?

Sam: One basic issue is how fast the Moon is traveling. I don't think it makes any sense it'd be going anywhere near the speed of light. But you'd have to be going that fast if you want to reach any other star systems... In *Star Trek* they get away with the distance and speed problem with their warp drive. In *Space: 1999*, the problem is just ignored.

Neil: *(inaudible speech)*

Roger: Comments, Neil?

Neil: *(voice becoming clear as he moves closer to the microphone)* ... is addressed in the <u>Moonbase Alpha Technical Notebook</u>, which gives the real timeline for the Moon's journey. It says that the Black Sun was encountered only 30 days after breakaway. This sent the Moon into an area of space which is way more dense than our outer arm of the Milky Way.

Sam: It's a question of how close the nearby stars could be.

Neil: If it's next to a galactic center, they'd be pretty close together!

Sam: Eagles were designed for travel to the Moon, not interstellar flight. If the Moon is moving fast and the planets are close together, the Alphans won't have much time on each planet.

Neil: Which is usually the case. The Alphans have to make their decision about a planet before it's out of range. That's exactly what happens.

Roger: So I think what we're saying is some attempt is made in the matten *[Editor's note: this is Roger's pronunciation of the acronym MATN, which stands for*

Moonbase Alpha Technical Notebook] to account for the real distances involved, and there are also efforts in those episodes involving planets to show that Eagles have real limitations.

Neil: Eagles can land and take off from planets without refueling. They really are interplanetary craft. If the stars are close enough and with sufficient provisions on the Eagles, they could also act as interstellar craft.

Sam: But they don't come close to the speed of light...

Neil: No no. That's right.

Roger: Okay. So Sam, another issue? Anything that needs some explanation?

Sam: Well, in *Star Trek* they have these security guards that always wear red uniforms, and they're usually the first to die when they land on a planet or encounter hostile aliens. This is very convenient for the script writers, having expendable characters. On Moonbase Alpha, you have the same thing. They have a whole group of people who are security guards and who carry weapons constantly. This is a problem.

Neil: It *solves* a lot of problems.

Sam: Yeah for the script writers and for Commander Koenig. But really did we send any security guards on Apollo? In Skylab? Of course not. If you have three hundred scientists and astronauts on a moonbase, why would you need security guards? Maybe the highest ranking officers would have access to some weapons, but really other than homesickness or insubordination, why would you need it?

Neil: There'll always be troublemakers.

Sam: Sure the script depends upon it. There has to be conflict. You've got aliens, Alphans possessed by aliens, you've got insurrections by Alphans... but on a moonbase you wouldn't expect those things. You're fairly close to Earth, so if you wig out on the Moon, you'll just get sedated and shipped back to Earth, where you can finish your career polishing bedpans in the NASA hospital for sick astronauts.

(sound of laughter: Roger, followed by Sam)

Neil: So why is it better on *Star Trek*?

Sam: Well the Enterprise from *Star Trek* is a military ship. The crew acts as diplomats and defenders for the Federation. It makes sense that soldiers and guards would have a place aboard that kind of ship. Really the Enterprise is *mostly* security personnel, with a few scientists and diplomats thrown in for the mission. On Alpha, it is supposed to be all scientists, very rational people. They shouldn't need babysitting by goons.

Neil: The purpose of the security personnel is to protect the Alphans, not babysit them.

Sam: But protect them from what? At breakaway, there were *no known aliens*. The planet Meta had been discovered and that signal received, but no confirmation of any aliens actually existing. So no enemy. Also your technical notebook shows that there was a war in the '80s and that, after that, prejudice and a lot of the international tension was resolved. So Alpha is a multinational project. Tanya Alexander is Russian, Sandra Benes is from Hungary, behind the Iron Curtain. There are Africans and so on. So there is no enemy.

On *Star Trek* you have the Federation versus the Klingons and Romulans. There's a neutral zone between those groups and it has to be patrolled and the peace kept. On Alpha, everyone co-operates. This is one of the ways that 1999 in fact shows a superior future than *Star Trek*.

Neil: *(laughs)* Glad to hear you say that…

Sam: *(laughs)* Yes. 1999 is better than Trek. (loud, from very close to the microphone) Did you get that? (laughs) The fact that world peace was achieved in this century, not in the 22nd, shows the 1999 universe is more advanced. They might not have warp drive yet, but on Moonbase Alpha the head doctor is a female. And she's not wearing a mini-skirt! But my point is that there's really no reason for security people on Alpha. It's just convenient for the script writers. It doesn't really make sense.

Neil: Maybe, but don't forget one of the reasons they're there is to protect the nuclear waste. That stuff could be used to make bombs and despite world peace breaking out, there's no doubt some bad guys would like to get their hands on that stuff.

We don't really know the state of private spaceflight, but probably it is already going on by 1999. So there could be criminals with access to spaceflight.

Sam: That's a good point but couldn't a laser cannon and some radar just as easily repel any invader? Why do you need a whole bunch of guys with side arms?

Neil: Maybe the criminals have some kind of cloaking device, so you wouldn't see them until they're in the travel tube.

Sam: Cloaking device?

Neil: Hey just because I can't watch *Star Trek* doesn't mean I haven't read it!

Roger: Whoa. Sacrilege.

(general laughter)

Roger: So I think we can conclude that despite some rough edges, 1999 is in fact a superior product and shows an even more optimistic future than *Star Trek*.

Neil: Absolutely.

Sam: Sure.

Roger: Glad that's settled! *(pause)* This is a good place to stop.

Entries from Roger Kay's 1976 Diary

Tuesday, November 16, 1976

While I was slinging heavy cases of Pic-A-Pop all last night, Neil was hobnobbing with Barry Morse! The judges watched several films and Neil was the projectionist. They were in a regular hotel room at the Holiday Inn. Neil said it was fascinating to listen to their discussions of the films, although mostly they just took notes.

At the end of the night, he approached 'Victor' and asked could he do an interview for the Association of Alphans? It's going ahead Friday night after the last movie is screened, around 9 pm! Neil says he'll need a tape recorder and a cassette, and I said no problem. He can buy a single cassette off me at a discount (I buy them in three packs) and borrow my recorder. But the deal is I get to hear the interview.

Neil runs the projector again tonight and then for the last time on Friday. Someone else from his advanced film class does it the other nights, but Neil got three out of six nights! How lucky can one person be??

Today after school he invited me over to the shed and asked me to bring the Budgie album. His brother Jerry was there and we all listened to side A. Jerry was talking about science fiction and the history of rock and roll and I had a brain wave. Why not interview him? Maybe I could write a general article about SF and Rock and sell it to that Association of Alphans? I agreed to give Jerry a cassette so he could tape Budgie. I think this helped 'close the deal'.

Friday, Nov 19, 1976

Tired today. Stayed up late last night reading <u>Man Plus</u> by Frederik Pohl. School was dull dull dull. Why do teachers stand at the front of the class and tell us all the things that we have to read in the textbook anyway? Why bother reading the book if you have to listen to it again? Or why listen if you are going to read it later? It just makes me sleepy.

In Ind. Arts we are finally screening our video projects. Ours turned out okay, with just a couple of problems. First, when we shot the scene against the window, simulating the planet surface, Sam turned into a silhouette. Second, her lines were a bit quiet. Also, for the scenes where I enter from the side, I didn't have a mic so my lines are also very quiet. My soft voice does not carry. The microphone was on the desk, so Neil's lines came out better. So, if you could actually hear what we were saying, our story was very good, but if you can't hear what is going on, then all is lost. When we played the tape for the class, I don't think they could make out a lot of what Sam and I were saying. Our video is excellent, but our audio sucks. Argh!

We watched all five productions and I wasn't surprised that most of it was crap. The funniest thing is when someone looks at the wrong camera. There was a lot of that, and people reading their lines in a very mechanical way. Maybe they should have enacted a story about robots?

Everyone had a marking sheet for each project with the different marking areas: script, acting, lighting, audio, switching, set design, team work, and overall entertainment value. We rated each project as we watched the final versions. Mr. Voerstadt says he will tally the results and we'll know our marks by Monday. I don't think I approve of the judging committee. It is the inmates running the asylum.

After school I walked back with Neil and Sam. Neil was excited about meeting Barry Morse but Sam is being really quiet these days. She hardly said a thing at lunch. Maybe it is just the ETV paper thing that's worrying her. I know she handed it in Monday but hasn't heard anything back yet. We walked her closer to her house than ever and then Neil and I zagged through St. Gerard's lot and back to my place so I could loan him my tape recorder for his big interview tonight.

Saturday, Nov 20, 1976

Neil came over around 11. He brought back my recorder but he didn't bring the interview tape! The interview went okay he said, but he didn't say much more about it. I got a bit pushy and said well let's go to your place and have a listen to it. No no he says, we can't do that right now. Why not, I demanded, we can just get the tape and bring it back here if we can't use the shed. No no he says, we can't do that. I kept pushing him until finally he said okay let's go. So we went to the shed and he played the interview tape on Jerry's component stereo. Right away I could see why he didn't want me to hear it; he stuttered really badly throughout the whole thing. It was pretty obvious he couldn't ask a lot of his prepared questions and was just asking whatever shortest, easiest to ask questions, he could think of. It must have been very frustrating. Also on the tape Mr. Morse seemed to be saying a lot of things about *Star Trek* being better because it had more 'human' stories. Neil did not challenge him on anything but just moved on to the next question.

As we listened I could see that Neil was embarrassed. I suggested we make another copy of the tape by placing my recorder right by his brother's speakers. We could copy Mr. Morse's answers but leave out or re-do the questions. Neil latched onto this idea right away and I ran back to my place to get another cassette. That left me with only one cassette, which I needed to record today's 1999 episode. So Neil got busy with his tape doctoring and I just went home.

1999 was "The AB Chrysalis" and I wrote a good summary and even typed it up.

Episode Summary: "The AB Chrysalis" (1636 words)
[Omitted.]

Comments on "The AB Chrysalis" (Roger Kay, 1994)

Devastating shockwaves are striking Alpha; they occur precisely every twelve hours and are growing more intense. A planet with a ring of moons is found to be the source. Koenig, Maya, and Alan Carter explore the new solar system with an Eagle. They discover that each moon contain an installation, run by robots, which emits the shockwaves to discourage visitors, friendly or otherwise, while their humanoid masters are in a vulnerable chrysalis state.

Koenig fails to convince the aliens' robotic minders that Alpha poses no threat and should be spared. His only option is to wait for the humanoid aliens to come out of chrysalis. Two aliens, beautiful naked women both, soon emerge from chrysalis, and vote on Koenig's request to delay or diminish the shockwaves. They vote: one in favor, one against. But time is running out quickly for Alpha and Koenig's Eagle already has insufficient fuel to return.

Favorite scene: Helena comes into Command Centre and gently confronts Koenig about Carter's story of beautiful, naked women on the planet. Gee, I didn't really notice, says Koenig. Helena repeats Carter's assertion that the women were beautiful, naked, and green. Really, deadpans Koenig, I don't recall them being green.

Barry Morse Interview
(Lionel O'Neill, 19 November 1976)

Q. When did you first hear about *Space: 1999*?

A. I had done a couple of other series in England for Lord Grade, that's the chap who is head of ITV, the Independent Television Network in England, the commercial network. I had done a series called *The Adventurer* with an actor named Gene Barry, an American actor, which was shot in England and then I did a series call *The Zoo Gang* which you might have seen, which was shot in the south of France and was based on a book by Paul Gallico. And so I had done two series for this ITV outfit and they told me they had an idea for a science fiction series.

Well to tell you the truth I don't know very much about science fiction and I'm not really very scientifically minded so I thought well I don't know what this is going to be like so they sent me a pilot script with an outline of what the scripts were going to be like and what the characters were going to be like and so forth and I had a look at all that and then they told me Martin Landau and Barbara Bain were going to play in it too and I know them of course. I've worked with them a lot in California in years gone by and we were good friends so I thought that's interesting, that would be attractive.

And this was all in about, now let me see, you say when, now I'm very bad with dates but as far as I can remember it must have been in the fall of 1974 I think because I think we started to shoot the shows somewhere around early November of 1974.

And as you know of course the shows were technically enormously complicated, you know the special effects were very elaborate, and all the photographic things especially things like the monitor screens and the little television sets we carried around on our belts, what were they called, commlocks?

Q. Right.

A. You see I've forgotten already. It's getting to be a few years ago since we started to shoot them. All those things are very complicated and the original plan was that every episode would take, I think it was, the idea was, that every episode would take about nine days to shoot, which is not bad, you know, for that kind of film. To shoot one episode, a one hour episode, in nine days is not bad. But as it turned out, our first episode took 32 days because we kept getting all kinds of problems with, you know, the difficulties with a very complex technical thing.

I won't bore you with it too much but since you're interested in the techniques of filming and television, you may be interested in this: when you are filming a picture which is being delivered on a television screen you get the problem of what is called flop-over. You know about this? And the synchronization of the film camera with the television image is terribly delicate and it so happened that in these studios where we were filming in England at Pinewood which is just outside London, they have a rather erratic power supply because they have their own power station and so the strength of the electricity, power, fluctuates slightly which means it is terribly difficult to overcome this flop-over problem and so in the event instead of our first episode being shot in 9 days it took 32 days and so we went on and on and on and I don't think we ever did get a show in 9 days. I think the quickest we ever shot one episode of *Space: 1999* was ten days. I think that was the fastest we ever did.

Q. Can you recall any humorous or amusing happenings that occurred during...

A. Oh endless, endless! Particularly on that first episode, as you can imagine, everything is going wrong. But one of the other very funny episodes we did was one, I'll always remember it, I can't remember what the title was, I'm not very good at remembering titles, but there was one which had, you'll remember probably when I describe to you, there was some kind of ectoplasm or force that we encountered which filled the whole of Alpha with detergent is what it amounted to. You remember that?

Q. "Space Brain"!

A. Was it called "Space Brain"? Okay. Well there you are, you remember better than I. Well they had very elaborate machinery from making all this foam and it was very effective, I'm sure you saw, and there was a sequence where the whole of Main Mission is filling up with this foam and Charles Crichton who was the director of this episode, a very nice chap, he's an older man and he said "Have you organized how the foam is to be made?", and the special effects guys said "Yes we have wonderful... we have a blowing system, we have tremendous blowers that will force the foam in and it will all rise up like this" and we couldn't wait to see.

So we said "We can't rehearse this. We'll just have to film it and hope for the best." So we rehearsed without the foam this sequence where the whole of Main Mission was going to be filled up and then we said "All right we'll go" and all the men with their machines were lined up and we turned over and the clapper boy you know the fellow who says 198 take one (*claps once*) bang clap was standing in the front of the set and they had started to blow in the foam and they said "We'll start the foam first and then we'll get the clapper boy to come in". So there was already a lot of this, soap it was, all over the floor. The clapper boy came on and he said "198 take one", clap, and fell flat on the floor under this foam!

He was buried in this foam and he started to get up and the director said "No no you stay there, we don't want you going across the shot. We'll see you. Just stay down there." So this poor boy was underneath the foam!

Now we are all playing this scene and the foam is rising, it is getting higher and higher and we're all standing up on our tip toes and all this and it was marvelous. We got the shot pretty well except there were a couple of things that didn't go quite right and so eventually they said "Cut!" just when we were all drowning in this detergent. We were all pressing it out of our noses and our hair and our ears.

Then Charles Crichton the director says "Right, get ready to go again".

Now the special effects fellows said "What?" He said "I want you to go again. Clear it all out and..." They had never thought about how to clear it all out!

The whole of Main Mission was filled to a depth of about eight feet with this detergent, foam and they said "Well, we don't know how to do that". He said "What? What are you gonna..." We spend almost the whole of the rest of the day waiting for these guys who were trying to... they got hold of great big pieces of plywood and tried to push all this foam out of the door, get it out of there. It took about four or five hours to get the set clean again for us to start the next day. So that was hilarious.

Oh we had lots of fun like that. We made laughs all the time, all the time, because when you are dealing with such serious things they are kind of funny you know. The next step is you start laughing of course. We laughed all the time.

Q. Did *Space: 1999* have a blooper reel?

A. I don't know. The technicians may have done. But as you probably know they did a number of episodes after I left the show, they wanted to go on and do another group of shows and I, by that time, had spent about a year and a half shooting the first batch of shows and truthfully I was getting a bit bored because we had scripts that were very similar to each other and I didn't think the scripts were getting any better and I wanted them to be better.

I mean the special effects were good but the scripts in terms of human characters I didn't think were good enough and so when they said they wanted to go on and do another batch I said hold on if you don't mind I think I would sooner arrange to fall off the back of the Moon and be lost because I had some other things that I wanted to do.

They never explained how I disappeared or why I disappeared did they?

Q. Yes.

A. Really?

Q. Yes, there are two explanations. One magazine reported your artificial heart broke down somehow and the <u>Moonbase</u>

Alpha Technical Notebook says you were working outside
Alpha, on a new ring of laser guns, when your oxygen tank
malfunctioned and you died.

A. Well I never heard that. Because after I had stopped
shooting the show I didn't see any of the scripts or know what
was happening and I've never seen the shows.

Q. What do you think was the best episode and the worst,
or least best episode of *Space: 1999*?

A. Well the best one for my money, the most interesting
script from a human point of view was an episode I think was
called "The Black Sun" in which Martin and I became a
thousand years old and there wasn't all that much in the way of
special effects but there was a great deal about
(*undecipherable*) yes and the script was mostly concerned with
what human beings think about and the idea of this cosmic
intelligence taking over our souls, our minds if you like and I
thought that was a very imaginative script and I wished that we
had had more scripts like that. Did you feel that was one of the
better ones?

Q. Yes, it was a fascinating episode.

A. One of the ones we did feel was a little foolish was
where we fetched up on some place that seemed to be full of
table tennis balls, what was that place, what was that episode?
We fetched up at a place where we all became very lazy. We
all lay about in heaps.

Q. "Guardian of Piri"?

A. That sounds rather like it. I don't know. There was a girl
who ran up and down the big flight of steps...

Q. Catherine Schell?

A. That's the one, you're right, yes, who afterwards came
into the series on a running basis. That episode I must say gave
us more laughs than most because I don't know there's
something very funny about landing on a planet that was full of
table tennis balls. It all had ping pong balls everywhere, didn't
it? And everybody is going to sleep and lying down. I thought
that was a bit silly. Did people who watched it think it was silly
too?

Q. No. I don't know. I haven't had much response on that.

A. Really. Ah. Now which did you think were the best episodes?

Q. I liked the first episode, although it wasn't absolutely technically correct.

A. The one where the Moon went out of orbit. Yeah, it had a lot of very good stuff in it, yeah.

Q. I also liked the one with Gwent.

A. Yes! Now that's very interesting because that script you may have noticed was written by the same guy who wrote "Black Sun" *[Editor's note: Barry is incorrect: the writers were different]* so that's the other good episode I was going to say the one that we enjoyed the most.

Wonderful actor named Leo McKern who played this old man. He's an old friend of mine. And it was I who suggested... originally there were two separate people and I said "No no no, we should make the man who is physically present and this governing voice, they should be the same person because it is he who has created this man who is his servant". And so the producers accepted that. They thought that was a very good idea. And we were lucky enough to get Leo McKern, wonderful actor, wonderful. He's an Australian you know.

And I thought that and "The Black Sun" were our two best episodes. And the interesting thing is they were both written by the same guy, by the same writer. Yes I enjoyed that enormously because those two episodes as well as having special effects had ideas and very stimulating ideas and that is what makes good television I think.

Q. If you were in charge of *Space: 1999* back then and could make any changes in the basic format, what do you think would have improved the show? In terms of characterization and such.

A. Oh, Martin and Barbara and I used to think a great deal and worry a great deal and agitate a great deal about enlarging the human characters because we never felt, and this is one of the reasons why I didn't continue with the show when it went into its second batch of shooting, I never felt that there was enough attention paid to human relationships and human character. And this is why I liked those two shows I mentioned because they had to do with human relationships, human characters and human ideas. So much of the time we were concerned merely with special effects and I don't think that you can make successful drama out of special effects. Drama comes out of human relationships, you know, people talking to each other.

There wasn't enough investigation. I would have liked to have seen much more investigation into how we felt about each other, what our weaknesses were. I would like to have seen the crew of Moonbase Alpha on more domestic occasions. When do we do our laundry, you know. Who falls in love? Who gets angry? Who gets frightened? Why do they get frightened, why do they quarrel, all those sorts of things.

There weren't enough things that we as human beings in the 1970s can relate to in terms of human behavior. That's what I would have liked to have seen, changed and enriched.

Q. Have you heard of *Starlog* magazine and if so, what do you think of it?

A. I think I have. Is that the magazine that is concerned with everything to do with science fiction?

Q. Exactly.

A. I think they wrote to me once and asked for an interview thing which I did do for them.

There is an organization too which organizes conventions. It is called the *Space: 1999 Alliance* I think and they arrange meetings, conventions. I believe one was held in Philadelphia and one was held in Pittsburgh and I unfortunately haven't been able to go because I happened to be working in some other part of the world when they were held but there is an enormous amount of enthusiasm and dedication to the series, isn't there? Despite the fact that, how recently were they shown here in Canada?

Q. Well, the first year ended in spring and the second season started this September...

A. There is a great delay you know between production and broadcast. In England people are always saying is it going to come back, will they ever do some more. I don't think they will because you know once a show is done...

Q. Except maybe for, uh...

A. Reruns, be back for reruns

Q. ... and the old classic *Star Trek* might have a movie but we won't get that for another ten years...

A. No, no. I'm afraid I think that *Star Trek* will wear better, will last better than *Space: 1999* because if you examine the nature of the scripts on *Star Trek*, they were all based on ideas and human relationships rather more than special effects.

Their special effects weren't particularly good, you know. They weren't at all elaborate. But their ideas, the contrast of the human characters and the conflict of human situations was very carefully examined and exploited. And in that respect I think although the show was not as technically elaborate as *Space: 1999*, I thought that in terms of human ideas it was better although it was done as you know a good long time before it.

Q. 1969...

A. Yeah. A long time ago. And things do change of course in that realm very quickly. Oh there'll be other series. I shall show up as somebody's scientific uncle again before long. It was pleasant, that was one nice thing about *Space: 1999.* It was very pleasant to be playing a character who was kind of everybody's uncle. I used to call myself a space uncle because he was the oldest guy in the outfit (*mumbling from Neil*) a sort of father figure. Were there some other older people?

Q. I'm not sure if he was older than you were... do you recall the episode with a spaceship from Earth and which had a drive which was extremely destructive and his name was Ernst Linden, or Queller maybe...

A. I don't remember that. Oh, yes yes yes.

Q. He was a rather old chap.

A. That's right. An actor called Jeremy Kemp played that character. Well, he's not as old as me.

Q. I can't tell.

A. I think he was in his late forties, or around fifty somewhere. He's probably ten years or more younger than me. But that's right yes I remember that episode. He was very good.

We had a lot of very good guest artists. My old friend Peter Cushing was in one, wasn't he? Peter and I were young actors together about forty years ago in the theater. I've known him all that long time. Yes we had a lot of very good guest artists.

There we are. I think we've about done.

Entries from Roger Kay's 1976 Diary

Sunday, November 21, 1976

Neil showed up at 1:30 and had the edited interview tape with him. When Sam got here we listened to the tape right away. She asked why Neil's voice is so much louder than Mr. Morse, and why there are loud snaps and pops between questions and answers so Neil had to admit he re-recorded his questions. But he didn't really say why, just that the original questions were not clear. I think Sam understood anyway.

We all thought "The AB Chrysalis" was a good episode, but we didn't discuss it. Instead we had a good general discussion about computers. I taped it. Sam seemed in a good mood again, even though Neil kept disagreeing with her. I think he is jealous or annoyed that both Sam and I can type (well Sam is just beginning) so he is left out on that.

Our discussion got interrupted by Grandma calling and then I forgot to tape the rest of the session. Oops!

Wrote a 500 word paper for Science explaining how the tilt of the Earth's axis causes seasons. 512 words.

21 November 1976
(audio tape from collection of Roger Kay)

Roger: Okay it's going. *(pause)* Today we continue our discussion of issues in *Space: 1999* with Samantha Renfield and Lionel O'Neill. I've got a new topic for today. In Main Mission, there're keypads for the main computer. There're different keypads in various areas, next to Paul Morrow's seated position, and for each Main Mission staff position, Kano, Sandra, Tanya Alexander... Then there're keypads for standing positions, not just in Main Mission but in other areas dedicated to computers. Like in "Ring Around The Moon" where Ted Clifford's taken over by aliens and he starts tapping away like crazy at these keypads. My problem with this is that the actual keys don't have any symbols on them. Is this just sloppy set construction, or if not, what's it tell us about the computer technology of 1999?

Sam: Let me start this with an unpopular view. I think it's simple lazy set construction. I just don't see any reason why they shouldn't have reproduced the symbols you see on a typewriter and put them on the keys. Really the computer keypads should be arranged just like a typewriter, so people can re-use their typing skills when they need to interact with the computer.

Neil: Well you don't need to be a typist to interact with the computer. Lots of time you see Koenig giving the computer voice commands. Obviously they have that technology so they don't need to have typists operating the computers.

Roger: Still I can see the need for something other than voice commands. Suppose you have a crisis and everyone in Main Mission is talking at once. How could the computer know who is talking to which computer? Also, how would it know if an Alphan was addressing a computer or another Alphan? Seems like a lot of room for error there. Some type of manual entry is probably essential.

Neil: But is it reasonable to assume that scientists and astronauts can type? Highly educated people have secretaries who perform all their typing. You can't bring a secretary along on every Eagle mission so that they can program their computers nonverbally...

Sam: If the primary way to communicate with the computer is some kind of electronic typewriter keys, then most people who are educated in the sciences *will* be able to type. It won't just be for journalists and secretaries.

Neil: It just doesn't seem to be very futuristic, to have electric typewriters hooked up to your computer...

Roger: I think the keypads would look much like 1999. Not an electric typewriter, but something that fits with the technology of the time. *(pause)* What about the having no symbols on the keys? Is there any sort of explanation for that?

Neil: Well if all astronauts and scientists have to learn to type, then perhaps they know what each button does and they don't need any symbols on them. Maybe this is a way to keep those who don't know how the keypads work away from them, a security thing?

Sam: Maybe each person would have a special identification word that put in then the computer knows it's them. I think there'd be a lot of typing errors if you couldn't see what keys you were hitting. I mean I'm learning to type and I can already type about 20 words per minute but I make all sorts of mistakes. So what happens in Main Mission when you punch all those nice blank buttons and then you can't see what you've typed? There'd be too many mistakes. People would die.

Roger: I suppose whether you enter a command with your voice or with a keypad, in either case you can make a mistake. Hopefully if it is something important, like opening an airlock, the computer will ask for confirmation before it does anything.

Neil: Which could cause dangerous delays...

Voice of Roger's Mother: Roger! Phone for you!!

Entries from Roger Kay's 1976 Diary

Monday, November 22, 1976

At 12 I ran down to the second floor to see if Mr. Voerstadt had posted the video project grades. He had. They were taped to the door of the Art room. We got a B but half the class was Bs! The other half was Cs, except Brian's group which got a D. Neil's name was on my team, but mysteriously Sam's was not.

Neil and Sam were in front of the music room, already eating their lunch. They knew about the B. Sam explained that she had been dragged into the principal's office this morning and he had torn a strip off her for that essay she wrote. Mr. Whyte admitted it was well-written, and he couldn't dispute some of her points, but said the paper itself was disrespectful and not what they had asked for. Sam told him that the nature of scientific learning was that sometimes you discovered one thing while doing something else, and that is exactly what happened to her. Mr. Whyte said "This was not a social experiment; it was an technical exercise". Sam said "Every thing and every day is an opportunity to learn for the engaged mind". He didn't like that. She got off with a warning and supposedly she will be getting the same 'B' that Neil and I got. We'll see if it has any real bearing on her Home Ec. final mark.

More good news: Neil has tickets for us to go to the viewing of the projects his advanced film class did. I hope his audio turns out better than on our ETV project. One problem is that the screening is this Thursday at 7:30, but I work 7-9.

Later... At work I asked Uncle Tim if there was some way I could get this Thursday off. He said, well, just work Tuesday night instead. That was easier than I thought! I'm very excited about my debut on the silver screen!

Thursday, November 25, 1976

I was pretty tired today because I've worked the last three nights in a row. But by the time evening rolled around, I was wide awake. I went over to Neil's then he and Jerry and I all walked down to the Regional together. Sam couldn't make it. Her family "is doing something". That's what she always says.

I'm starting to think she is a reverse vampire, when the Sun goes down she turns into a pumpkin or something. I had promised to tell her all about it, but then I re-thought and decided to smuggle my recorder in so I could tape the whole thing. This way, at least she'll be able to hear it.

There was a pretty good crowd. The theater was about half full and it's a big theater. Mr. Focault got up and made a speech about youth being the future and that all kids need opportunities to be creative, without the arts his own life would have been blah blah blah. Finally the lights dimmed and the films started. A lot of them were related to music. One group did a film where they pretended to be a band and they mouthed the words and pretended to play instruments while the real song played. Some BTO *[Editor's note: Bachman Turner Overdrive]* song that is a little 'blue collar' for me. Another film had a soundtrack of the first Black Sabbath song, called Black Sabbath, which showed a satanic rite in a graveyard. When the fast part of the song cuts in, they have shots of someone running (their perspective) with the camera jerking, and then shots of a looming black presence behind them. It ended with a shot of a headstone with a paper tacked over it: Under New Management. Kind of weird but enjoyable.

Our flick came next and Neil nudged me: this is it. A graphic announcing "*Karmic Whiplash* by Dharma Productions" starts it, with some classical music in the background. Then we are looking into a messy kitchen and we meet the two brothers who are the main characters. Neil is the younger brother. One of his film project guys is the older brother. It is clear that Neil, Abel he is called here, is a good guy and the older brother, Cain, is not so good.

Abel pleads with Cain to quit stealing groceries from the store, and says you can't borrow any more money from our friends, and if you did steal that money from the Darlingtons, then you better give it back.

Cain says, you gotta do what you gotta do to survive, there ain't no jobs around here, and Ma and Pa are dead and they can't help us.

There is a stop animation sequence where 'x' marks show up on a calendar, the days of June 1976 are passing fast. When we get to the end of the month, we are back in the kitchen and Cain answers the phone. It is good news, he says. He has been offered a job at a government car pool. It will pay quite well, and has benefits and security. They are happy and high-five each other. The brothers decide to take their last money and go out to buy something to celebrate.

We see them in OK Economy. Abel buys two steaks for them to eat. Cain buys a bottle of whiskey. You can't really buy booze at a grocery store of course, but this is part of the willing suspension of disbelief that movies require, perhaps.

When the two brothers get home, Cain proceeds to drink the whiskey and, after insisting on cooking the steaks himself, burns them. Abel does not drink, so Cain finishes his share of the bottle too and collapses on the floor.

We see a new sunrise. A clock shows 6 a.m.. Abel tries to wake Cain up. It is the first day for Cain's new job and he must get up. Come on, encourages Abel, I'll make you some eggs. But Cain does not want to get up, and says screw the job, I'm sleeping in.

They start to fight and Cain throws the frying pan, complete with boiling oil at Abel, good editing there, who takes the frying pan away. They struggle then Abel bashes Cain across the head with the frying pan and Cain falls to the floor, dead. The younger brother takes Cain's ID card and then sits at the kitchen table while he looks at the card a long time.

Finally the phone rings. Abel answers it and says yes, this is Cain California. Yes, I will be there. Sorry just having some problems with my younger brother. I'll definitely be there.

Next we see the scenes that Sam and I were involved in. Abel is at his new job; he opens the chain link fence, makes notes on his clipboard, closes the chain link fence.

Then I appear. Are you Cain California, I ask? You can make out what I'm saying but it is a bit faint.

Neil says, yes, I am Cain California.

I pull out a gun and say this is for attacking my sister you drunk son of a bitch, and shoot him. Neil does his death scene. Sam does a good job of following Neil with the camera as he falls to the ground.

The last part is in the interrogation room. Sam is a female police detective and she is telling the murderer (me!) that he has killed the younger brother, Abel, not the older brother, Cain, who incidentally has been missing for some time. I (the murderer) recount how my younger sister had been saved by Abel, who was the opposite of Cain, a good person in every way. It is this good person I have murdered, I then realize.

There is a close up of me with scrunched up eyes, moaning in pain, water glistening on my cheeks. The very last shot is of me slumping over the interrogation table, moaning piteously, one hand grasping my own hair, the other splayed out before me. The camera slowly trucks away from the table, and then the scene fades out.

The ending credits list the actors (including me and Sam!) while a death march type music plays.

There were a couple more films but I don't recall much. When we finally shuffled out of the theater I noticed some people were looking at me. They think I'm a star! Jerry was grabbing Neil and saying good job, good job and he grabbed my shoulder and said you did really well too. We are both fine actors according to Jerry. I felt a little cheated that that Sam couldn't be there.

Now I'm invited over to the shed tomorrow night to tape an interview with Jerry! I'm excited and exhausted. Is this the longest diary entry ever?? It is past 12:30. Good night!

Friday, November 26, 1976

Brian's older brother was in one of the films last night so he was there and saw *Karmic Whiplash* too. This morning he bugged me about my crying in the final scene of the film but I just said I wasn't *crying* I was *acting*. He is mistaking my character for me. I'm sure it happens to lots of actors.

At lunch time Neil and I told Sam all about the premiere of *Karmic Whiplash*. Her parts turned out really well we told her, which is the truth. I tried to find out why she couldn't get to the screening but she just said her parents are a pain. Neil says he'll hang onto *Karmic Whiplash* and when we finally get to high school, he'll talk to Mr. Focault and arrange to use a projector to show Sam the film. That's a long time to wait, but it's better than thinking she'll never get to see her own performance.

To be honest, I was so elated with my experience yesterday that I just sailed through today, not even noticing the double Phys-ed period at the end of the day. We played floor hockey but I don't even feel the bruises. When I wasn't thinking about my film debut last night, I was anticipating my interview tonight. Life seems to be accelerating now. I feel I am finally starting to live in a world of my own creation, rather than just being stuck in some hostile world that I never asked for.

After supper I scrambled over to Neil's shed. He was in there and we sat listening to records for a while before Jerry showed up, around 8. I cued up my cassette and we started the interview right away. Jerry's friend showed up around 9 and we had to stop. I said maybe I can come back tomorrow with a few more questions and Jerry said sure!Now I've already started working on the transcript for tonight's tape but it is a lot of work and I only managed to type about half a page before it was 11 and Mom said no more clickety-clack, time to sleep. Good night!

26 November 1976
(audio tape from collection of Roger Kay)

Roger: First, thanks to Jerry for agreeing to answer my questions. I know you've got a lot of knowledge and information about rock music and science fiction so I really want to thank you for letting me use your expertise.

Jerry: No problem kiddo. Lionel says you're a good guy, rock steady, and a good writer too. So maybe I'll wind up in *Rolling Stone* magazine?

Roger: Oh, I don't know.

Neil: He's humble too!

(laughter)

Roger: So can I start with the question: when did science fiction first begin to influence rock and roll?

Jerry: Well really the last eight or ten years or so is the music I'm interested in. Before that I don't think there was too much crossover between the two. Maybe I'm wrong but I think the real revolution in rock music came in the late sixties. That's the interesting stuff. Everybody now knows that and respects those artists.

I suppose by 1986 they might say the interesting stuff was in the late seventies. Maybe the reality is the average rock fan's record collection spans ten years or so. Hard to say. But for me, it started with the Beatles, the Rolling Stones, Jimi Hendrix, Spirit, stuff from the sixties, and then Black Sabbath, Deep Purple, Uriah Heep, Blue Oyster Cult in the seventies.

Originally pop music focused only on sex. I mean they talked in euphemisms, metaphors, riddles, but it was all about sex. "Hold my hand" means get in my bed. "Let's spend the night together", that's classic talking about sex without mentioning sex. What did you expect they're gonna do all night long? Talk about politics? No way.

(laughter)

Then starting in the late sixties, other genres of literature started to appear in music. Pop music was originally like a Harlequin Romance, but then science fiction, fantasy, and horror started to creep in. As harder rock was born, the romance got more explicit, so you now found lots of very sexy music too. Sometimes the lyrics talk about love, but if you look at the bands and the aggressive way they play, hard rock you know, then it's clear they're talking about sex, not hand holding. Anyway…

(sound of lighter igniting)

Hendrix did science fiction. From "EXP" where you hear a UFO landing to "Up From The Skies" where he is the alien, or "Third Stone From The Sun", same thing.

Even the Stones did science fiction. You remember "Twenty Thousand Light Years From Home"?

Uriah Heep brought fantasy into rock. *Demons And Wizards* is one album; another is The *Magician's Birthday*. Both Heep and Sabbath have a song called "The Wizard", very different songs though.

And it was Sabbath that really brought the horror genre into rock. "War Pigs", "Iron Man", "Children Of The Grave", all monsters of some kind. Their very first song, the eponymous "Black Sabbath", is a scene in a graveyard where witches gather to perform a human sacrifice, then the singer discovers *he's* the one gonna be sacrificed.

So a lot of stuff that used to be in books is now coming into music. Politics came into music in the sixties. First in folk and then into rock. Bob Dylan broke down that barrier and made it possible for rock to be more than just pop love songs.

Nowadays rock is a political force and young people use it as a way to express their ideas. I mean no one listens to young people and no one cares about their vote. Look how long the Vietnam war went on, despite huge protests from young Americans. No one cared.

Sure eventually they did stop the war, and maybe the music and culture helped speed that up a bit, but mostly the fact is old politicians and people over thirty just don't care about what young people need or want. They have their old ideas and they don't want to change anything. That's what you call the 'status quo', and there is a rock group called that too, but I think they're being ironic.

So, really I think it was the late sixties and the influx of new ideas from the young people that allowed science fiction to seep into the rock area.

But let's go back a little. A lot of walls were broken down back then, and that was just one of them. First of all, it was racism, so we had the civil rights changes in the States. Then it was sexism and Puritanism so we had the sexual revolution. Since the space age started to really take off, no pun intended,

(laughter)

we have a new perspective on the world. Standing on the Moon and looking back at our planet blew the minds of older people just as LSD was opening the minds of the younger generation.

All these revolutions, in race, sex, technology, drugs, more and more change is coming faster and faster and rather than writing books about it, we have rock and roll. It has become our newspaper and our encyclopedia. And the best part is that the status quo of the older people can't touch it. We control it and therefore we can create our own future.

How's that?

Roger: That's great. Um, how about, why or how does science fiction influence rock music?

Jerry: I'll start with why. I think there are images or archetypes in science fiction which resonate with rock musicians.

The idea of the rocket, the powerful engine that takes you places undreamed of, that can be a sexual type thing, what you call a phallic symbol: the rocket as a giant dick. The guitar is the same. Hendrix showed us this by sticking it out from in between his legs, or rubbing it against his amplifiers, and even in some of his lyrics which refer to women *sleeping* with his guitar. To Hendrix the guitar was both a sexy woman and a strong phallic symbol. He could make love to it, coaxing beautiful moans and sighs out of it, like a woman when you're in bed with her. And at the same time, he could play it like he was driving a powerful rocket, one that could take you from planet Earth to the great starry beyond in a few seconds.

And of course they want the guitar to be as loud as a rocket! The awe you might experience watching a Saturn V liftoff is the same feeling a rock fan gets when the amplifiers are cranked up and the whole building shakes. One thing escapes you into outer space, the other into your own mind, inner space. Rock can be very powerful and it becomes more powerful the more ideas and genres you allow along on the journey. Like scientific experiments you take on a space mission. You're going to the same place, but the more experiments you bring, the more you'll learn.

Another important thing is the idea of the outsider. Normal society fears and shuns the outsider. Anything that is different or that they can't understand, they fear and therefore hate. Now most rock musicians and true artists are outsiders of some variety. They pride themselves on their uniqueness. To stand out they grow their hair long, they wear unusual clothes. They shun anything normal or usual. The idea is to welcome the strange, the freak, and not to fear him. They are open to new ideas and experience.

Ask yourself, isn't that the exact same thing as a science fiction fan? You're fascinated by distant and strange worlds because you're sick of this one. You're interested in aliens, because you feel they might be more sympathetic than the people here on Earth. You're interested in the future, because you see the present here is deeply flawed. So you question why. Why does a river flow to the ocean? It's all water.

(pause and sound of lighter)

As for how, just go through the examples. Every song that carries some element of science fiction is another how.

Roger: So you're saying that both rock music and science fiction are revolutionary activities, things intended to change the world?

Jerry: Very good. You're as smart as Lionel says you are.

Roger: Thank you... Do you think rock really *can* change the world?

Jerry: If you get enough people and the right ideas, any revolution is unstoppable. So while science fiction inspires people to become engineers and scientists, the new rock music will inspire social and political awareness first and then, eventually, change. There will be resistance along the way, for sure.

A lot of people don't want change. Those words again: status quo. Them with the status wants to keep it. You can call them counter-revolutionaries, the ones with the power and money who do not want to see any change. They claim that there is no room in music for political dissent or social critique. They say you should just enjoy pop music for its beat or melody, not for any ideas that come with it. Pop music should be aimed at teenager's hormones, not at their brains.

Neil: They try to control us by using the weaknesses of our own bodies.

Jerry: Oh yeah, they sure do. They, and I mean the old people and the status quo, tell us that sex without love is meaningless, but when it comes to music, meaningless is what they encourage. I'd hate to turn thirty and then suddenly become aware that my record collection is all Patsy Gallant and Engelbert Humperdink.

(laughter)

I hope when I'm old my music still means something. All my old records should tell stories, tell me who I am, where I came from, and not just be a bunch of make out music. This generation will be the one to change that. Music has always been about love, about dating, about dancing. Now it is about the rest of life. The new music we have now will live on much longer than the old style pop songs.

(sound of sticky wooden door being pulled open)

Stuart: Hey Jerry, what's happening man?

Jerry: Hey Stu, come on in. Just sharing some wisdom with the young ones.

Stuart: Really? This one's way too smart already. You gotta watch him.

Jerry: *(laughs)* You good?

Entries from Roger Kay's 1976 Diary

Saturday, November 27, 1976
Didn't go downtown today. Lots of fresh snowing. Spent my time instead trying to type up a transcript of Jerry's interview. It is a lot of work.

1999 at 4 was "Catacombs of the Moon". I taped it.

Tonight I took a big chance. I thought Jerry might provide some even more revolutionary insights if he didn't think I was taping him. So I hid my recorder in my knapsack and wound the microphone cord through a small hole between the compartments so it could be close to the open air while the recorder itself was safe, deep inside, with the record and play buttons already pushed. I've done this a few times before, as far back as when I first started Grade 7. But I took such a beating that day, as did my knapsack, that I never tried to sneak my recorder into school again.

I went over to the shed around 7. Jerry and Neil were there. I set my knapsack down and activated the recorder with the switch on the microphone. I am James Bond. I had a pad of paper with me to take notes, to make it more realistic that I wasn't taping. Jerry did talk very freely then, even mentioning that he thought there could be aliens on Earth right now!

After Jerry left, Neil and I hung around and listened to some recorded music (a rare tape of a British radio broadcast) called *Potatoland*, by the group Spirit. It was cool and I thought I should tape it, so I pulled my recorder out of my knapsack. I didn't really need the microphone and I couldn't explain why the cord was threaded into the front compartment, so I just unplugged it before Neil could see. Instead I used my recorder's built-in condenser microphone by putting my recorder right next to the left speaker. We cranked *Potatoland* and it taped fine.

27 November 1976
(audio tape from collection of Roger Kay)

Jerry: ... pick up the groceries?

Neil: Yup. I went right after, um, this morning. It's all put away. Say Jerry, maybe you can tell Roger about *Potatoland*?

Jerry: That's not for everyone. (pause) But if you think he's worthy, okay.

(sound of chair scraping along floor)

Kiddo, you know last time I told you about the forces of change in both science fiction and rock music, and how the status quo wants to stop or at least control those changes? Well, the government is the worst part of the status quo - they're the central agent for all forces of social control. They're not afraid of getting their hands dirty, as long as they don't get caught. In the States they have the CIA, the FBI, the NSA, and a whole bunch of other organizations that look at what people are doing and try to control things.

Here in Canada we have the same things going on, but our secrecy is better because our citizens are unarmed and philosophically helpless to suspect what's really going on.

Maybe you've heard about the experiments where the CIA used psychedelic drugs, like LSD, to try to create super soldiers, or even just as a weapon against civilians. I wouldn't put anything past them. They take a tool of mind expansion and turn it into a weapon of mind control.

Most of the world is kept pacified, on a leash, with the few drugs, bad ones, they allow us. I'm talking about booze. It stops people from thinking clearly and ensures that large groups of people cannot act *together*. What if booze had been served at Woodstock? It would've turned the gathering into a giant melee and the message would have been lost.

Instead, as it happened, all was peaceful and it was a lost opportunity and harsh lesson too for the status quo.

To have us weakened and disorganized is in their interest. And this is what they've been doing to the mainstream all along by telling them that booze is fun and cool. It's not good for the brain or for society but it makes sure everyone is distracted and has lots of fun doing nothing.

Cigarettes are a deadly drug, so why are they not outlawed? Because they help keep people in line. You can kidnap people and force them to go through withdrawal against their will. You can make sure that a large proportion of the population is ingesting whatever chemicals and drugs you want to mix in with the government-approved packages of tobacco. Nobody grows their own tobacco, so nobody really knows what the hell is in them. If there aren't mind control drugs in your smokes already, that doesn't mean the government can't add them anytime it thinks it needs to.

Roger: But you smoke…

Jerry: Yeah I'm hooked. They got me. But I usually roll my own and if I ever noticed any strange effects from it, I'll quit right then. The thing is, I'm smart enough to see what they're trying to do, so it makes it that much harder for them to fool me.

(sound of lighter)

There are forces that are trying to stop the revolution. Black people, hippies, other discontents have always been excluded from the system. Rock music wants to include them, to remove the racism and the discrimination of old against young. The white status quo can't have that. You remember Martin Luther King?

(murmurs of agreement from Neil and Roger)

He was murdered. So was JFK, *and* his younger brother, Robert Kennedy. They were politicians that wanted to change things. So they had to be killed. In the rock world you have Jim Morrison, Jimi Hendrix, Janis Joplin, all dead under mysterious circumstances. I don't think they died by accident, or suicide. They were problems that had to be dealt with.

In the long run, the revolution is unstoppable - black artists will finally get the power they deserve and become a force to contend with. That is the reason the racist FBI continues to watch all the important people in rock. Any serious rock music lover will admit that the innovation for rock came from black people. For a long time they were ignored and it had to be a white cover act that could play the new rock music on the radio. If you listen to the old blues records it is absolutely clear that the black acts were far better than the local pretenders or the British invasion who copied the quote unquote *race music*.

I mean at least the British Invasion acted as publicity instead of just stealing work from the original black musicians. The more ethical of the white acts acknowledged the roots of the new music and tried to help the black artists who were still starving. Guys like Eric Clapton insisted on bringing black American bluesmen to London to play with them.

Because that original music is so much better, when it becomes dominant, maybe in ten years, it will be very powerful. The white status quo doesn't want to let this happen so they try to stop it with targeted assassinations and other bad influences. The FBI invented PCP, a dangerous drug. Maybe that is how Morrison was killed. I'm certain they made sure it was offered to Hendrix too.

The basic problem is that we live in an illusion of freedom. You can be free as long as you do what the government wants. Once you step out on your own, good luck, or more likely, good bye. You've read <u>1984</u>?

Roger: Yeah. Neil turned me on to it.

Jerry: Neil?

Roger: I mean Lionel.

Jerry: Right. *(pause)* There is a very important rock group called Spirit and they put out new music in 1972 that's been banned in North America by the government. But the government slipped up because it had already been played on BBC Radio in England. My friend there made me a copy of his recording. It's called *Potatoland* and talks about the idea of <u>1984</u> being closer than you think.

It's a concept album, basically an allegory about people being made from potatoes and how we get sliced up and fried and boiled in real life. It means that, to the people in power, we lowly masses are just commodities to be divided and digested after proper seasoning and cooking. The seasoning is our education, very carefully controlled by the government, and the cooking is how we age and become weak because of the chemicals they feed us, the rat race they force us into, accompanied by a heavy tax system, and the social hoops we're forced to jump through to become so-called upstanding citizens. We value appearance over substance all the time. This has been drilled into us. You have to *look* right. You have to make sure the neighbours don't think you're any different than them. If we're all the same, then we're so much easier to control. And easier for the forces of control to spot who needs that extra attention.

It was Randy California, the guitarist from Spirit, who created the ideas in *Potatoland*. I suspect he'll be killed soon, no doubt something that looks like an accident.

(pause)

You wonder why *Star Trek* was cancelled so early, after only three years and all the groundbreaking work they did. The show was getting more and more popular. So why did it disappear? The nonconformists finally had a platform and The Man couldn't stand it. I wonder if someone somewhere saw a script that came *a little too close* to the truth.

Roger: What truth is that?

Jerry: That we do not control our own destiny, that even the most powerful humans, the richest and supposedly wisest, don't truly understand what the future demands. Only an alien intelligence can understand and guide us.

Roger: What kind of alien?

Jerry: Not an alien alien. An alien intelligence. Most humans have closed minds. Their consciousness operates within strictly limited bounds, terrestrial bounds.

According to Timothy Leary there are different brain circuits within our nervous system. These circuits are common among the higher animals. Some of the circuits are active, but mostly they're dormant. Life on Earth requires only a few of the lower circuits to operate. If a human wants to live in space, which is where we're headed, then some higher level circuits need to turn on. These are the extra-terrestrial circuits which operate all the time in space-based civilizations. There are ways to turn these circuits on, certain drugs, but they pose a danger to the existing power structures here on Earth.

Only when humanity is ready, when enough people have their higher circuits activated, will we become aware of aliens. Until then, anyone who talks about it is liable to be called crazy.

Roger: Wow.

Neil: Can we listen to *Potatoland*?

Jerry: That's fine. I'm heading out with Stu at 9. Lionel, you handle the tape and be super careful, you know?

Neil: If we don't say where we got it, can Roger make a copy on his cassette recorder?

Jerry: All right. That's a good idea. Just be careful. I can't replace it. Come on. I'll get it for you.

(sound of sticky wooden door opening, and then slamming shut)

Episode Summary: "Catacombs Of The Moon"
(1239 words)
[Omitted.]

Comments on "Catacombs Of The Moon"
(Roger Kay, 1994)

Lunar mining chief Patrick Osgoode is having visions of Alpha being destroyed by fire. His wife Michelle requires a new, replacement heart but Alpha cannot spare any terranium to coat the replacement artificial organ. As a cloud of fiery gas approaches Alpha, Patrick declares his prophecy is manifesting, kidnaps his wife from Medical Centre, and takes her deep into the mining caverns of the Moon, safe from the firestorm but away from critical medical help.

Favorite scene: In the denouement, Tony offers his new batch of beer to Helena and is mocked. Tony says he is going to find Maya because if he is going to be insulted, he wants to be insulted by an expert.

Entries from Roger Kay's 1976 Diary

Sunday, November 28, 1976

Spent all morning writing my synopsis of "Catacombs Of The Moon". I was confused by a new character, a black doctor who works with Helena. He seems to be her main assistant or colleague now, but he is not good old Doctor Mathias. Did his spacesuit spring a leak too, like Professor Bergman's?? Hmm....

Neil and Sam were here this afternoon. We talked a bit about the new episode. It is not one of the better ones. I personally don't like the idea of mining in caverns on the Moon. How could you keep the work areas pressurized? Every time you blast open a new vein of rock, you are gambling with exposing yourself unexpectedly to vacuum. It would make a lot more sense if they wore spacesuits in those caverns. This may be another case of the dreaded 'set construction laziness' problem. It might be too uncomfortable or confusing to film all the actors wearing space suits and communicating only by radio, so they just don't. The reason might be as simple as that: ease of storytelling overrides technical accuracy. Like that never happens!

Sam didn't like the quasi-religious revelations that Patrick had. She likes her shows to be based on science and logic. If something appears magical, it is no doubt just advanced technology. Like Magus.

We listened back to Jerry's interview (the first one obviously!) because Sam was interested. After, I mentioned his idea of the status quo controlling society, trying to quash any revolution and that maybe it had even been involved in getting *Star Trek* canceled.

Sam picked up on Jerry's idea of revolution, saying *Star Trek* had a lot of stories that challenged the status quo, but through metaphors or allegory. A direct confrontation would never be aired, so *Star Trek* had to wrap their ideas in the camouflage of alien cultures and planets. She was a bit wound up today and also talked about faith, how the Alphans had faith in humanity, not faith in some external god. We all agreed that any type of humanoid god, in reality, is silly.

Neil left around 3:30 but Sam stuck around. We had to promise we wouldn't listen to my cassette of his *Karmic Whiplash* film without him here. Sam said she wanted to hear my new Budgie album, but when she got me alone, she started talking about Neil. She said that both she and him come from families that needed escaping from. But she didn't say why her family was a problem. I've never met them. She did say, they would be very mad if they found out what she's been doing. I didn't understand this. What has she been doing? Talking about a TV show? She wanted to know if Neil ever talked about girls. I said Neil is the gentleman type. He won't make degrading comments like many guys do. He doesn't wolf whistle. He doesn't look at girlie magazines, as far as I know. He had some older sisters, but I don't know what happened to them.

I was very honest with her except on one point. The truth is that I am crazy about her and fantasize that we could be together someday. I am okay with our friendship being only that, a friendship, but if things change and Neil and her became romantic, I'm not sure I could bear being left out. I understand why she would want Neil more than me, but that doesn't make it any easier on me. I could have told her that Neil is more interested in mind than body and he probably won't have a girlfriend until he has his Ph.D. but I didn't. Why do people always want what they can't have?

Spent the evening working on a transcript of my first Jerry interview. It is slow going and my depressed mood doesn't help.

Monday, November 29, 1976
The schedule for Xmas exams is out. We'll be spending almost a week writing ridiculously long (hour and a half) tests. At lunch, Sam talked about her parents for the first time. They are very religious and really strict. She has to lie whenever she goes out of the house, but because she has lots of brothers (five!) and they all lie too, she's learned how to deal with the situation and her parents are mostly powerless to control them.

The bizarre news is that Sam has invented imaginary school friends to stand in for Neil and I in her conversations with her parents. They would not approve of male friends, so I am 'Roxanne' and Neil is 'Nellie'. We had a good laugh over that. Sam is one amazing girl: brave, smart and very funny.

I really don't know if I should tell Neil about her crush on him. If he's not interested, I'm sure she'll be hurt, but if he is interested, I'll be devastated. I don't have a brother or sister to ask for advice so I'm kind of stumped how to get past this.

Tuesday, November 30, 1976

Real tired today. Stayed late at work last night because they had a big shipment and needed to re-arrange everything. New flavour: blackberry. Change is work. I'm starting to see the wisdom of preferring the status quo! Just kidding.

Wednesday, December 1, 1976

We got in a big argument at lunch. I was talking about <u>Man Plus</u> by Pohl, about the possibility of a merger between humans and robots in the future. I said we could extend our senses with cyborg elements: electronic eyes, ears, etc. We could replace weak body parts one by one as we age until eventually pretty much everything except the brain has been replaced with indestructible parts. We could live forever!

Neil thought this would be a good thing and added that, if we removed the hormone systems, people would become more rational and less emotional. Wars could be avoided, and therefore human science and knowledge would accelerate. This all seemed like a good thing, until Sam opened fire. She said that emotion, or at least positive emotion, was a good thing, and that if we replaced our flesh and blood with electronics we would lose the essence of our humanity. I said I don't think the basis of humanity is emotions. No, says Sam, but they are essential.

I tried to keep things calm, praising both their arguments and saying this was interesting stuff (like I wasn't sweating seeing my friends beat each other up, mentally anyway) but Sam and Neil seem to be squaring off on opposite sides. This is crazy. We've got to get back to our common Alphan roots.

I feel terrible about this, and to make it worse, my throat is very sore now.

Thursday, December 2, 1976

I am really sick today, coughing and sneezing, eyes and nose watering, head totally stuffed up. I have a fever of 101. Forget school, I'm staying in bed all day. Mom phoned Uncle Tim and told him I'd be missing work tonight too. I feel bad about that. Those bottles don't stack themselves, and I need the money. I thought I might do some writing, but this is all I can manage. My head is buzzing with weird images and ideas. Here I lie, exhausted but restless, flopping about in damp, sweaty blankets. Ugh.

Friday, December 3, 1976

Felt a little better today, but stayed home from school again. Neil called from school at lunch and I assured him I was fine and would be back on Monday. I said make sure you and Sam come over on Sunday as usual! I spent the day in bed, mostly resting and reading. I was going to do some transcript work, but Mom heard the typewriter and said no way, get back to bed. In the evening I listened to some of my 1999 cassettes.

Saturday, Dec 4, 1976

Didn't go anywhere today. Still a little tired, but my throat and lungs feel better. I watched cartoons in the morning. A show called *The Tomorrow People* was on at 1. It is kind of a kid's show, but still it is SF and I liked some of its ideas.

1999 at 4 was "Space Warp". I taped it, and then spent the evening writing a summary. Now I think I am pretty much recovered from my cold.

Episode Summary: "Space Warp" (1310 words)
[Omitted.]

Comments on "Space Warp" (Roger Kay, 1994)

While Koenig and Tony fly an Eagle to investigate a derelict alien spaceship, the Moon passes through a space warp and disappears. Meanwhile on Alpha, Maya has a high fever and rampages through the base.

The derelict spaceship provides clues to the location of the space warp, but even if Koenig and Tony can decipher the alien technology and find the space warp, how will they catch up to the Moon?

Favorite scene: A delusional Maya thinks she must return to Psychon. She accesses an Eagle but before she can lift off, the launch pad is lowered. Senseless in her feverish state, Maya fires the rocket motors anyway and tries to fly an Eagle while inside the maintenance hangar where rows of Eagles are parked. Much destruction results. Safety tip: never try to fly an Eagle in a confined space.

Entries from Roger Kay's 1976 Diary

Sunday, December 5, 1976

Sam showed up around 1:15 and Neil shortly after. I played them my cassette of *Karmic Whiplash*, stopping to explain some of the scenes that lacked dialogue. Sam was impressed with it and we all seemed to be getting along fine. We then had a long discussion that I taped. We got off topic a little, but I think it turned out okay.

Roger: Okay we've seen the new episode "Space Warp".
Let's start with Sam. How would you rate it?

Sam: Well it was quite entertaining. Maya, going crazy,
running wild, turning into all sorts of animals and aliens, that's
fun, but it's a sub-plot. This episode didn't have a strong
enough central plot so it needed a subplot! Because of this, I'd
put this one in the middle, better than some, not as good as
others.

Roger: Neil?

Neil: I think I agree. Not bad, but not great. I'll take some
points away for the awkward space warp plot. The alien crew
figures out how to track the space warp, builds the required
device, but then the whole crew is killed in an accident and the
leader happens to leave behind instructions on how to use the
space warp locator just in case someone else comes along and
needs it? That's quite the set of lucky circumstances.

Of course the alien recordings are in English too. And Tony
and Koenig understanding the alien technology? No offense to
them, but it would make more sense if the aliens spoke an
unknown language, maybe one that Maya knows, and maybe
Maya is on the Eagle and she can decipher the alien
technology. She is more advanced than the Alphans so that
would make more sense. But of course we need her back on
Alpha for the subplot.

Roger: Well, aliens speaking English is a problem we see
in a lot of science fiction.

Sam: *Star Trek* has a universal translator, which somehow
works even with totally unknown types of aliens. Or you can
have telepathic aliens, so maybe they don't understand your
words but they see your mental pictures and understand your
intent.

Roger: I'm usually disappointed with how aliens are
portrayed. You'd think they'd be something really exotic and
hard to understand, but mostly they're humanoid and speak

English. They may have some strange clothes or habits, but really they don't seem to differ from humans that much. Is it possible that all intelligent life forms could be so similar?

Neil: Well if they're physically similar to humans, they probably *do* have the same issues and therefore a lot in common. Now if you're an alien based on an intelligent spider, for example, you'd have a lot less in common with humans than any humanoid alien would.

Roger: I like when aliens are more highly evolved than humans. When the writer tries to give us a glimpse into our own possible future. You know the stereotypical UFO alien, a skinny, hairless, big-headed creature who communicates with telepathy. Some people say this is where the human race is headed, what we will evolve into.

Neil: Right. I'm not a big believer in UFOs, I'm a skeptic, but that's a compelling idea. As our technology improves, we'll have less use for our primitive bodies. Our brains'll become bigger, and our muscles will dwindle away.

Eventually as we become more mental and less physical, we'll be able to control our emotions and behave logically. This'll help the further development of even more technology, and reinforce the cycle. Eventually we'll just be big brains floating in space, contemplating all of existence.

Sam: So, your idea of evolving to space brains... how could that be considered human?

Neil: We'd be just like humans. We'd appreciate fine music, film, literature...

Sam: But what would the space brain literature be about? Other brains, thinking thoughts and watching films about other brains thinking thoughts...?

Neil: Sure, it's hard to imagine it here and now. But how hard would it be for animals to understand how advanced beings like humans enjoy life's intellectual pleasures: good music, films, books. In the same way animals can't imagine us, we can't imagine what our next step will be.

Maybe it seems weird and scary to you, but what if you offered an animal the chance to be human? Would it take the opportunity? Would it understand the choice? Same thing for us and the space brains. We won't be able to *understand* them until we *are* them.

Sam: I don't know. It just seems to me that you're describing a beautiful building where nobody lives. A world without war, greed, hatred. These space brains will be logical, rational. Their biology won't allow for any human-style emotion. So, really, how are they human?

I mean, this future space brain civilization, what good is it? You're defining an architecture, building the buildings, but you don't know what kind of creature will live there. Maybe they don't need buildings. Why do they need anything at all? It's like the "Guardian Of Piri" all over again. If you don't need anything, if you don't have to struggle, then how exactly are you human?

Neil: Well, as I assume humans are one step above animals on the evolutionary scale, so I assume there must be a next step further up the ladder. I'm simply trying to figure out what it could look like. Animals can accuse us of losing our animal heritage, and although I don't think we've lost that much of our animal nature, if we did, would it be so bad?

Sam: Perhaps being an animal is what gives us our compassion and meaning. We are warm blooded mammals. We have to take care of our offspring. We make physical love. We live and die in a finite frame of time. If you take that, that animal nature, away, what do we have left?

What did Gwent do when his companion was no longer there? He killed himself. Itself. He lost the last fragment of animal inside himself and then realized there was nothing left. Just cold machinery.

Neil: Gwent was not a space brain. He was a humanoid consciousness built or copied into a machine. A space brain would evolve over time into the new physical form which it would be comfortable with and enjoy.

An animal might look at us and say, hey too bad you don't have any fur to keep you warm, but we can put on and take off different furs and clothing at will. Much better than just having fur grow on your hide.

In the same way a space brain will have methods or technology to give them the best of animal or human existence, but none of the problems when you are locked into *only* that existence.

Sam: So the space brain could create a body and occupy it like we wear clothing?

Neil: Maybe! Who knows? The point is that we can't see up the evolutionary ladder. We can only guess.

Sam: Well this shedding of the human body in favor of a pure mental existence, that just doesn't seem like an improvement to me. Why can't our technology evolve and our physical form stay pretty much the way it is?

Neil: If our species meets extinction in an atomic war, then our passions will have destroyed us and you'll have your answer. How long can we continue with more and more powerful technology but the same old bodies, where hormones and chemicals cause irresistible passions that force us to compete against and kill each other?

Roger: But is it just the chemicals and hormones that control us? Do we really need a whole new body just to manage our existence? There's been progress in the world. New ideas have come. We pushed aside rule by kings and priests. Now we value men and women as equal.

Sam: Oh yeah?

Roger: At least in theory. Women can vote. Black people can vote. Ideas can change people, or at least a society over time. Maybe we don't need to change our bodies. We just need to change our minds.

Neil: It's a nice idea, idealistic, but there're going to be limits to what most people can do. If 99% of people subscribe to advanced ideas, but 1% are backward, you can still get into a catastrophic situation. Something more fundamental than ideas needs to change to secure the future for the long term.

Sam: Secure it for what? So that unfeeling robots can live for thousands of years?

Neil: You can't fight this type of change. The Luddites tried to stop progress, but they didn't succeed.

Sam: It's not that same thing. I'm not anti-technology, but I am pro-body. There is something anti-body about your idea.

Neil: I prefer 'pro-mind'.

Sam: Yeah, but it reminds me of my parents. They're very anti-body and anti-sex. They talk about animal urges all the time as a bad thing, but they have six kids! It's hypocritical. They talk about a love of God, but it excludes love of humanity, bodies or minds.

It seems somehow similar to your view that we must escape these bodies. Why can't we learn to deal with them in a smart way? Most people are not violent, and sex should be part of love, not some horrible animal instinct.

Neil: Sex too often is just disguised violence, or greed. You know, the conquest and the trophy wife, or trophy husband. Not much to do with love.

It's the body that confuses us about love and sex. We focus on the sex and forget about love. We focus on our bodies, our appearance and such, and we forget about the brain.

I'm not saying sex is bad. I'm just saying that it's dangerous and prone to misuse. Like a nuclear weapon. It's good we have it, maybe, but if we go ahead and use it, there are consequences.

Sam: If you're talking about pregnancy, there's the pill.

Neil: That's one consequence. Sure. But there are others. Promiscuity, even the threat of it, leads to jealousy and violence. So maybe it's not so good.

Roger: Not everyone is jealous. That's a cultural thing. On a different planet, promiscuity might lead to more community feeling, rather than jealousy. Doesn't it make sense that love is better than war? Isn't this what the hippies taught us?

Sam: It depends on your sex apparently. A promiscuous man is a hero, but a female is a slut. Likewise a picture of two women kissing is sexy, but two men, that just makes people go crazy. Isn't it better that they're kissing than killing each other?

(long pause)

All I'm saying is that animal instincts have a reason and a value. We can't just jettison them. Sure they need to be controlled, but so does intellect. No one wants a mad super genius to experiment with turning the Sun on and off, you know. Not safe.

Neil: On Moonbase Alpha they have a rule: no more children. Why do you think that is?

Sam: They have limited resources. They can't sustain more people.

Neil: But they've lost people. There are vacancies. There must be a reason why they don't allow it. In Year One it was clear that there were to be no weddings, no children, until the Alphans found their new home. Only now, in Year Two, do we see Alphans marrying. No children yet, but it seems like it might be permitted.

Sam: So what are you saying? Why did they change?

Neil: The writers changed it for their own reasons. They wanted more romance. To me Year One made a lot more sense. If you are on a ship with limited resources and a long dangerous trip, you don't allow fraternization among the crew. It leads to jealousy, fights, lots of problems.

Roger: But this year Alpha is more of a home than a ship.

Neil: Right! Which is what I'm saying. That's not realistic, or not a good story. We need them to be driven to find a new home. They can't comfortably sail past interesting planets every week.

Sam: I think they just got to the point where they said, this is crazy, we can't wait until half of us are dead, let's start pairing up now and then when we get to a planet, we'll have a head start on a new society.

Roger: Maybe they don't have the technology to create and clean all the diapers that they'd need!

Sam: Or maybe they just couldn't enforce the policy, so they gave up on it…

Neil: It'll be interesting to see where it goes. We haven't seen little Jackie Crawford from "Alpha Child" for a long time, but he's still there somewhere.

Sam: Maybe they'll spin off a new series: Teenage Alphan!
(laughter)
Roger: Commander, can I borrow the Eagle tonight?
Neil: Not until you've cleaned up the Hydroponics Section, junior!
(laughter)
Roger: Oh oh. Looks like it's about done.

Entries from Roger Kay's 1976 Diary

Tuesday, December 7, 1976

ORA this morning, really boring stuff they force us to read. There is nothing as dry as Canadian history. No matter how fast you read it, the yawning catches up with you. Lunch however was a real eye-opener. Sam is in big trouble with her parents. Seems they found out a few things, like her best friends are actually male. Also she apparently forged their signature on her class choices form at the start of the year: her parents thought she was taking Christian Ethics, but she signed herself up for Economics instead. Last night, our status quo loving principal phoned her parents for some reason, maybe the paper she wrote for our ETV project, and they soon uncovered the discrepancies in her class and friend choices. It is too late to switch classes for her, so she might escape Christian Ethics yet, and I thought there was nothing they could do about her friendships, but I didn't get to think that for too long.

After lunch, it comes on the loudspeaker: "Roger Kay and Lionel O'Neill, report to the principal's office!" Mr. Whyte was looking very stern. I didn't think friendship could be a crime, but it seems it is. He said that Sam's family has a right to raise their daughter according to their own values, and they feel it is inappropriate for Neil and I to be around her so much. She needs female friends. What sexist garbage, but we couldn't say anything. We are not as brave as Sam. Maybe I'll write a letter to the newspaper.

I didn't see Sam after school, or Neil. I didn't have the courage to go to the shed. If only Jerry is there, I'd hate to bug him with his friends, so I just stayed home. When I phoned, Neil's mom said he's out somewhere and will probably be back later. Not very helpful. What's going on? I feel like my life is falling apart.

Wednesday, December 8, 1976

Neil caught me in the hallway after English and said meet me at the southwest entrance for lunch. When I did, he and Sam were already there, eating away. This is our new hideaway. The entrance leads to the formal foyer for the auditorium (gymnasium). It was just last year I used to hide in the half height chair storage area off that foyer to eat my lunch, but now I've returned, not to that dark, cramped space, but to the bright entrance area. Really it is an airlock, but it is not terribly cold because the outer door never opens. No one uses the entrance during the day. Students are not allowed and adults would enter through the main entrance by the principal's office, so the airlock remains warm, sunny, and the floor is dry and clean, quite nice to sit on. We had a relaxing lunch with any arguments between us forgotten. Sam might not come over this Sunday, but she says it won't be long before she'll make up a new story and be able to sneak out again.

Work tonight was a breeze, literally. The cold air gets into the building and I got very chilled, especially my hands. Tomorrow I'm bringing my mitts to work. On the bright side, if people like their Pic-A-Pop cold, now is the time to come see us!

Saturday, Dec 11, 1976

When I got up, it was snowing again. Everything in the backyard is now buried in Winter's smothering weapon. Can't believe 1999 wasn't on today. That is not an early Christmas present. Neil read the TV listings too and called me around 10 to see if I knew. Yup. No joy today. We agreed to go downtown instead to look for some new, thin gloves Neil can use in the shed for drawing. We went to the Met, then to Woolworth's, where he did find a pair. Then we went upstairs to their lunch counter. I had a Pepsi and Neil had a burger with fries and a root beer. Neil says Jerry is working at The Stereo Hut on Betts now. They just did a big inventory, getting ready for Xmas, and Neil helped out too, so that's why he's got a few bucks today.

Around 2:30 we went to the library. No new LPs today. They say they'll have some new stuff, including rock, in the new year. Neil stayed there, reading, and I went home. I'm starting to think about a new chapter for Asteroid Beta. I haven't done anything for a while. This time I want the Betans to discover a very alien planet, maybe one populated with space brains.

Sunday, December 12, 1976

Quiet day. Did some writing for Asteroid Beta. Snowed all day. Windy and cold too. I shoveled the walk in the afternoon but otherwise stayed in. Neil called me (no misprint you read it here) at 7. He wanted me to come over. I did and we listened to some records in the shed. They have an electric heater in there, so it is not so bad, but still you have to wear your coat. Neil said Jerry was supposed to be back anytime, but he never showed up by the time I left, around 9:30.

I had a bath then watched some lowbrow TV.

Monday, December 13, 1976

So dark and cold in the morning now. Hard to get up. On the way to school, Brian and some of his friends were ahead of me but they were too busy bumper shining to harass me. Perfect. Bumper shining sounds like about as much fun as windshield bugging and they should enjoy themselves. Each time Brian would run to grab a car's bumper, his lackeys would cheer and hoot. The ground is very icy, but not completely. So I knew it was coming: the coup de bumper shine. Brian grabbed the metal rump of this chocolate brown Chrysler Imperial, a huge car, but as he was being pulled along his boots must have caught a dry patch because his head suddenly pitched forward, smashing into the bumper. The car kept going, probably not realizing anything happened. Brian had lost his grip and was left on the road, his nose bloody. He packed some cold snow against it and it did stop bleeding by the time he got to school, but he looked like a bloodied zombie. Mrs. Wilson saw him and dragged him away to get cleaned up. Guess we don't want people to look like bloody axe murderers, even if they might be in their heart!

Neil was worried at lunch because Jerry didn't come home last night. I said don't worry, he's probably at a party or met a girl. No, says Neil, he's not like that, I always know where he is. I think Jerry is a free spirit.

Sam was asking us what we wanted for Xmas! I've never really bought gifts for anyone but my folks, but I'm willing. I'm still working three nights a week so my cash flow is good. If I could buy something to make Sam understand how I feel about her, I'd do it.

The whole school is a slop fest. A million snowy boots have deposited an archeologist's delight of layers of soil and debris onto the floors. After eating lunch on the floor we were all quite dusty. No hassles from the Man though, our continuing co-ed friendship is flying under the radar of the principal and his spies.

Work was busy. Strange for a Monday, but Xmas is coming and people are stocking up on their pop I guess.

Tuesday, December 14, 1976

Jerry is missing. Neil's mom called the police yesterday, but was told she'd have to wait until tonight to file a report. You have to be missing 48 hours apparently. Neil is taking it very hard. At lunch he was almost in tears. Sam and I feel terrible about this. I really hope something bad didn't happened to Jerry. Neil phoned Stu last night, but he hadn't seen Jerry either. I really hope he's just shacked up with a girl somewhere in town, and not dead, frozen in a snow bank somewhere.

I tried to write some, but couldn't. Too tense, too distracted. I phoned Neil around 8:30 but there was no answer. They are probably down at the police station.

Wednesday, December 15, 1976

Still no Jerry. What the hell is going on? After lunch I got called to the principal's office. A policeman named Detective Hooper was there and he asked me when I had last seen Jerry. Not for a couple weeks I'd guess. Since the day after *Karmic Whiplash*? I had heard Jerry was working at The Stereo Hut though. And we were waiting for him in the shed on Sunday night but he never showed up.

Hooper also quizzed me carefully about when I had hung with Neil. I said I could provide better answers if I could consult my diary and he said he'd like to see my diary! My big mouth. I promised to bring it down to the station tonight. It'll remain strictly confidential he assured me. Yeah right, trust The System.

I took my diary to work and then right after I was done, I went to the Post Office building, where the RCMP *[Editor's note: Royal Canadian Mounted Police]* are. Hooper made a copy of several pages from my diary (Dec 11-13). He then read them carefully and asked me how snow could be considered a weapon, and why I thought Brian was an axe murderer. I tried to explain why I said those things, but I don't think he really understood. I asked him to black out, on his copy, the line where I admit how I feel about Sam. He used a big marker to do so, but he also made notes at the same time, so I think it is still in his notes. Not cool.

I left the police station around 10:00 pm and walked to the shed. Neil was in there, with Solo, the guy from the pool hall. They were smoking up a storm. Neil filled me in on what had happened after they filed the report yesterday: the police had questioned everyone in his family, including him, plus Jerry's friends Stu and Steve, plus some people at The Stereo Hut.

When I came home I said, don't worry I'm not smoking, it's just the shed and Neil's nervous chain smoking. My clothes smelled strongly of tobacco but I had not a single puff. My folks declined to argue. Now it is after 11:00 and I am exhausted. Good night!

Thursday, December 16, 1976

Neil was not in school today. Sam and I had lunch in the southwest entrance, just the two of us, but it was not a happy occasion. Her parents are still angry that she forged their signature, despite the fact that this is something her brothers have been doing for years. I guess they're not used to a girl doing it. We talked about Neil's family. I didn't give any secrets away, but I did tell her that from my interview with Jerry, I knew he was a very interesting and intelligent guy. Just because someone doesn't have a job, that doesn't make them stupid. Sometimes true genius has to lie fallow for a period before it can begin to flower. This is how Neil feels about Jerry. He has told me he is convinced his brother is a genius and will write a great book or create something extraordinary someday. I hope it's still true.

After lunch as I was getting my books together for Social Studies, Brian snatched my lock and then locked it, upside down, onto Sandra's locker. As I tried to spin the dial on the upside down lock, not as easy as it sounds, Sandra came along and I had to explain how my lock got on her locker. She was not impressed. I didn't really care. The whole thing is just silly compared to the real troubles going around.

Work was crazy tonight. The place is as full as I've ever seen it. Not enough room to maneuver around all those extra pallets, so I was using the pallet mover to stack up the empty ones. I didn't see Uncle Tim come into the back but when he saw what I was doing, he came over and demanded I move the empty pallets by hand! I said why waste all that effort when we have a machine to do it? He got mad and yelled in my face: just put on your work gloves and do what I say! Also he said: why do you always think you know best? I didn't answer him but I thought: when you're surrounded by idiots, you likely do know best. Adults don't like it when you think for yourself and find a shortcut they didn't.

It is a long dark cold crunch through the snow to walk home. The wind picked up and it is feeling much colder than the advertised 10 below. I hope Neil is doing okay. I had a bath, wrote this, and went to bed.

Friday, December 17, 1976

Today was the last day of actual classes. Next week, exams start. Most of the day the teachers spent reviewing what areas would be on each test. A probably worthwhile but definitely boring exercise. The exception was in Math class where Mr. Peebles decided he'd have some fun and show us how calculus works: derivatives and integrals. Integrals are apparently a way to measure the cumulative value of a function by measuring the area under the graph, while derivatives are the slope (amount of upward angle as a ratio) of the graph at a certain point that shows how much the function is accelerating or decelerating. It sounded fascinating, but he lost the class in about five minutes. I will definitely take calculus in university.

Neil was back today and we had lunch with Sam. He snuck out after we ate and had a cigarette just outside our lunch spot. We waited and opened the door to let him back in. His smoking is getting worse. I asked both Neil and Sam if they wanted to come over tonight, but Sam can't, no surprise, because her folks are still watching too closely, and Neil can't because he is going to The Stereo Hut to help out.

I thought it was going to be a boring night but then I got a call from Uncle Tim. He said I could work a couple hours if I wanted, so I did. I moved a million empty cases right next to the loading dock.

Got home around 9:20. I noticed the little ridges on my favorite black corduroy pants have become totally worn down above the knees. Something must be rubbing while I work. I showed them to Mom and she said to add a new pair to my Xmas list. Then she fixed me with a deep gaze and asked me if I smoked. No I sure don't, I protested. Well, she said, Neil has a rough life, but he is an intelligent boy so as long as you promise you won't smoke, you can keep on being his friend. But this stink has to stop. She showed me how to operate the washer and dryer, and where she keeps the detergent and the freshener. If you come home stinking of cigarette smoke, you have to change your clothes, and if you have a lot of dirty clothes because of this, then you have to take responsibility and wash them yourself. No problem I said. I go to school, work part-time, am in the middle of writing my first novel plus preparing submissions for the *Association of Alphans Newsletter*, and now my best friend's brother has disappeared. Extra chores? Why not.

Saturday, December 18, 1976

A little warmer today. Still a trudge getting through all the snow, but less wind means less unpleasant. I went downtown looking for Xmas presents for my friends. Went into a couple of stores but didn't see anything. Decided I would buy them both a record so I went to Sam The Record Man. I didn't go to

The Stereo Hut because Neil might be there and I didn't want him finding out about the gift.

Also, Rudy is my 'record man' and helpfully pointed out a lot of cool new stuff. I had it down to either Black Sabbath *Technical Ecstasy* or Blue Oyster Cult *Agent Of Fortune* for Neil, and either David Bowie *Station To Station*, or Queen *A Day At The Races* for Sam. Finally decided on Black Sabbath for Neil and Queen for Sam. The two LPs were almost $16 together, but I think they are impressive gifts.

I snuck my purchases home before heading to the public library. Neil was there, reading, sitting in a chair far back in the adult section, a stack of books beside him. Most of the books were about missing persons, not surprising. As soon as he saw me he said: "Agatha Christie disappeared for eleven days in the 1920s after suffering a case of temporary amnesia".

Tomorrow is one week that Jerry's been gone. It hurts to think about. Neil and I walked to the Yorkton Hotel. We each had a plate of fries and gravy. He told me he's working at The Stereo Hut again tonight. The manager there has basically given him Jerry's job.

I said: Shades of *Karmic Whiplash*!

But Neil took it wrong and said: I didn't kill my brother!

Ouch. No, of course not, I told him. Jerry is still alive. My stupid mouth.

Came home feeling depressed and just moped around. No 1999 today, again. Wrapped the two LPs. Did some studying. Not really into it.

Sunday, December 19, 1976

I wasn't really expecting anyone today, so I was very pleasantly surprised to see Sam at 1:30. I presented my wrapped gift for her, and she had a gift for me too; it is a long, cylindrical package, possibly a poster. I put it under the tree. We both have a gift for Neil, so I called over there. No answer, no surprise, so we walked over.

Neil was sitting in the shed, smoking, and working on some drawings. He is going to create the complete set of Moonbase Alpha blueprints using the information in the MATN as a starting point. He also showed us some rough drafts of other drawings he already submitted to the Association of Alphans: a blueprint of the alien ship from "Earthbound"; an anatomical drawing of those aliens, the Caldorians; a detailed drawing of the life detector device that Prof. Bergman used in "Guardian of Piri"; plus a blueprint of the standard double living quarters on Alpha. Very interesting stuff. We presented him our gifts and he was quite excited. He opened them right away. Sam got him a 1999 poster, with Alpha on the bottom and an approaching Eagle above. Very nice.

I was going to hang around some more, but finals start tomorrow and my folks expect me to study all today, so I reluctantly left them there and went home. For tomorrow, I felt okay about Science, but my French did need some work.

Monday, December 20, 1976

Slept in a bit. First exam wasn't until 9:30. It was French and it wasn't easy. I'm just not that interested in learning another language, sorry Quebecers. I think I passed, but I don't think I aced it by any means. It took me a long time to write the exam. Left the school around 10:45, only fifteen minutes from the end of the test. Came back at 1:00 for the Science test. It was much easier. I reviewed my answers and still managed to leave at 2:00, a half hour early. Brian gave me a dirty look as I left. Too bad. Now who's the weakling, you mental midget!

Spent the rest of the afternoon studying for tomorrow's tests. Algebra should be no problem, but there is lots of stuff to memorize for Health.

Work is still very busy. We are moving a lot of product, literally in my case. Ooh. Bad pun.

Tuesday, December 21, 1976

First exam was Health. It was multiple choice, so not as bad as I feared. Why don't they tell us in advance about these things? I could have studied a lot less. Algebra in the afternoon was a breeze. I left just before 2:00, and was the first to hand in my paper.

Dropped over to Neil's shed after supper and he was there. Solo was there too. They was listening to the new Sabbath record I gave him. I'm glad he likes it. I asked Neil how his finals were coming and he didn't really answer me. He's got a lot more on his mind than school these days. I left at 8 to do more studying.

Wednesday, December 22, 1976

Today's first exam was English. There were plenty of short answer, quite a few long answer, and one essay question. I had a lot to say for most of the answers so I wrote a lot. By the time I finished my hand was sore and it was 10:55. I used the whole 90 minutes! Afternoon was the Economics test. It was all multiple choice and I blazed through it. I was the first one out at 1:50. Now my last problem is Social Studies tomorrow. There is a lot to memorize there but Mr. Peebles has already said it will be mostly multiple guess.

Work was crazy again. It's like everyone in Yorkton suddenly decided that Pic-A-Pop is the only thing you can drink on holidays. Haven't you people ever heard of eggnog?

Thursday, December 23, 1976

The final day of finals! Social Studies in the morning, and sure enough it was all multiple choice. That's a relief. I did really well and was out of there by 10:15. Bumped into Sam on the way out of the school and walked her home, or at least to the corner of Darlington and 2nd, which is the closest either Neil or I ever get to her house.

The TV schedule in the paper showed no 1999 again this Saturday but I suggested we three try to get together on Monday, instead of Sunday. I promised to pass the word on to Neil, and Sam agreed she'd be here at 1:30.

After lunch I had the Music final. Not too tough! I was done by 2:00 and gone.

Sat around the house after that, smelling the tree and sipping eggnog with cinnamon. I phoned Neil's. His mom answered and, shock upon shock, actually put him on the phone. He must have been inside the house for once. He says he is doing okay, but I can tell by his voice there is a lot of pain under his calm. He agreed to come over Monday afternoon.

Last work shift before Xmas! All went smooth.

Friday, December 24, 1976

Did my final gift wrapping in the morning: a bottle of wine for Dad and the Catherine MacKinnon LP *Everybody's Talking* for my Mom. It is the only one she does not have.

I phoned Neil in the afternoon. He says he is hanging on, he's fine. Not sure if I believe that. What kind of holiday can he have with his father away and his brother missing? Mom was busy making cookies today and the house smelled terrific. We have to go to church tonight so I'll just end this entry here.

Saturday, December 25, 1976

Woke up early, of course, and we got at the tree just before noon, after a sumptuous brunch. I got some very cool stuff (see attached list) but the coolest are my new stereo and the Mark IX Hawk model. My new stereo is a Lloyds and it has a turntable, AM/FM radio, plus two tape decks so you can copy from one tape to another with very high quality! You can also record directly from the turntable or the radio to tape. There are two big bookshelf speakers and it sounds really terrific! The Hawk model is incredible. I've only seen pictures of this thing so I won't be waiting long to assemble it.

My gift from Sam was, as I suspected, a 1999 poster, similar to the one she gave Neil but not quite identical. I have an Alpha landscape with two giant Koenig and Russell heads floating above it. There are some small pictures around the top and bottom border. Very cool. I will find a place of honor on my wall for it.

At 7, we had a huge meal with turkey and all the trimmings. Grandma and Karen were here too. After supper we hung in the living room listening to Xmas records, folk music, and Mom's new LP too. I ate a lot of cookies and little cakes.

I phoned Neil's around 9 but no answer. I hope he's doing okay.

Sunday, December 26, 1976

Had to go to church this morning. For every reaction there is an equal and opposite reaction, or, what comes around goes around. Surely I didn't think all this Christian largesse would come without a price tag? Oh well. It was worth it. I might not believe in the Christian God but I am no enemy of the small 'c' Christian philosophy, despite the arguments of Ayn Rand.

I put my new stereo speakers high up on my model shelf and they sound phenomenal. Now I can listen to high fidelity music while I type in my room. So long decrepit basement record player!

Uncle Tim and Aunt Rose came for supper. I thanked them in person for their gift: a double album of Beatles music. That's one less thank you note to write. The closest thing to SF on it is a song called "Across The Universe". Overall, it's okay but kind of mellow. They look more hard rock on the cover than they sound.

I got a call from Sam! She was using the extension in her parents' bedroom. Very sneaky! She likes the Queen album I got her, I'm very glad to report, and I thanked her for the poster. I told her I haven't heard from Neil since Friday. She will be coming over tomorrow she promised. I'm spending the rest of the evening listening to my new Beatle double LP and working on some <u>Asteroid Beta</u>.

Later. It's almost 11:00 now. Neil just called. He and his mom just got back from the morgue. Jerry's body was found near JayCee Beach yesterday. I can't believe it. I told him how sorry I was, and he said: I had to call and tell you but I'll talk to you tomorrow. Then he hung up. My folks are shocked. I feel terrible.

Monday, December 27, 1976

Sam and Neil did come over this afternoon. I hid my recorder under my bed and taped our whole conversation. Not sure why I did that. It just feels like there is too much changing right now and I need to grab it so I can slow things down and understand what is going on. Or maybe Jerry being gone means I now see the unique value of my recordings of him, so now I want to have more recordings of my friends too. Also I'm not sure when I'll be able to tell Neil about the second Jerry recording. How will he view my secretive actions? I don't want to risk our friendship.

I outsmarted myself today though, because I wound up with two tapes of our conversation. The first tape they were not aware of, and the second tape, they requested!

27 December 1976
(audio tape from collection of Roger Kay)

Roger: *(yelling)* Okay! I'll get it!
(two minute pause)
... since last night. It's just unbelievable. He was such a cool guy. I dunno why anyone would want to hurt him. And at Christmas time too.

Sam: Poor Neil. I'm not sure if we should probe the subject or simply give him our sympathy and leave it at that. Let him say as much or as little as he needs to.

Roger: He might prefer we just do our regular session. I doubt he'll want to hear any outlandish speculation, I mean, about Jerry.

Sam: Right. *(pause)* So what's going on here?

Roger: Working on my new Hawk model.

Sam: You got a lot of paint.

Roger: I've been buying them, a few at a time, ever since summer. Now it's quite a few. Some of this isn't quite dry yet. That smell is varsol. I use it to clean my brushes. The window is open a bit because if you smell too much varsol you'll see pink elephants.

Sam: *(laughs)* Oh!

Roger: How do you like my new poster?

Sam: Hey it looks good up there! This is your new stereo? Far out! Looks great! I'd love to hear some Queen on it!

Roger: Anytime. Come on down! *[Editor's note: the previous intoned in the manner of Bob Barker welcoming a new contestant on The Price Is Right.]* I like Queen too.

Sam: My problem is I can't listen to rock when my folks are around. They don't like me having rock records either. James, my oldest brother, he's pretty cool. He lets me keep my records in with his collection. I've got *A Night At The Opera*, that's the previous one. It's incredibly diverse. Not like most groups that sound the same all the way through.

Roger: Right, with the new hit single, "Tie Your Mother Down"?

Sam: Yeah!

Roger: That's a rocker! Very different than "Bohemian Rhapsody", that opera song.

Sam: They have an incredible range because they're all brilliant composers. The final song on the new album, they sing in Japanese.

Roger: Whoa, really?

Sam: Yeah! Their lead singer, Freddie Mercury, is *so* handsome and smart. He's almost as cool as David Bowie.

Roger: Their lives must be incredibly exciting. And here we are stuck in Nowhere, Saskatchewan.

Sam: We'll get out of here. Just don't lose your dream. Keep writing.

Roger: I think I'd like to live in New York. That's where the action is. Imagine all the things that would happen there every single day.

Sam: We'll drop this town like a rotten-

(sound of doorbell)

Roger: -that's gotta be Neil. Hang on, I'll bring him up.

(sound of footfalls descending stairs; some paper rustling nearby, then muffled voice of Roger as he and Neil ascend the stairs)

Roger: …upstairs in my bedroom today. You gotta see my new stereo.

Neil: Hey man, thanks again for the Sabbath record. You're a good friend. Hi Sam!

Sam: Hi Neil! I'm so sorry…

(fifteen second pause)

Neil: I think I'm in some kind of shock, like I'm watching a movie, you know, this is not happening to me. I saw Earl this morning.

Roger: Your father.

Neil: My Mom's parents are Jewish and they're doing this Shiva thing. It's like a wake, but it lasts seven days. Today they can't cook. Other people are supposed to bring food over. I wonder if anyone will show up. Earl's an asshole but Mom's parents are just as bad, and they don't mix well. Technically,

Shiva is only for the deceased's closest generations, that means his parents and any kids. It is not supposed to include the grandparents, but they like to steal the show. Very self-centered, like Earl. Maybe that's why they don't get along. They are more alike than they admit. Now they're trying to completely take over.

This Shiva thing shouldn't even be starting yet - Jerry isn't even buried. I didn't want to go this morning, but we did. Maybe Mom thought her family might actually comfort her but that was way off. They treated her like a dog. I said: let's go. But the thing is, you're not supposed to leave! Mom's still there but I walked out.

Sam: Did you get in a fight? Is that how your shirt got ripped?

Neil: No. This is a sign of mourning. My stupid grandpa did it. Like I'm not mourning enough and I need him to rip my good shirt to prove my love for Jerry. I'm not a stupid Jew or a bloody Christian. I'm an atheist. This religious stuff is not helping.

Roger: What about the funeral?

Neil: Earl is planning it for Wednesday. It'll be in a Catholic church which should really piss off Mom's side of the family.

Sam: Do they know what happened...?

Neil: No, not yet. They're doing a full autopsy. That's why the funeral is delayed. It doesn't make much sense. There's no reason for him to be at JayCee Beach at all. The whole place is frozen up. There's nothing going on. I think he must've been murdered and then dumped there.

Sam: Does Jerry have any enemies?

Neil: No. I don't know. (long pause) The police are at my house right now.

Roger: What?

Neil: Yeah, they're searching the whole place. When I got back from my Mom's folks place, the cops were waiting outside. Now they're swarming all over and they have a search warrant so they can take whatever they want.

Roger: Well I hope the truth comes out.

(long pause)

Sam: Well maybe we should have our regular1999 discussion. You want to tape us again Roger?

Roger: Oh, uh. I don't know. We don't have to tape it.

Sam: Really? Why not? Last time when you played it back for me, it was hilarious. I didn't know I sounded like that.

Roger: I could record it with my new stereo. See, the microphone plugs in here. Also I can record from tape to tape, so I can make excellent copies of any tape you have. You know, Neil, we could make a couple of good copies of *Potatoland*.

Sam: *Potatoland*?

Neil: It's a very rare tape from England, a radio broadcast of a banned concept album.

Roger: Sort of like George Orwell's <u>1984</u>. It is a warning to society about the system and how it eats us up like so many french fries.

Sam: Cool! You could make me a copy of it too, if I had a blank cassette, right?

Roger: Sure. I'd do that. If you want. So, we can tape our conversation. I got a blank right here. There. Easy as that. And we're rolling...

Sam: Welcome to the 100th International Festival of Why *Space: 1999* Is Better Than *Star Trek*.

Roger: *(laughs)* So no new episodes for the last three weeks which has been pure torture. We know there's more episodes, the matten *[Editor's note: MATN]* and Starlog both agree on that.

Sam: Yeah. I have a question or topic. From reading *Starlog* it seems that the force behind *Space: 1999* is Gerry Anderson. For Year Two they also talk about Fred Freiberger, but no one talks about Sylvia Anderson.

Roger: Who's she?

Sam: See? She was the producer of Year One. Gerry was the executive producer, and her husband. Now in Year Two there's no mention of her *anywhere*. I bet there's an interesting story behind her disappearance.

Neil: She disappeared?

Sam: Disappeared from the series. Gerry Anderson is taking all the credit this year. Maybe rather than us worrying about what the addition of Fred Freiberger will do to the series, we should be worrying about what the subtraction of Sylvia Anderson has already done to Year Two!

Roger: Did they get divorced? Maybe she got the house and he got the moonbase?

Sam: (laughs) Could be. Have you guys seen the book The Making of Space: 1999? My brother James got it for me.

Roger: No. No way.

Sam: It's really cool. This thick, with a bunch of photos in the middle. It's also got an episode guide and loads of info about the people who work on the series. But no mention of Sylvia.

They gave her the proper credit for Year One, which I suppose they had to, but otherwise they don't mention her at all in the book. As usual, the woman gets screwed out of the credit.

And have you noticed a decline in the standards for female behavior in Year Two? While the women might be more human, they're also more stereotypical. I liked the cold, icy, professional head of Medical Center that was Dr. Helena Russell in Year One. In Year Two, sometimes it seems like she's just Koenig's girlfriend.

Roger: Well we do have Maya. She's smarter and stronger than anyone else on Alpha. That's a definite increase of female main characters for the second season.

Sam: Not really. What about Sandra Benes? She's no longer getting much screen time. She's even missing for whole episodes. Sorry Neil. And Tanya Alexander? She's completely gone.

Roger: Yeah I noticed Sandra's absence. They didn't give any reason for it. I don't know why they don't just say, oh

Sandra is nursing a broken leg this week, like they did with Paul in that one episode last year.

Sam: Do they think we won't notice she's missing because she's female??

Roger: They didn't say anything when Bergman went missing. And Bergman was a very important, very central character.

Neil: Bergman's not missing. He's dead. His spacesuit leaked.

Roger: Yeah, so says the matten.

Sam: Maybe they should create a movie of what happened between Year One and Year Two. Then they could kill off Bergman, Morrow, Kano, and Tanya in a really dramatic way. You should be working on the script for that one!

Roger: *(exhales noisily)* Well. That's something to think about.

(ten second silence)

Neil: I gotta take off. I should see if Mom or Earl came back.

Roger: No problem man, we totally understand.

Entries from Roger Kay's 1976 Diary

Tuesday, December 28, 1976

This afternoon I was over at Neil's shed. It was thick with smoke in there, even though he didn't have one while I was there. He was working on some drawings and just sat on his stool, facing away from me, the whole time. He was saying something about Gary (?!) Anderson, that he was deliberately messing up *Space: 1999*, that his decision to kill off Bergman would destroy the series. I was confused until I realized he meant Gerry Anderson, not Gary. I know it starts with 'G' but it is definitely not 'Gary'. He doesn't seem able to say 'Gerry'. (Because it sounds like Jerry?) I didn't question him on it.

Before I left he gave me the *Potatoland* cassette. At that point he turned to face me and looking very intense said: Don't let this tape fall into the wrong hands, protect it with your life. Okay, no problem. I promised to make three copies. One for me, one for Sam, and an a third to put in safe keeping. It took most of the afternoon to make the three copies, but I got it all done.

When I went back this evening, I felt compelled for some reason to bring my tape recorder hidden in my backpack along again. I didn't realize the gold or the guilt I would get for doing so. I now have Neil admitting on tape that he is not interested in Sam. The smoking gun that I can never use.

28 December 1976
(audio tape from collection of Roger Kay)

Roger: That should be safe there.

Neil: Thanks for doing these tapes. The more copies there are, the better. You know, I can't help but think maybe the government had something to do with this. There isn't anyone I know who is more aware of the power of the system and the status quo than Jerry, and if they can pick off rock stars and politicians, Jerry'd be a walk in the park.

Roger: But why him? What harm could he really do?

Neil: You forget. These tapes don't exist anywhere in North America, except for these copies. And although there's a new president in the States, he won't be sworn in until next year, so in the meantime the old president will be trying to clean up any loose ends. President Ford was Nixon's buddy. He pardoned Nixon's crimes! So we know how corrupt he is. Maybe this new guy, President Carter's not part of the problem. Unlikely, but we'll see.

Roger: How's your Mom doing?

(ten second pause)

Neil: She's okay. She's inside and Marilyn is still here too, but she's going back to Canora tomorrow.

Roger: Are you going in there to talk to them? You probably need some family about now...?

Neil: What the fuck man, like I'm going in there and let them blame everything on me? No way!

Roger: Sorry.

Neil: No, well, it's not your fault. The world is fucked, that's all.

Roger: It's not your fault either. I don't see how they can blame anything on you.

Neil: I'm through taking chances on people. There are certain people in this world you can trust, and a whole lot that you can't and shouldn't. For example, I'm sick of being a slave to my Mom. She sits around drinking and expects me to go buy all the groceries, buy her cigarettes, and clean everything myself.

As soon as I can I'm out of here. Like Nancy, my oldest sister, I'm going to university and I'm never coming back.

Roger: Well you can count on our friendship. I love you like the brother I never had, and Sam loves you too. Although I think her love might not be very sisterly.

Neil: Are you in love with Sam?

(long pause)

Roger: She's my best friend, I mean you're both my best friends. But I think she has a crush on you.

Neil: Well I'm not looking for a girlfriend right now. Life is too complicated and I don't need people taking ownership of me and trying to change me. Jerry told me all about girlfriends. If you like her, you can have her. I'm not interested.

Roger: I don't… we're just friends.

Neil: Well that's good enough for now then. Look, I gotta go downtown to see someone. Sorry for kicking you out.

Roger: No, not a problem. I'll just grab my stuff.

Entries from Roger Kay's 1976 Diary

Wednesday, December 29, 1976

Today was Jerry's funeral. I got up around 9 and moped around a bit until it was time to put on my suit. The funeral was at 11:00 at St. Gerard's. I walked over at 10:30 to meet Sam. We hung in the lobby for a few minutes, just absorbing the alien atmosphere of the Catholic church. Then we went inside. There were a few teachers there, but it was a small crowd. The service was not very long. The priest was the only one who spoke, and it was clear that he didn't know Jerry well. Neil sat in the front row with his family. His father, or Earl as he calls him, sat by the aisle, then Neil, then his mom, then one other woman, who I later found out was Marilyn, one of Neil's sisters. Some really old people sat behind them, probably grandparents.

After the service Mr. Voerstadt saw Sam and I and asked us if we needed a ride to the cemetery. It is way too cold to walk across town so we said sure. Also, it had just started to snow.

As they lowered the coffin into the ground I could see Neil's face was stony and darker than usual. His mom looked sad, but kind of unfocussed. Marilyn was crying. Sam started to cry too, but just quietly. I put my arm around her and she didn't resist. I felt like a cad as delicious tingles ran through my whole body. I think I really am in love with her.

Mr. Voerstadt dropped us off at my house and Sam came in for a hot chocolate. I think she wasn't ready to go home and face her parents. She had to lie and sneak out to get to the funeral. How sad is that? I invited her to come over New Year's Eve and she said she might!

10 pm. I came back from work and had a bath. Uncle Tim said I could work all day Thursday, and then Friday afternoon too if I wanted. Why not? Now I'll probably stay up and watch a movie if there's anything decent.

Friday, December 31, 1976

I worked yesterday, a full day, so I'm sorry for not writing, my Dear Diary. Today I only worked until 4 so afterward I went to The Stereo Hut and bought the new Blue Oyster Cult record *Agents Of Fortune*. It was playing in the store and irresistible, on sale at $6.67, marked down from $7.29. I really like that song: 'Extra Terrestrial Intelligence'. "The saucer!!"

After supper I found Neil in his shed. Solo was there too, but he left in a few minutes. Then Stu, Jerry's best friend, came in. He said he's taking Neil to a party tonight, to cheer him up. That seems odd. Maybe Stu is the one who needs cheering up. That is all well and good but if Neil is taking the place of Jerry for Stu, who'll take the place of Neil for me? I think I need my friend more than Stu does, but what do I know, I'm just a kid. Argh.

Just as I got home, Sam called. She can't come over either. Her parental vigilance is unyielding today. Bummer.

My folks have decided I am now old enough to trust with the house for an evening. This means no babysitter tonight, and I remain here all alone while they party.

Later. I've made progress with Chapter 4 of my Asteroid Beta novel. The Betans encounter a planet that appears Earth-like but unoccupied by intelligent life. When they land they discover that some of the clouds are actually intelligent beings, Neil's space brains, essentially. These cloud aliens are telepathic and can read emotional humans easiest. When the brains realize the Earthlings are carnivores, and some of them harbor very unpleasant inner lives, they not only don't want the Betans to settle on their planet, but because of the ugliness of human nature, decide to destroy them.

We're out of chocolate ice cream.

Now I've written the ending: One space brain falls in love with a beautiful, kindly female Betan. Of course their love must remain unrequited. However the love-stricken space brain does convince the rest of its kind that the humans should not be destroyed. Each human is unique, it has learned, and at least a few deserve to live. So although the Betans cannot settle on space brain planet, they are allowed to leave to continue their journey. Tout fini!

It is now 12:05. Happy New Year! Tomorrow I begin my nifty new black leather-bound diary.

Entries from Roger Kay's 1977 Diary

Saturday, January 1, 1977

My dear, newest Diary,

I understand the importance of words. Words are the most important thing in the song, probably the most important thing we have. We create them, and we store knowledge with them. I want to use them. Maybe people will recognize me in themselves when they read these words, an extension of my personality. If you collected all the words I ever wrote, would that equal my personality, my soul? I suppose you could just as well argue dance is a language and you could capture every motion, every change of position of the body throughout your life, and say that equals the personality. You is just a word too. So is I.

Today *Space: 1999* was cancelled due to the Rose Bowl, an inauspicious beginning for this supposedly brightest of years, lucky double sevens.

It is a snowy frigid day, and I have no desire to go outside. Everything is whiteness. So a big cold empty day to start another year of my big cold empty life.

I phoned Neil's but his mom said he wasn't around. She promised he'd phone me when he gets in. A rare concession. The library is closed today, and most of the stores. After supper I checked the shed, but it was dark and quiet. I wonder where he is. This year must seem terrible and dark to him, and emptier than even I can imagine.

Sunday, January 2, 1977

Nobody coming over today. I miss Sam and Neil. They both have their own problems so I understand why they can't be here, but all the same it is a drag.

Neil phoned around lunch. I told him about my new Chapter 4 for Asteroid Beta and he said I should work on some short fiction for the Association of Alphans, a *Space: 1999* story. Dare I?

I started to type up my corrected draft of Chapter 4 when Dad poked his head into my room and saw me surrounded by stacks of paper.

Getting a head start on the paper work for the new year? he joked.

This gave me the idea I needed. In less than an hour I had my first draft of a short story about how Moonbase Alpha is contacted by friendly aliens who offer the Alphans another chance to return to Earth (this is after "Journey To Where"). The catch is that they must complete the paperwork, of which there is such a ridiculous amount that they eventually give up. I typed up a two page, corrected draft of my story. I call it "Gilligan's Moon" after everyone's favorite castaway.

Steaks for supper. Then watched *Six Million Dollar Man*, and *Switch*. That Robert Wagner sure is a smooth talker. Had a bath.

Monday, January 3, 1977

It was dark when I got up early today. I slept in during all the holidays, so this was a shock all over again. It feels like you are walking to school in the middle of the night. 1977 sounds so futuristic, but here we are again and nothing has changed. Sure we have new classes, but they are the same as the old classes from the first half of the school year. They just chopped them in two so we could be bothered with comprehensive exams twice a year instead of only once. How thoughtful.

Brian asked me in class if it was true that Neil's brother was dead. I nodded. He just smirked and I looked away. If you ignore them they lose interest.

At lunch, I met Sam and Neil at the southwest entrance. For some reason I had felt like I'd never see them again so it felt really good to sit on that cold floor with them. I had my corrected and typed draft of "Gilligan's Moon" which they both then read. Neil said it showed 'hyperbolic realism', whatever that is. Sam thought it was funny. I gave the pages to Neil so he could submit them to the Association of Alphans. Wish me luck! They both said they'll definitely make it over to my place this Sunday, whether there is a new episode to discuss or not.

In homeroom, at the end of the day, Mr. Peebles handed out the report cards. I did quite well: all As except for some Bs in French, Art and Music. Also, I got a D in Phys-ed.

Neil and I walked Sam to 2nd and Darlington and then he asked me to come over for a few minutes. We went to the shed and he gathered up some papers. Time to meet your first publisher, he said.

We walked back around the corner of his block and to the fourth house in, where Ron from the Association of Alphans lives. We went to the back door and rang the bell. Ron's mom answered. She is older than my or Neil's mom, but seems nice and called Ron to the door. Ron is a skinny and pale guy with long brown hair. Not that different from me: a little older, a little taller, a little tougher. He listened carefully when Neil talked.

Neil introduced us and gave Ron a sheaf of papers, the work Neil had shown me, plus my own story. Ron barely glanced at my story before he said he didn't like the title. But at least he promised to read it. That was about it. He didn't invite us in. We just stood in his back entrance and talked for a couple of minutes and then out we went. Maybe he would have judged my story more fairly if he hadn't seen me. I don't know.

Work was pretty quiet.

Tuesday, January 4, 1977

School is just zedfull (my new word for boring; it rhymes with dreadful). Is there anyone who cares about the Treaty of Westphalia anymore?

At lunch Sam seemed in a good mood, or maybe she was just trying to cheer up glum Neil. She said she had a fight with her parents and actually won! They cannot control her and she will be living her life the way she wants, regardless. So you can come hang out at the shed tonight, asks Neil. Well no, but I will make it to Roger's on Sunday afternoon. That's definitely better than nothing. Maybe not quite the victory she makes it out to be, but at least we're not losing any ground. She looked really nice today and when she smiles it is like a thousand watt bulb illuminates my heart.

After school I walked all the way to Accent On Books and bought that new book: <u>The Making Of Space: 1999</u> for $1.95, a pretty good price for an inch thick paperback with many pages of photos.

Now I'm back from the shed. I went over around 7. Solo was there too. We talked about Eagles. When I got home, around 10, the folks were glued to the TV so I snuck by them, put my clothes into the washer, then started it. Crawled into bed, wrote this last bit, and then read my new book until I was zedfull. ZZZZZ.

On Talking About Eagles (Roger Kay, 1994)

In my diary, there is mention of 'talking about Eagles'. To the trained investigator, these statements might stand out as odd because I never give any details. There is a reason for this: it is a code. In several cases in my 1977 diary, when I say I went to Neil's shed and was 'talking about Eagles', it actually means we smoked marijuana.

The fact that my parents had already discovered and accepted Neil's smoking of cigarettes allowed me to hide this new activity. No doubt my clothes became quite malodorous from all the smoke, tobacco and otherwise, that lingered in that cold shed, but because Mom had already instructed me on how to launder my own clothes I was able to minimize the risk of discovery.

Our house was smoke free. My Mom had smoked in her youth, before I was born, but quit when she became pregnant. Looking back now, this seems even more intelligent than it was in those days. However it was not easy for her to quit. To this day she cannot stand being in a room where someone is smoking, and she can instantly smell any smoky residuum on cigarette users' clothes.

Luckily for me, she never smoked marijuana. Not that I ever asked her, but I must assume this was the case as she was never able to detect its smell on me. Perhaps she just wanted to stay far enough away from any tobacco smell that she never approached close enough to smell the other.

I only did it a few times. I was jealous and distrustful of the relationship Solo had developed so quickly and thoroughly with Neil after Jerry was gone and that lead to my associating grass with Solo and all the bad things that came after Jerry's disappearance. So although I would have followed Neil anywhere, the participation of Solo in the drug use limited my willingness to experiment.

Entries from Roger Kay's 1977 Diary

Friday, January 7, 1977

Still dark getting up for school, but the afternoon was bright and clear, although cold. At lunch Neil was absent and I ate with Sam. We talked about Jerry's death. We still don't know precisely how he died. Did he get stoned and fall asleep outside and freeze to death?

Double Phys-ed right after lunch. Did a bunch of running and different exercises and then they divided us into four teams to compete in shooting baskets. The losing team would have to do extra exercises. Our team went first and we shot 3/10. I thought that's it, we will lose, but the next team shot 2/10, and the next 2/10, and the last team 1/10! They had to do numerous burpees. Dodged a bullet there.

After school I walked with Sam to the corner of Darlington. She is preparing plans (meaning: lies) to create new false-friend identities that can cover up some potential evening activities with her real, Alphan friends. I'd love to see her more often, and away from the school would be nice. I told her how much our friendship means to me, both her's and Neil's, and she said the feeling was mutual. My other feelings I didn't mention.

7 pm now. I've recorded a cassette of my Budgie album, both sides, and even written up the index card with all the song titles and length info. Finally, I drew a budgie on the front of the cassette insert. It's kind of funny looking, but Neil should get the idea. It is a gift for him. I'm heading over there now.

Almost 11 now. Back from Neil's. Just put my clothes in the washer. I made another secret tape of our discussions. He was talking revolution, imitating Jerry perhaps. Solo showed up around 9 and we soon discussed Eagles. Gonna turn the lights out and listen to *Potatoland* on headphones. Good night!

Roger: Cool. How long did that take you?

Neil: Each page takes between an hour and maybe three, depending on how complicated the section is.

Roger: I like that the travel tubes are in there too.

Neil: It agrees completely with the Technical Notebook, what do you call it, the matten?

Roger: And there's Koenig's quarters, just down the hall from Main Mission.

Neil: We saw that in "Space Brain".

Roger: Right. I've got something for you.

Neil: Hey, nice artwork. Put it on!

(sound of song "Anne Neggen" starting)

Neil: How much was the cassette?

Roger: Don't worry about it. My gift to you.

Neil: Wow thanks. These guys are good. (pause) Seems like they've chosen their side.

Roger: Their side?

Neil: In the revolution against the status quo. Look at the album cover. Those space budgies are armed with missiles and ready to fight. It may be cute, or whimsical, or whatever, but if you take it as serious and purposeful, then the meaning becomes clear. Budgie is in a war against the great empire of Brittania, which means the British government. Budgie are British. The title of the album shows their intent: they want to change the rules of the empire.

Roger: "If I Were Brittania I'd Waive The Rules"...

Neil: They mean change the laws. Change more than that too. Once the new generation comes in, the old ideas will be swept away. That is what revolution literally means: things get turned around.

Roger: Oh yeah. I never thought of it like that.

Neil: Check out the song titles.

"You're Opening Doors": that's about opening our minds to the deeper meaning of their music.

"Quacktors and Bureaucats": that's a putdown of the people behind the status quo.

"Sky High Percentage": that's about the costs of being part of the system. A lot of bands have to sell their soul for commercial success. Not these guys.

"Heaven Knows Our Name": that means: no one else does. So their identity is hidden. They don't want the Man to know they're onto him.

"Black Velvet Stallion": that's a beautiful strong animal, which might represent youth, who are the target of their message. Also makes me think of those black velvet paint-by-number paintings, which is like us filling in the blanks as we decipher their message. It all fits together amazingly.

Roger: Well, what about the first song: "Anne Neggan"?

Neil: It's brilliant misdirection, or disinformation. They start the song singing "I don't see in the future" then they spend the rest of the album defining their role in the future, talking about the revolution. Also I like the use of the same-sound phrases: 'Anne Neggan' versus 'and again'. The title is not a woman's name as you might think - it's a subliminal reminder for us to listen to the album again Anne Neggan until we get the real meaning.

(ten second pause)

Roger: So it sounds like something innocent to old people.

Neil: Plausible deniability they call it. Hopefully enough so that MI5 doesn't target them.

Roger: That's the British CIA?

Neil: Pretty much. Every so-called free nation has a spy service directed against its own people. I don't know what it's called in Canada, but no doubt it's a secret branch of the RCMP. That's why I'm not happy about the RCMP investigating Jerry's murder.

Roger: So he was murdered?

Neil: They admit it's suspicious but there's no suspect yet. If it was the RCMP themselves, then we'll never find out, or they'll set up a patsy, like they did with JFK.

Roger: The newspaper just said that foul play wasn't ruled out.

Neil: Oh it's ruled in. The body was moved, and he didn't freeze to death. That's all they'll tell me. I spent most of today being interrogated by the RCMP, 'interviewing' me they call it.

Roger: So that's where you were. They can't think *you* had anything to do with it?

Neil: No. Especially if they did it! Although one hand might not know what the other is doing. The local cops probably don't know anything about these types of actions.

Roger: What did they ask you?

Neil: Well, questions about Jerry's friends, his activities, our family. They'd love to pin this on Earl.

Roger: My god. That's horrible.

Neil: I don't think he did it. Not even Earl would kill his own kid. Or if he did, it would be in such a blind, drunken rage that it would be obvious, you know, blood all over the place.

(ten second pause)

Roger: I walked home with Sam today. She's working on new cover identities for us.

Neil: No more Nellie and Roxanne?

(laughter, pause, second side of the Budgie LP begins to play)

Roger: Man, does your heater go up any higher?

Neil: No. Stand up and move around a bit. You'll warm up.

Roger: I sure hope 1999 is on tomorrow. Seems like months since we've seen a new episode.

Neil: Yeah. I'm still waiting for Year Two to be as good as Year One. They can do it, if they just focus on ideas and get their scripts right. This action-adventure approach is bogus. Turning the Alphans into ordinary people is stupid. You don't build a statue of a real, average, boring person. Who wants to see that? You want to relate to them, but you also want to be inspired by them. That's one thing I like about Ayn Rand, her views on art.

Roger: Really? What does she say?

Neil: She defines art as the selective re-creation of reality. Not just a slice of actual life. It's a creation carefully constructed to provide meaning and a message, not just a series of action-oriented adventures. The hero is just that, a hero. He's not a patsy, or an accident. He's a destination for our goals. Who we want to become. Even if he dies at the end of the movie, we feel his life was worthwhile because of what it meant.

Roger: So it's not enough to just blow up the monster.

Neil: Exactly. It's *how* you do it. Do you sacrifice others, yourself, your ideals? What's the cost of victory, and how do you make the decision whether to pay that cost? That's the human conflict we can be proud to observe. Just watching some asshole with a big gun killing aliens isn't art. It's entertainment, low-brow entertainment.

Roger: Art versus entertainment, maybe that should be our topic tomorrow.

Neil: Yeah. Sure. Give it some thought.

Roger: I think Sam would probably-

Entries from Roger Kay's 1977 Diary

Saturday, Jan 8, 1977

Slept in this morning. Still pretty cold. Walked down to Logan's Drugs in the afternoon then stopped by the library but Neil wasn't there. I took out <u>Rendezvous With Rama</u>, an Arthur C. Clarke book.

Went home and typed up a good draft of <u>Asteroid Beta</u>, Chapter 4: "Planet of the Space Brains". Can't wait to show it off tomorrow.

At 4, finally a new episode of *Space: 1999*, called "A Matter of Balance". Taped it and then spent most of the evening writing and editing my episode summary. At 10:30, I watched King of Kensington with Mom and Dad. Then watched a late movie, "Evil Roy Slade". It was a western but very funny in a demented way.

Episode Summary: "A Matter Of Balance"
(1889 words)
[Omitted.]

Comments on "A Matter Of Balance" (Roger Kay, 1994)

Tony is cultivating another version of his alleged beer, this time with the help of Shermeen, a pretty young botanist from the Hydroponics Section. The new version is a flop and Shermeen, who has a crush on Tony, takes it badly.

As the Alphans explore another new planet, the emotionally vulnerable Shermeen is manipulated by a male phantom figure named Vindrus into attacking other Alphans and stealing a portable power generator for his evil purposes.

Favorite scene: When Shermeen disappears from the landing party, Maya finds her in the mysterious alien temple and is shocked to see that Shermeen is unafraid of the ugly, spear-wielding alien guard creature that prevents anyone else from entering. Shermeen's nonchalance is unnatural and unnerving.

Entries from Roger Kay's 1977 Diary

Sunday, January 9, 1977

Good news and bad news. The good news is that Sam and
Neil made it over today and we spent the afternoon talking
about 1999. The bad news is that I managed to somehow not
tape our discussion. The little switch on the microphone that
can start and stop recording is very useful, except if you mean
to be recording but forget to flick it on! Then you spend the
whole event glancing at the recorder and being falsely
reassured by the fact that the play and record buttons are both
clearly pushed down, but all the while not noticing the wheels
are not turning so nothing is being recorded. Rat salad!

So let's see what I remember. It is 4:30 now and they both
left about half an hour ago. Neil got here first, but Sam was
only a few minutes behind. I played my new Blue Oyster Cult
album for them.

So, regarding "A Matter of Balance". Both Neil and Sam
had problems with the guest star Shermeen acting like a
'teenager'. How can a trained scientist wind up betraying the
people on Alpha just because of a crush gone wrong? If the
astronaut selection process is that faulty and a bad apple
somehow gets through, or maybe becomes rotten due to the
stress, then can they ever really trust her again? In the final
scene, Shermeen is back among the Alphans and her treachery
appears forgotten. This seems wrong. It would have made more
sense to have her die at the end of the episode, we all agreed.

Shake 'n Bake chicken for supper! Yum! I'll be back in
about four pieces of chicken.

Later. Neil pointed out that at 1702 days since breakaway,
the Alphans have been on their journey for over four years.
Everyone on Alpha should know each other very well by now,
and anybody who was 'young and foolish' would probably have
already been killed off.

I mentioned that in "One Moment of Humanity", Koenig
admits to their robot hosts that he loves Helena and that Tony
loves Maya. We checked the MATN, and that episode occurs

only 400 days after breakaway. So what has Tony been doing in the last three years? Maya has been on Alpha for three years and Shermeen doesn't realize that the female Tony is interested in is the alien who can instantly turn into a nightmare bug-eyed monster? On a small base like Alpha, Shermeen should know.

Sam said the scriptwriters should quit trying to make the females look weak and should instead focus on creating exciting, heroic characters. Which Neil jumped on to start the art versus entertainment discussion.

His point is, if you are just interested in seeing stuff blow up, it doesn't matter much who pushes the button, but if you want real drama, you have to care about the characters because they have redeeming qualities. What was Shermeen's redeeming quality? She is in no way a hero, just a convenient cause of problems. Our main characters are the real heroes of course so we can consider 1999 art, but that doesn't mean there aren't many elements that are in place for the sake of entertainment only. This is usually where the scripts go wrong. The action-adventure approach usually results in entertainment, not art, says Neil.

There was more discussion about Tony and his flaws. Neil contrasted him with Professor Bergman. While Tony is action-oriented, Bergman was idea-oriented. Neil said he didn't think the death of Bergman as described in the MATN was right. How could he die in a simple accident after all they had survived, passing through a black hole, passing through the space brain, collision with Arra's giant planet, and so on? I asked him what he meant by 'right' and he said it just doesn't make sense, sort of like Spock dying in a transporter accident between episodes. No fan could ever accept something like that. We had to agree.

I have one nicely typed copy of <u>Asteroid Beta</u> Chapter 4. Sam read it first, but passed the pages to Neil as she went. I got some good feedback from them. Neil suggested I change the ending so the space brain that falls in love with the Betan woman gives up its energy-body and becomes human. Then

Asteroid Beta could have a resident alien like Alpha does. Interesting thought!

My hand is sore now.

Monday, January 10, 1977

Very cold, dark day. I had lunch with Sam and she told me that Neil was not in school today. Now what?

We talked about my maybe incorporating an alien character into Asteroid Beta. Sam says that the space brain creatures would be neither male nor female, and that upon becoming human, this would be the greatest shock to it. She suggested I could have the creature inadvertently become a human just like the woman it loves (mind love not body love) so that it becomes a woman too! This would pose some problems for the female Betan it loves, and could raise lots of issues. Plus it means adding a female character, not a male one, to my novel. This is all very interesting, but I don't think I'm ready to write that chapter yet.

Before work I dropped by Radio Shack to pick up some more cassettes. Bought three packs of three. Also bought some fresh batteries. I hate it when they die in the middle of something, especially if you can't see the recorder and therefore don't know about it when it stops!!

Uncle Tim wasn't at work today. He's got the flu. His assistant, Delmer, who I usually never have to deal with, isn't as nice. He wasn't around last summer when I was working full time, but now he thinks he needs to keep telling me how to do my job. Maybe he should spend more time doing his job instead of watching me work.

When I got home I had a bowl of chocolate ice cream and watched Front Page Challenge with the folks.

Tuesday, January 11, 1977

Snowing this morning. Someone tried to hit me with a snowball as I walked past the courthouse. You'd think that would be a safe area, but no. The icy missile barely missed my head and I trudged a little faster to get away from the firing zone.

Mr. Peebles is out with the flu and we have a substitute teacher for homeroom, Math, and Social Studies. It is Ms. Koch again but she looks old now. Her hair is tied back tightly against her head, and she is wearing older people clothes. I still like her. Brian was talking in class, being a jerk and paying her no attention but then he sure jumped when she slammed a yardstick down on his desk.

Neil did show up today. At lunch he was telling us that the police now have a suspect or maybe just a 'person of interest' in Jerry's case. They won't tell him who it is, but they admit there are some forensic tests being done on a car they think was used to move the body. If the results are incriminating, we'll find out who the suspect is.

Neil was very tense as he told us this. He kept making a fist with one hand and grabbing it with the other, then doing back stretches and rotating his head like all the muscles in his body were sore or he had ants in his shirt. Obviously this causes him pain to talk about, but I'm glad he's sharing these new facts.

I said if the body was moved by car, likely it is a murder type of thing instead of a random attack. This means Neil might know the killer, and maybe even is in danger himself. Neil said he already thought of this and keeps a big knife in the shed now.

Sam and I agreed that we would be at the shed Friday at 7. Sam coming out at night! I'll believe it when I see it!

After school I went to Logan's Drugs and bought *Starlog* #3. Strangely, the cover resembles a MAD magazine: Spock and other Trek characters are swinging from a chandelier while a crowd with signs like 'beam me up' are below, almost chasing them. There is an in-depth article on a big *Star Trek* convention being held in the States. Oh. More importantly, there is an article on 1999 with awesome color photos and descriptions of some Year Two episodes. I read the whole thing, cover to cover.

Finished reading <u>Rendezvous With Rama</u>. Are there two more books in the series to come?

It was just too cold to go over to the shed. Had a bath. My hair is finally getting nice and long again. I'm not going to let Dad cut it so short again next summer.

Friday, January 14, 1977

Cold, snowy and windy this morning. Can't tell if it is snowing, or just blowing around. Uncle Doug on The Top O' The Morning Show said it is actually snowing. Who wouldn't believe a man with a hand puppet? My earmuffs broke when I was adjusting them, about half way to school, so my ears nearly froze solid. Why do they build them out of such cheap plastic? I'm moving to California after university.

Mr. Peebles is back, but he still has a sore throat. He talks softly, when at all. Most of our time today we spent reading and doing problems because of this. Here the good news is that I've got absolutely no homework, but the bad news is the day takes even longer when he's not boring us with his long windedness.

After supper I went over to see Neil, but Solo was there too. He just wants to talk about Eagles all the time so I only stayed for a little while. Sam never showed up, which is probably a good thing. It is way too cold in there.

Saturday, 15 January, 1977

Got up early. It is overcast, but a little warmer. Wind has eased off its usual fury. I walked down to the library around 1. Neil was there, in his favorite chair, a pile of psychology books beside him. He was reading something called <u>Man's Search For Meaning</u>. I asked him if he had found any meaning yet and he said: just in dictionaries. I think that was a joke.

We walked over to Sam The Record Man's and looked through the bins. Rudy played a new LP by a group called Prism, who are Canadian. The first song is "Spaceship Superstar". I liked it and bought one: $6.99.

I invited Neil over to listen to it, but he declined, saying the album was pop and had too much keyboard. I was a little insulted but didn't let on, and just said, well maybe I'll drop around tonight.

Which I did. But again Solo was there and they were only interested in talking about Eagles. So I left.

Spent the night working on my summary for today's 1999 episode, a new one, "The Beta Cloud", and listened to my new album. It does have some love songs on it, so I see what Neil meant. Maybe it is not art, but it is entertaining to me.

Had a bath and then stayed up for a far out late movie called *Silent Running*. It is about a future where humans have sent giant spaceships to orbit Saturn. These ships have domes which house habitats for the few remaining plants and animals from planet Earth. When the order comes to destroy the domes, one man (Bruce Dern) rebels. He kills one of his crew and then flees in the final surviving ship with only three small robots for company. It has a sad ending but is a powerful film. The spaceships and robots were incredibly believable, rivaling 1999 I must admit. I should have taped it.

Episode Summary: "The Beta Cloud" (1271 words)
[Omitted.]

Comments on "The Beta Cloud" (Roger Kay, 1994)

An orange-yellow space cloud crosses the Moon's path and leaves most of the Alphans in a strange state of lassitude. Only a skeleton crew remain fit for duty. When an Eagle dispatched days earlier to investigate the cloud finally returns, the crew is gone but a hulking space creature emerges and begins to wreak havoc on the base. A message comes from the cloud: Give us your life support system or we will destroy you.

Nothing seems to stop the space creature. Strangely, Maya cannot transform into it. At one point when things look especially desperate, Tony confesses to Maya that "Psychon is my favorite planet" and kisses her passionately.

Favorite scene: In the denouement, Maya is visiting the injured Tony in Medical Centre. She brings him flowers, chocolates, games, books. She starts to explain to him how to play three dimensional solitaire when he says, you know, I hope you didn't get the wrong idea with all that wild garbage I was saying earlier...

Wild garbage? Was that what it was, Maya asks him.

Well you know we were under murderous pressure and a guy can say some wild things, replies Tony. Without another word, Maya packs all the treats she has brought and leaves the room.

Well, says Tony aloud, I guess she *is* crazy about me!

16 January 1977
(audio tape from collection of Roger Kay)

Roger: Okay, we're definitely rolling.

Sam: You sure? We don't want you committing hari-kari.

Roger: No no, just kidding about that. *(pause)* So today we have Samantha Renfield and Lionel O'Neill and we'll be discussing "The Beta Cloud".

Neil: How many of these sessions do you have now?

Roger: A few. These are my 1999 episodes, and these are other movies and shows. Then the stuff we've recorded together is here.

Neil: Does that include the session with Jerry?

Roger: No. I have them in a safe place.

Neil: Them?

Roger: I mean 'it'. It's one tape. Yeah, I'm pretty sure.

Neil: Do you think I could get a copy of it?

Roger: No problem, man. I'd be happy to make one for you. Maybe, bring back the *Karmic Whiplash* copy I made and I'll put my Jerry interview on the other side.

Sam: You interviewed Jerry?

Roger: Yeah. We talked about science fiction in rock and roll. He's really a fascinating guy, and brilliant.

Sam: I wish I could've met him.

Neil: Well, they think they know who killed him now.

(simultaneously:) **Sam:** Oh my god! **Roger:** What? Who is it?

Neil: Albert Kiblah.

Roger: You mean Mr. Kiblah, the Phys-ed teacher from Dr. Brass?

Neil: There were tire prints where they found Jerry. The cops matched them to Kiblah's little foreign car. Then they found Jerry's blood in the trunk.

Roger: But did Jerry ever go to Dr. Brass?

Neil: He did. Back when it was a junior high. But Kiblah didn't teach there those years.

Roger: So how would he know Kiblah? What could possibly be the motive?

Neil: They don't know.

Sam: I'm so sorry.

Neil: I hope they string him up. But it'll take a while.

Roger: It's monstrous. When did you find out?

Neil: Yesterday. Anyway there's nothing we can do about it right now. Let's do our 1999 thing.

Roger: Sure. We can do that. Maybe I'll throw some music on. Any requests?

Neil: Yeah, anything but Prism.

Sam: Not good?

Roger: How about some Rush? *2112*?

Neil: Side 2?

Roger: Sure, if... yeah.

("A Passage To Bangkok" by Rush begins to play)

Roger: So... what about that Beta Cloud?

Sam: Well, Maya saved them again. She's their ace in the hole. I don't understand why Tony is playing those games with her.

Roger: Sorry, games?

Sam: He tells her he loves her when he's in danger, and then when the danger passes, he pretends he didn't say it. But like you said last week, Koenig has already let the cat out of the bag, and *years* are passing. It's like *he's* the teenager, not Shermeen.

Neil: Tony, there's something about that guy. I mean he replaced Paul, and Victor, and even Kano. He's head of security. He's second only to Koenig. It's possible he could have arranged their deaths. He certainly had a motive. And as you say, he's not very mature or consistent, so I wouldn't put it past him.

(twenty second pause)

Sam: Tony's supposed to be a good guy.

Neil: Nobody with that much power is a good guy.

Roger: Well, Koenig...

Neil: Yeah, yeah, there's Koenig. But this Tony, he comes bubbling up through the ranks as people go missing. Pretty suspicious.

Roger: If Bergman was murdered, you'd think they'd figure it out. He was very important to Alpha.

Sam: Well, he was just written out. That's why no one mentions him.

Neil: Maybe. Another possible interpretation is that Bergman did something so horrible, so monstrous, that they can no longer bear to talk about him.

Sam: They should make a movie about what happened between Year One and Year Two. A lot must have happened. Something scared them into abandoning Main Mission.

Roger: *And* something scared them into changing the style of their uniforms.

Sam: *(laughs)* You should write that as a short story. I bet that Association of Alphans would be interested.

Neil: He keeps pushing back the date he's gonna publish. He hasn't put out one newsletter yet.

Roger: Did he say anything about my story?

Neil: I'll ask him this week.

Sam: Writers and their egos!

Roger: Hey if I get published, I'm definitely getting an ego.

Sam: *(laughs)* So, anyway, we'll see what happens next with Maya and Tony. Something should happen.

Roger: I think they'll get together.

Neil: It doesn't make a difference really. That's the problem with Freiberger. He's changing the focus from the mystery of space to boy meets girl. The show really doesn't need it. And you're right Sam. Maya *is* the most important Alphan now. Without her they'd be sunk. She's smarter than the Alphans, and considering her talent for molecular transformation, she can be stronger, faster, larger, smaller, whatever she wants. If Tony thinks he can replace all those others, you know, Paul and Victor, he's dreaming. Maya is their replacement. Tony is expendable. I really do think Maya is a great character, but they need to show how she's different from the Alphans. She's an alien. Other than her one talent, they're not using that fact as much as they should.

Sam: One of the best *Star Trek* episodes ever involves Spock going back to his home planet Vulcan to participate in a mating ritual. Seeing other Vulcans and being introduced to their ways is fascinating for the viewer.

Neil: Hey no Trek examples. What is this, *Starlog*?

(Sam and Roger laugh)

Roger: Can you believe they put *Star Trek* on the cover again? *(pause)* Hey I thought of a good question. Why is it the Beta Cloud? That just means second cloud in Greek, right? So what happened to the Alpha Cloud?

Sam: It got torn apart by Asteroid Beta.

Roger: *(laughs)* There's my Chapter 5 idea!

Sam: No charge. *(pause)* Hey how'd you like this?

Roger: It's very good. From the public library. I'm taking it back soon. It's almost due.

Sam: Let me know when you do and I'll go grab it.

Roger: Sure.

Entries from Roger Kay's 1977 Diary

Sunday, January 16, 1977
Snowy again today but it didn't stop Neil and Sam from showing up. I taped our session. We discussed yesterday's episode plus other more startling matters, like an arrest in Jerry's case: his Phys-ed teacher from Grade 6, Al Kiblah. No ideas on motive yet. Neil didn't really want to talk about it. He just told us, and then we dropped the subject. Whatever gets him through, that's what we'll do.

I don't know how much more winter I can take. These short, dark days make me feel like I'm living at the bottom of a deep hole.

Sam was looking more beautiful than ever today. She must have gone to church and then snuck out because she showed up wearing a dress, white pantyhose, and a frilly blouse. Man she looks good like that.

I don't understand Neil. If I had a shot at her, I'd grab it. Here we are, over halfway through Grade 9. Next year we'll be in high school. To enter high school with a girlfriend by your side, that would be the ultimate in cool.

I made a copy of the first Jerry interview tape for Neil on a fresh tape. No charge.

Tried to do some writing. Nothing coming.

Monday, January 17, 1977
Back to the grind today. Slogged through mounds of snow just to get to a stinky building overrun by rivers of foul slush and torrents of juvenile odor. The senses reel!

At lunch I gave Neil the Jerry tape copy. He told us Kiblah was claiming self-defense, that Jerry had broken into his house. That makes no sense as Jerry never stole a thing in his life, according to Neil. Kiblah is obviously lying, but we don't know why.

Swung by the YPL on the way to work and dropped my Rama book into the after-hours return slot.

At Pic-A-Pop, Uncle Tim was back and Delmer was under control. I'm glad because I don't know how long I can put up with that idiot.

Business was slow so Uncle Tim let me go half an hour early. I think I'm still getting paid for it.

Tuesday, January 18, 1977

Boring day at school. Why do we try to educate smart and dumb people in the same classes? The dumb people inevitably wind up hating and harassing the smart people. Brian started calling me Roger Codger today which is not really an insult or all that bad, but after a lot of repetition it does annoy. I am not an old codger. He thinks anyone who doesn't say "ain't" is high-falutin'. Brian will be an old man by the time he is 20. He'll knock up some really stupid broad and then live in a trailer with his evil, deficient children. So in 10 years he'll be feeding more little bullies into the school system. Very helpful.

Lunch was really nice, just me and Sam today. I was asking her about her plans for the future, and she talked about university and becoming a scientist someday. Did she want to have kids I bravely asked? No, but she'd still like to get married though. Oh yeah, me too, I added nonchalantly. Keep your head Roger, cool is the way.

After school I stopped by the shed, but Neil wasn't there. After supper I stopped by again, around 6:45, and he was in, but he seemed distracted and upset. He had spent all day talking to various police detectives. They wanted his help trying to understand if there was a connection between Jerry and Kiblah. If there is no connection then they must assume, they said, that this was just a break and enter gone bad. This upsets Neil because it implies Jerry was in the wrong. Neil was quick to point out that if someone breaks into your house and you accidentally kill them while defending yourself, you don't dump the body at JayCee Beach.

The police also came back and took more of Jerry's stuff. They didn't take his albums, but they did take all his cassettes, including *Potatoland* and the copy of Jerry's interview that I gave to Neil. They didn't care that Neil said it was his tape, not

Jerry's. It was in their bedroom with the other tapes and they just took it. They also found some marijuana in the shed so now the police have the stupid idea that Jerry was doing B&Es *[Editor's note: 'break and enters' or burglary]* to finance his drug habit. I'm starting to think Jerry's theories aren't so crazy. The cops seem to be trying everything possible to cast him as the villain.

Despite all this, Solo showed up at 9 and they started talking about Eagles so I left. Came home and threw my clothes into the washer. Neil is smoking more than ever.

Friday, January 21, 1977

The Leader Post had something on Jerry's case today: charges were laid against Kiblah, who is reported as a 37 year old school teacher with no criminal record. It also said he is on paid leave from the school pending the outcome of the case. I found this out today at lunch because Lucky brought it to Neil's attention this morning (who would have thought Lucky could even read a newspaper?) and said something like: you better watch out, if another teacher wants a paid vacation, they'll do you too. Sam, sitting next to Neil, overheard this and saw what happened next: Neil grabbed Lucky by the neck and pulled him right out of his desk! After a moment Neil just disengaged and stood back, quiet as a statue, tears streaming down his face. Mrs. Wilson took pity and instead of sending Neil to the principal's office, sent him home.

I went over to the shed around 7 and Neil was there, working on his Alpha floorplans. He didn't want to talk too much but I hung around until 9 when like clockwork Solo showed up again. I didn't stay after that.

On Surviving the Aftermath of Murder
(Lionel O'Neill, 1988)

I can't describe the pain and anguish I went through in those months after Jerry died. Some people tried to help me, like Roger and Sam, but other people pushed me to the edge.

At school, the day we found out the murder charge had been laid, one of my classmates said something very insensitive to me. I became enraged. I picked him up by the neck, then dropped him onto the floor. Then when I saw the marks on his neck, they reminded me of the marks I saw on Jerry's neck at the morgue. This was devastating. An equivalence, however tentative, between myself and Jerry's murderer was more than I could bear. I cried in public for the first time, and I didn't even care. I don't think they ever punished me for that assault. They just sent me home. There was nothing they could do to hurt me at that point anyway.

After that, I threw myself headlong into my work, drawing the complete blueprints of Moonbase Alpha. This provided a valuable escape for me, keeping my brain engaged and creative while letting me disengage from my miserable reality. It did help for a while.

Entries from Roger Kay's 1977 Diary

Saturday, January 22, 1977

A sunny day finally but feeling lazy. Watched TV all morning: *Flintstones*, *Rat Patrol*, *Gilligan's Island*, and *Wolfman Jack*.

Went downtown in the afternoon, Logan's Drugs, The Stereo Hut. Stopped in at the YPL but Neil was nowhere around. Read some magazines then came home.

Taped 1999 at 4, a new episode called "The Lambda Factor". This one takes place 800 days after last week's episode. That is more than two years! These episodes are way out of order.

Spent all evening writing up the episode summary and then half of the night watching a movie: *It's a Mad, Mad, Mad, Mad World*. It was quite funny but almost three hours long. Snuck up from the basement like a mouse and now it is 2:15 a.m. Good night!

Episode Summary: "The Lambda Factor" (2322 words)
[Omitted.]

Comments on "The Lambda Factor" (Roger Kay, 1994)

A murder has occurred on Moonbase Alpha. Meanwhile Koenig is losing his self-control due to lack of sleep. As the murder investigation starts to focus on Carolyn Powell, Helena discovers that a mysterious space object is emitting lambda waves which are correlated to ESP powers in humans. It soon becomes clear that the murderess has strong ESP powers.

Favorite scene: Koenig facing his waking nightmares, the accusations of his best friends Sam and Tess who blame him for leaving them behind at a space station doomed by its infection with Venusian plague.

Entries from Roger Kay's 1977 Diary

Sunday, January 23, 1977
Slept in till 11. I was worried Neil wouldn't show up today, but he did. I think it is important for him to keep living his life, even if he feels like it has ended. Sam made it too. I taped our discussion, but it ended a bit abruptly when the tape ran out. At first Neil was being kind of quiet, but towards the end he warmed up and seemed his old self. He even stuck around after Sam left and asked me if we could make another copy of *Potatoland* for him. We made the tape together, listening to it again. He tried to give me 75 cents for the cassette but I said no, just take it.

23 January 1977
(audio tape from collection of Roger Kay)

Roger: Repeat what you just said.

Sam: If we're now 2308 days after breakaway, that's more than six years! So my theory on Bergman is that, possibly, he died of old age.

(laughter: Roger and Sam)

Neil: Well he wasn't super old. Younger than Ernst Queller anyway.

Roger: This is actually two years after the Beta Cloud episode. So all the characters might die of old age before we get to Year Three.

Neil: If they leave that big of gaps between episodes, you wonder what they're leaving out. Maybe more than just the true story of what happened to Bergman.

Roger: What do you mean? Like what?

Neil: Anything could have happened, but if you look at the evidence, some things are clear. No one talks about Bergman, so likely he did something bad. Did an alien give him super powers and he was corrupted and had to be killed, or did they seal him in a spaceship like on "Earthbound", or inside an asteroid, like on "End of Eternity"? When the Alphans built the new Command Centre, far underground, what threat were they reacting to specifically? We aren't told. Maybe the threat was Bergman himself. Maybe these gaps between episodes prevent us from seeing what really happened.

Roger: What *really* happened?

Sam: Do you think they're saving some story points for a movie?

Neil: No I don't think they'll make a movie out of a TV series. That'd be different.

Sam: Actually it did happen. The British series *Doctor Who*. They did a movie in like 1966, with Peter Cushing, based on their low budget TV series. I know you both think the rumors of a *Star Trek* movie won't amount to anything, but it's not impossible.

Roger: I've seen *Doctor Who* books. Did you see the show in Regina?

Sam: No, but my brother did. It was on long ago. I think in black and white. And they kept changing the actor who played the main character!

Roger: *(laughing)* That can't help.

Sam: No. But the really cool thing about Doctor Who is that he never carries a gun. He always beats the aliens by talking to them, finding out about their problems, then solving them. So although it is not a deep show, the hero certainly stands out from the usual OK Corral approach.

Neil: You know that shot in the opening credits of each 1999 episode, where Koenig spins around in his chair, then jumps up and fires his stun gun? What the hell is he firing at? Is this supposed to be the new dynamic Koenig?

Compare that to Year One, where he is standing, and just pivots slowly towards the camera. He looks much more dignified, more intelligent there. Maybe the years in space have changed him, made him more reactive, less trusting or thoughtful.

Sam: They've been in space a long time now. Two years since the Beta Cloud even. And still no progress in the Maya-Tony relationship. How long does he plan to leave it? Not much *action* there.

Roger: Maybe he's scared of rejection.

Sam: Tony? He's a very confident guy.

Roger: The Alphans can be funny though. Remember how quickly Helena started to suspect Tony of poisoning her in "One Moment of Humanity"? And Maya being an alien, some barriers there I suppose.

Sam: Not so much if her parents are out of the way.

(laughter: Roger and Sam)

Neil: Maybe Tony is affected by a Mysterious Unknown Force.

Sam: Yeah I can't believe *Starlog* said that. Sure 1999 used the Mysterious Unknown Force a lot in Year One, but it was very effective. It made you think.

Neil: Exactly. In Year Two, the Mysterious Unknown Force manifests itself as the motivations of the aliens. The cosmos itself is rational, and it's the aliens who are inscrutable but eventually decide to spare the Alphans despite their strangeness, like in the "AB Chrysalis".

Hang on. I think the most important thing for the Alphans to do is to chase after that Force, not some primitive mating urge, but the urge toward the transcendent, something by definition unknown and requiring imagination even to approach.

Action-adventure takes a simplistic approach to good and evil, sweeping any chance for thought under the rug, and letting aggression resolve things to achieve the so-called good outcome. This is simply 'the end justifies the means'. Not a very advanced morality.

Sam: Well, in "The Lambda Factor", they do seem to be dealing with Mysterious Unknown Forces. There's both the space phenomenon and Carolyn's mental powers. As far as morality, this is the usual case of absolute power corrupting absolutely. Once Carolyn understands that she has these awesome powers, she begins to see the other Alphans as toys or pawns. If they don't obey her, she'll kill them.

Roger: We can classify this as one of the Bad Alphan episodes.

(laughter: Sam)

Roger: Like "Lambda Factor", "A Matter of Balance", even "Catacombs of the Moon". Or in Year One, "The Troubled Spirit", or "Force of Life".

Neil: Whoa. In "Force of Life" technician Anton Zoref is taken over by an alien entity. That's not his fault. At least in "The Troubled Spirit" Mateo was performing experiments against Koenig's orders. Maybe that qualifies him as a bad Alphan.

Roger: Right. Okay we exclude Zoref from the list.

Sam: Maybe that's a writing assignment for you: when good Alphans go bad.

Roger: *(laughs)* Maybe so.

Sam: One thing I liked about this episode was we get the rest of the story Koenig started in "The Exiles", about his crewmates with the Venusian plague who had to be left behind to die. This shows the sensitivity of Koenig. After all those years, these deaths still haunt him and he can't forgive himself.

Neil: The fact that they didn't take the easy way out at the end, that Carolyn wasn't okay after the big battle, that deserves credit. You don't want everything to completely return to normal after the conflicts are resolved. I mean, it has to be normal enough so that you can do the next episode, but you also need some cumulative effect from all these adventures too. You can't travel through space, have all these adventures, and not be affected. Experience causes change. You can't ignore that.

Roger: Neil, can I go back a sec. What did you mean by what 'really happened' to Bergman? I mean, you've *met* Barry Morse.

Neil: Of course. What I meant was, what is the canonical view of what happened to Bergman, like what is the accepted wisdom.

We can believe what's in the *Starlog* canon, which includes the matten as you call it, and that talks about an accidental death. Or we can look to the Anderson canon, which is silent on the matter, and that implies something very different.

It's a bit like having four gospels which contradict each other. Or Paul and James; they contradict each other when they talk about Jesus. You have to decide which one applies in which situation.

Sam: Echh. I'm not looking for a bible discussion here.

Neil: No I'm not in favor of religion either. I'm just using it as an example.

Roger: But you obviously know something about it.

Neil: 'Know thy enemy' is good advice.

Sam: I'm more a 'flee my enemy' type of girl.

Roger: You? *(disbelieving)* Yeah right!

(laughter: Roger and Sam)

Entries from Roger Kay's 1977 Diary

Tuesday, January 25, 1977

Double Phys-ed this morning. I think the rest of the Phys-ed teachers are pissed off that one of their own got caught doing something terrible and they are punishing us. Or they are just their usual sadistic selves, making up all sorts of games that help define the losers so they can be more easily singled out and picked on. After an hour and a half of grunting and abuse, my reward is to clearly understand that I am a loser. Very helpful in my development, thanks.

So at lunch, still all sweaty and stinky, I didn't want to sit right next to Sam. Neil was very quiet. I told them about *Silent Running*. Nothing. Then at the end of lunch suddenly he opens up, talking about 'Gary' Anderson and how Professor Bergman might have been responsible for the destruction of the original Main Mission. Did I miss an episode? I thought he liked to draw, but today he seemed to be more into writing new episodes, or at least talking about his ideas.

I dropped over to the shed after supper and he was working on his Alpha blueprints. He pulled out an album by a group named Electric Flag called *A Long Time Coming*. It opens with a quote from somewhere about 'the dignity of man' which is then followed by audience laughter. He says this is the clue that the album will be about revolution against the status quo, which he is now calling 'the fascists'.

These fascists are trying hard to ensure that alcohol is the drug of choice for the next generation. Its detrimental effects on the revolutionaries is the only thing that can stop the change. He played the song "Wine" and there is a line about Janis Joplin liking wine. This is the fascists encouraging the hippies to move to alcohol. Instead of 'turn on, tune in, drop out' it will be 'conform, drink up, fall down'.

I said I wasn't clear which side of the revolution this Electric Flag group is on. Both sides, he says. The white players are on the side of status quo, and the black players are on the side for change. Each is trying to sneak in information or subliminal messages for their own purposes.

Janis Joplin did die from booze, so it's not too far fetched I suppose. Neil is starting to sound more like his brother. Maybe this is his way of making sure Jerry is not forgotten.

Solo showed up around 9 and I left. Neil knows I don't like hanging out with Solo. Neil says he's cool with that but anyway I should come around on Friday and even bring my recorder.

Thursday, January 27, 1977

In study period, just before lunch, Mr. Peebles came over and said: come with me. He took me to the Principal's office and Detective Hooper was there. He said do you mind answering a few more questions and I said sure. I didn't realize he meant at the police station! So Det. Hooper takes me down there in his squad car (front seat at least) and puts me in a small room with a table, two chairs, and a one-way glass window just like in the movies. At first I think everything is okay. He gives me a can of Coke and says I can help the investigation if I want and that it is important I tell the truth. Sure. Then the questions start: how long have you known Neil and Jerry? Easy question. Did Jerry ever mention Kiblah? No. Did Jerry have any enemies? No. Did Neil have any enemies? Well, the likes of Lucky and Brian. He probed on this and I had to mention the milkshake incident.

Have you seen any evidence of violence or lawbreaking in their lives? I said I thought it was likely that Jerry liked to smoke grass but I hadn't seen it myself. I said Neil didn't do that, but he smokes cigarettes.

Detective Hooper got a little less friendly after that. What about violence he asked? Jerry, never. Neil, nothing I'd seen. I don't count (or mention) things done to protect me.

Where were you on the night of December 12? Just like my diary says, I said, I was in the shed for most of the evening. Did I know what Neil was doing that afternoon? No. Do I know what happened after 9:30? No. Don't I have to admit it was possible that Neil accompanied Jerry to Kiblah's house that afternoon? Calls for speculation, I said. How would I know?

He showed me the taped copy of Budgie I made Jerry. Did I create this? Yes. Do I realize that I am breaking copyright laws and could be fined thousands of dollars? No. Then he really threatened me. If I don't tell the truth, my parents will wind up in a police car in front of our house, where the neighbours will see them, and the cops will ransack our house, reading all of my diary, confiscating all my tapes. Things will get broken. I had no choice. So I admitted that Neil grabbed Lucky by the throat in class last week. I didn't see it, so I've not lied. I only heard about it, so why mention hearsay? You will mention hearsay, he tells me.

Do you think that Jerry was mentally unbalanced? No way. The police are the status quo but they protect our society, I said. That gave him pause.

He asked the same questions over and over. At one point he showed me a picture of Jerry, dead, with black marks splotted around his neck. I tried not to look at it. I kept my answers the same and as short as possible. After several hours, I said shouldn't I have a lawyer? You're too young, he said. Can I talk to my parents, then? The questions stopped and I waited in that little windowless room, forever it seemed.

Eventually he let me go. It was already dark outside (5:10pm) and I was late for supper. The folks were shocked I had spent so long with the police. Dad was angry. I said don't worry about it.

If Neil is right, the police are part of the conspiracy to stop change. If you blatantly challenge them, you might wind up like Jerry. I feel they are trying to make Neil a scapegoat for Jerry's murder.

Worked until 9. Now it is 11:40 and I am just not having any luck getting to sleep. Very worried about Neil.

Friday, January 28, 1977

I may be a better artist than I thought. In Art period Mrs. Adams was being lazy and said just go ahead, use the large paper, and do whatever watercolor you want. I was making a view of the Earth from the Moon. I had the Earth and the lunar surface done when Mike Webb came up and said what a cool painting. He was on a free period and finishing up a charcoal sketch of a clump of basketball players, all arms and legs. He's a lot higher up on the social ladder than me (tall, suave) so I wasn't expecting any comment, especially a positive one.

Brian must have overheard because when I turned my back he dropped a big blob of yellow paint on my Earth. Undeterred, I just changed the blob into a giant explosion then colored all the background black for void. Now I have a picture of the Earth breaking out of solar orbit. Mike came back later and asked me to explain the altered picture. When I said it was an inversion or variation on the idea of *Space: 1999*, he said I was very creative! I called my painting *Breakaway: 1977*.

At lunch I told Sam and Neil about my painting and Mike's comments. I was a little disappointed that Neil jumped on the technical accuracy high horse and said that as the Earth moved away from the Sun, the oceans would freeze and everyone would die. It's just a painting.

Neil made sure I was coming over with my recorder tonight saying: you have to tape everything so I can prove what I've been saying. I'm not sure what he means. He also invited Sam and she promised again she would make it but she hasn't yet. Now it is after school and I need a cassette with a mostly blank side to take with me.

Roger: Okay. The tape is gonna pick up every *(unintelligible)*

Neil: Check!

Roger: That made the light flash. Okay. Tonight, I have Lionel O'Neill and Samantha Renfield with me. Welcome to the Alphan Clubhouse, Sam!

Sam: Nice to finally be here, although it's a little cold. I'm glad I've got my mitts.

Roger: Not as cold as the void of space!

Sam: *(laughs)* Well, almost!

Neil: It's on full blast. Put your feet in front of it.

Roger: To start, we're going to talk about Moonbase Alpha. Neil, you've been spending a lot of time lately working on *blueprints* of Alpha, right?

Neil: Yes. The base is a manifestation of my subconscious desire for a proper environment, a secure place where I can evolve.

Roger: You don't live there ...

Neil: No, no. It's fiction, but it comes from the same source as my own feelings. It's not only that it speaks to me, but it's saying what I've wanted to say. The future is fantastic, amazing. Brave people with trust in the future and no fear of the unknown will prevail. The opposite of here today, where cowards strike out in fear and hate.

Roger: You think our space program has cowards?

Neil: No, man. The programs are good; it's the rest of Earth. The governments and the different groups. That is what the hippies were trying to say: our present reality is not groovy. But they come up a bit short on the solution because they don't have the technology. That's what the future is about, the technology.

Roger: The technology will give us more info and then we won't have to be afraid of the unknown or the future?

Neil: Yeah. But to create the technology you have to co-operate. You can't kick people around because they're short, or Indian, or whatever. You've got to respect their talents and let them on the team. People *not* working together isn't going to get us to the future any faster.

Sam: I think you're right about technology and change going together. And the pace of change keeps increasing. Look how different our world is to fifty years ago, and then compare a hundred years ago. Change is coming faster and faster. Technology is like a snowball and once it really gets rolling, we'll see a lot of big changes.

Roger: So you think 1999 is a reasonable time frame for a moon base?

Sam: Definitely. We know a space shuttle is on the way. Once that's going, we'll have the means to build stuff in space. I think we might even see something by the end of the 80s. By 1999 we might be far beyond what we see on *Space: 1999.*

Roger: Neil, do you agree with Sam's assessment of where we're going in the next couple of decades?

Neil: Well it depends who controls the technology. If it's the big corporations and government, I'm not so sure. If it's individuals, then it's possible. Things are happening faster and faster, both in technology and in culture so anything's possible. But it's also easy for fascists to derail real progress.

Sam: But when the new generation controls the corporations and government then everything *will* change.

Neil: That depends on that new generation. If they've been bred to be sheep, then any autocratic ruler can slow change to a crawl.

Roger: What do you think about Commander Koenig's autocratic ruling style?

Neil: Well I don't think he is ruling, or a ruler.

Roger: He's a yardstick! *(laughs)*

Neil: Sure. The measure of all men. But he's on Alpha because he's accepted a responsibility to help them. He's not trying to mess with anyone. Without a crisis, he'd let his staff carry on until they needed a command decision.

Roger: But there always *is* a crisis.

Sam: The show must go on!

(laughter: Roger and Sam)

Neil: You're right though. He's got a dictator-like position on Alpha. It's a wonder that it hasn't corrupted him. I mean, this is why he's such a hero. He views command as more responsibility than power. Survival is the only status quo he wants to maintain.

Roger: In "Another Time, Another Place" we see the Alphans re-populate a dead Earth. They disperse into small groups throughout the only habitable valley on that ravaged future Earth. Koenig does gives up his authority over his people at that point, so he can't be a dictator.

Sam: Roger, Koenig was dead at that point, crashed in an Eagle on the Moon. It was probably Paul's decision to let the Alphans spread out into different groups. Or maybe he didn't have any control over them at that point.

Neil: I agree. You can't read too much into that.

Roger: Okay, let's get back to your Alpha blueprints. As you draw, what assumptions are you making about the lives of the Alphans?

Neil: I'm not so much assuming as interpolating.

Roger: Not sure what that means.

Neil: I'm taking known, general facts about Alpha and turning them into specifics. For instance we know that the Alphans wear standard uniforms. So there's got to be a central laundry. We know there's a large recreation building, so I can be fairly sure it'll contain similar entertainments as we have today, a theatre, a cinema, a library. We are told that Alpha is self-sufficient, so that means they need fabrication facilities for fabrics, for plastics, for electronics, and so on. All these details can be supported by general facts or specific instances in episodes.

(pause with sound of papers rustling)

Sam: These are really detailed. Are you going to give them to that Association of Alphans?

Neil: I might. Mostly I'm doing it for myself right now.

Roger: Your subconscious desire... what'd you say?

Neil: Alpha represents hope to me. A place in the future where people are worthy of your trust, authority is trying to help you, intellect is respected, and discrimination is part of the past. Only there can I reach my full potential. When I started the first drawing I thought it was just my love of this type of drafting, this technical art, the visualization of spaces, but as it went on I realized there was a deeper reason why I was doing it. This is where I want to be.

Roger: Drawing in the shed?

Neil: No! On Moonbase Alpha! If I could live somewhere where people were authentic, not robots programmed by their culture... thinking about that type of existence gives me hope. I may be stuck here in body, but my mind is free. Even the government can't take that away from me.

Sam: The government?

Roger: You mean the status quo, or the government?

Neil: The government is the primary agent of the status quo. All the institutions in society work to enforce the status quo: schools, government, corporations. That's the reason I wanted you to tape this tonight. You have to understand you're being molded by forces with reasons of their own, and not your best interests in mind. If you want change, you're going to have to get past the short term interests of the entrenched power class. They won't give up power willingly and you need to be reminded of this. When people go missing, those left behind have to speak out. If I go missing at least you'll still have this tape to prove I was here and what I was about.

(fifteen second pause)

Sam: You think the government is going to snatch you?

Neil: I don't know what I believe anymore. How can I explain what happened to Jerry? I know he was aware of a vast inter-generation power struggle. Who else was? And then he goes missing and we find out that a teacher is responsible. Teachers are the ones responsible for indoctrinating children. If that fails, maybe they're responsible for the cleanup of loose ends too.

Sam: That's chilling. If teachers are involved, it's a vast conspiracy.

Neil: When you rule out the impossible, whatever remains, no matter how improbable, must be true. Sherlock Holmes.

Sam: I can't believe all of our teachers would be in on something like that.

Neil: It doesn't have to be all of them. The powerful ones will select for advancement the younger ones who are willing to take on the dirty tasks. I don't know why you resist the idea. You've seen them gang up on you when you wanted to take TV production with the boys. That was a change they didn't like, and they tried to stop you, making you write that ridiculous paper.

Sam: That's not the same as murdering someone.

Neil: It's just a first step. If you persist in being a problem, steps will escalate.

Sam: I don't blame you Neil, but you've got a pretty dark view of humanity. I've always viewed the church as an oppressive institution, brainwashers, you know? But you see everything like that. If that's the way it is, then who can you trust?

Neil: Only the young. And only *some* of them. There are probably thinkers and artists of all ages in this battle, but in Saskatchewan?

Roger: Nothing, huh?

Sam: You need to get out of here. Graduate, move away, live your own life. It's the small town no-thinking trap that's behind all this. I'm sure it's not an organized thing. Most old people hate change. They have more to lose.

Neil: It's a murmur, that turns into a whisper, that becomes a defiant statement, that explodes into an angry shout, and finally, beaten, retreats with a whimper. It's the cycle of conflict. As we get stronger and organize, those against us grow stronger and organize too. It's a natural law of conflict that things worsen slowly until a breaking point is reached. We're near that point now.

Sam: I don't know.

Roger: If that's the case, what can we do about it?

Neil: You're doing it. Tape what I have to say. Think about it. Think about everything society asks you to do, and then *question* it. Is it in the interests of the status quo, or in your own interest? Does it take the world further ahead, or does it just help the powerful?

Sam: So you're advocating awareness, not action?

Neil: No. Awareness *leads* to action. If you know something is wrong, then you're more likely to act against it. Thinking is not solely an ivory tower exercise. It should point your feet in the right direction.

Roger: So you want us to tell others about the … um…

Neil: I've told *you* because I trust you. I've got to trust *someone*. I'm not recommending you shout this from the roof tops because that'll only attract the attention of the fascists and you'll be singled out for… handling. You've got to be discreet. Find trustworthy people. Do what you can, but be careful.

Sam: Speaking of careful, my folks will be home soon and I've got to get there first. Really Neil, I can't believe all the stuff you've got in here.

Neil: Most of the books are Jerry's but I've read a lot of them. The stereo is his too. He bought a lot of these records used. Only a few are mine. The chairs came from our old house on Circlebrooke Drive. When we moved to this little house, there was no room for all our old furniture and we got rid of most of it, but Jerry insisted these chairs come with us. On Circlebrooke we had a rec room in the basement with a bar and a dartboard. I used to sit at that bar and Jerry would pour me a cold glass of water with ice cubes. We'd talk about the future. We were going somewhere far away and wonderful some day. I remember shaking my drink, listening to the ice cubes clink.

Roger: Wouldn't be hard to make ice cubes in here.

Sam: You must really miss him.

Neil: Yeah.

Sam: It's okay. You'll be okay. Don't let this destroy your life. Jerry would want to see you succeed. You've got to beat the system for him.

Neil: You guys are great. I don't know what I'd do without you.

(sound of wooden door opening, then slamming shut)

Solo: Hey, you've got a crowd tonight!

Neil: This is Sam. Sam, my friend Solo.

Sam: Hi. Are you a science fiction fan too?

Solo: More of a music fan really. I was like Jerry's best friend.

Sam: Ah. You're Jerry's age?

Solo: Yeah pretty close. Hey, Professor Armstrong, what's happening man?

Neil: This conversation's being taped right now. *(in imperative voice:) Roger.*

Roger: Didn't you wanna tape everything?

Entries from Roger Kay's 1977 Diary

Friday, January 28, 1977 (2nd entry)

Just after 10 pm now. Taped almost a whole side in the shed. When Solo showed up, Sam and I left. We are very concerned about Neil. He seems to be turning into a fiery revolutionary. If he straps an ammunition belt across his chest, we may consider having lunch with someone else. This Jerry thing has really turned him inside out.

Sam and I walked to Victoria School and sat on the steps of the boy's entrance, where it is sheltered from the wind, to talk. She is very thoughtful and caring. I think she's in love with Neil. We agreed we would stick by him no matter what.

I was elated to have her alone with me, but after only a couple of minutes in the brutal cold I started to shiver uncontrollably. Sam was surprised but I told her it was perfectly normal for me. I have a low tolerance for cold. Then my nose started to run. The conversation was going important places, but my nose wouldn't stop and I didn't have a Kleenex. I was so embarrassed. I had to say I was cold (I wasn't that cold) and go home. I didn't even walk her to 2nd because I was afraid the snot streaming down my face would gross her out. Shit! My stupid weak body!

Afterwards I was sitting in my room with my head in my hands and Dad came in and asked me what was wrong. I just said that there is a girl I like but I think I looked like a fool in front of her because my weak body won't let me do even normal everyday things. He said I was just too self-conscious and wouldn't I rather have a weak body than a weak mind? I had to agree with him but this time it didn't make me feel any better.

Saturday, January 29, 1977

Woke up very depressed. Laid around the house for a while. Watched TV all morning. Still very cold out but I thought I'd drop by the shed and see if Neil was there instead of at the YPL and I was right.

He was working on his Alpha blueprints again; for the Hydroponics Section he was drawing laboratories with large garden plots, shading in the soil areas. He showed me a paper cut on his thumb and claimed that the government was thinning the paper to make it more dangerous to use so they could discourage 'planning and expression'. Actually he wasn't all that talkative and I left after half an hour.

Came home, changed back into my pajamas, readied my tape recorder and settled in to watch/tape a new 1999 episode called "The Séance Spectre". Spent the evening writing up my summary.

Episode Summary: "The Séance Spectre" (1755 words)
[Omitted.]

Comments on "The Séance Spectre" (Roger Kay, 1994)

Alpha moves towards the space cloud Tora which might or might not have a solid core. Command Centre is keeping a tight lid on information. This does not sit well with some Alphans who feel that Koenig is trying to suppress information about a habitable planet in order to prolong his dictatorship. The ringleader of the discontent is Sanderson, head of the lunar exploration team that has spent more time than anyone else isolated on expeditions across the lunar surface.

When Koenig admits there is a planet within the cloud but claims the atmosphere is poisonous and they must explode nuclear waste in order to divert the Moon from colliding with it, Sanderson and team are not convinced and go guerilla to interfere with the plan.

Favorite scene: In the denouement, Helena has ordered all Alphans to spend hours looking at pictures of Nature from planet Earth to proactively treat the 'Green Sickness' that drove Sanderson to mutiny. She catches Tony and Alan viewing pictures of scantily clad woman. Now that's natural.

Entries from Roger Kay's 1977 Diary

Sunday, January 30, 1977
Sam didn't show up today. Neil was right on time. He says she might have gotten into trouble because she stayed out late last night. I hope not.

I'm just not feeling great today. I felt okay until after Neil was here, then I started to feel worse. For the first time I feel excluded from our Alphan triumvirate. What happens if Sam and Neil fall in love? I'd be left out in the cold and lose everything. It would be the end for me.

(Side two of the Black Sabbath LP Paranoid *is playing throughout)*

Roger: Today we are discussing the *Space: 1999* episode "The Séance Spectre". I have Lionel O'Neill with me.

Neil: And you are Roger Kay.

Roger: Yes I am. Thanks for reminding me. So what's your impression of "The Séance Spectre"?

Neil: No, no. Host first. What did you think?

Roger: Oh, okay. Thanks. Well, it has one of the best Eagle crashes of all time. And Maya turning into a plant to produce oxygen was inspired. Also, it really ties in to what we were talking about last night. Sanderson and friends believe Koenig's a dictator only interested in upholding the status quo.

Neil: I think this is definitely one of the, what did you call them, Bad Alphan episodes?

Roger: That's right!

Neil: Sanderson thinks Koenig is trying to keep everyone trapped on the moonbase so he can remain dictator. I think if it wasn't for Koenig in that command chair, if Gorski or Commissioner Simmonds were in charge, or maybe Tony, they probably would go fascist at some point.

Roger: But Tony's a good guy...

Neil: He's head of security. Koenig and Maya's expectations keep him in line. We don't know what he'd be like without their presence.

Roger: Huh.

Neil: One thing, and a little disturbing too. This whole séance thing- they didn't really explain it, but Sanderson is made to appear deranged with his references to prophecy. I think that's a little unnecessary. It's not unreasonable to assume Koenig is keeping a habitable planet from the others. Okay, not correct in this case, but not totally unreasonable.

Roger: This episode happens over two thousand days after breakaway. That's like *six years*. I think some Alphans *would* go crazy spending that long cooped up with the same people.

Neil: Yeah, the Green Sickness thing made sense.

Roger: Did you see when Koenig and Sanderson were fighting on the lunar surface? One time, Sanderson hits the ground and his spacesuit helmet visor slips open like an inch or so. I'm surprised they didn't re-shoot that scene.

Neil: No I didn't notice. Good eye.

(pause and sound of lighter igniting)

Neil: Some of the best episodes involve Koenig losing his command. Like "Seed of Destruction" or "Collision Course".

Roger: I really like it when they find an alien planet. The stranger the better.

Neil: Yeah that's cool. You can say this about "The Séance Spectre": we get to see some new Alphans and they actually have significant parts. There's got to be a lot of interesting people on Alpha. We should see more of them. And less Tony.

Roger: According to the matten there's five more episodes left this year. One is a two-parter, so really there's six hours left. Do you think it'll be significantly different this fall when it returns for the third season?

Neil: Impossible to predict. Depends if Freiberger is still around I suppose. And what actors they decide to go with. I wouldn't mind them dumping Tony, but it's not likely because he's Maya's love interest.

Roger: Although, as Sam likes to say, he's still waiting to make his move.

Neil: That's fine by me. She can date Alan next season, if she must. But unfortunately he seems a little immature too.

Roger: Alan immature? Why would you say that?

Neil: At the end of this episode, they're ogling pictures of women from the computer library. The script writers need to decide whether these guys are scientists or teenagers. They can't be both.

Roger: Scientists don't look at pictures of sexy women?

Neil: They have wives or girlfriends. That's what they're interested in. Not pictures. How does it make the female Alphans feel when the men are sitting around looking at that stuff and getting sweaty? Not cool.

Roger: We could ask Sam about that. If she were here.

Neil: She might've gotten into trouble last night. When she came back she stayed past 11. I doubt her parents didn't notice that.

Roger: She came back last night?

Neil: Yeah, Solo and I were smoking, talking about Eagles, after you left. Half an hour later, she came back and sat with us until almost eleven thirty. She's really worried about me.

Roger: It was so cold last night.

Neil: It got colder too. We were really huddled around the heater at the end.

Roger: Sam was talking about Eagles?

Neil: Yeah a little, but she's better at it than you.

Roger: Hang on. I'm gonna stop the tape.

On Samantha Renfield (Lionel O'Neill, 1988)

I first laid eyes on Samantha, or Sam as we called her, in my first Grade 9 homeroom period. For some reason I thought she was a farm girl. Maybe it was the simple, straight down the sides haircut. She sat to my right, I next to the door and she further into the front row. I had no inkling she was a special creature until Roger Kay introduced me to her on the second day of class.

It wasn't until years later that I realized Sam had had a crush on me. Certainly we enjoyed a stimulating intellectual rapport and spent time together, but for me this was always platonic. Roger, Sam and I were all good friends and I didn't see anything unequal about the relationship.

My first clue should have been that Sam was always trying to get me alone with her. That first day we had lunch together, when Roger introduced us, I think we wound up walking home without him. She had made some excuse about having to leave right away after school and I took the chance to go along. Her house was on 2nd Avenue North, a white two storey that looked quite prosperous. I was glad we didn't have to go past my own house, as it was tiny and miserable in comparison. We would spend longer saying goodbye than was reasonably required. Some things are clearer in retrospect.

Another clue was that whenever we argued about SF, whether it was technical details or artistic merit, she always seemed to be more upset at the idea I was disagreeing with her than the reasons I was opposed to her ideas. Again, clearer in retrospect.

I remember, after Jerry had disappeared, Sam was over at the shed one time, trying to comfort me. She moved to hug me and although I let her, as soon as she touched me, my mind went far away. I'm not sure if it was a romantic hug or just a reassuring one, but it was not something I was used to and I could not tolerate it emotionally, especially in that tumultuous time. If her intent was to bring us closer together, that hug failed. It drove me far further from her and reality. I wish I could have been more than a friend to her, but for me it was impossible. My fear and disgust at my own body was greater than any fascination with the female form.

On Fundamentalist Neil (Samantha Renfield, 1988)

By January 1977, my crush on Neil had me convinced he was in love with me but wouldn't admit it even to himself, such was his fear of destroying the triangle of friendship we had with Roger. I was convinced that if I got him alone, I could get past that protective barrier.

Neil talked a lot about the importance of the mind and that the body (sometimes referenced as 'emotions', or 'hormones') was the basis only for problems and destruction. At first I took this to be a pro-feminist, anti-sexist stand, and it was very attractive to my ideals. Here was a guy who said I will not judge you on beauty and I will not let my mind succumb to the temptations of the body. He would love with his mind first, and his body later. Problem was, the later part never came.

It was in coldest January that first evening I spent in Neil's shed. Roger was there and I think he was taping our conversations about *Space: 1999*. Roger and I left the shed early enough that I could get back to my house before my parents returned, but we stopped in front of Victoria School to talk about Neil. We were both very concerned, of course, as his brother had been murdered and a teacher had been accused of it. Neil had been very close to his brother. At that time we had no idea how sick Neil was getting, but we did notice that he seemed to be becoming more paranoid and increasingly difficult to understand. I'm sure Roger knew this because we talked about it that night. Then he got so cold, Roger had to abandon our discussion and go home.

After I said goodnight to Roger, I started towards home, but then I had a sudden impulse that Neil needed me, or maybe here was my chance to get him alone. So I turned back and returned to the shed.

I was very disappointed when I got there because Solomon was still inside with Neil. Everything was upside down. Solomon seemed happy to see me, but Neil was being very quiet. Soon I understood why. They were stoned.

I had heard about marijuana before and like everything my strict parents were so desperate to keep me away from, the mysterious substance compelled my interest. Neil certainly had primed me for this, with all his talk of alcohol being the devil that society uses to control you, while marijuana was the tool the young used to break their programming. So I tried it for the first time that night. The effect upon me was minimal, a bit of giddiness and strangeness, but that could have been a placebo effect. It did however affect Neil and Solomon quite more severely.

As I said, Solomon did seem glad to see me, but looking back this was less a personal commendation than just the effects of the dope. After he smoked, he was giddy and happy, making stupid jokes or laughing at non sequiturs. Neil was the opposite case. The more he smoked, the quieter he became, and the less sense he made. His non sequiturs were more problematic.

I didn't say much. And eventually what I was waiting for finally happened: Solomon left.

I remember I made a show of being cold and moved closer to the heater, which meant standing right next to Neil. I think I said: "You can always count on me" or some similar sentiment, and draped my arms around him in a friendly, let's stay warm way. Neil smiled briefly, and he didn't force me away, but that was all I got out of him.

We stood there for a few minutes. He had the best chance a guy ever had in this world to kiss a girl and he didn't take it. I had to assume he didn't want to, although when I finally gave up and moved away, I could tell he was aroused.

Just before that, he had delivered the coup de grace. He said "I'm so glad you guys are my friends." Then as if realizing the blatant inadequacy of this pronouncement, he added "You *are* very important to me." Then he patted my back a little, and went limp. But not everywhere. I could tell his body wanted me but his mind wasn't about to let biology get the better of him.

So that was it. I was part of 'you guys'. Important, apparently, but only as a non-sexual entity. At that point I began to see the parallels between his asexuality and the philosophy of my parents and their ridiculous religion: no sex until marriage and even then, don't enjoy it!

This would not be the philosophy for my future. This I would make certain.

Entries from Roger Kay's 1977 Diary

Monday, January 31, 1977

Neil was absent again today. Sam and I had lunch, but she seemed strange. I look at her and I'm not sure she's even the same person. She admitted she went back to the shed on Sunday, saying: I was just so worried about Neil that I had to check on him. We agree that Solo is not a good influence on him. She didn't mention exactly why, but we both know.

At the end of lunch hour, Mike Webb came and sat with us. He said he had watched "The Séance Spectre" and liked it. He mentioned my Earth breakaway painting again and said it was very imaginative.

Uncle Tim was away tonight and I had to work with Delmer again. What a pain. Everything I do, the guy says do it another way. It is like he expects I am going to do the wrong thing, or that I am not thinking about what I am doing. Just because you're older doesn't mean you know everything. What is worse, he didn't charge the pallet loader before I got there so it died about half way through the night and I had to move some cases by hand. Exhausting physical labour! Not what I signed up for.

Time is now 11:05. Very tired.

Tuesday, February 1, 1977

Neil was at school today. Sad that this qualifies as news. He said he was tired yesterday. Sam said she was really glad to see him, but didn't say much after that. Neil did open up at one point and said that the world was sliding towards a third world war. There was a lot of development of new weapons going on, both by the USSR and the USA, which the public would not know about until it was too late. I asked him if he saw this on TV and he denied it, sounding a little insulted.

I had to do my speech in English today. The asteroid belt was my subject and I made it through without too much terror. I was trying to look up at the audience and not just read it from the cards, but Mr. Peebles said I did not succeed. Good content, bad presentation. What am I, a PR hack? Writers don't have to read their own lines. They have specialists for that, actors and anchormen. I got a B+.

9-32 started speeches today too. Neil tried a new way of giving a speech. Rather than preparing cards to read, he decided to just draw on the board and talk about his subject. He presented 'Ayn Rand's Moral Basis for Capitalism'. Not sure how you'd draw that on the board, but Sam says he drew clusters of dollar signs next to stick figures and illustrated how wealth moved from individual to individual in a fair way only with a capitalist system. His main points: greed is good, selfishness is efficient, government intervention is fascist.

Neil got pretty far into it and was doing quite well until Mr. Peebles (he teaches English to all the Grade 9s) interjected that Neil was using a word incorrectly: 'fascist' only refers to WW2 Italians who fought for Mussolini. Neil disagreed but at that point he couldn't talk anymore, and after a few sputters just sat down. He says he only got about halfway through his speech. Neil is way too smart to be in this school.

Near the end of lunch, Webb came over and told Neil that his topic was fascinating, and the teacher shouldn't have interrupted him. Neil struggled to answer this, saying that we would soon all know more about fascists than we ever wanted. And they wouldn't be Italian.

His stutter is much worse when he's not talking to just Sam or me. With us, sometimes his words will catch a little, but mostly he is fine. With Webb, Neil was struggling and had to stop and take a breath a few times to get over a bump. I hardly ever see him in that type of situation anymore, so it is easy to forget that he has that problem.

I dropped over to the shed after supper. Both Neil and Solo were there but I didn't stay long because it was very smoky in there. Neil was telling Solo about how the fascists were going to take over the world. They were listening to old LPs of Jerry's and coming up with outlandish ideas that each song had a hidden meaning tied to the coming revolution. I wasn't sure if they were serious, but Solo sure seemed to be encouraging him, waving around *Blows Against The Empire* by Jefferson

Starship. I think Solo is a fake friend but I can't risk getting on the wrong side of him, so I just left.

When I got home I realized my clothes were all stinky again and now I'm completely out of clean clothes. I changed into pajamas and ran a wash and then a dry cycle. This took most of the night. I had barely enough time to put it all away before bedtime. What a pain.

Thursday, February 3, 1977

No Neil at school again today. Sam and I had lunch in our usual spot and guess who dropped around to talk to us. Webb of course. He and Sam both gave their speeches today.

Sam's was on Transcendental Meditation, which is basically a way for people to temporarily leave their body and travel around in a ghost-like 'astral body'. I asked her if she really believed in it and she said no, but like UFOs, there is a small chance of some grain of truth to it, and it is interesting. I read her speech from her cards and the whole TM thing does not seem very scientific to me.

Sam really liked Webb's speech and she insisted he hand over his cards for me to read while she extolled it to the heavens. His speech focuses on the *Star Trek* character Spock and how he is an outsider who must try to get along with those very different from him. It is actually a very compassionate speech and I can see why Sam fell for it. The teacher did too; Webb got an A.

The thing Webb never mentions is that he himself is not an outsider, so any empathy he has does not come from real experience. This good looking, popular, strong guy writes a speech about what it is like to be an outsider and everyone falls over themselves congratulating him. While the real outsiders look on in stunned amazement. It is like John Wayne writing about what it would be like to be the world's first female jet fighter pilot.

At 5 I got a call from Uncle Tim. The pallet mover isn't working properly so if you can't stack cases without it, he said, don't bother coming in. Well I can't, so I won't, I told him. No problem, he says, we'll get someone else. So that's it, I've lost my job. I bet Delmer sabotaged the pallet mover just to screw me.

After supper I dropped over to the shed and found Neil and Solo there. They were listening to music and Neil was right out of it, not saying anything. Eventually he asked me what time it was and I said 8. He said a.m. or p.m. and I don't think he was kidding. When I asked him why he wasn't at school, he said it didn't matter and that he had important experiments to do instead.

To me, it looked like they were just sitting around, listening to music. They had the case of Pic-A-Pop that I always give to Neil on Sundays. Usually it stays in the house and lasts all week. Tonight they had it in the shed, and it was almost empty. Solo offered me one. Maybe he doesn't realize who they come from. I took the last root beer.

Solo seemed to have commandeered the stereo because he restarted the record when it ended. How many times can you listen to "Strawberry Fields Forever"? Twice is more than enough for me. Then Neil suggested we all go on a clay hunting expedition behind Leon's. Now that I know the water runoff channel where Neil gets his clay is actually sewage runoff, and because I have no desire to fall through ice into a warm pool of sewage, I said: not for me, no thanks.

Friday, February 4, 1977

I've been slacking off my French lately, I have to admit. We had a quiz today and I only scored 6/10. Didn't tell the folks about that.

At lunch Sam and Webb showed up at our spot, but Neil wasn't around. They spent the whole lunch hour talking about *Star Trek*. I feel like I've been stabbed in the heart, or maybe the brain. I didn't say much.

After school I dropped by the shed. No Neil. After supper I tried again. Still no Neil. I went home and laid around in a daze. Is it day or night? Who cares.

Saturday, February 5, 1977

Today was much better. I woke up early and watched a lot of silly shows, although I do like *Wolfman Jack*, and then went downtown after lunch.

Stopped in at The Stereo Hut, but didn't buy anything. Then I went to Logan's Drugs and bought the new *Kamandi* comic. When I stopped at the YPL I was not expecting Neil to be there, but he was! He seemed okay and laughed when I asked him if he knew if it was morning or night. He said: what's the difference, at this time of year it is dark for both.

On his advice I took out an SF book Ubik by a new (to me) author: Philip K. Dick.

We went for coffee at the Summit Café and he told me that he and Solo were on an acid trip when I was over on Thursday. He says I should have come with them because they spent the night lying in a snow bank, somewhere behind Leon's Manufacturing, watching the stars play hide and seek behind batches of clouds. If it was with just Neil and Sam, I'd consider doing it, but not with Solo. He's not our age and I just don't trust him, supposed friend of Jerry's or not.

Neil wanted to show me a drawing he did so I walked back with him. When we got to the shed, Solo was already inside with some hippy looking girl, his age, not ours. She left after only a minute or two.

Neil's drawing was of a giant spiral galaxy and instead of stars, it was all eyes. The eyes streaming down the nearest spiral arm in the foreground have vein lines in them, like maybe they are older than the eyes at the center of the galaxy. Neil didn't describe what it meant so I was just confused. It was almost 4 so I had to rush home to tape 1999.

As usual, spent the evening re-listening to parts of the episode tape and assembling my summary. Then I stayed up late, reading Ubik.

Episode Summary: "The Bringers Of Wonder, Part 1"
(1526 words)
[Omitted.]

Comments on "The Bringers Of Wonder, Part 1"
(Roger Kay, 1994)

Koenig exhibits bizarre behavior, flying an Eagle erratically, whooping and laughing while swooping much too close to the nuclear waste domes. When his Eagle inevitably crashes, Helena puts him on an experimental brain machine to induce sleep and healing.

An Earth Superswift spacecraft appears over Alpha, piloted by Tony's hyper-competitive brother Guido. The Alphans are going home! Dr. Shaw, Helena's urbane medical mentor, is with the Superswift crew, as well as Diana Morris, a barracuda from Koenig's past.

The only problem is when Koenig awakes, apparently fully healed, he doesn't see friends from Earth. He sees horrifying putrescent aliens!

Favorite scene: Tony introduces Maya to Diana, explaining that the Psychon is the last of her kind. Diana comments that "she is not surprised" and turns away, dismissively. Tony has to give Maya a severe warning look as she transforms into one of her favorite scary space monsters and prepares to grab Diana from behind.

(Space: 1999 soundtrack LP side 1 plays throughout)
Roger: Okay. Today we're discussing "The Bringers of Wonder", part one of two. Any opening comments, Samantha Renfield?

Sam: Yes, Roger Kay, I think if we're grouping episodes under general headings, you know, you mentioned Bad Alphan episodes, then I think this one, or two, should belong to the Believe Koenig set of episodes, where everybody but Koenig is wrong, and he has to either convince them or use threats to get his way and save the day.

Roger: Yeah, there's "Collision Course", "Guardian of Piri"...

Sam: And then "Seed of Destruction" which combines Bad Alphan and Believe Koenig styles.

Roger: Right! Koenig says believe me, but *he's* the bad alphan!

(laughter: Roger and Sam)

Neil: I find the Elendorf machine a fascinating idea. If you could massage people's brains so that all illusion drops away, that could change the world. People depend so much on illusion instead of reality. We think of things as permanent, but they're not. We view people as predictable and known, but they're not. We think we exist, but do we?

Sam: I think a certain amount of illusion is required in most people's lives. That's why we have religion. It takes a very strong person to say, there's no great overseer in the sky looking after me. When I die, I'm done. That fear of death would drive the average person insane.

Neil: I agree. And what would happen if you strip away all the illusion of society, of roles, and labels. If we didn't have these little compartments to put ourselves in, how would we define ourselves?

Sam: Maybe by our relations to others, our family, friends. That's not illusion.

Neil: No, I don't know about that. Married people divorce. Families break up. Friends turn on you. Those ties are no less fragile to personal whim than religious belief is to rational thought.

Sam: Okay. If you want to talk about illusion, look at people's sex lives. We spend all of our time worrying about covering up our bodies, or hiding our desires. The hippies tried to change this with free love, but they only scratched the surface of our inability to face our own sexuality.

Roger: Do you believe in free love?

Sam: More than I do marriage.

Neil: Sex is a powerful force for sure. If we just let it out without regard to the consequences, people will get hurt.

Sam: A lot of people get hurt by *keeping* it bottled up. Seems to me it would cause less harm if people dealt with it in an open manner.

Neil: But what about the confusion between love and sex? If people were clear about which was which, there'd be less problems. I agree with that.

Sam: Still, people have the right to use their own bodies for their own purposes. For parents to say their kids shouldn't have sex until they're married isn't very realistic. It's usually very hypocritical. There's illusion, then there's just plain lying, which is what a lot of adults do to justify their own behavior.

Roger: Okay. I think we're a bit off topic. "The Bringers of Wonder"…?

Sam: It's a good episode because we get to meet a lot of people from the Alphans' past. Usually guest stars are limited to aliens, so this is a real opportunity for the script writers to fill in some detail on the history of our favorite Alphans. This plus the extreme drama of a Believe Koenig situation, you know, his closest friends thinking him crazy, that makes for some terrific conflict.

Roger: You'd think by now everyone would just accept *whatever* Koenig told them.

Sam: Maybe by next season.

(laughter: Roger)

Neil: These aliens are really insidious. How do we know the Moon isn't still orbiting the Earth and the aliens are responsible for everything the Alphans have experienced since September 1999?

Roger: Once you open that door, it's very hard to close.

Sam: Loss of illusion can be devastating. There's no going back. You can only go forward with the truth you've found, which is probably an illusion too.

Neil: Do you ever get the feeling that things are really different from what we think?

Roger: Like the government is controlling us?

Neil: I mean beyond that. Like the nature of time and reality itself. Our little brains see the cage around us, but we have no idea that there's a house outside our cage, and a city and a planet beyond the house too.

Roger: You mean like other planets?

Neil: No, more like an entirely different universe. Like we're sleeping and dreaming and when we wake up, we'll find out that we're not who we thought we were at all. And it's not the same world as in the dream.

Roger: I wish for that all the time.

Sam: *(laughs)* Roger, Roger. You are blessed with a beautiful brain and many talents. Don't let this backwater life get to you.

Roger: Thanks. So, okay, if we go the other way, what didn't we like in this episode?

Neil: Well, that Diana Morris character. First she seems to be competing with Dr. Russell for Koenig. Then five minutes later she's after Tony. I don't know if she's the same as the real Diana, but I doubt Koenig would be interested in that type of woman. She's very shallow. It's the sex and power of being in the role of Koenig's girlfriend that she's after. Not love.

Roger: What do you mean, the real Diana?

Neil: The one Koenig remembers, the human on Earth, not this projection by the aliens.

Sam: Well she isn't very likeable, but that doesn't mean she's not believable. I mean Tony's brother Guido is not much different.

Neil: You're right. He's a crappy brother. Coming onto Maya in front of Tony like that. Not cool.

Sam: Yeah. Another problem is the timeline again. If this is six years after breakaway, the people from Earth should've aged and changed. I don't think anybody commented on that happening.

For example, Ben Vincent's fiancé. Ben's been gone six years, assumed dead or at least lost forever, and his fiancé does not move on with her life? These are the clues the Alphans should've picked up on. They could detect this illusion if they allowed themselves a suspicion.

Roger: Maybe that's it. They're so happy to see these people, and so anxious to go home, they're not thinking carefully.

Neil: It really is brilliant the way the Alphans' latest challenge is a reflection of the problem facing our generation today. Think about it: we'll inherit great technology and great power, very good things, but at the same time we have this huge curtain of illusion hiding the true nature of our government, our culture, ourselves, and perhaps physical reality itself. But we don't dare strip away all that's false because what's left underneath may be much less attractive. The Alphans have to strip away their illusion to survive, and humanity will have to do it too.

From the Ayn Rand perspective, this art is worthwhile because it recreates for us in ideal form an issue that we need to, and can, face.

Sam: Until we get past these illusions, I don't think we'll get the really good technologies: interstellar travel, medicine to re-grow limbs, reverse disease, and maybe, eventually, halt aging.

Neil: You didn't seem interested in eternal life before…

Sam: Not if you're just copying my brain pattern into a robot body.

Neil: Well it wouldn't be a robot as we think of them now. More like a cyborg.

Roger: Like Steve Austin's cyborg arm and legs. They feel very real to him.

Sam: Yeah, that seems worthwhile. As long as you don't wind up owing six million to Oscar Goldman.

Roger: *(laughs)* He cost OSI an arm and a leg!

Sam: Two legs! But hey it's probably very satisfying battling the forces of evil.

Roger: Oh oh. I think we're running on fumes here.

Entries from Roger Kay's 1977 Diary

Sunday, February 6, 1977

Had a sleepy morning. Neil and Sam were here this afternoon. I taped our conversation about the BOW, Part 1. It was a good session. Despite everything, Neil seems back to normal.

I spent some time, or wasted some time, reading the jobs section in the paper. My problem is I can't get a real job until this summer when I turn 16, and in the meantime I'd hate to go back to delivering papers. After being paid literally dollars per hour, I can't go back to just pennies per newspaper.

I don't understand what went wrong with my Pic-A-Pop job. I got along fine with everyone, well except Delmer. The problem is that Delmer has been working for Uncle Tim forever and if he wants to get me in trouble by sabotaging equipment or spreading lies to ruin my reputation, then I can't do much about it. I suppose I could get Mom to talk to him, but I don't want to resort to that. It is all really very unfair.

Had a bath and went to bed early: 10:45. Good night.

Monday, February 7, 1977

School was okay. No job to go to tonight. The reality of this is starting to hit home. I feel I am entering a period of extreme poverty. How long can my savings last? Too upset to write more.

Tuesday, February 8, 1977

Science quiz in first period. I got 9/10. I saw Brian's paper and he got 5/10. Good pass job, moron! I made sure he didn't see my grade.

Neil and Sam were around for lunch and for the first time Webb joined us to make it four. Webb seemed kind of wary of Neil, like Neil might punch him if he talked to Sam. But Sam is not Neil's girlfriend and it is not like that. I like to see Webb cringe when Neil finally says something.

If Webb wants Sam he is going to have to re-think his approach. We talked about careers and Sam was saying that she wants to get a Ph.D. and work at a university. She's not sure exactly what type of science she's interested in, but figures that will become clear in high school. I said I wanted to be a writer but Webb just ignored me and asked Sam how long she'd teach before she got married and had kids. I had to stop myself from laughing out loud. Sam's eyes went wide and she was furious. I could tell because when she's angry she talks very clearly and slowly, like she's talking to an idiot. Which makes sense. So she starts explaining to Webb that first of all, she won't be teaching, she'll be doing research. And, second, it won't make a difference when she decides to have children because her husband will be staying home to look after them. That shut him up. She has mentioned before that she doesn't want kids, so I think her answer was more designed to stymie his come-on than answer his (stupid) question. So long Mr. Trek!

I was gonna drop by Neil's tonight but Mom made me stay in and do laundry. I still have enough clothes for a couple more days, but she said the hamper is full, so now is the time. Serves me right for putting my clothes in the hamper! Sort, fold, and hang. Ah, the golden hours of childhood.

Later. I discovered a Kleenex was left in a pocket and now it is dissolved all over my clothes, dried into a sort of permanent dandruff. What a painful waste of an evening. I am not happy.

Wednesday, February 9, 1977

Marvin and I were playing fetch in study hall. He would snatch the pen out of my hand and throw it across the room. When I went to get it, he'd take something else from my desk and throw it the other way. This went on for a while until I got wise and knocked everything off his desk. Of course then Mr. Peebles comes in and says: what did you do Roger? Yeah, it was all me.

At lunch Webb was nowhere to be seen. Sam was telling us that her parents had taken on a new role in their church and would be out in the evening a lot. Her younger brother Peter is now responsible for looking after her (how sexist!) which is excellent because he will let Sam do whatever she wants, and then cover up as required. I've been kidding her that she is a werewolf, the only possible explanation for her never being around after dark, but now she says she will howl at the Moon.

Neil said, you can howl all you want, but just make sure you are on the Moon when it breaks away. He has a really dry sense of humor sometimes.

After supper I went over to the shed to hang with Neil. He showed me some more of his Moonbase Alpha blueprints. He is well over half done the above ground levels in all the buildings. The drawings are interesting but the lettering is shaky and hard to read, giving it an amateur look. Also he is very inconsistent with the size of details, like windows and doors. I didn't mention this. He seems entirely oblivious to the shortcomings of his work.

Around 8 who should show up but Sam! This is only her second time. We listened to a Jethro Tull record called *Aqualung*. It has a remarkable parody of scripture on the back which ingeniously reverses a key Bible idea: Man created God in his own image. Sam was impressed by this, saying it would explain why God is a white male saddled with ideas from a long dead era.

Beyond the cover, the record has some really rocking songs ("Locomotive Breath") plus a lot of good lyrics for a religion cynic. At one point he sings that God is "not the kind you have to wind up on Sunday". Take that, religious hypocrites! I think Sam has a lot of anger towards her parents who spend all their time helping out at the church but have no time for their own kids.

Solo showed up eventually and everybody talked about Eagles except me. I find it too tiring.

Neil got fired up at one point and explained Ayn Rand's view of altruism, that helping other people just for the idea of helping other people was not a good thing. You should only help those who deserve your help. By that he means those who will pay you back eventually. Ayn Rand doesn't believe in something for nothing. An act is 'good' if it is 'good for you', nothing else. This of course is the opposite of Christianity, so Sam was pretty intrigued. Solo mostly just listened but I don't like the way he looks at Sam. Doesn't he have a girlfriend his own age?

Came home and threw my stinky clothes into the hamper. Mom said she talked to Uncle Tim and I can have my job back! I didn't ask her to do it, but she says that I've been looking very sad the last couple of days so she went ahead and called him anyway.

Very tired now but I also feel good, sort of optimistic.

Thursday, February 10, 1977

Neil missed school again today. Webb saw Sam and I having lunch and he tried to join us. Sam asked him point blank: Do you believe Jesus Christ is the Lord, Our Savior? He said, well sure, as if it was obvious. So Sam says: okay then, fuck off! I laughed and laughed after he left.

I was happy to be back at Pic-A-Pop tonight. Uncle Tim told Delmer and me that if Delmer forgets to charge the pallet mover during the day, he will have to help me move cases at night until the work is done. That should solve that. I still don't think Delmer likes me, but at least now he won't mess with me because he knows Uncle Tim won't stand for it. Rocking!

There is a new guy too: Stanley. He mostly helps Delmer in the front, talking to customers and hauling cases to their car if the customer is really old. He said 'pleased to meet you' and seems nice. He is about Solo's age, with long hair too, but he doesn't have a carney vibe like Solo.

At 9 I stopped by Neil's but the shed was quiet and dark. There was a light on in the house and I heard some music so I knocked on their back door. When Neil's mom opened the door, I think she was expecting someone else because her face dropped as soon as she saw me. She was wearing a housecoat and maybe not much else because when she moved I saw a lot of the skin of her leg. Also I don't think she was wearing a bra. I was sort of embarrassed and she was a little angry saying: if he's not in the shed, you should use the telephone so you don't disturb us! Not sure who 'us' is. Isn't Neil's dad living in Saskatoon now? If his mom is messing around maybe that is where Neil gets his distaste for 'animal desires'.

Saturday, February 12, 1977

Big dump of snow last night. Had to shovel the front walk and it took most of the morning. Then it starts snowing again of course.

After lunch I went to the YPL. Neil was there but we didn't go anywhere. He was really tired and just seemed to be hanging out, not even reading. He has spent the last couple days in Saskatoon with 'Earl'. Not sure why. He says he won't be home tonight either, but he'll be over on Sunday.

I took out a double LP *Uriah Heep Live*. Sweet Lorraine, there's a party going on!

Today was the second part of "Bringers of Wonder". Taped it at 4 and then spent the evening working on the summary.

Now it is 1:15. The late movie was *Beneath the Planet of the Apes*. I understand why Charlton Heston pushed the button at the end. I live with grunting, fighting subhumans every day.

Episode Summary: "The Bringers Of Wonder, Part 2"
(1988 words)
[Omitted.]

Comments on "The Bringers Of Wonder, Part 2"
(Roger Kay, 1994)

The aliens have the ability to manipulate humans by changing the reality they perceive based on details from their victim's memories. This is how they convinced the Alphans they are friends from Earth. After Koenig persuades Maya to undergo the same healing procedure as he had on the experimental brain machine, she too is immune from their influence and illusions. Now the fight is on to disillusion the rest of Moonbase Alpha.

Favorite scene: The settings in New York City and the Australian outback that the nuclear waste monitoring team believe they are experiencing when in fact they are readying Alpha's nuclear waste for a gigantic explosion intended to feed the starving aliens.

13 February 1977
(audio tape from collection of Roger Kay)

Roger: Okay today is February 13, 1977 and I have Samantha Renfield and Lionel O'Neill in the room to discuss "The Bringers of Wonder". Now that we've seen the finale to this two part episode, how would we rate it? Neil?

Neil: I think the idea of living in an illusion is profound. The aliens give the Alphans an alternative to their fate on Alpha: they can spend a few moments, in reality dying, but in their own minds, enjoying a long and happy life on an Earth constructed from their memories and desires. Koenig makes the same decision as he's made before, on the planet Piri: on behalf of all Alphans, Koenig says no thanks.

Sam: I think any great story does that for us. It strips away a layer of illusion and lets us see things normally hidden. Whether you have a little self-discovery, or for the first time empathize with a character you thought unsympathetic, you learn something by discarding some false shell of belief.

Roger: Isn't that where all understanding comes from, removing a crust of belief that has been built up over time and getting down to the original material, still fresh inside.

Sam: You make the quest for knowledge sound like an Oreo!

Roger: *(laughs)* Mmmm... sweet knowledge...

Neil: Sometimes the truth is very sour at its center. We think we live in a world of grownups and ideals but, in truth, most adults are very childish, and most people over thirty who spout ideals don't believe in those ideas but just mouth them because it supports their own status quo. There are a million examples.

Roger: One will do.

Neil: Take World War Two. We fought against the idea of a ruthless empire, German, Japanese, whatever. A lot of people died and most of Europe was destroyed. We found out that the empire, or Reich, was even more cold blooded than we thought. Putting people in ovens, slave labour, genocide, you

---

name it. So one generation later, what do we have to remind us of our epic struggle: *Hogan's Heroes*, a situation comedy about life among prisoners in a German POW camp. We see the evil German empire as a bunch of lazy, self-absorbed idiots who get run circles around by the quirky, fun-loving, and healthy prisoners. How ridiculous. How demeaning to those who actually spent time in those camps and faced the horrific threat of the Nazis.

Roger: Did your, I mean, was Earl a POW?

Neil: No, no. His family is Irish. My Mom's parents were German Jews but they emigrated in the nineteen thirties, before things got really nasty there. I've heard the tale many times of my uncle who spent months as a slave labourer in Buchenwald. He was lucky. He survived and lives in the States now. He's got a number tattooed on his arm.

Sam: Insanity.

Neil: My point is that by enjoying *Hogan's Heroes* you're layering a big blanket of no-big-deal on WW2. How can we avoid future wars if we don't recognize the true and horrific nature of what we've already gone through?

Roger: Those who do not learn from history are condemned to repeat it.

Neil: Exactly. If people still remembered clearly the hell of war in Europe, we'd never have gone into Vietnam.

Sam: What do you mean 'we'?

Neil: Hey if it's 'our' space program then I guess it has to be 'our' war too.

Roger: As long it's not 'our' president.

Sam: He's nobody's president now.

Roger: Now they got peanut guy.

Sam: Don't laugh. If he pays the federal government with his peanuts, maybe they'll be able to afford peanut farms in space.

Roger: *(laughs)* That'd be a very good thing. But getting back to the episode... Did you guys wonder about those nuclear waste dumps? Didn't they blow up the last of them in "Séance

Spectre"? Should there even be anything left after breakaway? Both nuclear waste areas blew up on September 13, 1999...

Sam: Which episode comes first? "Bringers of Wonder", or "Séance Spectre"?

Roger: I'll check the matten.

Neil: Alpha has three Nuclear Generating Areas and various nuclear waste domes attached to Alpha with travel tubes. Anton Zoref blew up one generator, so they still have two left, assuming one nuclear generator per area. The nuclear waste areas were for waste from Earth. The nuclear waste domes, it's pretty clear, are for their own wastes created by Alpha's generators. So they'll have more and more waste as time goes by.

Roger: Here it is. Huh. It says "Séance Spectre" is *after* "Bringers of Wonder". So that's okay then. In "Bringers" no waste was exploded, so that leaves lots for "Séance Spectre". The only problem is... *(sound of papers shuffling)* according to my episode summary, "Bringers" is like 2500 days after breakaway, about 500 days past the time given for "Séance Spectre" in the matten. So the matten definitely gives the wrong date for "Bringers".

If we believe the matten data for "Séance Spectre", which means it's only 2012 days after breakaway, then "Séance Spectre" is before "Bringers", which doesn't make sense.

Neil: I guess it's a question of how much waste was used in "Séance Spectre". If only a little is needed, then perhaps it was the fresh stuff.

Sam: Fresh? *(laughs)* You make nuclear waste sound like orange juice!

Neil: What can I say? I'm pro-nuclear energy.

Roger: I think there's a mistake in the matten. Dr. Russell clearly says it is 2515 days after breakaway in "Bringers" part two. The matten says 1912 days.

Sam: There's a lot of info in there. I guess a couple of errors shouldn't surprise us. Remember it is put together by the people at *Starlog*. They were probably busy thinking about *Star Trek*.

Roger: *(laughs)* Oh no! I don't think they'd let trekkies work on the matten.

Sam: You're an idealist, Roger.

Roger: And loving it.

Sam: Well we're getting close. I better run. Peter can only cover for me until 4. If I'm not there to help prepare supper, the Book of Revelation will unfold.

Roger: *(laughs)* No problem. We'll stop here.

Entries from Roger Kay's 1977 Diary

Sunday, February 13, 1977

Slept in until 10. At 1, Sam came over. We waited more than half an hour for Neil but he didn't show so we walked over to the shed but Solo was alone in there. He offered us $2 if we would walk over to Steve Bishop's girlfriend's sister's apartment and came back with an LP of his. We weren't too keen but he convinced us Neil had been there the previous night and so he was probably there now too, having uncharacteristically forgotten our plan to meet. I admit we took the bait.

The apartment is a vast, many limbed body of old brick buildings near the water tower, on the south side of downtown. I believe it used to be the hospital during WW2, before they built the Yorkton Union Hospital in the newer, farthest south part of Yorkton. It took us a while to get there and find the right apartment because the place has multiple entrances and miles of corridors. Of course we started on the wrong end, on the wrong floor.

Eventually we found the door with the right number, around a corner in the basement, but (should I be surprised?) no Neil. There were two girls there, from what I could see peering in from the hallway. The one who answered the door I recognized as having been in the shed with Solo a few days ago. She is Janet and was quite nice. The other girl must have been her sister, similar looking but a couple years older. I don't know her name. She didn't say a word, just sat on the couch looking away from us.

So Janet doesn't invite us in, maybe because she wants to avoid cleaning up after our snowy boots. Or maybe we're just too young to be considered cool. Instead she just hands us the LP. I asked her if she knew where Neil was, but she says I think he's with Solo in the clubhouse. That is what Jerry used to call the shed.

A little annoyed at this wild goose chase, we head back to Neil's. As we hit Smith and 5th I say, let's maybe jag over a block to the Summit Café and have a quick warm-up. If Neil is indeed home and we want to hang around that frigid 'clubhouse' it's better not to be too cold when you get there. I was very happy Sam agreed.

We both ordered a mug of hot chocolate and then had a closer look at the LP. The cover is all white with a picture of a man on fire shaking another man's hand. The back cover is a figure (empty suit of clothes) standing on a sand dune. It is called *Wish You Were Here* by Pink Floyd. Never heard of them. The inner sleeve is nice solid cardboard and has two more strange pictures as well as some lyrics. Sam figured out quickly that the four pictures represented the so-called (as the ancients saw it) four elements: Fire, Earth, Water and Air.

We got a surprise when we looked inside the inner sleeve: next to the record was an envelope. Inside it, we found a bunch of tiny squares of paper, maybe the size of a thumbnail each. There were plenty of them so we decided I should withhold a couple for ourselves. I wrapped them in a napkin and stuffed it in my back pocket.

When we got back to the shed, Neil was there. He said he had been out buying smokes for his mom and had missed us by only a minute at my house. Solo wasn't apologetic about misleading us. Instead he just grinned and waved a two dollar bill in my face saying: easy money, huh?

Sam and I had agreed we would not ask Solo about the envelope, but we would instead ask him to play the record right away, to see if he knew about the hidden cargo. He casually agreed to play the record, but he turned his back on us to remove the record from the sleeve and must have pocketed the envelope because we didn't see it again. The record was strange, very slow moving, not my usual taste in rock music. We listened for only a couple of minutes and I asked Neil if we should just forget about our 1999 discussion at my house. He said, no, we can still do it, so we left Solo by himself in the shed, still listening. Doesn't this guy have a home?

I taped our conversation but it was fairly short because of the time we wasted on Solo's wild goose chase.

I'm feeling pretty good. I'm putting together an idea for a new chapter of Asteroid Beta. One of the Betans, science specialist Astrali, is taken over by an alien intelligence. The alien-Astrali claims that she is amnesiac, but this seems odd because she remembers details about their trajectory, but doesn't know how to use chopsticks (she's Thai). Then when the real Astrali is found in an alien spacecraft hidden on the other side of the asteroid, they think she is an alien because she is stuck inside the alien's body and cannot communicate using its ultrasonic voice. The alien gathers intelligence by posing as Astrali, and keeps the real Astrali out of the way, and the Betans off balance with the switcheroo and the mystery of the alien spacecraft. I intend a happy ending.

Hand very sore now. Good night!

Monday, February 14, 1977

When I got up Mom gave me a heart-shaped tin of chocolates! Sometimes she can be really kind. I thought that, instead of opening it, I should give it to Sam, so I tucked it in my knapsack.

At lunch I was disappointed because Sam said it was sexist for me to give her candy on Valentine's Day. I tried to protest that I was just giving it to her as a friend, but she jumped on that and said, exactly! If you gave one to Neil and also one to me, then that would make sense, but because it is only to her, it is sexist. I said, well we can all share the candy then. So I opened it and we each had a piece, but I was left with it at the end of lunch. That didn't work out too well.

Sam was talking about going over to Neil's tonight so I'm a little concerned that he (or much worse, Solo) will get more solo time with her and I'll miss out because of my job. I'm already at a major disadvantage because she is in 9-32. Sometimes I think I should play her the tape where Neil rejects her, but then I stop myself with the thought it would probably backfire on me and make her blame me and want him all the more. Here's a storyline worthy of Shakespeare.

So I don't know what I missed tonight because of work.
What did Jim Morrison say? Trade in your hours for a handful
of dimes...

Tuesday, February 15, 1977

School was the pits. We had skating and Brian stole my
toque. I don't know where he threw it but I couldn't find it and
it is still damn cold outside. What a dimwatt (my newest
insult).

Sam and Neil were both around for lunch. Turns out that
Sam couldn't get out last night anyway so all my worrying was
for nothing.

We were talking about life after death and how she has
come to the conclusion that TM *[Editor's note: transcendental
meditation]* is bullshit because it relies on the assumption that
we have a soul. What else could it be that is attached to the
body with a silver cord but can roam freely all around the
universe as TM claims? Ridiculous, she says, we are body and
mind but there is no soul. We are no more eternal than animals.
Neil and I both agree with her. Religion is just a reaction to the
fear of death.

It was really weird at Neil's. I went over after supper and
Neil was alone, drawing. He was talking about Alpha like it
was a real place, saying that on it survived the best of
humanity, the 'supermen', while back on Earth the malicious
and weak of mind were left behind, the 'hollow men'. Almost
like the Moon broke away because the Alphans wanted to
escape the dimwatt hordes on Earth, that Alpha was not just a
sample of the advanced humanity we find in *Space: 1999*
(advances we had long all agreed were better and earlier than in
the 22nd century of *Star Trek*) but instead the entire elite
group.

This contradicts things Koenig previously said, about a war
on the Earth in the 1980s, the aftermath of which was the
extinction of racism and prejudice all around the globe. Neil
says Koenig is fooling himself by believing this propaganda,
which is likely just some politicians trying to put a positive
spin on a military fiasco. When Neil argues like this I don't

know how to respond. I have the episodes, the books, some magazine articles, and of course my holy grail, the MATN, but he seems to pull ideas out of the air (or really, unrelated library books) and then import it all into the 1999 universe. That's not playing fair.

Thursday, February 17, 1977

Had a social studies quiz today. Only scored 7/10. Oops. Better study next time. I don't think it is worth much towards the final mark anyway.

At lunch Neil was in a weird mood and Sam noticed it too. He was talking about acid rock and how the government tries to make its own acid which, if you ever got any, you would be in deep doo-doo because it guarantees a bad trip and when you recover you're a mind-numbed conformist forever after. Kind of scary considering how would you know which is the government acid and which the pure stuff?

When I asked Neil about that *Wish You Were Here* LP, supposedly acid rock, if it was really his or Solo's, I accidentally called it 'Pink Freud'. Sam thought that was hilarious and said it wasn't quite a Freudian slip but I might need psychiatric help all the same. Ouch. It actually was Solo's album, so at least he was honest on that count.

Worked on <u>Asteroid Beta</u>, Chapter 5 some more after supper, then off to Pic-A-Pop for more fun with Stanley and Delmer. I asked Stanley if he ever heard of Pink Floyd or that record and he said yes, it was a very good album and that they were a much more mature and intelligent group than most of the rock groups coming out now. Maybe I'll have to give it another listen.

Friday, February 18, 1977

Neil told us at lunch that Kiblah is out on bail and still claiming Jerry came to his house and attacked him. Neil is very concerned Kiblah might get off scot-free. If that happens, I'll be joining Neil's revolution full-patch.

Finally, a night off work. I went over to Neil's. Solo was there and Sam showed up too! I smuggled in my tape recorder, hidden inside my knapsack, and taped some of our conversation.

I finally learned how to spell Nietzsche. I think Sam really likes the fact he says God is dead. Then she doesn't have to go to the trouble of killing him herself.

Sam's new freedom is making a big difference. She stayed the whole evening. Even when I left at 10:30 she stayed behind. Solo seems way too interested in her. He spent a long time talking to her about family and how they always try to restrict young people. I don't think he's just interested in her brain.

Threw my clothes in the hamper. Nothing good for the late movie.

18 February 1977
(audio tape from collection of Roger Kay)

(The Doors' first LP, side B, is playing)
Solo: Why do you carry that at night anyway? You smuggling drugs?

Roger: *(nervously laughs)* No, just a few books.

Neil: The facilities on Alpha are incredible. The most advanced recreation, the best learning opportunities. Most of them have Ph.D.s.

Sam: No doubt, but there must be lots of smart people left back on Earth.

Neil: The point is that these are the best. If the Earth was destroyed after breakaway, then it's not the end of the world, so to speak.

Sam: You think *all* the worthwhile people are on Alpha?

Neil: There's not very many good people in the world. How many good people are there in Yorkton?

Roger: Three?

Solo: Hey!

Roger: Maybe, four?

Neil: Exactly. There are lots of old people who, maybe, used to be worthwhile, but now it's all cattle and parasites. Ayn Rand calls it 'second-hand lives'. People waste their lives following what the government wants, following the rules, following their family, instead of doing anything authentic.

Sam: Yeah, the religious view is you get your reward in Heaven. So work hard here, don't think about yourself, and you'll reap big benefits in the afterlife.

Solo: Bullshit, eh? Jim Morrison said 'No eternal reward will forgive you for wasting the dawn'. You've got one life to live, in other words, so don't waste it.

Sam: To trade your whole life for the off chance you'll be rewarded in the afterlife seems a tad stupid. I know, because my parents are like that. They only care about what the church thinks.

Roger: So they spend all their time propping up a façade of righteousness?

Sam: Yeah they do. If it makes them look good, they'll do it. But if no one is watching, then look out, you're gonna get smacked.

Neil: Nietzsche did believe in a sort of afterlife, but it's the same life. He suggests a cyclical universe where you live your life, and then, when the universe re-runs later and everything repeats, you get to live your life again, the exact same life. This means that whatever you do with your life, you better be sure you like it, because you'll be repeating it for all eternity.

Sam: So if you're counting on living an altruistic life here and then scoring big in Heaven, you're gonna be very disappointed.

Neil: Right.

Roger: Nothing worse than being dead *and* disappointed.

(laughter: Sam and Roger)

Neil: You don't know for certain you're in a cyclical universe. But if you can figure it out early enough then you can take advantage by living thirty years the way you want, instead of ninety years kowtowing to the status quo.

Roger: You planning on doing something fun that takes sixty years off your life?

Neil: Nietzsche's idea 'will to power' means that you do whatever makes you feel stronger, more alive.

Solo: Like sex?

(laughter: Sam)

Neil: No that's not what he means at all. You have the freedom to do what you want, that's true, but his focus is more on intellectual achievement, artistic freedom, academic bravery, that type of thing. He calls it The Eternal Recurrence. You guys know the Big Bang theory?

Solo: Sounds fun...

(the album We're An American Band *by* Grand Funk *begins playing)*

Neil: We know that we live in an expanding universe. I won't bore you with the details, but by extrapolating backwards we can see that the universe began as a small ultra-dense clump of proto-matter that exploded long ago, then later evolved into our cooling and expanding universe.

Now, if there is sufficient mass in our universe, then eventually, someday in the far future, it will all pull itself back together into a single lump again.

If that lump is the same lump as existed just before the Big Bang, then you have a basis for the same universe to be born and to unfold in the exact same way as the last one.

Solo: So you're saying his idea of a repeating universe is backed up by science?

Neil: Nietzsche wasn't a physicist, but his ideas were very advanced. There's no real proof, but his theory seems possible if you look at the science.

Roger: So in a billion billion years, once the universe has spread out, then collapsed back into itself, then exploded again, everything will unfold the same way and we'll be having this exact same conversation?

Sam: Doesn't that rule out free will?

Neil: Not at all. It's just that you're the same person each time, with the same experience and thoughts, so you make all the same choices. But each time, it's based on your free will.

Solo: Sounds like a good excuse to rob a bank, enjoy a few good years, and then off yourself.

Neil: Well you could do the same thing as a Catholic. You simply repent on your deathbed. And in either case, you'll never know if you were right.

Roger: Unless you wake up in Hell.

(laughter: Sam, Solo)

Solo: You don't believe in Hell?

Neil: It's a juvenile idea. I believe in a hell on this Earth. If you don't live your life authentically, you wind up in a hell here and now, not in an afterlife. When breakaway occurs in 1999, the Moon becomes Heaven, and the Earth, Hell.

The Alphans are the most authentic people and they have a chance to live a real life, but the masses left behind on Earth drown in their own ignorance. The Alphans can't control their future, but they make the right choices every day and go forward. The people on the Earth meanwhile wallow in their mental and moral laziness.

Sam: You make breakaway sound like the Rapture.

Neil: Maybe it is. A more scientific Rapture, but maybe they are saved.

Roger: But Earth does go forward. We see the future of the Earth in "Journey to Where".

Neil: In "Journey to Where" the Earth population is reduced to living in domes because the rest of the planet is a wasteland, a hell if you will. Plus look at the Earth people the Alphans talked to: some pompous bureaucrat who screws up the transfer by ignoring earthquake warnings, and some of his fawning underlings. It's a hierarchical system and it's clearly not based on competence.

So the Earth people are *not* more evolved than the Alphans. Their technology may have some good points, but they had a lot of time to develop it. Hundreds of years. Probably the Alphans could develop similar technology in less time.

Roger: And there's only about three hundred Alphans. So that may make technical progress a bit slow.

Neil: Very true.

Solo: Here.

Roger: No thanks.

Sam: Thanks.

Roger: And without Professor Bergman, that'll slow them down too. He was the one who designed the towers that saved them from the black sun.

Sam: But Maya's even smarter, and she's got knowledge of very advanced alien technology.

Neil: Yeah, was a great stroke of luck for the Alphans to save her. But if she ever turns on them, they won't survive. I think Bergman's betrayal was bad enough. I don't doubt the other important Alphans who went missing in Year Two are the direct result of his actions. As well as their decision to move out of Main Mission into the more secure Command Centre, deep underground.

Sam: Why do you think Bergman was involved in all that?

Neil: Working on these blueprints has brought me very close to day-to-day Alphan life. I feel I understand them much better now. I can read a lot from small details. I can't really put my finger on it. It is intuition perhaps, but a boatload of small things just don't add up, or don't add up to the agreed sum.

Sam: Such as?

Neil: They never mention Bergman again. At all. No memorial for him, no wondering aloud in difficult situations how he might've helped. This means he is infamous. There're a lot of other unexplained events, so the simplest approach is to assume they're related. Once you do that, the pieces fall into place.

Solo: He might be a hollow man, right Professor Armstrong?

Neil: That is one theory. Maybe he became what Raan showed him as, someone open to altering his principles if it gets in the way of his goals. The alien spaceship Bergman discovered had room for three. Perhaps it was Bergman, Kano, and instead of Koenig, Paul that took it.

Roger: That means Kano and Paul were involved in some kind of mutiny too.

Neil: It's not impossible. Kano was never happy on Alpha. He was the main computer guy, a very important position on Alpha, but it didn't get much recognition. Blame is all he got. Whenever computer couldn't come up with an answer or was acting strange, usually when it was taken over by an alien like in "Guardian of Piri", they *blamed* him.

Also the computer/brain interface he allowed to be installed in his skull showed how he had made great sacrifices for science and Alpha, but it never really helped him.

Then there's Paul. Remember how the future Paul in "Another Time, Another Place" stood up to the present Koenig, saying the second set of Alphans couldn't populate the Earth alongside the first Alphans? This gives us a clue: Paul is not so happy just being second banana. Also, when Paul ingests the lunar mushrooms, or manna or whatever it was, in "The Last

Sunset", he's anxious to get away from Alpha, from the chain of command. Maybe the drug let him see more clearly the true status quo on Alpha.

Roger: But Koenig is a good guy, not ...

Neil: Sure, he's no Richard Nixon, but Paul might not feel that way.

Sam: But you have no proof. You're just slandering these three Alphans!

Neil: Just because you don't have proof doesn't mean something isn't true. Lighter?

Sam: No, but you have to base your ideas on something.

Neil: I've spent hundreds of hours on my Alpha work, documenting set details and drawing up blueprints. If there's anyone in the world who's more familiar with 1999...

Sam: Well I don't doubt that, but you still need some proof for your ideas.

Neil: Once I complete these blueprints, they'll be coming for my ideas. In my imagination is the true history of Alpha, all of the inhabitants, not just those Year Two has left intact.

People don't disappear without an impact. You can't tell me that Bergman dies from a faulty spacesuit and no one ever mentions his name again. It doesn't make sense.

You have to look at the details and come up with what fits. *Starlog* didn't do that with the Technical Notebook so we have to assume it is non-canonical.

Solo: Not cannon what?

Neil: Not the correct version, not what we should believe.

Sam: It's a religious term meaning something not in the Gospel.

Solo: Oh. But we're talking about a fictional future, not the past...

Neil: How people think makes a difference. If we believe in one type of future, we'll work towards making it come true. If we believe in something else, say something that doesn't inspire us, then we won't work to make our ideals come true. So change will not come.

Likewise if we believe in one version of the past, it can affect how we live our lives and what we think is possible in the future.

These matters may appear hypothetical, but they do impact us, maybe subtly, but deeply too. No less than the music we listen to. What you surround yourself with, the ideas, the people, the sense of life, eventually you cannot escape them. You have to face them or you have to change your life. If they are not authentic, eventually you will suffer.

To put it another way, it is like Nietzsche's death of God. If you believe it, the ripples that flow into your life change everything. The same if you think He, or She, well, It does exist. Your assumptions can change your life.

Roger: How do you spell that?

(the song "Black Licorice" is playing)

Solo: Check it out. When he says licorice it sounds like lick her ass! Ha ha! Did you grok that, Professor?

Roger: It's 10:30. I should go.

Entries from Roger Kay's 1977 Diary

Saturday, February 19, 1977

Had a lazy morning. In the afternoon I did my usual rounds downtown, checked out some records at STRM *[Editor's note: Sam The Record Man]* and some magazines at Logan's Drugs. Nothing interesting.

Neil was not at the YPL so I dropped by the shed and he was still in there. Solo was there too and they seemed kind of out of it. Neil was looking at a cool astronomy book, pictures of star clusters and galaxies, but he wasn't talkative. I left after a few minutes.

1999 at 4 was "Dorzak", a really good episode! I taped it and then worked on my summary through the evening. This time I wrote the first draft longhand, corrected it, and then when I was happy with my messy, blotched but updated sheets, I started to type the whole thing. But my hands are quite sore so that's all for today.

No good late movie!? A cowboy flick and then really really old dramas. Come on Shamrock Stations, you can do better!

Episode Summary: "Dorzak" (1965 words)
[Omitted.]

Comments on "Dorzak" (Roger Kay, 1994)

Sahala, the beautiful captain of the Croton Federation ship floating over Alpha, requests medical assistance. She has a criminal on board, in stasis, and an injured crew woman. When the criminal turns out to be Dorzak, a Psychon known to Maya as a philosopher and a poet, doubt is cast on his guilt.

Favorite scene: Alan Carter is attracted to Sahala and when they say their goodbyes, he kisses her. When he asks her how they say goodbye on Croton, she says I like your way better and kisses him back.

Entries from Roger Kay's 1977 Diary

Sunday, February 20, 1977

Well today turned out to be a fiasco. Sam came over at 1 and she was mad at Neil. She went to the shed last night and both Neil and Solo were acting weird. When I saw Neil yesterday afternoon I assumed he was tripping so I didn't stick around. When she got there much later, Neil was unresponsive and Solo was being manic.

Solo was raving about free love as a solution to the world's problems, but it seems he meant more like 'free sex' because he tried to talk Sam into taking her clothes off so that Neil could see "there was nothing to be afraid of". This freaked her out but what bothered her even more was Neil saying if she wanted to do it, she could, but he wasn't going to stick around to watch, and then left her alone with Solo!

She says Solo then offered to take off his clothes first, to put her at ease. Why doesn't he try to seduce someone his own age? Needless to write, she doesn't like Solo but just puts up with him out of respect for Neil. So she stepped out of the shed and found Neil sitting on the cold ground next to the house. She told him point blank that she has no interest in Solo and he said "well it is your decision" like he would approve their going out. That really hurt her, she reports.

Guess I won't need my incriminating tape at all.

Neil didn't come over today and I didn't tape anything so let me try to recall what all Sam said. I think her main points were:

1) Solo is a bad guy, not a friend of Neil's
2) Neil is deeply in denial about his own body and physical reality
3) Solo is responsible for feeding Neil bad drugs
4) Neil needs to stop wallowing in self-pity about Jerry's death and look after himself
5) Roger is a good friend and a rock in a storm

I agreed on all counts.

And what of Solo always calling Neil 'Professor Armstrong'? It is like he is making fun of the nickname I gave Lionel (feels funny to write his real name). There's nothing wrong or funny about being a Professor, but I don't think Neil Armstrong can be considered one so it just doesn't make sense and feels to me, and Sam agrees, like Solo is just making fun of Neil.

We also talked about "Dorzak" and agreed that just as Maya was wrong about "Dorzak", Neil is wrong about Solo. We need to implant some jamming devices in our heads whenever Solo is around because he is up to no good and we must not allow him to influence us. I'm really glad I know where Sam is at Solo-wise.

We walked over to the shed intending to confront Neil and give him a Solo-or-us ultimatum but there was no one there. We knocked on the back door of the house too, but no answer. Back at my place, we phoned over. Neil's mom answered but said that if Neil wasn't in the shed, he was out, and that's that. Sam and I agreed to talk to Neil about this at school tomorrow.

Later... I stopped by the shed again around 7 but no one was there. Neil has never stood us up like he did this afternoon, so I went back again, at 8, and then he was there, gloriously alone. He said he had been over at Stu's grandparents for supper and was expecting Solo shortly. We listened to some music and Neil smoked.

When Solo showed up with two high school girls, I could smell the booze on him. Neil smelled it too and asked if he had been drinking. Solo said yes, but that booze was much better for scoring ladies than acid. The two girls didn't even blink at that. They seemed eager to party with us but Neil grew irate and said: no booze in the clubhouse!

Solo: "Come on, loosen up, you can't live in your head all the time, you have to experience life's pleasures!".

Neil: "You know how I feel about booze. You have to respect me or get out."

And get out is what Solo did! Neil held firm and I was never so proud of him. After that it was just the two of us. We listened to Spirit's *Dr. Sardonicus*. I stuck around until 9:30 then I had to head home for a bath. With Solo out of the picture, maybe things can get back to normal!

On Solomon (Lionel O'Neill, 1978)

On philosophy, I differed diametrically from Solo. He was pro-strength; I am pro-underdog. I believe the intellectual is the underdog right now in society. Music has moved to dance and disco, electronic music, synthesizers. Everything is falsified. The relationship between man and instrument is blocked by the bulk of technology. Luckily the writer and his inky paper are currently safe, no foreseeable behemoth threatens it with irrelevance.

Computers will take over music as a fascist philosophy emerges. The truly cunning and power mad will gain the top positions and ensure all the slaves are kept subdued with violence, drugs, brain deadening music, whatever they can muster, or encourage. Decadence is a positive feedback loop. Just feed the decadent what they want and they dissolve.

Solo believed in existential determination. He lived alone, without any god or absolute guidance. He held no criteria for selecting his daily behavior other than the seeking of pleasure or the avoidance of pain. He wanted to be the top dog in the power society.

Like him, I am bereft existentially, but unlike him, I posit a worthy value, humanity. Not the species, I mean the behavior of being human. Not just humane, but seeking to understand the universe and wanting to cooperate with others, human, alien, and animal, to achieve mutually beneficial ends.

To me, Solo personified Objectivism reduced to narcissism amid a morality-free zone of existential nihilism. This type of thinking encourages a fascism of the strong (mind or body), of the beautiful, of the powerful, instead of a society that rewards the truly advanced. Weak people can be advanced and productive in society, but unenlightened strong people, while appearing very productive, in fact try to work the system for their own narrow advantage and when seen in a wider context, should be understood to be counterproductive. I see the strong abuse their power. I will not join them willingly. My goal is to change the system itself.

Entries from Roger Kay's 1977 Diary

Monday, February 21, 1977

Something horrible has happened to Neil. 9-32 had Art this morning and they worked on water color paintings. Neil had drawn a picture of a face that he said was 'Gary Anderson' with all sorts of bloody and broken body parts floating all around it. When Mrs. Adams saw what it was, she asked him why he would draw such a thing and he said it was a voodoo drawing that would prevent 'Gary' hurting anyone else.

She then asked, who has he hurt?

The answer was 'many many Alphans so far, but others if we don't stop him.' Sam says Neil was talking a lot of nonsense before that, about how Alpha had to be saved because the Earth was already destroyed.

At the end of the period, they all hung their pictures up on the wall to let them dry, and Webb snuck over to Neil's and drew a little Starship Enterprise on the bottom. I guess he thought he was being funny, but when Neil saw the alteration he grabbed Webb by the neck and started choking him.

Some of the guys in the class tried to separate them but it was a big struggle. They got Neil off Webb eventually but then he just started smashing things so they locked the Art Room with him inside until the police came.

The stupid thing is that when Sam talked to Neil before that, in homeroom period, she liked what she heard. Neil said that Solo was trying to poison him and his friends and that he'd do anything to protect his friends. Now she realizes it was quite a paranoid rant, but Neil needs to be paranoid of Solo so it sounded reasonable at the time. She didn't expect him to go psycho in the very next period.

I heard the sirens and saw two RCMP cars pull up behind the school. 9-31 faces that way, so everyone crowded to the window to see. Two burly cops got out and entered the back of the old building. They brought Neil out in cuffs, put him in the backseat, and drove away.

We were stunned. Mr. Whyte made an announcement that there had been 'an incident' in the Art Room and that Art classes for the rest of the day were canceled. No mention of who or what.

At lunch Sam filled me in completely and then Webb came over and apologized for drawing on Neil's painting. He said if he had known it would trigger that sort of reaction from Neil, he would not have done it. I could see he still had marks on his neck from Neil's grip.

After school Sam and I loitered around the cenotaph, talking about Neil. This type of violence is so unlike him. He has always been protective and gentle towards us. We walked to the payphone outside United Grocery and called Neil's. No answer.

At supper I told my parents what happened and they were shocked. What really bugged me was that they said, well if he is violent, then maybe his brother was too, so it makes sense that Mr. Kiblah had to defend himself.

I was so angry I stood up at the table and started to shout and cry at the same time. They said well if you're too upset to go to work we'll just call Uncle Tim and cancel. No way I'd let that happen so I managed to settle down and very calmly insist there had to be another explanation.

I went to Pic-A-Pop and Uncle Tim had heard the cops had to go to St. Joe's and wanted to know more. I had no desire to tell the story so I just said I don't know. I did use the phone however when no one was looking and called Neil's house a couple times. No answer until after 8:30. Then I got his mom and she said that Neil was very sick and would be in the hospital for a couple of days. Sick with what, I asked. Sick in the head, she screamed and hung up.

I phoned the hospital to see if he was admitted and they said yes, but he can't have any visitors because he is in the isolation wing of the psychiatric center. What a crock. Probably dosed with government acid by Solo because he was pissed about the alcohol/shed incident.

10:30 now and I'm very tired. Like Fleetwood Mac says, the world's in a tangle. I'm gonna build myself a cave and move down in the ground.

On a Visit to Moonbase Alpha (Lionel O'Neill, 1988)

I had finally completed the creation of my Moonbase Alpha blueprint set when my break with reality occurred. The significance of the architecture and inhabitants of that place became all absorbing. My attention fell into a trance state such that I thought I actually was at that possibility of a lunar locale. I was in the future and all that had gone before had long departed. Only the severe, monochromatic lunar landscape and the gentle, consistently patterned walls of the moonbase corridors confronted me. I was among heroes. I was home, a creature in a fragile uniform facing a hostile environment, always only a centimeter or two away from the void and certain death.

If one lived in a primitive garden, you could be forgiven for thinking any God was a loving provider, but if you live in the absolute cold and desolation of the universal void, then your choice is simple. Give up or go forward. You would not be forgiven for weakness nor would you be rewarded for kindness. Any meaning you could create in your own mind, based on your own values and situation, would be your sole comfort. There was no external definition of reality to wrestle order and coherence from the chaos of creation.

I found myself on Alpha. I was an astronaut, a senior Alphan. I do not know if breakaway had yet occurred. It was a dreamlike sequence. I remember what I thought, and much of what I saw, but there are also huge gaps in the logic of the scenario that should have precluded its credibility. I think I knew it was a dream, or a hallucination, or some combination of such faux experience, but I clung to it anyway. There was a dread in me, that was why I was here, some part of my brain knew my real situation and infinitely preferred this detour.

It seemed as if I knew I was not supposed to be on Alpha. I don't know if it was something I had done or just a scheduling reality, but I knew I must not be discovered and so I began to take steps to assure my anonymity. I freed my commlock from my belt, turning the side with my photo and identification details in towards the palm of my left hand. Somehow this might help me avoid detection.

The room was filled with Alphans I did not recognize. The opposite of the situation in "Bringers Of Wonder". But then I caught a glimpse of Professor Victor Bergman behind the grand dual doors to the Commander's Office that swept shut as I peered from the sunken operations level of Main Mission. I calmly turned away, toward the bank of windows on the exterior wall and looked out upon the lunar landscape.

In the distance, beyond the steep rim of Plato, my naked eye could detect a series of circular disruptions, craters with subsidiary ejecta depressions. On the dark floor of Plato, tire tracks and footprints were everywhere. This at least made sense; those marks would last forever (or until another "Last Sunset" when atmosphere might revisit the Moon and disrupt eternity's dusty canvas).

I was excited but terrified at the same time. Something was coming. I had to hide. On each side of the 'Big Screen' in Main Mission is an arched passage. They both fed a small connecting corridor behind. The row of windows I was enjoying continued along the exterior wall and into that connecting corridor. I stepped through one arch and looked again at lunatic Nature from this less conspicuous vantage. The stars had an unearthly clarity, the Milky Way a diamond sash clothing a black satin background, mottled with a diversity of cosmic objects, galaxies and stars of all colors and configurations, dramatic gas clouds, clusters in collision, unfamiliar ringed planets. This seemed proof enough that we had already left the Solar System. The beauty held me for a moment and then my sense kicked in. Time to hide. Behind me, facing the anterior of the 'Big Screen' was a door, full of curvilinear polygons, no doubt familiar to those already steeped in Alphan interior design, with a small well-centered sign that read simply: Office Supplies. The room was small and windowless. There I hid.

As I waited for the danger to pass, I considered what I thought I knew. There was no God, no purpose, no rescue from the void. The universe was cyclical. If your life was a happy one, this might provide comfort, but mine was not.

If the universe was to repeat, would it be because of Mankind, or in spite of us? Was the Eternal Recurrence a phenomenon of Nature, or was it the culmination of determined humanist action? In other words, would the universe reform and cycle through its next identical incarnation, its next Big Bang, without any help from us, or was there an active role required of intelligent life to ensure that all time would be recycled, repeated, conserved?

If it was the latter, then I might have some part in derailing the scheme. The complexity of the goal of ensuring the universe would return to its initial state when all its time had been expended and collapse was upon us would require much human evolution, social and technological, as well as ingenuity, and determination. Was it human destiny to assume the role of Creator and stage manage the death of this universe to ensure we would return, to live again? This was the most optimistic cosmology I could conceive and yet I wanted no part of it. Better to die with finality, to end suffering and rest eternally than to drink the poison of the same unbearable life again and again.

If this non-metaphysical reincarnation was a purely natural phenomenon, needing no help from Mankind, then God was the demi-urge and we were all cursed to exist in his torture chamber without escape.

If the universe is infinite, then our possibilities should be infinite, life should be infinite. To recycle the same existence ad infinitum would devalue its meaning. So-called random factors would take on a premeditated and anthropomorphic villainy. True understanding would invoke paranoia, not enlightenment. When infinity shrinks to a single point, it is no longer infinite, no matter how dense the matter involved.

The office supply room had no electronics, no viewscreens, the walls were fully covered with shelving holding a full capacity of nondescript boxes. I sat on the floor, incommunicado and feeling incapable of action while these thoughts raced through my mind.

It seemed to me that a demon was eating the universe, destroying its potential, and the demon was us. The actions of the human race would ultimately result in a repetition of all that had gone before, and destroy any chance of escape from the wheel of torture that was our existence. There would be no release from this samsara for us.

When I later returned or awoke, I was sitting on the floor of the shed, my legs numb from the cold. I recalled that I had kicked Solo out of the shed for the final time the previous night. I crawled into my bed, exhausted and fearful.

Entries from Roger Kay's 1977 Diary

Tuesday, February 22, 1977

Today was a horrible drag. I felt like a robot, dragging myself from class to class, mechanically taking notes, all the while feeling nothing. Sam and I had lunch and Webb joined us. He seems genuinely sorry about what happened to Neil so I didn't protest. Maybe he's not as bad as I thought, but I still don't want him cozying up to Sam.

When I told Sam that Neil was in the Psych Centre, she looked like she was going to cry. I said let's try to go see him tonight. She agreed.

I can't phone her house, because there's no way to tell who is there and who might answer the phone, so we agreed she would come to my place and we'd set off together at 7:30. Dad offered to drive us, which was really nice because it is a hell of a long walk and still very cold.

When we got to the hospital, Dad waited in the car. Sam and I went into the Psych Centre but the nurse there said we couldn't see Neil. Only family is allowed. Well he's like the brother I never had so this angered me. I told the nurse that Neil has very little family and I was like family, but she just checked her sheet and said, well his next of kin is his mother and she lives in town, so that's who gets to visit him. Maybe come back in a few days and we'll see… She's just being an obstructive pain.

Dad insisted on dropping Sam off at her house, which came close to causing a major problem. But then she told him her house was halfway down the block, far past the real one. So hopefully no one in her family saw us and her alibi, being with her brother Peter, will hold.

The world without Neil is a horrible thing to contemplate.

Wednesday, Februrary 23, 1977

I phoned the hospital from work and they said Neil is no longer a patient there, so I phoned Neil's and his mom answered. It is true: he has been released! His mom said he is mostly okay but still on the mend and getting used to his medication, and if we really had to, we could come over for a few minutes on Thursday. I said, well I work Thursdays, how about Friday? She said, if that is what is important to you, fine. I think that is a yes. What a bag. Still, I can't wait to give the good news to Sam. Neil is going to be fine!

Thursday, February 24, 1977

Can hardly write today. Uh, what happened at school? Don't care. We get to see Neil tomorrow finally. Sam was happy at lunch when I told her. She seems to have forgotten all about his less than stellar behavior when Solo was coming on to her. Personally I'd rather see her interested in Neil than someone like Webb, so I didn't remind her.

After school as I was walking home Stu College (I think that's his nickname, not his real name) was driving by in his awesome black and yellow Monza Spyder. He pulled over and invited me to hop in. He said he was concerned about Neil, and because Neil is Jerry's little brother, he feels protective of him. Well good, someone needs to be, I said.

Stu said he heard Solo has been hanging around Neil a lot recently. I confirmed this, and that they were getting into bad things. Stu knows all about this and he predicts Solo will try to take over their old clubhouse for evil purposes.

I told Stu about the booze incident and that Solo was now kicked out of the shed. Stu seemed pleased with this but told me to keep a lookout. He offered me his phone number just in case. I'm not sure when or why I'd call him, but I was glad, thanked him, and took the number.

Work was slow and crushingly dull.

Friday, February 25, 1977

Aced a math quiz today. Lunch with Sam, and Webb came over of course. When he heard we were going to see Neil tonight he asked us to send him his 'get well' wishes. How big of him. Also during lunch, Sam admitted to me that her second oldest brother, Paul, is driving her to and from school on a directive from her parents to keep a close eye on her, she being the delicate female of the brood. Would be horrible to have her shame the family by walking home unescorted with a male school friend! (note my sarcasm) I guess some of her escapades recently have disturbed their parental hibernation. Paul is her least favorite brother because he mostly toes the family/church line.

Suffered through a double Phys-ed period of floor hockey this afternoon. Not sure what exactly you have to do to qualify for 'high sticking' around here. Also, would using your stick to joust with someone on your own team not qualify for a penalty? Apparently not.

Sam's here! Time to go!

Almost 10 now and I'm back. Its been a long time since I was inside Neil's house. I think I've only been in there two or three times really. Neil always told me to feel free to go use their bathroom when we hung in the clubhouse (that does sound nicer than 'shed') but I've always tried to avoid his mom.

The back half of the house is basically the kitchen, the bathroom, and the kids' bedroom. An arched opening in the kitchen leads to the front half, which is just living room and front bedroom. I don't remember it from the first time I was there, but definitely every other time I was inside there was this dark drapery across the archway that divided the house from front to back. This prevented you from seeing into the living room from the kitchen and vice versa. Those few times I did use their bathroom, I couldn't see into the front of the house and I felt like a burglar, sneaking around the back half of the house.

That dark and dusty drape divided the house into two isolated units and signaled You Are Not Welcome to me, which is exactly the same feeling I got whenever I bumped into Neil's mom.

It wasn't easy to go up to the front door and ring the bell, but there was no one in the shed and we desperately needed to see Neil, so of course we did. His mom peered at us from the front window for a few moments and then, apparently quite reluctantly, motioned for us to come in through the front door.

She remained in her chair where she has a good view of the front window and the TV, which unfortunately was on and quite loud. Neil was sitting on the couch and, as soon as we rid ourselves of boots and coats, we sat next to him. Sam in the middle, I on the far end of the couch.

We asked him how he was, but he seemed unfocussed, like he was sleepy. He said he was fine but he had been diagnosed with paranoid schizophrenia. Was there a cure, what was the prognosis, we probed. There is some kind of medication that can stop the symptoms but there is no cure. The medication makes him sleepy and he can't think as clearly which annoys him.

He doesn't remember much of what happened in the Art room; he just remembers fighting for his life, that someone had destroyed something he needed to sustain his own existence. We passed on Webb's apology for defacing Neil's work and his eyes lit a little when he remembered the painting. He asked if it still existed and we had to admit we didn't know. We promised to find out for him but then he said well it's not important.

He said he wasn't trying to hurt anyone and that if there was anything he did that hurt Sam or me, he was very sorry. We assured him that was not the case. All this conversation is going on while his mom is watching TV and we have to strain to hear what he's saying. Neil was never a loud talker, but I don't recall him talking that softly before. Probably this is just the medication too.

After only half an hour his mom suddenly announces, kids, Neil is getting tired, you better go. This threw me into a panic, when would we see him again, would he be back at school? I tried to ask his mom but she just said, we'll see. I felt like crying. I think the thought that it might upset Neil was the only thing that stopped me. We put our boots and coats back on and left.

I walked Sam part way home. We stopped in St. Gerard's parking lot and sat on the concrete ledge there and then Sam did cry. I put my arm around her and tried to be comforting even though I felt the same way. I promised her things I had no control over: Neil will be fine, he'll be back in school in no time, his disease is under control and everything will be alright.

I said we all love each other and that is what counts. I pecked her on the cheek to emphasize this, but it was a mistake I think.

Life is all screwed up. Don't mind the smudged ink. I'm so exhausted I can't even check the late movie listings.

Saturday, February 26, 1977

Woke up early. The sun was shining, some snow had fallen and it looked fresh and clean outside. What a lie. I was practically crying at breakfast and had to confess to Mom about Neil's disease. She said I may have to prepare myself to see Neil disappear into an institution for years, or forever. That didn't help.

I went down to the YPL and read up on paranoid schizophrenia. Neil is in some really bad company with his PS, murderers and cannibals and such. That doesn't make sense to me because I know Neil really well. Some of his theories about the status quo sound a bit like PS rantings, but I can't accept they are crazy because they were originally Jerry's ideas and nobody said Jerry had PS. What are the odds of both brothers having it?

Maybe the government did spike something he took and made him react like this because they don't like where his ideas lead. If I believe that, does that mean I have PS too?

I came back and taped 1999 at 4. "The Immunity Syndrome" is the best episode in a long time. The alien entity reminds me of Neil, a powerful being who has difficulty relating to or understanding beings so different from himself. When he tries to communicate, he risks destroying them, or maybe just giving them PS.

After that, I tried to call Neil but there was no answer at his house. I walked over and the clubhouse was quiet too.

Spent the evening working on my episode summary. If Neil never gets better, what do I do about the Association of Alphans? Will Ron deal with me, or do I give up trying to get into his publication? Not fun to think about.

Episode Summary: "The Immunity Syndrome"
(1951 words)
[Omitted.]

Comments on "The Immunity Syndrome"
(Roger Kay, 1994)

The Alphans land on a new planet and their first tests indicate it is habitable. However Tony soon encounters an alien the mere sight of which leaves him homicidally insane. Because the alien is entirely alone and without a physical body, it does not understand identity or life. Only when Koenig bravely engages it, does it realize there are intelligent life forms external to itself and it must take care not to harm them.

Favorite scene: When Eagles cannot be used because of a degenerative atmosphere, Helena and Maya elect to make a one-way trip on a plastic glider down to the planet surface.

Entries from Roger Kay's 1977 Diary

Sunday, February 27, 1977

Woke up early, especially for a Sunday. Tried to do some work on Asteroid Beta but no inspiration. Just re-read what I did two weeks ago. How to go forward?

Mom made bacon and eggs and tried to cheer me up. I didn't even want to get dressed but I knew there was a small chance Sam would come over. Glad I did because at one o'clock the doorbell rang and there she was at the back door.

There wasn't any question this time of trying to discuss 1999 without Neil around so we quickly decided to drop over to his place and see what was up. The shed was abandoned but there were fresh tracks in the snow at their backdoor. I knocked; no answer. I was convinced Neil's mom was in there but just refusing to acknowledge us. We stood there for a few minutes trying to think what to do. Was Neil back in the hospital? With his father? Where was he? Should we give up? But then Neil trudged up, churning fresh snow and carving a new path along the alley.

He seemed more alert than Friday and quickly opened the shed and turned on the heater, inviting us in to wait for him while he dealt with his mom. It took longer than you'd think necessary to hand over some cigarettes and change and when he re-entered the shed he explained that his mom was being a pain about his having friends over. Even though the friends were not actually in the house itself.

I think we're the best things in his life and here is his mom trying to ruin it for him. Parents can be very stupid sometimes, not realizing what their kids really need. Food and a roof over your head is not sufficient. Maybe you were overjoyed to have at least or only that during the Great Depression, but we have our own depressions now and they're individual and no less fierce for it.

The shed was in an unusual state of mess, a pizza box with bits of cheese and frozen toppings still clinging to its clam-like mouth abandoned atop his drawing board and a bottle of unknown liquid (no label) sitting on the floor. It wasn't frozen so it must've been booze. Neil just poured the contents out on the ground while I folded and crammed the pizza box into the garbage barrel beside the house.

All this made me very happy, the most normal thing in the world, clean out the clubhouse with your friends. Then reality set in as Neil sat at his drawing table and we started to talk. He is still very medicated. He can't focus on topics properly and doesn't seem to want to speak his mind anymore. Sam took his hand in hers and told him that what happened before doesn't matter. All that matters is that his friends are with him and he can take his time to recover the pieces of his life. I felt a little jealous and then immediately felt like a jerk. This is my best friend. He needs every bit of attention and affection we can give him.

Neil didn't want to listen to any music, saying it just makes his anxious, a side effect of his medication. He asked again about his 'Gary' Anderson painting but we had no more news to give him.

I offered to bring Neil some books from the YPL or St. Joe's library, but he said no thanks. He hasn't been reading since his medication started. No books and no music? He must be very sick in that case because these things are our lifeblood, our intellectual oxygen. We sing the mind electric, not the body. What next, time to forget about outer space and focus on dreary old Earth? It is absurd.

We sat in silence for a while, neither Sam nor I wanting to drive the conversation anywhere, just waiting to see what he would say, but nothing came. Finally, seeming to sense the conversational void, he admitted his doctor was still adjusting his medication dosage and so maybe he would be better company soon. We denied he was bad company and professed our joy to be back with him, but soon he was rubbing his head, complaining of a headache, and saying he had to go back in the house to beg a smoke from his mom. We agreed to come over again very soon.

After we left, Sam was shiny eyed, saying that the Neil she loved was gone. I argued with her saying he was still there, and all he needed was a little time for the doctors to get the medication right. Sam smiled at me, said I was a true and loyal friend, then hugged me. All my troubles disappeared for those few seconds. I hope she is right about me and wrong about Neil. Now I'm worried that if Neil doesn't recover, will she still want to be my friend?

Is she my friend, or are we both just Neil's friends? As long as Neil is around, I'll never have to face the answer to that question.

Pot roast for supper. Mom and Dad wanted to know all about Neil. I just said that the medication was working and he should be much better soon. Then they started talking about crazy people and how dangerous they were, like that Charles Manson. This is a totally unfair and ignorant comparison. I slammed my fork down so hard my plate chipped.

I spent the evening in my room cooling off. Mom came in just before bedtime and said she was sorry my friend was sick but I was going to have to be realistic about it. I said: he'll get better, you'll see. She said that is what she wants too, so we are on the same side.

Monday, February 28, 1977
No Neil at school today. Sam and I had lunch together but Webb somehow migrated closer as the hour waned and wanted to know how Neil was doing. We said he was getting better but not quite better. Webb had watched 1999 on Saturday and liked "The Immunity Syndrome". I'm not sure if I believe him. Maybe he just wants to get closer to Sam.

Back to work this evening. Uncle Tim said he was sorry about my friend. I could see Delmer smirking in the background but I just ignored him.

Tuesday, March 1, 1977
Today is March 1st, but it still looks like January outside. Some kids set up a snowball ambush at the entrance, but I was quick enough to avoid getting hit. Arvid wasn't that lucky; an ice chunk hit him in the head and broke his glasses. He was

pretty upset and Mr. Peebles helped him tape his glasses together so he could see the board.

Sam and I had started lunch just the two of us when Webb came over and asked to sit with us. Sam said okay before I could say no and he ate his smelly sandwiches with us. He kept talking about *Star Trek* and he really pissed me off. How I miss Neil.

After lunch, Arvid came up to me and we talked about Neil for a while. We haven't talked in a long time. Arvid has a theory that Neil's disease is due to some traumatic event from early childhood, like in *Tommy* that movie by The Who we studied last year. I listened politely but I don't believe it. I didn't give him my theory.

After school I walked downtown and bought *Starlog* #4 at Logan's Drugs. The cover is a drawing of the Six Million Dollar Man and the Bionic Woman with a giant Oscar Goldman head prominent between them. This issue has an interview with Nick Tate! Also there is an article on the new space shuttle and how NASA is looking for astronaut recruits. I hope they're still looking when I graduate from university.

Later. I'm just now back from the shed and it is after 9. I was surprised and disappointed to see Solo there. Neil says his mom decided she needs help looking after him so Solo was invited to move in. This seems bass ackwards to me because it is usually Neil looking after his mom, not the other way around. And to prove the point, as soon as I got there, Solo says he needs more smokes and sends Neil and I off to Mark's Grocery to buy an Export A green pack for him.

Neil did not seem entirely better. He was more alert and talkative but he continues to rant about how 'Gary' Anderson is trying to mess up his life. I mentioned "The Immunity Syndrome" to him and he confirmed he did see it. He's not that crazy. He liked the idea of the entity with no body, and mused that if there was such a creature on Earth people might confuse it with a ghost. Maybe ghosts were just aliens.

When we returned, two other guys, both about Solo's age, were in the shed. They left in like one minute after promising to catch up with Solo on the weekend. Where would he be on the weekend? In the shed, Solo replies. Great. So then he's smoking and Neil is smoking and I'm not, but I'm choking on it. I ask to open the door for a minute and Neil is apologetic and says maybe everyone should smoke outside instead. Solo just overrules this, like it is his place, and says, nah, a little smoke will toughen you up. Yeah and a bullet in the head makes you smarter I guess.

In another few minutes, another friend of Solo's shows up. The guy says he 'wants two' and Solo takes an envelope from his jacket pocket, hands him two little bits of paper and accepts a ten dollar bill. Now I understand why he wants to occupy the shed. It is the perfect place to move some of his illegal product.

While Neil has a cigarette outside, I quiz him. Yes he knows what is going on, but he lets it go on because, one, it is not a dangerous drug like alcohol, and two, Solo lets him do whatever he wants, including ditching his medicine. Neil admitted he had talked about Eagles with Solo earlier today and had already also stopped taking his medication. Neil thinks that if his head clears he'll be able to better understand and face his problems. I hope he's right. He said Solo returned Sunday night and has been sleeping on their couch ever since.

I asked him when he'll be back at school but his doctor thinks he should avoid that excitement until they have his medication completely figured out.

I showed Neil the new *Starlog* and he was so fascinated that I said keep it for a couple days. I've already read it completely, but just once through.

I thought maybe Sam would show up, but by 9 there was no sign of her and I had to leave. As I walked towards home, down the alley, I saw someone enter the alley from Darlington. Another customer for Solo.

My clothes reeked of cigarettes when I got home and I had to explain to Mom that Solo is a heavy smoker and that's the cause of the smell. The last thing I want is for her to blame Neil for something else.

Heard a new song on the radio: "Hotel California" by the Eagles. I love their name and the song has mysterious poetic lyrics. You can check out but you can never leave, they sing. What is the Hotel California? Neil would know, or at least have some good theories.

Wednesday, March 2, 1977

Once again Neil is not in school. I think he won't ever recover if Solo takes over Jerry's role. Solo is no Jerry. He thinks only of himself and continually takes advantage of those around him.

I had to do something about this so after school I walked down to the police station and asked for Detective Hooper. He was there and invited me into his office right away.

I told him Solo was selling acid out of Neil's shed but that Neil had nothing to do with it. I can provide proof against Solo, but only if they agree not to do anything to Neil.

Hooper said, don't worry, Neil is a minor and we're not interested in him for drug offenses. But they are very interested in Solo. So I gave him the two little bits of paper I had fished out of the envelope hidden in the Pink Floyd album. I explained where they came from and Hooper made notes.

What apartment number was it at the old hospital building, he wanted to know. I told him.

Where does Solo keep his stash in the shed? In an envelope on him, in a coat pocket.

Good, says Hooper, that means he can't disown it and say it was Jerry's or Neil's. He made me promise not to tell anyone what I had told him or that I had talked to him at all. I walked home and had supper in a daze. I tried not to think too much about what I had done. Have I betrayed my friend or saved him?

Work was okay I guess.

Thursday, March 3, 1977

Learned about Louis Riel in Social Studies today. Some people view him as a brave revolutionary, others as a traitor. He was hanged in Regina in 1885 so I guess the traitor view won out. I wonder what we'll think of Neil's theories in twenty years.

After school Stu College stopped and offered me a ride again. He told me Solo has been arrested! He asked if I had anything to do with it and I said, maybe, maybe not, well, no. He just laughed at that and said my secret was safe with him. He said Neil needs a good friend like me and I should make sure that he takes his medication. Stu's a pretty cool guy.

Delmer is bugging me at work again but this time he is being more subtle. Every time he wants to put something down he refers to it as 'crazy'. Leaving the light on in the bathroom after I'm done is a 'crazy waste' of power and money. Leaving my work gloves on the pallet mover is 'crazy careless' and just asking to lose them. Working three nights a week and then taking the whole weekend off is a 'crazy schedule' that probably hurts my homework quality and lets me get into all sorts of trouble, with my 'crazy friends'. I'm trying not to react but I'm starting to fight back by calling everything he is associated with ugly. His ugly attitude towards customers, ugly clothing which must have saved him money, ugly haircut which is low maintenance, ugly mood because he has no friends. It is the battle of the adjectives.

Friday, March 4, 1977

Webb joined us for lunch again today. He didn't even ask, he just plopped himself down. Sam and he were talking about the Starship Enterprise from *Star Trek* and I didn't really join in. I wonder if she's forgotten who her friends really are. I asked her if she wanted to go with me to Neil's tonight but she said, no, he needs more time to recuperate. Seems a bit like she's given up on him. I'm very disappointed in her. Neil needs us more than ever.

After school I dropped down to STRM and picked up that new Eagles record, *Hotel California*. I spun it once before supper. My favorite track, next to "Hotel California" itself, is "Life In The Fast Lane", a tale of rock star success and excess.

After supper I went down to Neil's and found him on his drawing stool, working on yet another sheet of his blueprints. I showed him the Eagles album, asked to put it on. He said sure. He seemed absorbed by his drawing and not really aware of me. I think it is good he is finding his passion for drawing again. This can only help.

I got my *Starlog* #4 back from him. There was a crease on the back cover but I didn't say anything.

After my record played, nothing else was said and I started to get bored. I asked Neil if he planned to be back in school on Monday and he said, no, that would be too much of a risk. He wouldn't explain what the risk was. He did however promise to come over on Sunday to discuss tomorrow's 1999 episode. Maybe all will be back to normal by then.

Tonight there is a late movie called *Moon Zero Two*. It takes place on the Moon and stars Catherine Schell! Apparently Alpha was not the first or only place on the Moon that Maya visited! The blurb in the paper says it is a 'space western'. I will tape it. I've got the cassette picked out already, a nice 120 minute one with a bunch of disposable music from YPL vinyl copied onto it.

Saturday, March 5, 1977

Slept in until almost 11. After lunch I went down to the YPL. Neil was there but he wasn't reading. He had a notebook with him and was drawing a large, complicated spaceship. It looked like it had scary monsters/animals growing all over it. He says the design will be added to his 1999 spaceship guide. I didn't recognize the ship and asked what episode it was from. No episode he says, it is Gary (huh?) Anderson's ship, which he agrees we haven't seen yet but he claims is bound to turn up eventually.

Neil says he has now completed his Alpha blueprints and is very pleased with how they turned out. He said we only have seven years until Moonbase Alpha construction begins, as according to the gospel of the MATN. I got mad and said, so do we plan for a nuclear war in 1983 as well then, which is also in the MATN? He wouldn't look at me after that but eventually said: you can't change history.

I asked him point blank if he was still taking his medication and he said of course but then he gathered his things and headed out without really inviting me along. I called after him "see you Sunday!" and he nodded over his shoulder and waved as he left.

I came home and taped 1999. Spent the evening writing a detailed summary.

I'm still stuck on Chapter 5 of <u>Asteroid Beta</u>. My creative juices seem to have dried up.

Episode Summary: "Devil's Planet"
(1901 words)
[Omitted.]

Comments on "Devil's Planet" (Roger Kay, 1994)

Koenig is held captive at a penal colony on a moon run by sexy female aliens dressed in red tights. The alien leader finds Koenig attractive but has an explosive secret: the planet from which they are exiled is dead. The prospect of eventual return to their home planet is the only thing that keeps the prisoners from revolt.

Favorite scene: With whip-happy female guards hot on his tail, Koenig returns to his damaged Eagle. Although he finds it scavenged and disabled, Koenig manages to escape his pursuers by dropping through a never-before-seen exit hatch on the bottom of the Eagle nosecone.

Entries from Roger Kay's 1977 Diary

Sunday, March 6, 1977

Today was very sunny and the snow is beginning to melt. Sam came over at 1 and I was quite happy until it became clear that Neil wasn't going to show up and Sam had only come over to tell me our eternal trio was finished. She says Neil is really sick and needs a friend who will be honest with him (what, that's not me and her?) and that although she counts me as a dear friend she gets the feeling I would like something more, so in the interests of not leading me on, we shouldn't hang out so much anymore. I asked her if she was interested in Webb and she denied it, saying Neil was very special to her and she is not in a position to open her heart to anyone else right now. I'm kind of glad I didn't tape it. At least I won't have to listen to it again. A crushing defeat, if you'll allow the pun. So by two we had given up on Neil coming over, she had blown off my friendship, and I had been left to wonder what went wrong.

What did I think of "Devil's Planet", dear diary? I'm glad you asked. It is great to have friends who value your opinion. I gave it high marks. I think it is interesting that the premise of the leader trying to keep his flock from leaving the nest, as we earlier saw in "Séance Spectre", is so turned on its head.

Instead of Koenig, it is Elizia who wants to keep her sheep under her thumb. The similarity is that in both cases the desired destination of the flock is actually a poisonous planet. The difference is that in Koenig's case he was telling the truth about it, but in Elizia's case she is lying. And their motives are different too

[Editor's note: In the original, a ink line continues after the last cursive word, extending down the page, and wrapping around itself to form a nebulous ball of blue spaghetti that fills the majority of the blank, one-third remainder of the page. It signals frustration and suppressed rage.]

Monday, March 7, 1977

I woke up at 6 a.m. because a giant bolt of lightning struck right next to my window. It felt like it was inches from my head - I don't remember waking up, just a giant flash of light and I jumped right out of bed. I was standing, shaking, before I was even awake. It must have passed very quickly because as I ate my breakfast I could see no trace of rainfall outside. Some snow was still there, half-demolished, dirt-specked piles of the stuff, but every bare patch of concrete or dead brown grass was bone dry. Maybe I only dreamt it.

Did I mention I went over to Neil's last night but couldn't find him? I found the shed unlocked, the heater and lights on, but no Neil. I waited inside for a few minutes but still no one. I could not bring myself to knock on the house door so I reluctantly left. I had a weird feeling I was being watched. Is Neil avoiding me?

Today at lunch I sat with Sam and Webb. I tried to talk about "Devil's Planet" with them, but it felt just too damn strange. Maybe I should give up SF and go back to hanging around with Arvid. How crappy is it when your identity depends upon your friends accepting that identity? I want to be a SF writer and I want to be surrounded by people who see me on that path. Is that too much to ask?

After supper, I walked to the shed and this time did find Neil there, and no Solo in sight! I asked him where Solo got to, trying to appear the innocent, but Neil surprised me by revealing that Solo had been arrested… but was already released on bail!

And what is worse, Solo came back to their house and Neil's mom again extended an invitation for him to stay. Now Solo sleeps nights inside the house, on their couch, and expects Neil to run for smokes, buy the groceries, do all the chores, etc. Solo likes to cook, but he doesn't know how to do dishes. Yeah right.

But the very worst part, Neil confided, is that Solo has changed since he came back. He is now possessed by the alien intelligence that Neil refers to as Gary Anderson. I told him I don't understand what that means and Neil said not to worry, there is no way to understand such an alien creature, but he is uniquely qualified to deal with him.

I don't understand what Neil is talking about but this is probably one of the symptoms that his medication will resolve. He does seem to have improved in alertness and energy. He is no longer tired or listless and we are listening to music again. I'm glad to report that it is possible his recovery is around the corner.

Tuesday, March 8, 1977

Very disappointed with Sam today. At lunch, with Webb hanging around of course, I raised the idea we should go visit Neil as soon as possible, but she shot it down. Neil needs time to recover and the excitement of company is probably the last thing he needs, she claims. On what is this based? I think he needs us more than ever. And we need to keep an eye on him, make sure he is taking his medicine, etc. Could she possibly think that we can entrust this to Solo?? I wonder if she is happy to just jettison us both as more trouble than we're worth.

At one point she said, look we can still be friends, but we don't have to hang around that shed. I think she is not being honest. She is either pissed off with Solo or Neil or all three of us. I feel this is very unfair because I personally have done nothing wrong. I could accept her being interested in Neil, but in ditching both of us, when we need her the most, she has truly hurt me. I hope I never feel pain like this again.

Almost 7 and I have to go to Pic-A-Pop now. I feel more like hurling cases of the stuff instead of stacking them, but I am too professional for that.

Neil's house has burned down! As I'm coming home from work, I see smoke rising from behind Victoria School. At first I'm kind of excited, like it would be cool to see something burn down, maybe I could use it in my writing, but then when I walk past Victoria School I see fire trucks and police cars blocking off Darlington between 4th and 5th. I backtrack to the alley behind the school and approach Neil's house that way. Then I can tell his house is definitely the source of the smoke.

Halfway down the alley, right behind Ron's actually, a police car is blocking the alley. A cop starts to shoo me away but I say: "Is Neil in there? Did you check the shed?" When the cop realizes I know something, he asks me who lives there. I tell him Neil, Neil's mom, and Solo. No, I don't know his last name.

I ask if there was anyone inside. He won't tell me. The house looks like a total loss. Wouldn't they be able to get out in time? It is a small place. Just bust a window or step outside. This isn't the middle of the night. Everyone should be okay.

I watched the house smolder and disintegrate for a while. An ambulance arrived, then the cop told me to leave. He assured me the crowd out front would also be dispersed. No one would be allowed to watch the removal of any bodies. I couldn't believe my ears. I walk home, my brain racing, is Neil okay?

But there he was, in Shaw Park, sitting at a damp picnic table, facing towards the smoke plume. I would have seen him from the front window of our living room if I had missed him on the walk home.

I rush to him, saying his house is destroyed. He said he had caught his mom and Solo doing something bad, there had been a fight, and he had left. He had then walked along the train tracks down the little valley behind 6th Avenue, a quiet place to collect his thoughts.

Now, Neil said, he finally understood. Solo had killed his mother and burned down their house, managing to destroy all of Jerry's revolutionary materials and proofs. All that remained of his brother's legacy was what was in the shed, which I must save at all costs. His Alpha blueprints were in there. Suddenly he was very concerned about that. Next, did I still have a copy of *Potatoland*?

Yes, I assured him.

Don't let them deep-fry you, he said.

I said "I eat french fries for breakfast." Which I know doesn't make much sense, but I was trying to be fearless and comforting within the confines of the potato metaphor.

A police car spotted us and abruptly stopped. They got out and asked if we knew or had seen Lionel O'Neill. Neil took off running. One cop grabbed me and the other chased Neil down.

Is that him? Yes it is, I admitted. You can't outrun a cop and I have to maintain good relations with them because of my deal with Detective Hooper. They put Neil in the backseat of their car and drove away.

Now it is midnight and I can't sleep. This is like a bad movie. It doesn't make sense. Why would Solo burn down their house? Did he know I ratted on him? Would he come after me next? Would our house succumb to arson? What if he killed my parents? What would it be like to be raised by Uncle Tim? Horrible, unthinkable. I'm going to have nightmares, if I sleep at all.

Saturday, March 12, 1977

Last episode of *Space: 1999* Year Two, or ever, aired today. See my summary.

Episode Summary: "The Dorcons" (1858 words)
[Omitted.]

Comments on "The Dorcons" (Roger Kay, 1994)

The Dorcons are a powerful race and the Psychons' dreaded
enemy: they use Psychon brain stems to achieve immortality.
The Dorcon flagship arrives at Alpha and demands Maya be
handed over. Their decrepit leader requires her brainstem for
the good of all Dorcons everywhere. The Alphans are no
match, but Koenig jumps into the transfer beam and winds up
aboard their flagship where he begins a desperate battle to save
Maya.

Favorite scene: When she understands the Dorcons will
soon take her, Maya pleads with Helena to shoot her.

Selected Entries from Roger Kay's 1977 Diary

Tuesday, April 12, 1977

Hello my dear diary,

I am writing to you in this fresh notebook because your previous incarnation is now in the hands of the RCMP. How could I have known as I intimately updated you on all the private aspects of my life that my words would be consumed by these barging horsemen? It will take all my composure and restraint to remain true and frank in my writing. If I wind up in the gulag, that will be the most forceful evidence yet for Jerry's theory of status quo domination.

A lot has happened in the last couple of days. Some details about the fire at the O'Neill's have come out. Neil's mom and Solo were both in the house at the time of the fire and are dead. The fire started in the kitchen and looks accidental but the cops are still calling the two deaths suspicious.

The house was completely destroyed. There is no roof and only remnants of the walls stand, short blackened stumps that corral the charred mess that remains of the contents. The police have taped off the area.

You can walk by the house on the alley side and get pretty close to the shed, but it also has a police sticker sealing the door. The ice from all the water used to fight the fire has frozen into thick layers that also coat the shed and all the yard debris.

Neil remains at the Psych Centre. The nurses confirm he is there, but they wouldn't let me see him last week when I tried because only next of kin are allowed.

Today I bumped into Stu College at The Stereo Hut. His real last name is Schmidt. Stu says he and his girlfriend managed to see Neil by claiming that she was Neil's sister Nancy. Neil was happy to see them, a bit drowsy but lucid, his medication working again. He thinks he will be out in another week, but the bad news is that he won't be returning to St. Joe's. Earl will take him to live in Saskatoon and he'll be dumped into some school up there.

I envy Neil's moving to a much larger city but I pity myself left behind to deal with all the fallout. I don't know if he ever got his Alpha blueprints out of the shed. I hope he managed to recover some of his stuff. On the other hand, maybe it would be good for him just to start completely fresh. All that happened here is stuff he won't want to be reminded of.

It was the Saturday after the fire that the last 1999 episode aired, "The Dorcons". I knew it was the last one when I watched it because of the episode guides from the MATN and from *Starlog*.

As I watched it, I had to think of Neil. Here were aliens come to take away the one person on Alpha who was way smarter and more knowledgeable about the galaxy than any of them. I always thought of Neil as the alien, the misfit. With his incredible powers he was plain different from everyone else, just like Maya. Somewhere high in orbit, Neil's brainstem is being transplanted into the cranium of a withered supreme galactic leader.

I think he knew he was that person too. He always identified with the outsider. He was an alien who came from inner space, a void that existed only within him. We could hear him but we could not see him. He was lost in the blackness. The mental capacity and creativity that powered his breakaway from an unworthy Earth was glorious and full of promise, but his collision with the ugly realities of 1970s life was inevitable and fatal to his flight path among the stars. Have I written his epitaph? Will mine read: his wordiness was appreciated by ink producers everywhere?

I must admit I was disappointed in that last, final episode. The Dorcons might be better labeled "The Dorkons" for so faulty were their security and fighting skills. In this episode the Mysterious Unknown Force is the idiocy of the Dorkons. How can the rulers of an entire galaxy be so inept? Who builds a spaceship with air ducts so large that you can crawl around in them? I have seen this in so many low quality shows, giant ventilation ductwork providing an escape path. What kind of duct can support a 200 pound man? The Mysterious Unknown

Force from *Space: 1999* Year One that *Starlog* complained about makes MORE sense than this air duct copout.

I don't get to see Sam too much anymore. After the fire she seemed to lose all interest in our friendship. At first we did lunch together still, but our Sunday get-togethers were over. Webb was more and more in the picture. Eventually other people got involved and I was no longer welcome.

I don't want to write about that.

I've been spending more time with my old friend Arvid. He is now playing the guitar and I have taken up the bass. The thing about bass is that it is a lot easier than guitar. While Arvid has to do all sorts of complicated chords and single note runs, I can just bop along repeatedly hitting the same note for the entire bar (four beats). Plus there are a million guitar players and every one of them needs a bass player. Right now we are learning some Nazareth songs like "Hair Of The Dog". It is pretty hard but I like the new type of challenge.

What else. Oh yes! I am excited and pleased to report that I am now working at a gas station: Broadway Texaco. I get adult minimum wage which is three dollars per hour. That is twice what I was earning before!

Goodbye lime-flavored Pic-A-Pop! I am so sick of you. Also, I have learned it is not a good idea to work for relatives. There seem to be advantages at first, but later you find out they expect you to do everything and anything without a single question. They seem hurt when you quit, even if they tried to fire you before and don't listen to your complaints about older staff who should know better than to be stupid on the job. Enough said. Things are looking up for me. Only a couple more months and I say goodbye forever to St. Joseph's Junior High Prison.

...

Wednesday, June 29, 1977

Logan's Drugs had *Starlog* #6 and it says right on the cover that *Space: 1999* is canceled. There will be no third season. To be honest, I'm not that surprised. The second season certainly didn't live up to the promise of the first. This reminds me that

<u>Asteroid Beta</u> is sitting stagnant, still only five chapters long. I think I need a new premise.

...

Thursday, December 29, 1977

Saw *Star Wars* today. They left a lot of the book out. I was happy but I was sad. Happy for SF fans everywhere that they have a new excitement to shiver them and feed their wonder, but sad for Neil who no doubt sees this as a capitulation of SF into the (not deep) pit of action-adventure.

I can't help but feel that he would prefer *Close Encounters Of The Third Kind* and would think that we, I mean the world, were still going in the wrong direction. For me, I agree but I don't care. Some SF can be mainstream. That doesn't mean there won't be alternatives for the more reflective among us. Great art is never appreciated by the masses until the artist is long dead and grown mythic in his grave. Or at least until after the show is cancelled.

On a Happy Childhood (Lionel O'Neill, 1988)

I do have some happy memories of childhood, but they are few. I recall one sun-burnished afternoon at Manitou Beach that benefited from the unlikely confluence of my father being sober, my mother being aware she was alive, and both of them being focused primarily and positively on my well-being.

Although I don't recall any gifts or a cake, I think we were celebrating my seventh birthday. Miraculously, Jerry and my sisters were all there and somehow I felt it was my special day. And it was special. There we were at Manitou Beach as a family and seemingly happy.

My mother had packed a picnic lunch for us. In this memory the jelly salads were less watery than usual. We lunched contentedly after spending a morning floating in that mineral-rich and therefore amazingly buoyant lake named by the Indians after their deity, the Great Manitou.

I remember the feel of the moss at the bottom of the lake squishing between my toes as I bounced up and down, the heavy green mineral water forcing me to the surface and then me wiggling about until gravity overcame buoyancy and my feet struck bottom again. It felt slimy yet not unclean. I couldn't see the moss but it felt like it must be vibrant green and completely healthy. I idled and was lulled in this womb of warm cosmic oneness.

As we drove to the lake, for once my parents were not arguing. They commented on the beautiful weather and promised I would love the lake. They were right. I did. I wish there were more to love about my childhood.

On Swimming (Lionel O'Neill, 1988)

When I was much younger I had some terrible things happen to
me. My Grade Six Phys-ed teacher was Mr. Kiblah and at first
I thought he was a great guy. I had a real fear of swimming and
water. Since my trip to Manitou Beach I had been greatly
disappointed and disillusioned to find that other bodies of water
were much less forgiving. You could not count on floating
without effort. This came as a surprise and I swallowed a lot of
water and endured the laughter of my schoolmates a few times
before I realized I truly could not swim. Manitou Beach had
been an anomaly.

So I began to hate the water. The chlorine smell of a pool
was like slow death to me. I dreaded the enforced wading and
soaking I endured while others floated and swam. It seemed I
was marked for failure.

But Mr. Kiblah took pity on me. I had one note from my
Mom stating I had the flu and therefore should not be in the
pool. I reused that note each and every pool period we had.
When it became clear this scam was working, I was elated at
having escaped from my own personal hell of water torture.

Eventually and inevitably, the other shoe dropped. After a
pool period one afternoon I sat reading in the library, where I
usually hid after deploying the well-worn note yet again, when
Mr. Kiblah appeared looking serious and concerned. He strode
right to where I sat and stated we would have to meet at his
office after school so we could discuss the eligibility of my
swim note. That is exactly what he said and it threw me into a
confusion. Was the note going to be debunked and confiscated?
Would my life of aquatic hell return?

So at four o'clock, as directed, I went to his office, adjacent
to the gymnasium. He explained he was not going to force me
to swim but he wanted to understand what my problem was. I
tried to tell him that I feared the water because the forces of
Manitou had deserted me and I could no longer swim, but he
quickly dismissed this idea as nonsense and instead suggested
the real problem was that I was not comfortable with my body.

He explained in a gentle voice that my body was changing and I would have to accept it, and not worry about it, because it was all perfectly natural. He persuaded me that I had to convince him my body was normal. He made me strip off my clothes and began an unhurried inspection of my corporeal form, or at least my genitals. I had not yet reached puberty and so lacked pubic hair. He lifted my penis and manipulated my testicles reassuring me all the time, yes this is perfectly normal, you shouldn't worry about anything. He explained that soon my body would change and that my penis would become much bigger. Girls would want to put it into their mouths and other parts of their bodies but I should resist such things until I was much older and knew "what I wanted from life". To illustrate the expected growth, he contended he would have to show me his. Which he did. He suggested I touch it so I could better understand where mine was headed. I declined and he told me to relax.

After I had dressed, he was still acting soft-spoken and friendly. He told me there would be no problem with my continuing to use the swim note but then just as I thought the ordeal was over, he demanded I appear at his office for private health lessons after each pool period. I won't list the topics of these weekly lessons but they started with the how and why of erections. This carried on until the end of the year when we all gathered for the last Phys-ed class. He presented me with the ridiculously inappropriate Most Improved Swimmer award which the rest of the class found justifiably risible.

On Causality and Conscience (Lionel O'Neill, 1988)

When Jerry didn't return home that fateful Sunday, the part of my mind associated with my confession or disclosure of the previous night, twitched. A spark of pain said, maybe, not for sure, but maybe, this is the reason, this is the root cause. The information you released has caused someone to react in a negative way that could have been predicted and prevented if the information had been safeguarded. What happens if you tell your brother that you had been mistreated by aliens and he winds up ineffectually attacking those aliens and therefore being needlessly killed himself? A story idea I should have presented to Roger.

I can thank the drug Cephapax for my new clarity. I can remember things, or parts of things, and often a truer significance emerges. This is my first visibility into an area corroded with madness and impossibilities.

Only now can I recall what I said to Jerry that night before he disappeared. It was Saturday and we had worked an evening shift together at The Stereo Hut where Jerry had a new job, probably as temporary staff for the Christmas season. His boss allowed me to tag along half the hourly rate he had promised Jerry, i.e. one dollar an hour.

We had worked the Friday evening together and been paid cash. The next day I bought a pair of gloves downtown with Roger, spent the afternoon reading at the library, and then spent the evening again working with Jerry.

Later that night we returned to Jerry's clubhouse, our shed, and I admit I smoked marijuana with him. This may have "loosened the screws at the back of the tongue". I told Jerry I had learned a valuable lesson seeing him stand up to Earl back in October '75, and how after that I would never again let anyone get away with hurting me or my friends.

Jerry was not one to miss details and he asked if someone had hurt me in the past. I said no, not really, I haven't had any real problems since Mr. Kiblah. This was the moment of my undoing, my great failure to remain silent when it counted.

Then the seals on this closed file had been broken. I did explain to Jerry what Kiblah had done to the younger me, what he had shown me, and what he had said. Jerry tried to appear calm but I knew below the surface he was livid.

When Jerry disappeared the next day, deep inside I knew that he had gone to confront Kiblah. When that bastard was eventually tied to Jerry's murder, I knew who the real blame for the whole situation fell on. It was my own fault. I was numb with guilt. After that, sometimes my brain would just stop and I floated in a void. It was like I was already dead but my body didn't realize it. Before long the delusions had started. They didn't stop for years.

Horrible as this is, I am glad to finally understand the etiology of it all.

On the Onset of Schizophrenia (Lionel O'Neill, 1988)

I was struck with a profound psychotic break on the morning of February 21 1977. For some time I had been having unusual flights of thought. Sometimes I would find strange conclusions already fully formed within my mind. Mundane coincidences took on heightened significance.

Because LSD is a psychomimetic drug (it mimics schizophrenia) I was already acquainted with some of the disease symptoms and so did not realize when I crossed over from a temporary, desired unreality of fun and wonder to a permanent, undesired unreality of terror and confusion.

I woke up that morning listening to my clock radio, only it wasn't on any correct frequency. Perhaps half-awake I had clumsily bumped the tuning button off-station, to a band of frequency where only static reigned. As I laid in bed listening to the electronic mush, feeling an unusual fright squeeze my brain, I began to detect swirls and ripples in the electromagnetic susurration, then a soft voice whispering like a gentle stream trickled into my ears. Only what it said was horrible. It called me all sorts of names and made accusations that I knew (or at least hoped) were false.

Then the music came. Reminiscent of Pink Floyd's "Welcome To The Machine", a churning, shuddering blaze of industrial percussion that threatened to pulverize my brain. The noise grew louder and more distinct.

Certainly it couldn't be coming from my radio I thought. I rolled over and then back again, opening and closing my eyes, trying to reset the situation. The noise continued. It was behind me. I turned over. Still behind me. No matter which way I turned, it was coming from behind me, not from the radio anymore.

The din continued its assault for some time while I cringed in my bed, sweating profusely, my heart racing. I was almost completely overwhelmed and paralyzed and then I could bear the house no longer. It did not feel safe.

So I fled to the shed in which I had fallen asleep the previous night and then woken around 2 a.m. chilled by more than the cruel cold: a stark memory of hiding in the office supply room beside Main Mission while awaiting the final and fatal arrival of Gary Anderson, the entity that would destroy free will and leave the universe locked into a loop of horror and pain.

Now it was a few minutes past seven in the morning, still dark outside. I knew where Solo had cached two hits of blotter acid and I retrieved one. In half an hour I was pleasantly tripping and the soul-devouring noise was almost forgotten. It would return along with terrifying thoughts of imminent death only a couple of hours later in Art class, heralding the destruction of my former life.

On His Mother's Death (Lionel O'Neill, 1988)

On the night my mother died, I did visit violence upon Solomon. I had no intention of killing anyone, Solomon nor my mother, but when I entered our house and found him sexually assaulting her, I had to act.

In Grade 7 Industrial Arts class I had carved a block of wood into the shape of the word 'words'. This meta ethic was a gentle whimsy I employed with unconscious irony when I presented it as a present to my mother that Christmas.

She knew words were important to me, viz my ravenous reading habits and favored retreat of the Yorkton Public Library.

Now I know there were things I could have or should have told her that might have avoided the tragic path which would unfold for both her and Solomon, but at the time the carved wooden gift represented a diplomatic oeuvre from son to mother. It was a promise of future communication and understanding.

The estrangement from my father Earl had just begun and I wanted to impress upon her the importance of the efficacious intercourse that the clear and structured medium of language could avail. She complimented me on my craftsmanship but I don't believe her understanding surpassed that lowly baseline.

When I happened upon them that night in flagrante delicto, as the Italians say, my reaction erupted from both delusional and firmly grounded precepts.

It seemed clear to me that Solomon was attacking my mother in a sexual way, but additionally I believed that he was both an entity I referred to as Gary Anderson, an evil being from the future that could and had disguised itself as Gerry Anderson, the creator of *Space: 1999*, to pass along coded warnings and messages to SF viewers about a coming alien invasion, as well as Solomon Malakowski, a hallucinogen supplier for my deceased brother, who had now latched onto my home and family in an attempt to quash my unintended intercept of those same clandestine warnings.

'Words', the wooden carving, was selected based on proximity to the coitus interruptus. She and he were positioned on the couch in the living room, a dusty chamber darkened and isolated via thick drapes over the sole window facing Darlington Avenue. She was crouched forward, bent over the couch, he behind and choking her neck while perpetrating the sex assault. The wooden carving was on top of the TV, an iniquitous position for an object so inherently signifying values counter to that glass teat.

Regardless, I grabbed it and swung it heavily into Solomon's head, causing him to recoil and lose his balance. My mother began to scream, demanding I desist, but in my fervor to deal with Solomon I pushed her with unrestrained force towards her bedroom door and I don't recall seeing her again after that.

Meanwhile Solomon had recovered himself and rejoined the battle. I believe he was a little drunk because he was not much of a fighter. I grabbed his neck and squeezed. He grabbed my hair and yanked. I loosened my grip and with one additional swing of the self-referential carving, I left him unconscious on the floor. At precisely that point I fled.

In every tragedy there are mistakes the protagonist makes. Mine was that I did not see the pot of oil coming to a boil on our stove. Missing that detail changed everything that followed in a dramatically negative fashion.

Looking back on the scene, I understand better now that I have matured and seen more closely the underbelly of the world of prurient desires and interests. It is clear that Solomon was not raping my mother. They were engaging in a dangerous game of sexual intercourse heightened by asphyxiation. Perhaps my mother developed a taste for this during her time with Earl, a man who I can easily suspect of such a malevolent depravity. Perhaps it was something which Solomon introduced to her. Whatever the actual case may be, it was my perception and actions that turned that unlovely embrace into a perceived assault, and turned a moment of debased desires into the destruction of much more than two lives.

For years I have suppressed these memories, or had a lot of trouble deciphering their reality from the delusions I had simultaneously suffered. The fact I was mentally ill also projected a patina of blameworthiness upon myself. Had I been clear of mind and very early indicated what my real intentions were, and what mistakes I made, resolution of the impact of these issues upon my own life would have come long before now. Instead I suffered years in institutions while the real story slowly emerged and gained credibility.

Agreed Statement of Fact by Lionel O'Neill
(source: RCMP, 1980)

1. Voluntary Declaration of Crime
During the evening of September 13, 1979, I went to the home of Mr. Albert Kiblah, to wit, apartment 211 of 351 Allanbrooke Drive. Mr. Kiblah had been acquitted of the murder of my brother, Jeremiah, a year earlier but I could not accept this verdict.

I confronted Mr. Kiblah regarding his unacknowledged guilt and a physical altercation ensued. During that contretemps, I squeezed his neck with both my hands until the bones snapped, and his larynx was crushed. This physical damage resulted in his death.

2. Additional Statement regarding Motivation and Frame of Mind
I now regret this action but at the time I was suffering from a delusional state brought on by inadequate or inappropriate anti-psychotic drugs and a pre-existing case of paranoid schizophrenia. This state was aggravated or provoked by an earlier undisclosed history of sexual abuse by this teacher upon myself, his former student.

My state of mind at the time of the death of Mr. Kiblah was delusional. I believed he had been colluding with aliens and some fictional characters from the future to alter the history of the Earth. More specifically, I believed the producer of the television series *Space: 1999*, Mr. Gary (sic, Gerry) Anderson, in collusion with the actor who played Professor Victor Bergman, had portrayed the true future of humanity in the first year of the series but subsequently aliens had taken control of them, forcing alterations in the second season of the program.

As well I believed that the aliens plus the 'real' Professor Bergman from the future now assumed key positions on the Earth with the mission to ensure that the bright future I had seen on the show would never come to pass.

I believed this future was something worth fighting for, and the debacle of my history with Mr. Kiblah and the death of my brother convinced me that Kiblah was also involved in this alien conspiracy.

My brother Jerry was key to that imagined brighter future. His philosophy was essential for the new era which was to come, but Mr. Kiblah had snuffed out his light. When I confronted Mr. Kiblah in his apartment, I accused him not only of murdering my brother, but of murdering the future of all humanity. Viewed in that context, his death seemed necessary and right.

It was not until effective medication for my condition was administered that I began to understand the folly of my deluded actions. I know that Mr. Kiblah killed Jerry. I blame myself for that murder because if I had not confided in my brother about the abuse, he would never have confronted Mr. Kiblah.

It is clear to me now that I was very likely not the only victim of abuse by Mr. Kiblah. There were lines not crossed in his abuse of me that indicate he was early in his career as an abuser. If Mr. Kiblah had crossed the final rubicon of perversion with me, perhaps Jerry would be alive today. I mean, if he had done more than just confuse and disgust me, if he had tried to complete his molestation, to sexually interact to bring me to the point of orgasm, my reaction might have become quite volatile, and as a result his secrets would have been rapidly revealed to the authorities. It is very painful for me to think through this contingent reality and it will no doubt haunt me to my last breath.

On Reconnecting with Neil (Roger Kay, 1989)

Early last year I received a card from Neil. This was the first contact we have had since the night of the fire.

Although I had imagined that Neil subsequently lived at his grandparent's farm and attended school in Saskatoon, I never did confirm this. Perhaps I would have tried harder to find Neil if Detective Hooper had not specifically warned me to stay away from him.

I remember reading about the trial of Al Kiblah during 1979 and was shocked when this killer was acquitted. The pundits at the time suggested the Crown had made a fatal error by charging Kiblah with murder instead of manslaughter. While there was ample indication of manslaughter, the murder charge would not stick due to gaps in the logic of the case. Why did Jerry go to Kiblah's place? What was Kiblah's motive to kill Jerry? Without these blanks filled in, the jury could not be certain that murder was what had occurred.

Why other charges were not brought against Kiblah, I cannot say. The fact that he moved Jerry's body, then covered up what had happened and really never explained it satisfactorily, should have given the police ample opportunity to assign other criminal charges such as interfering with an investigation, lying to the police, moving a body, etc. Why the police did not take further actions against Kiblah is one for the conspiracy theorists. Unemployed youth shows up at respected teacher's house, to which he has no connection, then winds up dead. Who is to blame?

At that point I still held out some hope that Neil would be (forgive me) rehabilitated. But when he returned to Yorkton and committed murder himself, eliminating the only witness to Jerry's murder and no doubt a source of great mental anguish for himself, all my hopes were dashed. I knew then that I would not be seeing my friend again for many years. If ever. Perhaps my friend did not exist at all, and was just an illusion I had superimposed on what then seemed revealed as one very dysfunctional person. This is not how a genius solves his problems.

Neil was sentenced to life in prison. I cried when I heard his sentence but those tears also cleansed my heart of the trouble and horror I had been through. Finally I moved on.

Almost 10 years later, Neil's sister Nancy contacted me. Neil had been released and she was planning a book on his life. Her approach would be to gather statements from Neil, as well as his friends back in the day, in an attempt to prove that Neil's actions, although extreme, were not arbitrary. He would be portrayed, if not as an actual victim, at least with sympathy.

What she planned at that time bears little resemblance to this work. Hers was the initial and germinal idea, but once I admitted that I had references contemporary to the key events in my old diaries, the ingredients for this project were adjusted.

That note I received from Neil was short and polite. It said he didn't place any blame on me for anything in the past, he was grateful for my friendship, he was aware of my discussions with Nancy, and I should feel free to contact him.

Neil is now living in a small, low rent apartment, actually the basement of a house, in the Cathedral area of Regina. Across the street is a small bar, Blue Horizons, at which I left my girlfriend on the night I finally went to visit my old friend.

These days I have a micro-cassette recorder and I often tape meetings. Rarely do I admit that I am. This book may breach that secret. As for Neil's reference to others parsing our private conversation, I must admit, that he was correct in this case and perhaps there is a fine line between psychic and psychotic.

On Lionel (Samantha Renfield, 1988)

I remember Lionel O'Neill. We called him Neil. He was a very intelligent young man who was devastated by mental illness. To be truthful, we were quite close and I had an enormous crush on him in Grade Nine.

He was the opposite of everything I rebelled against in my family. I came from a large family that was run as a religious patriarchy; they were anti-intellectual and anti-sex. I saw the autonomy that Neil had in his life, virtually no interference from his parents. It was incredible to me. His brother played the role of a friend, not an agent of his parents.

Neil was very intellectual and it was the saddest thing that a man who relied on his brain for every type of satisfaction in life was targeted by a disease that attacked the very thing he valued most. Or the only thing he valued. Imagine an athlete becoming physically disabled. That sad.

I remember trying and failing to communicate my affection to him. It should have been a simple thing, but nothing was simple for Neil.

I agreed with his pro-mind stand. The enforced ignorance and unquestioned dogma of my family's church was anathema to me, and Neil's embrace of books and science fiction refreshing and exciting. I wanted new ideas and new places to go, terrestrial or not.

We were both against the stream of conformity at that time, but what originally presented as Neil's anti-sexism, I eventually discovered was closer to an anti-sex ideology. I mistook his fear of woman as respect. This manifested in Neil as a disconnection from his body and eventually became an insurmountable obstacle for my romantic hopes for us.

Neil thought pop music was intended to make you stupid and think only with your genitals. It would make you waste your youthful energy on hormonal concerns so that the status quo could survive unquestioned. I admit I did mistake this political conspiracy view as a pro-female, anti-sexist stand. Initially his worldview was very attractive to me, but when I came to understand that he valued my brain too much to even think of my body, I knew our love was not to be.

Beyond his high IQ, I also found very attractive Neil's loyalty and steadfastness in friendship. His best friend was Roger Kay, a slight boy who always seemed very nervous around me. I knew Neil stuck up for Roger against the bullies at our school. So, despite his inability to show physical affection, I knew Neil had the proverbial heart of gold.

After the horrific deaths by fire at the O'Neill's, we didn't know what Neil had or hadn't done. Was Neil homicidally insane? It seemed preposterous on some level, but you always hear about the easygoing neighbor that turns out to be a serial killer. I incorrectly assumed the worst and this had a carryover negative effect upon my friendship with Neil and Roger. I do regret this.

After high school, our paths diverged. I fell in love with and subsequently married Michael Webb. My unfavorable early impressions of him mellowed and aged over our high school years, and by graduation we were deeply in love. I completed my Education degree with a minor in Psychology at the University of Regina in 1985. I now provide career and social guidance to the 487 high school students at the Yorkton Regional High School.

When Nancy O'Neill and Roger were contemplating this book, she approached me to request my reminiscences. I admit I was a bit reticent, not wanting to disturb old wounds, but Nancy convinced me that I could not and should not ignore the past no matter how painful. She being an expert herself on that type of situation, I had to agree.

Both Nancy and I came from families that we later repudiated in order to safeguard our own sanity and potential. Nancy succeeded in university (Social Work) despite her family and has never allowed her upbringing to get in the way of what she feels is right. I had to come to my own awakening in this regard.

I now realize it was the extreme dogmatism of my parents that drove their children either into the arms of dysfunctional dependency, be it on an institution or group, meaning the church, or intoxicants. The only exceptions to this fate were my brother James and myself.

James was an artistic soul, my original impetus and inspiration to seek out truth in science fiction and rock music. He could not survive the continual moralistic scrutiny of my parents. After high school he headed down east and lived for a time in Toronto. We kept in touch and I still have all his letters. His death due to HIV complications a few years later drove a knife into my heart and increased my empathy for Neil. Only after suffering the death of a sibling myself did I realize how harshly I had judged Neil and his reactions to the key traumas of his life.

As extreme as Neil's reactions were, I cannot deny mine were similarly life-altering. The difference is, in my case, it was solely my own life that was affected. I turned away from the path of self-righteous confrontation and reactionary revolution to seek my own place in society, and to make my own positive contribution within established academia, a world free of the strangulation of counter-productive and baseless illusions.

I harbour no ill will towards Neil. I understand he is selling a fan publication of his Moonbase Alpha blueprints. I wish him good health and every good fortune in his creative projects.

Roger Kay's comments to the author
upon reading a pre-publication draft of
"The Crash & Rescue Of Professor Neil L. Armstrong"
for
End Times magazine
(December, 2005)

Maybe Neil always was paranoid. I remember one of the first times he came over to my house, he and Samantha, and we were talking about *Space: 1999*. I have the tape of that conversation. I think it was September '76.

Anyway we were talking about how the show was changing and he said it was turning into a second *Star Trek*, then he leaned over and without any warning just shut off my tape recorder, rather brazen for anybody but him for I was master of my own tape recorder of course, and then he started acting all spooky, like 'shh, don't tell anyone, wink wink'.

I thought it was quite funny and I think Sam did too because she was smiling and laughing I remember, but Neil was saying "don't say *Star Trek*, they might hear you". Maybe he was kidding, but thinking back on it, he never shut off my tape machine again, and rarely did we discuss *Star Trek* after that. It was an episodic thing. I can't believe I just said that.

Neil was up some days and down others. I enjoyed his peaks, the manic stream of ideas and his generally right on sense of humor. And the down days, he was quiet, passive. Completely retreated into himself. But that day it was a bit of a joke and we all had a good time.

Appendix: Additional Documents and Tape Cache

13 September 1989
(audio tape from collection of Roger Kay)

Roger: It's so good to see you after all this time.

Neil: Yeah, man. You too. Come on down. You want a beer?

Roger: Sure, that'd be great. Hey, when did *you* start drinking?

Neil: In jail.

Roger: Oh. Well at least it's not illegal.

Neil: It is in jail.

Roger: I brought you something. Remember the Association of Alphans? Well Ron finally published his magazine in 1979, and we both made the cut. I don't know if you've seen it, but I have a copy for you.

Neil: No, I haven't. Thanks. That's my photo of Barry Morse on the cover.

Roger: From your interview. There's a few of your drawings inside too.

Neil: Wow. This typeface is pretty crappy. Even worse than your old typewriter.

Roger: I'm surprised you remember!

Neil: I'm not one to forget things easily. Looks like he used a bunch of my stuff. And your "Gilligan's Moon" story is in here too.

Roger: My first sale.

Neil: Did he give you anything for it?

Roger: Couple of free copies. I haven't published anything since.

Neil: Really? Why? You were doing so much writing when I knew you, that book you were always working on, and your episode guide too.

Roger: After the cops seized all my stuff I gradually lost the urge to commit anything to paper. I was in university before I finally got anything back. I had to chase it all down myself.

Neil: You know my sister Nancy is helping me publish my Alpha blueprints? You could write an introduction for it. Value added. I'd cut you into the proceeds.

Roger: I haven't written anything in a long time.

Neil: Okay, but you shouldn't give up the fight. They haven't gotten you yet.

Roger: The cops?

Neil: And who's behind them. You know Sam is working at the Regional as a guidance counselor?

Roger: Yeah...

Neil: Well that's a case of giving in to the status quo. In her position she'll be able to influence young minds and steer them into obedience.

Roger: I don't think it's like that.

Neil: No? Then how is it?

Roger: She's probably just trying to help. She knew a lot of messed up kids so it is understandable she'd want to help.

Neil: Like me?

Roger: I was thinking more of her own family. She's got like five brothers and two sisters, you know. They had a lot of problems too.

Neil: Well she turned her back on both of us, didn't she?

Roger: I guess. It was a difficult time.

Neil: Right. She had it pretty hard.

Roger: Look I'm sorry about how the Kiblah thing turned out.

Neil: I don't really want to talk about it.

Roger: No, I understand.

Neil: You know, you might think I'm crazy. It's an idea a few people have had. But I don't think you do.

I may have been derailed by some evil people, but you're free. You still have a chance to find the truth.

Maybe you think I'm kidding when I say that the status quo is a real force. But it is. No matter how much some people want to change the world for the better, there are other people who want just as badly to keep it exactly the way it is. And they don't care who gets hurt.

Now, yes, I do know that Gary Anderson was an illusion, but that doesn't mean there wasn't a grain of truth to it. Even this conversation, it's still important. It still interests them. Someday, somewhere, dark entities will be going over these words, looking for enemies. But there is little more they can do to me.

You want to smoke?

Roger: No I'm good. Actually I should get going. Pam is waiting for me, my girlfriend. I left her at the karaoke bar across the street.

Neil: Is she a singer?

Roger: Not really. But she likes to try sometimes.

Neil: I used to be like that.

Roger: You used to sing?

Neil: No. I used to try.

Roger: I'm sorry but the smoke in here is killing me.

Neil: Should be much better in the bar.

Roger: I've got a business card. Let me give it to you.

Neil: Sure. Don't be a stranger.

Roger: You too.

3 September 1974
(audio tape from collection of Roger Kay)

(Sound of rhythmic rubbing, the microphone is bumping something as Roger walks)

Roger: Today is Tuesday, September 3, 1974, first day of Grade 7 at St. Joe's Junior High. I've just entered the building.

(more rhythmic noise, then some crowd noise)

Roger: Hey Marvin, what's up?

Marvin: Just waitin' for our homerooms. Nice knapsack.

Roger: Thanks. It's new, it's full, and it's heavy! I'll be glad to get a locker and dump all this crap.

Lucky: *(angrily)* Hey watch it kid!

Roger: Oh sorry! My knapsack's a little big. Sorry!

Lucky: Well take it the fuck off or I'll shove it down your throat.

Roger: No problem, sorry.

(muffled sounds of microphone rubbing and items re-ordering as Roger slings his knapsack to the ground)

Marvin: Hey man, you shouldn't mess with him. He knows karate.

Lucky: Oh yeah? He's pretty small.

Marvin: Small, but deadly.

Lucky: Oh yeah?

Brian: Hey Jolly Roger! It's Jolly Roger!

Roger: Why do you call me that?

Brian: Because you're dangerous, like a pirate, right?

Roger: What the hell are you guys talking about?

Marvin: One chop he'd split you in half.

Roger: Bug off man. I'm not a karate master.

Marvin: A true karate master has to be humble.

Lucky: You think you're a karate master?

Brian: He's only a master of bullshitting.

Lucky: You're a fucking runt that's all.

Roger: What did you choose this year Marvin?

Lucky: What did you choose this year Marvin? What the fuck do you think he chose? He's a frog-loving Jew. French for him, and economics because they invented it. What about you grasshopper, you a Jew too?

Roger: It doesn't matter, but I'm an atheist.

Brian: Ooh. Big word. Takes you three minutes just to say it. Nay-theee-ist. What the fuck is that? Jesus not good enough for you?

Roger: You can believe what you want to believe. It's a free world, well except for the USSR, China, Vietnam… but you're free to take Christian Ethics if you want. And Ukrainian is a beautiful language, very useful locally.

Brian: Sla-ven-yuh-vee-kee.

(sound of microphone jostling)

Roger: Ooof!

Lucky: Watch it! Fucking faggot.

Roger: Careful, that's breakable.

Brian: Then don't fall on it, stupid.

Loudspeaker voice: Attention. We have the homeroom assignments. They will be posted on the door shortly. Everyone please line up. Have a look at the list and then go to your assigned homeroom. No pushing. Be quiet and orderly. This shouldn't take more than a few minutes.

Roger: I feel like a steer at a slaughter house. When we get to the front of the line, a big hammer jumps out and hits us in the head, knocking us dead.

Marvin: It won't be *that* easy.

(ten minutes of indecipherable crowd murmurs)

Hooper: All right. You understand that anything you say here can be held against you in court? If you lie or mislead us, you could go to prison.

Kay: I understand.

Hooper: Because you're a minor, you have a right to have a parent present. You have waived this right. Is that correct?

Kay: Yeah, but I'm not under arrest for anything.

Hooper: No, and if you're truthful with us, we won't worry about the small stuff. And your parents won't have to hear about it either. For example, we know that there were drugs in that shed.

Kay: Any drugs in there would have been Solo's, I mean Solomon's, not Neil's.

Hooper: Neil? You mean Lionel?

Kay: Yeah, Neil is what I call Lionel.

Hooper: Okay, so Neil, was he ever angry with his mother?

Kay: No I don't think so. I know he helped her out a lot, buying groceries, taking clothes to the laundromat, making meals...

Hooper: That's right, there was no washer or dryer found in the house.

Kay: No. They were a pretty poor family. It was feast or famine. Sometimes he'd have money at the start of the month, but by the end, they would be getting pretty desperate.

Hooper: 'They' meaning Jerry and, uh, Neil? That's a nod. Could this desperation have translated into violence?

Kay: They never knocked over a grocery store if that's what you mean.

Hooper: Did you ever hear Jerry or Neil make threats or wish their mother was dead?

Kay: No, really the opposite. Neil told me that his parents used to fight a lot, but by the time I met him, they were pretty much split. His father didn't spend much time at the house on Darlington and his mom was usually drunk or sleeping.

We spent most of our time behind the house, in the shed. We didn't talk about his parents much but I do remember he said that at least once Jerry had stuck up for his mom and, you know, like squared off against his father.

Hooper: So their anger was directed more at their father?

Kay: I guess you could say that.

Hooper: What about Solomon? What was his relationship with Mrs. O'Neill?

Kay: I don't think he had any. He was Jerry's friend and I guess later he was Neil's friend, although I don't think he was a very good friend.

Hooper: Solomon never said anything about Mrs. O'Neill? You never saw them together?

Kay: No of course not.

Hooper: What was your relationship with Mrs. O'Neill?

Kay: Me? I didn't know her very well. I talked to her a few times, trying to get a hold of Neil. I've only been in their house a few times, and mostly I never see her. The living room doorway to the kitchen was covered with a sheet so if I went into the house to use the bathroom, I couldn't see her or anyone who might be in the living room. Usually it was very quiet, sometimes you could hear the TV, but I don't recall any voices.

Hooper: You used the bathroom. So you never spent any time in the living room, or saw Mrs. O'Neill talking to anyone there?

Kay: No I don't think so.

Hooper: You never hung out in the kitchen, maybe do some cooking? Make some fries?

Kay: No I don't know how to cook anything. I don't even know how to boil toast.

Hooper: What does that mean?

Kay: Just a joke. I can't cook. We hung out in the shed, as I said.

Hooper: So you have no explanation as to how your fingerprints could have been on the pot that started the fire?

Kay: No that's impossible.

Hooper: So you only ever entered the house to use the bathroom?

Kay: That's right.

Hooper: Well what did you usually drink out in the shed? Tap water? Beer?

Kay: No. I worked at Pic-A-Pop and I got a free case of pop every week. Usually I'd bring that over and we'd share it.

Hooper: So you kept the pop in the shed?

Kay: Well, no. In the winter the shed gets very cold, especially overnight when the heater is off, so we kept the pop in the kitchen, close to the back door.

Hooper: So you could nip in and grab a couple bottles easily?

Kay: Exactly.

Hooper: Did you share this pop with other people, friends of Neil's, perhaps?

Kay: Sure. Whoever came over to the shed, probably we'd have a pop. Twenty four bottles of pop a week is more than I could drink so I was happy to share.

Hooper: Did Jerry drink this free pop too?

Kay: Sometimes.

Hooper: Did you offer it to him, or did he help himself?

Kay: I would offer him sometimes, but I think he knew I wanted him to have it too. Jerry was very nice to me and I was glad to share.

Hooper: When did you get the free pop each week?

Kay: At the end of work each Thursday I got a crate.

Hooper: A crate is twenty four bottles?

Kay: Right. I'd keep five or six bottles for myself and Neil would pick up the rest on Sunday. Usually he'd bring over the empty crate from the last week and take the new crate with him. This was our routine.

Hooper: So eighteen bottles, more or less, would wind up over at the O'Neill's?

Kay: Right.

Hooper: During the week, how many bottles of that pop would you consume when you were over there?

Kay: At the shed? I don't know. I'd go over and drink a couple of bottles maybe. Do that a couple of times a week...

Hooper: And Neil would drink with you?

Kay: Yeah.

Hooper: How about Jerry? Did he drink a lot of your pop?

Kay: Maybe. Either Jerry or Neil. Or maybe some other friends.

Hooper: Such as?

Kay: I'm just guessing. Maybe some of Jerry's friends?

Hooper: Anyone in particular?

Kay: No, I didn't see anyone there usually.

Hooper: So most of the pop, you didn't even see who drank it. And this didn't bother you? You're feeding this guy's family a whole crate of pop every week, and you're okay with that?

Kay: Sure. He was a good friend. He didn't have much. I was glad to help.

Hooper: You never felt used, or cheated?

Kay: No. Neil and his brother treated me with respect. They were thankful for what I gave them, but really they gave me a lot more.

Hooper: Oh? What did they give you?

Kay: Well not real things, but, you know, friendship and respect. That means a lot. It's not what people take from you, it is how they take it.

Hooper: So because they respected you, it was okay, you were happy.

Kay: Sure I was.

Hooper: When did you first meet Solomon Malakowski?

Kay: I think it was in the pool hall on Betts Avenue. He was a friend of Jerry's.

Hooper: When did you meet him?

Kay: More than a year ago I guess. But I didn't see him very often. It was only after Jerry disappeared that he started coming around the shed, or that I saw him in the shed.

Hooper: You didn't like Solomon, did you?

Kay: I don't think he was a good friend to Neil. The guy was trouble.

Hooper: Well, we know about his drug dealing. Is that what you mean by trouble?

Kay: Sure, partially. But also he didn't really respect anyone. I don't know how he treated Jerry, but he didn't treat Neil very well.

Hooper: What do you mean?

Kay: Well, he called him Professor, or Professor Armstrong.

Hooper: As in Neil Armstrong? Is that where his nickname comes from?

Kay: Sort of. But Neil Armstrong is an astronaut, not a professor. When Solo called Neil that, well it seemed like he was making fun of his intellect.

Hooper: Lionel, or Neil, he's not retarded...

Kay: No, for sure not. But in my class people make fun of you if you're smart, not if you're dumb. Although I'm sure there's some of that too.

Hooper: So other than calling him 'Professor', how else did Solomon disrespect Neil?

Kay: He brought alcohol into the shed. That's a big no-no. Both Neil and his brother thought that alcohol was a very bad thing. Probably because their parents drank.

Hooper: Did you ever see Solomon inside the house, maybe drinking with Mrs. O'Neill?

Kay: No, Neil wouldn't have stood for it.

Hooper: You think seeing his mother drinking alcohol with the young Solomon could have driven Neil to violence?

Kay: No I just mean their friendship wouldn't survive. Solo could hang in the shed with us, or in the house with Neil's mom, but no way could he do both. It would be the end of his friendship with Neil.

Hooper: Did Solomon ever drink any of that free pop?

Kay: Well it's not free, it's part of my wages.

Hooper: From your illegal, underage job?

Kay: Well yeah. But you said you weren't gonna worry about that!

Hooper: No that's fine, carry on. I'm not going to raise that issue unless of course you are lying to me.

Kay: I'm not lying!

Hooper: No, okay, don't worry about that. Just answer honestly. Did Solomon drink any of the pop you brought over, every week, without fail.

Kay: Well yeah, I'm sure he did. Anyone who came to the shed got offered one.

Hooper: Would Neil leave you in the shed and fetch the pop for the guests?

Kay: Well no, I usually did. We had a bottle opener in the shed, but we didn't keep the case in there because, as I said, it gets too cold.

Hooper: So you'd play the servant and run in the house to get drinks for any guests that showed up, drinks that you already paid for with the sweat of your brow?

Kay: Well, yeah. But I was happy to do it. Neil was the best friend I ever had. I completely trusted the guy. I knew we were unequal financially... I did help him out often, but was *happy* to do it! He was like my big brother. A mentor, a protector.

Hooper: Right. Now I've talked with the principal at your school. He says there are at least four incidents, that he knows of, of Neil fighting or choking other students.

Kay: That's not right. Except for when Neil got sick and attacked Mike Webb, he didn't start any fights. One time he got in a fight with a student who stole some food from him, but it was the other student who started the fight. He was expelled, not Neil.

Hooper: Yes. The student you mention claims that Neil tried to poison him, and you were in on the scheme. Does that ring a bell?

Kay: I've never knowingly tried to hurt anyone in my life.

Hooper: So when you'd go inside the house to pick up some pop for the guests, did you have to move anything to get to the pop? Were dirty dishes piled on top, or pot lids, or anything in your way to access those crates of pop?

Kay: One crate of Pic-A-Pop , and it was right by the back door. Sometimes there'd be stuff on top of it, maybe some garbage.

Hooper: They'd put garbage on top of your drinks?

Kay: Well yeah, his mom would sometimes put garbage by the back door and Neil was supposed to take it out. Sometimes it wound up on top of the pop crate. I got the impression that his mom didn't like having the pop there, by the back door. She was kind of controlling.

Neil always said that if you were in earshot, she'd have a chore for you. So they stayed out of earshot.

Also, maybe she didn't like someone else providing for her kids. Crazy as it sounds, I think she was jealous of anyone who was close to Neil. She didn't treat his friends well. Like after Neil got sick. She made no effort to really help him and she didn't like Sam and I coming around. We didn't get to see him again until he was well enough to ignore her and insist on seeing us himself, again not in the house, but in the shed.

Hooper: So you'd maybe have to dig a bit to get at the pop in the house.

Kay: A bit, sometimes.

Hooper: But no pots or pans did you ever touch?

Kay: Not that I recall.

Hooper: So you didn't like Solomon at all?

Kay: No, I don't think I did. You know the trouble he caused. You arrested him before.

Hooper: True. And you didn't like Mrs. O'Neill?

Kay: No, not too much really.

Hooper: So when Solomon started drinking in the house with Mrs. O'Neill, you weren't too happy?

Kay: I didn't know that was going on.

Hooper: Neil never mentioned it?

Kay: Absolutely not.

Hooper: And you didn't talk to Neil on the night of the fire?

Kay: No, yes I did. After the fire. He was in Shaw Park. That's where the police found him.

Hooper: Found you both.

Kay: Well yeah. Neil thought that Solo had burned down the house.

Hooper: Your diary says that Neil admitted a fight occurred when he found his mother and Solomon in the house together.

Kay: I don't know if that was a verbal fight or a physical fight.

Hooper: So your best friend is suffering from a mental disease, and his mother and his other so-called best friend are causing him a lot of grief. Wouldn't it be nice for him if they both went away?

Kay: Well no, Neil needs his family. His father's a real jerk. He drinks a lot and he's hit his kids before. Neil didn't want to live with him.

Hooper: Would he have preferred a drug addict to take his father's place, someone the same age as his deceased brother, someone who has turned his trust upside down?

Kay: No. I'm sure not. But that's not a reason to kill him.

Hooper: But wouldn't it have solved a lot of problems at once?

Let's imagine a scenario. Neil comes home and finds his mother drinking with this grease ball. He knocks them both two ways from Sunday and, being the sick confused puppy he is, he leaves. In a few minutes, along comes his best friend, little old Roger Kay. Now Roger knows the score about the trouble these two had been causing his best friend. He sees them unconscious and believes Neil has killed them. He panics. To cover up his friend's crime, he puts a pot of cooking oil on the stove and sets it on high, knowing that it will soon boil, overflow, and start a plausibly deniable house fire that can destroy all the evidence.

Of course not all the evidence is destroyed. Like the strangulation marks on both corpses. Like the fingerprints on the pot on the stove.

Kay: Are you saying they weren't dead before the fire?

Hooper: You seem upset. Did you think they were dead?

Kay: I wasn't there. I don't think Neil killed anyone, and I certainly didn't. I think the fire was an accident.

Hooper: They weren't napping when the fire started. We didn't find them snug in their beds. There was evidence of violence.

Kay: Maybe they fought each other. Maybe it was a murder suicide thing. You can't just say that Neil or someone else started the fire unless you have proof.

Hooper: What about the fingerprints on the pot? How's that for proof?

Kay: You're lying. That's impossible.

Hooper: Why would I lie?

Kay: I don't know. I've helped you before. I'm a good guy.

Hooper: Ninety nine percent of snitches are criminals.

Kay: I want to call my parents now.

Introduction to Lionel O'Neill's
Moonbase Alpha Blueprints
(Roger Kay, 1991)

First let me say that it is a bit strange, less than a decade shy of
the eagerly awaited 1999, to be commenting upon 'futuristic'
blueprints that were drawn with an HB pencil in 1977. Because
I knew Lionel well at the time that he drafted this, if I am
permitted to say 'drafted' of it, and because I am one of perhaps
only two people who ever saw the initial stages and designs for
this work, I am uniquely qualified to comment.

I remember finding Lionel hunched over the work bench in
his family's shed. He was perhaps sixteen at the time and he
looked like a lot of kids from the 1970s, long shaggy hair, a
scant moustache, bad skin, t-shirt and bell bottom jeans, two
inch high platform shoes. He was not very tall, indeed he was
very short, but he seemed the tallest kid in the school to me. He
was my best friend, protector, and just an incredibly loyal,
steadying, and yet creative force in my life, despite all his own
troubles and catastrophes.

So there he would sit, the light issuing from the flexible
pod of a high intensity desk lamp clamped to a wall bracket
and arranged to rest just above his hair, almost threatening to
set him on fire for his lack of due awareness was he so
distracted to find himself in the hallways and corridors of
Moonbase Alpha. I'm sure it was a happy place for him.

I saw how he would lay his paper on a long but broken
piece of arborite that covered the scarred work bench to
provide a smooth writing surface, how he worked without t-
square or drafting tools, referencing the <u>Moonbase Alpha
Technical Notebook</u> (MATN) for the shape of the many
buildings and levels that make up the lunar base, noting and
incorporating these 'known' dimensions. Every travel tube,
every elevator, every corridor, all these he detailed, finding
specifics to fill in variously from his sketch archive created
during his original viewings of *Space: 1999*, and from his

imagination such that he performed an extrapolation of 1975 technology into the future as he had been shown it.

Looking back now, with the benefit of hindsight, it appears there are some bad assumptions and basic fallacies built into his conception, for he was no prophet, only my friend.

The first thing I would point out is the use of paper resources on Moonbase Alpha. Fans of the show are aware that computer expert Kano was more likely to tear off a slip of paper and read computer results as inked there rather than just looking at a computer monitor as we know them.

There can be no excuse from Gerry and Sylvia Anderson for this one. Even in *Star Trek*, which came several years prior, the heroes read information from computer displays and had an electronic clipboard that obviated any need for paper supplies on the Enterprise, at least for printing purposes. On Moonbase Alpha we instead must expect that there is a stockpile of small rolls of paper somewhere, which are occasionally replenished from the handy, nearby, original planet Earth.

Lionel made the choice to have that paper goods stock room absolutely proximate to Main Mission, in fact, as a room the portal of which faces directly on the posterior of the 'big screen' in Main Mission. In retrospect, this is hilarious.

Another issue is the general misunderstanding of computers. Again this is not blameworthy as Lionel takes his miscues from the series itself. Rather than understanding that one well-placed full QWERTY keyboard is all that is needed to operate a well-networked moonbase, we see on Alpha a myriad of function-specific stations which are often not remotely accessible.

Recall the scene: Professor Bergman pushes a button under the 'big screen' in Main Mission, then walks over and up a couple of stair to the main computer, where he pushes two buttons and a piece of adding machine paper is fed out.

Sometimes the computer seems all knowing and uber-capable, as when Koenig asks it a question verbally and receives an answer in kind. But sometimes it seems like the computer is not really paying very close attention, as when it allows aliens to imitate Koenig's voice to give priority commands, while Koenig and his commlock are elsewhere on the base. Would that not raise a red flag with the main computer, that Koenig is apparently in two places at once?

This issue of function-specific controls versus a general computer interface is also evident in the Eagles. Lionel drew a diagram of all the controls in an Eagle Command Module (nose cone) and it is interesting that there is indeed no keyboard evident, only sets of function-specific buttons. Again, he is just reflecting the shortcomings of the original series.

To underline these original shortcomings, consider the one tool continually carried and used by each Alphan: the 'commlock'. A combination audio/video communicator and door activation device, the commlock is drawn and explained in detail in the MATN where its single function mindedness is apparent and presents a microcosm of the Alphan technological paradigm. Specifically, note the button denoted 'Geiger Counter' in the MATN drawing. A scroll wheel for options, or an on-screen menu was not yet envisioned. Instead, every option maps to a unique button and every choice requires a dedicated hardware switch. To activate the Geiger counter, you must depress the Geiger counter button.

In 1975, each button had a fixed cost so the increase of button versus option cost was linear, 1:1. A crucial paradigm shift that signaled option quantity could approach infinity with marginal incremental costs via the use of advanced human-machine interfaces (virtual control panels and menus) had not yet arrived.

To parallel the myopic view of single function controls, single function rooms prevail throughout his design. Every lab is denoted with a purpose and every space science purpose or Alphan need that can be imagined is assigned a room somewhere among the various buildings or 'sections' that comprise Moonbase Alpha. The idea of the multi-purpose, or flexible-use room was not considered even by Lionel as he drafted his vision.

Obviously, Lionel was no engineer. He glosses over how a small moon base, with a maximum complement of 311 personnel, can meet all the needs of a lunar society. There are labs for fabrication of textiles, plastics, electronics. It is not assumed that Earth is in the re-supply loop; he does not duck from the effort to give Moonbase Alpha full technological independence, aggregating faint circles and rectangles to create large machines named categorically: electronic component fabrication, cloth fabrication, synthocrete fabrication. Details about the necessary inputs for these industrial processes were, unsurprisingly, not provided.

In a sense Lionel's idealism was unrealistic. No one gets to work on a moonbase, even as a security guard, in *our* future. The Moon is again unreachable. We are heading in the wrong direction.

At that time, *Star Wars* was on the horizon, a comic book taking the place of serious science fiction, and a comic book about *war* at that. Peace doesn't sell it had been definitively proven by late 1977.

Like the rock group ELO which evolved from *On The Third Day* to *Discovery*, moving to a sleeker look, a new style, a change in the environment demanded mutation. But let's be clear, they are following the trend not creating it. Very disappointing artistically. Fiery young new talents burn out and turn into salesmen.

The 90s started just like the 70s ended. In 1979 Ian Curtis of the band Joy Division hung himself on a laundry drying mechanism in his kitchen. In 1991 Kurt Cobain of the band Nirvana blew a hole in his head while hid out in his secluded greenhouse. Both were young talents unexpectedly stumbling onto success in a rare moment in music history when feeling supersedes technique. Or as Commander Koenig put it to Raan: "Feeling is more important than thinking".

Neil might not agree with this sentiment, but that doesn't mean it isn't true.

Addendum to Second Edition:
On Lionel's Last Days (Roger Kay, 2027)

After the initial publication of Breakaway: 1977 in 2010, I never again laid eyes upon Lionel. Our final meeting was in 1989, and our correspondence thereafter was very limited. He sent a short message thanking me for writing the introduction to his Moonbase Alpha Blueprints. It was polite and formulaic. I don't believe he trusted me anymore.

Once Lionel's drawings became available to *Space: 1999* fandom, a strange thing happened. Interest grew. In an age when video and computer games were the *sine qua non* of entertainment, Lionel's messy pencil drawings actually garnered page views or 'hits' on the internet, much to the surprise of all. The original version of this book provided just enough background on his difficult and storied life to establish a sheen of danger and glamour to all the trauma he had suffered. He began to give interviews for oddball (and mostly online) magazines. Often they referred to him as 'Professor Neil J. Armstrong', which was a pseudonym he had used just one time, when he had first published his blueprints online. There was talk of a movie at one point in the blogosphere and this chatter snowballed into further attention for this little book as well as Lionel's own works online.

I myself was approached several times and provided comments that were used in various online magazines such as End Times, Science Fantasist, and Future Doom. I regret giving those interviews. Back in the mid-nineties I was no child or adolescent. I should have known better. The piranhas of media have little inclination for mercy. For the works of a sick person to be so widely disseminated and voraciously dissected was no ameliorative to his condition. More plainly said, the publicity didn't help him.

When Lionel disappeared in 2012, it was a shock but not entirely unexpected. I read some of his later writing and it was full of suspicion and despair. The fact that his blog was last updated on the date of the end of the world according to Mayan

Prophecy (another pile of hogwash), December 21, 2012, drove home the point that he was under the influence of a dangerously faulty perspective. Whether his illusions were the result of a breakdown of sanity, or a breakthrough to a less subjective layer of reality is beside the point. They did not serve him well.

At this point in my life, I can no longer refer to my long lost friend as Neil. That person disappeared into a police car long ago, never to return. Perhaps he was killed along with his brother. My friend did not believe in revenge. That person who killed Kiblah was not my friend.

I am almost too old now for regrets. Or am I too old for anything but? My 65th birthday was last weekend. My life has become a series of magnified, minor annoyances. I have money, but not enough to waste. I have a wife, but she is very tired. I have interests, but they do not raise my passion anymore. My children are all that matter to me these days, and they are far away. I look forward to their visits during the holidays. In the meantime, my arthritis occupies me. It takes all day to exercise away the stiffness and pain that each morning brings. Life is pain, perhaps constant pain, but there are moments that I would not trade for any ease or abundance of vitality.

What do I think of *Space: 1999* now? Certainly it was a decent show in its day. It had an air of mystery that enthralled audiences and the heroicism of its main characters reflected the simpler ethical considerations of its day, more than half a century ago. But ultimately, it was not something that could have constituted a philosophy or way-of-life for teenagers lost in the ditch beside the road to identity. This is not to denigrate the show in any way. I think it is common for adolescents to latch onto something they feel is uniquely theirs and to import to it all the virtues of a full-fledged religion or philosophy. It is all or nothing in one's youth. *Space: 1999* was our all.

How foolish it is, in hindsight, to pin all of one's hopes and dreams into what was intended as simple entertainment. Today is no different. Virtual environments are more compelling to youth than anything that exists in old-fashioned reality. Who cares about true reality these days? The important thing is one's avatars and the worlds in which they exist.

Should I complain if my generation performed the same magical feat of disappearing themselves into an illusion that was created for commercial reasons? My generation was lost in TV, lost in movies, lost in music. Why would I think that the next generation would be any different? Shouldn't they too barricade themselves inside faux realities that are more amenable to their own desires and interpretations than the sterile, inflexible worlds of adults?

Neil (and I use the name on purpose here) was concerned with the influence that great social powers wielded over the individual. He was especially concerned about collusion amongst powerful adult institutions such as business and government. He did not see the purveyors of cultural landmarks such as music, cinema and TV in the same dangerous light but perhaps he should have. While the so-called adult influences tried to impress certain values upon us, our self-selected artistic influences impressed alternate values upon us. Without looking at the content of the values, there is not much to distinguish these two. We were prone to accept one slate of values or the other.

We could accept society, or we could accept the counterculture. There was no room for a third way, a way based upon our own individuality and unique requirements.

Neil, Sam and I were not typical teenagers. We tried to find that third way. We were ahead of our time. If anyone had a shot at deciphering the puzzle of maturity, it was us. You can see the green shoots of our thought in this book's long-ago entries. But we did not succeed. The thing we loved most, our cultural ephemera, no matter how inviting, exciting or intoxicating, was no basis for a life.

I wonder if we had concentrated more on the creation of our own works, we could have escaped some of the inevitable mediocrity and disappointment that greets us all somewhere north of the midpoint of life.

Ultimately, you must either prove or disavow conspiracy. You must choose between the hypothetical and the real. You need to take responsibility for your own situation and determine your own goals. Heroes are fine, but they can inspire obsession and stagnation. Those things that you find most stimulating may someday appear to you as the most confining and narrowing of influences. Keep your mind open. Nothing is sacred, except life itself.

Breakaway: 1977 (2010, Biography)
Addendum A001 (Lionel O'Neill)
13 September 2099
Global Library of Literature (A2010018799)

Today is my 137th birthday! Hooray for me! I am alive and I don't mind. Life is good. How are you? Are you sure? How does the song go – it is later than you think.

By now, enough time has certainly passed that a dispassionate update on the events and people chronicled in this 'book' is possible. I am the sole survivor of the tale. Let me recount the final days of the others.

Roger died in 2028. I had not seen him for many decades, and that final meeting was rather brief. If you've read the book then you've read the transcription of that last encounter which Roger secretly recorded. Ultimately, my sister Nancy was closer to him than I. They spent significant time working together on the book in the nineties and zeroes and remained friends after that.

Nancy later told me that Roger aged rapidly during the twenties. Roger had always been passionate about his career but it was somewhat unrequited, or perhaps dysfunctional. A career in research and development management consumed his final years. What was meant to be a rebound from an earlier undeserved fiasco in telecommunications engineering, only served to echo and underline it. This requires some explanation.

Throughout the nineties Roger wrote software for a succession of telecommunications and networking giants. During that period, Nancy saw him transform from a fresh-faced and self-driven idealist to a dissipated middle-aged inertial mass. Apparently there were many stresses in his industry. As the decade wore on he was confronted with extreme corporate down-sizing and increased pressure for performance increments. He was well-paid, but foolishly encouraged to put his nest-egg into the company stock. A streak of irrational exuberance gripped the internet industries in the late nineties. Stock prices seemed to climb without fail until finally, in 2000, they began to slide. That slide turned into a plummet. By 2001 Roger was overweight, depressed, and near broke. Nancy reported that around that time, he considered himself "financially broken" because he had missed the "housing escalator". House prices had risen dramatically throughout the decade, but being too busy at work he had remained a renter. Not being on the property ladder meant he was unlikely to fully own a home for many years. This plus the high-tech stock crash meant his nest egg had messily Humpty Dumptied.

Drawing on a reserve of resilience, Roger shook off these setbacks and embarked on a path of self-renewal. He cashed in his RRSPs and financed a Master's Degree in Nano-robotics. Roger returned to his career track with a vengeance, rapidly moving from an engineering role to management.

When Nancy last saw him, just a few months before his death, it appeared that history had repeated. The job stresses and demands had again inspired neglect of his own health. He was forced into retirement by Global Nanobotics just before they went bankrupt. It appeared that his retirement pension would be held up and likely decimated by the bankruptcy proceedings. He was only 65 and it is ironic that the products of his own company might have saved him. (Of course not if the bots were from that Singapore lot that caused the great "Botch of '27", the casualties and lawsuits from which led directly to GN's bankruptcy.) The official, but reductive, cause of death was heart attack. Roger was a generally very loyal fellow, kowtowing to a corporate status quo, and this may have led him to his final impasse.

As far as the Detective Hooper interview and his hypothesis that Roger was behind the fire at the Darlington house, I maintain that Roger was not a big rule-breaker. His behavior since then has reinforced this. I do admit that in my darkest days, just before my new dawn in 2018 (more on this shortly), I did consider Hooper's theory. I vividly recall one dark moment when I excoriated my friend. In a paranoid fury, I paced my flop room listening to the song "Fish Fry Road" from *Potatoland*. The lyrics about "the flames shooting higher" suddenly took on a new significance as I considered how they might relate to Roger and his alleged decision to destroy my home. Was his motivation to protect me or was he in league with the status quo and Gary Anderson?

This was perhaps the nadir of my illness. I could bravely face the terrors of my mind, but the horror of finding my friend grotesque was unbearable.

I've come to accept that memory is a tricky thing. When I went into that living room to find Mom and Solomon, I'm pretty sure the burner was cold. If they'd just turned it on that very minute, that would explain it. But to me it felt like I spent half an hour in there. This is no doubt some kind of time compression effect due to the stressful conflict situation. Probably, or logically, I'm sure I could not have been in there more than five minutes. I left in such a furor that I might not have noticed the glowing red burner. So let's put that to rest.

My friend Samantha has disappeared into the mists of time. I know that she divorced Webb in the 1990s and remarried, but I cannot find the message Nancy sent me containing Sam's second husband's name. It seems odd to me that she would not revert to and retain her original surname, especially after a failed marriage, but I must admit my understanding of her has been faulty throughout our acquaintance.

Additionally, after 2018 I sought to start life anew. There was no desire to revisit my tumultuous past.

So what is new since 2018? Bots running amok in '27. The impulse wars in the Thirties, culminating in The Big Wipe. Then the pan-Asian conflict, colloquially known as Last Stan, which was ultimately resolved via the Treaty of Delhi in '55. And of course the calumnies of 2098 I will not recount here for I will not give succor to their perpetrators nor grace my pages with their names. History is academic, but politics are now.

For me personally, things are much better now. I work in a strawberry farm, running the pruning bots. It is meditative work.

I felt I *had* to disappear in 2012 as the (this) book and public facade thing got to be too much. I changed my name to Gilbert McLintsky. A horrible name for a horrible time. I changed it back in 2018 when I finally came to grips with my schizophrenia and drug addictions. Thank you Trizopam. Since 2018 I don't think even a hundred copies of this book have sold. My fears did not materialize, which resembles my whole life.

The whole space travel thing never took off. I mean sure there's asteroid mining now and some great maps of far-off planets, but no ETI contact and no FTL drive.

The bot thing, of course, is huge. I would be long dead if not for my blood bots. I am one of the lucky few for whom the bots keep everything in balance and aging is perpetually (fingers crossed!) kept at bay. It is unclear how old I can become. My genes have finally paid a dividend. Schizophrenia be damned, here comes immortality! Perhaps in more ways than one.

My family provides a degree of immortality that even nanobots cannot deliver. I know that I must die someday, however far in the future that day might lurk, but the branches of my family tree are strong and will, I am certain, endure.

Nancy died tragically in a car accident over two decades ago. With her final (and definitely improved) husband Ted she produced two daughters, Lilith and Jezebel.

Lilith married Yao and begat Chi and Geo. Chi and Param begat Hercules. Hercules and Ania begat David.

Jezebel married Anthony and had triplets, Matthew, Mark and Luke.

Matthew and Deidre begat Blazer and Nova. Blazer and Dyanne begat Fenix and Sugar. Nova and Barrack begat Alpha.

Luke and Diamond begat Athena. Athena and Vijay begat Timbali.

My other sister Marilyn had a son, Joseph, way back in the 20th Century. Joseph married Susan and had a son Aaron who may have some descendants that are unknown to me.

Joseph also had two children from a second marriage to a woman named Joy: Corinthia and Timothia.

Corinthia and Bel begat Augusto.

Timothia and Ulysses begat Hera and Hero.

Not enumerating step-relations, my two sisters are responsible for at least twenty-three descendants!

Little Alpha is now three years old and is the sweetest little boy imaginable. No relation to Moonbase Alpha. Just a happy coincidence.

One question that still confronts me, at my advanced age, is the nature of immortality. My family thrives and I am alive, but aren't these blood ties just evolution's tribalism? Why should I value my family more than any other contemporary human? As you see I remain a contrarian, fighting Nature to my last.

I admit I have asked the question, but I also admit that I am disingenuous poser. Yes I do value my own tribe more. Little Alpha means more to me than a billion Australians.

Let me question myself too. How much of who I was in 1977 remains who I am today? I remain an avid bass player, inspired by Geddy Lee of the rock group Rush. In 1977 my favorite Rush album was *2112*. In 1981 it was *Moving Pictures*. But by 2002, it was *Vapor Trails*. Does this demonstrate my closely following the evolution of an artist, or is it a symptom of an increasingly nebulous identity? Are my preferences regressing towards a mean, the mainstream? Does this flux represent dynamism or conformity?

The passing of my father Earl at the respectable age of 139 also made me confront the question of identity. On his deathbed, Earl mistook young family members for their ancestors, calling then-little Blazer by the name Jerry. Was this the same Earl who drank and fought in our little house on Darlington Avenue?

The human body replaces even the longest-lived cell-type within fifteen years. A complete somatic turnover of all cells within a decade and a half. After such renewal, do we remain the same person? And if so, perhaps it is by choice. We remember who we are and we sustain it by choice, or we don't.

And when enough time has passed, those small choices, even if we cling intently to continuity, have rendered us unrecognizable to our earlier selves. I will not evaluate this process; I simply report it here for your elucidation.

In honour of my long-loved science fiction 'television' drama, I have waited and submitted this likely final update on the centennial date that, to me, will always symbolize Fate as part departure and part decision. We choose our path, but we can never know what awaits us.

About the author

R. M. Kozan lives in Ottawa with his girlfriend Lois and seven guitars. He disavows life as a mechanical process devoid of organic authenticity and enjoys sweet dark seedless grapes.

www.ingramcontent.com/pod-product-compliance
Lightning Source LLC
Chambersburg PA
CBHW020925020726
47495CB00002B/348